I0681018

GOD'S LOOKING GLASS

Also By Steve Jaffe

Fiction

Children with Invisible Faces
The Haven House Chronicles-The Conspiracy

The Mind Diet Series Books

Re-Defining Stress to Prevent Disease
Count Your Life With Smiles Not Tears
 Healing From Within, Emotionally Surviving Cancer
A Recipe for Healing, Coming Together as a Team
Beyond Valentine's Day, Making Love All Year Long

Preview all books at www.stevejaffebooks.com

GOD'S LOOKING GLASS
A Suspense Thriller

Steve Jaffe
Lightning Source Publishing
www.stevejaffebooks.com

Steve Jaffe Books
www.stevejaffebooks.com

God's Looking Glass Copyright ©2010 by Steve Jaffe
ISBN 978-0-9819410-2-8
Revised from original first printing of The Devil's Poison ©2002

Acknowledgements

I want to first thank my wife Nancy for her helpful insight and thoughts about this story. You are the best sounding board for my ideas, even after so many rewrites. I could not do my writing without your support.

I have to thank two friends, Richard Bentley and Paul Dijulio, who read *God's Looking Glass* and gave me the needed encouragement to say it was ready for publication. To both of you, I am not sure if I will ever tell you how I come up with my tales, but I will let you buy me a drink or two to see if you can squeeze it out of me.

Lastly, I need to thank my mother, Edythe, who always reads my manuscripts with a loving mother's heart. Thank you for your wonderful support.

Dedication

To Nancy, who has taught me that faith, hope and prayer really works.

Author's Message

Throughout this novel, God is mentioned numerous times. A few biblical stories are addressed, as well as this author's thoughts about them. This story was born from the turmoil our world faces each day and in most instances seems to be generated from misguided religious beliefs.

I have the deepest respect for the hundreds of millions of people who believe in a divine power and practice the true tenets of their religion. In no way was this story intended to insult any person's religious beliefs.

It has always been my desire, wishes that people, not politicians or religious leaders, step up, and show the world that we can all live without fighting and express to *everyone* the love in our hearts.

PART I

THE ULTIMATUM

PROLOGUE

Esther squirmed in her chair as she listened to the orders from the Council president, his voice rattling unchecked in her headphones. The Council had reached a decision—it was no longer debatable. Their new mission had a short lead-time and it had to be swift.

The Chancellor was unwilling to mince words. He reminded Esther that she and her family had failed ten years ago. Unwilling to sugarcoat the truth, the leader of the council spelled out to her in crystal-clear terms the exact nature of Operation Genesis: Reduce the world to rubble and cleanse it of the all-pervasive evil that tainted its very core.

While the Chancellor's words crackled in her ears, Esther glanced at her husband. Jacob knew precisely what was happening; he could read it on her face. She knew he would object strenuously to the Council's directive. Jacob, along with his children, guided himself with compassion and empathy, not by blind, remorseless "justice."

Esther recalled the naive attempt the world had made to stop terrorism ten years earlier. She had stood by her husband then as he fought hard to maintain his peaceful stance. It had been difficult to watch the non-Muslim world as it feebly attempted to weed out all the terrorist cells, the sources of their support, and the seemingly endless reservoir of hate they tapped. The attempts by the United States only further corrupted its government that was once admired around the world, while adding fuel to the hatred Muslims felt toward all non-followers of Allah.

Esther knew Jacob was a good man and would want to follow his heart to save the world, even go against the orders from the Council. However, she knew it could not be done. The world had too much poison, and, as the Council insisted, it must be dealt with.

Now she had to explain the Council's decision to her husband and children. She reluctantly looked at her family, their anticipation building as she struggled to hold back her own anxiety. What her family could not hear was the harsh verbal lashing she had just received from the Chancellor.

She removed the headphones and turned slowly in her chair to face her defiant family.

Hindsight was no longer a luxury. Their mission had been clear ten years ago, but Jacob wanted to see one last time what the world would do after a horrific event. Could the world finally rally and become united against evil? Could even the peaceful Muslims support the war of terrorism?

What had happened to the United States should have inspired the world bringing terrorism to its knees. It should have brought all believers of God together to stop the "New Gangster" that was masquerading as revolutionaries. Instead, a new breed of evil was born, amassing weapons of mass destruction and was about to draw the world into a war that would destroy the most powerful nations and open up the world to never-ending evil.

The most vile, horrible people would be elevated to a position that had never been witnessed before in the history of the planet, all led by Dável and his family, Jacobs mortal enemy.

Esther's expression was stone cold, as she steeled herself to explain to her family what had to be done. "We have our new orders," she said. "We have no choice this time. If we can't rid man of the evil poison that's inside him and bring peace to this world, everything has to be destroyed."

"I can't do that." Her husband's hands trembled as he defied her words and the authority of the Council. "Too many innocent people will die. The world is infected with a small percentage of evil, and I won't destroy everyone to punish the few."

She hated the way he acted when he defied her, how he would look away from her disapproving eyes. Her head dropped to her chest as he turned his chair to face his children.

"I have a plan," Jacob said. "If it doesn't work. . . well, I'll capitulate. We'll have just enough time."

Esther did not like Jacob's stubbornness and feared the punishment they would face for disobeying the Council. She watched her children, the remaining soldiers of their cause, as they listened to their father and his plan for each of them.

"Jacob," she called out desperately, "I feel it's time to start over."

She looked away after Jacob turned his gaze back toward her, his icy stare draining the blood from her face.

"I'm still in charge. I will not give up on my original mission," he scolded her. "That's final."

She saw the looks of defiance on her children's faces. She knew she was outvoted.

* * * * *

Esther had refused to talk to Jacob during and after their evening meal. He knew he had hurt her feelings but he was confident she would get over it. He gazed out the porthole, lost in thought, only his eyes moved as the fish from the dark ocean passed before him.

He had always felt guilty and responsible for not preventing the atrocities that plagued the world.

He had the power. He just had too much faith in man's goodness to interfere.

He knew of the evil and stood by while it destroyed the world he loved so much. He looked at the weapon that had been entrusted to him to rid the world of its poison. He had hated himself for letting a lunatic, another Hitler methodically implement the attacks that jolted the world ten years ago. He had hoped in 1993 that the United States would fight back against the fanatics who killed so many at their embassies in Africa. He had hoped they would set a positive example, unite a world that needed to come together, but President Clinton was too weak and he failed miserably. Then, again, when one of their Navy ships was bombed, they did nothing of any significance. Even their own experts were ignored as they warned of a more serious event that would rock the world. Jacob buried his head in his hands and wept as he remembered what had happened that September. It was not tears for the thousands that died that day, but for what it symbolized about the human condition that was evaporating before his eyes. While Christians, Jews and Muslims that all worship the same God, allowed false leaders to manipulate HIS original message, HIS powerful words that were supposed to be humankind's rulebook for survival, were now on the brink of destruction.

Jacob's heart was breaking as he witnessed God's, children about to destroy themselves because of hatred and fear, as well as for the greed that wars create.

"So many dead," he mumbled to himself. "And now it's going to happen again. The world hasn't learned its lesson, and now I must intervene."

Jacob shivered the cold metal bulkheads and black ocean currents chilling his room. He stood up and reached for his Staff, steadying himself as the ship rocked.

"Rebecca!" he shouted. "Ian! David!"

Within moments, his children were standing in front of him, their hands by their sides, waiting for his command to be at ease. He waved his hand, signaling them to sit.

"Father, is everything okay?" Rebecca asked. She was the oldest, and the leader of their small army.

"It's time to begin what we should have done ten years ago. You all know what needs to be done. No deviations. Rebecca, do you understand?"

"Yes, Father," she replied.

"We have thirty days to complete our assignment, so be off with all of you."

Rebecca bent over, kissed her father on his cheek and vanished. She met up with her brothers in the corridor.

"Ian, you and David have your assignment," she said. "We'll meet up with each other in two days. Any questions?"

They shook their heads.

* * * *

Esther stood by the door, staring at her husband. Her face was ashen with the thought of what they were about to set in motion.

"I hope you know what you're doing," she said softly, her voice cracking. "I don't want to lose any more of our children."

"I have no choice," he said harshly. "This time it will work. Just stick to your job, and let me do mine."

He looked up to see that she was already gone and had not heard his words.

Esther returned to her computer. She waited for the connection to be completed and trembled knowing she was about to betray her husband.

CHAPTER ONE

Allan Vincent had miscalculated the time he needed to make his flight, and, as his car sputtered to a halt a hundred miles from nowhere, Murphy's Law kicked in.

"Damn!" he shouted, hitting the steering wheel with his fist.

It was not just being stuck that pissed him off. It was that he had to drive himself—something he hated doing because his overweight body barely fit into the driver's seat.

His thick glasses fogged up as he rubbed his arm against the side window to see where he was. He was leaving the country for good. The worst he could imagine in his sordid and twisted life was about to happen, thanks to him, and he wanted to be somewhere far away from the fallout.

His abrupt stop seemed fitting. The heavy, relentless rain and high winds had made visibility impossible. His wiper blades struggled to clear the mud that caked his windshield. He was hopelessly late for his flight. Was God finally sending him to hell for all his evil deeds?

He perspired profusely even when he was calm, but now the panic had broken the dam and his body was wet, a slimy film of stink.

"Fuck this cell phone," he cursed, staring at the readout. *"No Service"*. "What else can go wrong?" He loosened his belt to release the five rolls of fat around his waist.

He wanted to shoot everyone at his office. He blamed them for his delay and the desperate situation in which he found himself.

His meeting had dragged on an extra two hours at his company, United Weapon Systems. He knew the extra time he had allocated had been necessary in order to solidify the sale of his highly advanced impulse carbine: the Pulsar XR-36. This was the weapon of the future, but for a better price, he had perfected it sooner than the United States military expected. It was going to the highest bidder and it was not the United States. He was now a traitor and hoped his new friends would find a place for him in their new world order.

He recalled how impatient the military had become after the attack on America, how they demanded a weapon be built that could make them impervious to any further terrorist attacks. The paranoia grew, and the new president tightened the restrictions on the American public, reducing the country to a police state, its economy effectively shut down. It was no longer easy to distinguish between the terrorists' tactics and America's response. Who was good, and who was evil?

Allan Vincent knew he was under scrutiny, that soon his action would be discovered. No one would believe the corruption he had seen within the new administration, its weak president essentially a pawn of his advisors, especially his Vice-president.

His watch beeped, bringing him back to the present. It was his nerdy scientists, like always, explaining everything to him in their own high-tech jargon. He believed they did it just to frustrate him. Nevertheless, he had no choice and took their abuse.

"Just speak fucking English!" he remembered shouting at them as he kept looking at his watch impatiently.

The storm continued to pelt his car as he trembled at the thought of the men he would soon be meeting in South America. He knew they were ruthless killers—a new breed of terrorists that made Bin Laden look like a reasonable man. He knew if he did not show up on time and they felt they were being screwed on this deal, he was a dead man.

He looked at his watch again. He would not make the evening party, but he was confident that if he could get in the air within the next five hours, he would be at his meeting on time.

"Where's the goddamn highway?" he screamed, slamming his fist against the side window.

The Pulsar XR-36 prototype was safely in his truck and ready for its demonstration. If they liked what it could do and transferred the five-billion dollars in his offshore account, they would have a thousand weapons that would bring any country to their knees. The transaction for one thousand units was almost complete. At first, what he had created scared him. Anyone using his weapon would have at his or her fingertips a deadly weapon capable of inflicting unimaginable devastation. Unlike conventional rifles, this one, with its range and wide beam, could eliminate a hundred soldiers with one pull of the trigger. A battle would be over within seconds, bodies ripped apart from a high impulse beam that tore through skin and shredded internal organs.

This sale would be his first—and last. He planned to spend the rest of his life lounging on some secluded beach in the Caribbean, where he could work on a dark tan and sip those tropical drinks with the cute umbrellas all day long.

Allan Vincent feared no one, but his situation had shattered his confidence. He understood that his money and power, along with his grating behavior toward others, made him the most unlikable character to command a multibillion-dollar corporation. However, he could not have cared less what people thought of him. He had been laughed at most of his life and now, with his wealth and his power, he was getting the last laugh.

Nevertheless, now he was alone and helpless.

Like all men with power, he had the military courting him for the new toys he could make for them. His biggest and most profitable customers were the world's most feared terrorists. Off the books, he was getting paid billions of dollars for the weapons he would supply them—weapons he knew would kill American soldiers and US civilians.

He understood the golden rule of terrorists: never trust anyone. A few weeks earlier, he had finally completed the RX—666, the only defensive weapon against the Pulsar. He had it hidden, along with the plans, at his home in the Cayman Islands, an insurance policy in case his new friends had other plans for him.

With all the rumors buzzing on Capitol Hill regarding the criminal investigation against him, he had kept his campaign contributions flowing to the politicians who favored his arms business. Thus paid, they continued voting favorably for his industry, all the while impeding the criminal investigation that was being mounted against him. He was ruthless with his money and blackmailed enough of his political cronies to overlook his illegal arms sales, even though the lives and safety of Americans around the world were threatened. He had looked on smugly as gun control legislation remained locked in congressional committees, while crime throughout the United States and around the world escalated out of control. The fanatics who didn't want to lose their precious handguns and hunting rifles kept him in business with their incoherent and outdated arguments about constitutional rights.

However, being stuck in the middle of nowhere did not exactly fit into his plans. He guessed the problem was electrical, since the car had simply coasted to a halt, coughing its last sign of life on the black desert. He usually employed a driver, but he had not wanted anyone to know he was leaving the country permanently.

Not one with a keen sense of direction, especially at night, he had made a wrong turn and found himself on some desert road with no signs or markers. If he had not been cruising at ninety miles per hour, he might have spotted the small interstate sign on a service road ten miles back that would have taken him to the main highway and the forty miles to McCarran Field, where his private jet was fueled and ready to whisk him to Sunrise Island, South America.

The rain, which had been hammering the car for the last two hours, had finally stopped, giving way to sixty-mile-per-hour winds that howled through the empty desert, kicking up wet sand in their wake. Unable to see out of his car windows, he stepped out into a torrent of flying desert mud that instantly covered his entire body in a warm, wet overcoat.

"Shit!" he screamed, his sounds muffled by the high, whistling winds. He wiped the sticky sand from his glasses with his handkerchief. "Where the hell am I?"

He squinted, putting his glasses back on. He could just make out a light flickering in the distance, its shining silhouette barely discernible through the swirling sandstorm that nearly blinded him as he closed his car door. He carefully inched his way along the muddy desert field, his feet being stuck in rain-soaked crevices. His three-hundred-pound frame struggled toward the pulsating beam as he lifted his heavy legs with his arms.

After walking a hundred yards or so, his shoes caked with mud, his Armani double-breasted wool suit totally ruined, and his face looking as if he had just had a mudpack at the spa, he discovered the illumination to be a porch light attached to an old shack beat up from years of harsh sandstorms. The high winds continued to howl, shaking the structure to its shabby foundation.

Relieved and excited to find sanctuary from the storm, Allan failed to notice the exposed wires of the flickering light. They dangled, the connection broken.

He knocked, pounding his fist against the door, hoping someone was there to offer help. After ten seconds, his frustration got the best of him and he impatiently tried the door, which opened freely. The room was bright, inviting him into its shelter. But something did not seem right to him. The single light bulb dangled from an exposed ceiling outlet, flickered its yellow beam, yet the room seemed illuminated by something other than this lone light bulb.

Rusty hinges squeaked as the door closed by itself behind him. He heard a click and, to his surprise, found himself locked inside. The howling wind disappeared as if he had been sucked inside a powerful vacuum chamber. His overweight body heaved as he sucked in large breaths, the room growing ever brighter.

Like the inside of a ghost's tomb, the cabin reeked with the caustic smell of mold and decay. He gagged, simultaneously walking through a cobweb that spiraled down from the ceiling. In the center of the room was a broken table with one chair that had seen better days. Over by what had once been, a window stood the remains of a kitchen sink. Next to the window, cabinets hung loosely, their doors dangling on broken, rusty hinges. A small cot with a mattress that had most of its stuffing popping out occupied the opposite corner.

Tired and scared, Allan shuffled over to the chair by the table, brushing the cobwebs off his shoulders. His weight was too much for the rickety chair, though, and it splintered into several pieces. On his back, he could see that the roof was mostly gone, the night sky and a million stars staring back at him. He could see the sand swirling over the roof.

But the cabin remained silent inside, beyond dead quiet. The sound of his shallow breathing and pounding heartbeat echoed inside his head, growing steadily into a high-pitched, screeching chorus that rang cacophonously like the bells in a cathedral tower. He clutched at his ears in pain.

Then, nothing.

He was alone. But he was sure he was being watched. He

could feel thousands of fingers moving over his body, tracing his spine from his neck to his lower back. His breathing and heartbeat grew faint, their throbbing rhythm muffled by a subsonic, superhuman hum. He trembled, cold. Something was touching his body.

Inside his mind, a voice spoke.

"You are being punished for the terror you have brought into the world," the almost feminine voice intoned. *"Tonight your body will die. Then the bodies of your associates will die. And once again, the world will be safe."*

He tried to speak, moving his lips. But nothing came out. His thoughts imploded as the room spun around him. He held his hands out in front of his face and watched in disbelief as his limbs began to disappear, one at a time, as though his life was being sucked from him. He tried to scream, but again, nothing. Finally, a bright flash of light blinded him briefly before everything went dark. All that remained were his thoughts, jumbled and alone, which floated somewhere in quiet darkness.

* * * * *

"Did you get the weapon?" Rebecca asked her brother Ian.

"Yes. I couldn't find the plans for the RX-666. We need to check his company for the blueprints."

"We can handle that later. I just hope this will end it, once and for all," Rebecca said as she adjusted her robe. "Father's waiting. Ian, take this back to him. I'll clean up this mess."

CHAPTER TWO

Chief of Police Robert Philips tried to focus his eyes as he approached the crime scene. His men had closed down SR 35 using yards of crime scene tape. They were blocking the early bird commuters, mostly commercial trucks, to a snail's pace. His head ached from a hangover, which made any facial movement painful. *It's going to be one of those days,* he thought.

Springs River was a sleepy retirement community, sheltered from murders, sexual crimes, and burglaries. However, today, as he pulled up to the victim's car and the yellow tape stretched around it, Philips viewed the first probable murder in Springs River since he became chief of police.

He spied his small team of officers, which consisted of one rookie and one experienced officer, and noticed that the two men looked exhausted, as though it had taken them several hours to cordon off the crime scene. He scanned the area around the victim's car and then stuck his head out the open window.

"What happened?" Philips asked Officer Davis, the senior of the two officers.

"I haven't found any evidence that this was nothing more than a guy who died of natural causes," said a dumbfounded Davis, shrugging his shoulders.

Robert Philips knew the small retirement community where they worked was ill prepared to handle a crime scene, especially a possible murder. He also knew Davis would make a hasty conclusion just so he could get back to his warm office.

Philips had arrived at the scene forty-five minutes after his two officers. Five-thirty in the morning was excessively early to venture out into the cold desert air, especially with a pounding headache from a long line of late-night binges.

As he stepped out of his Jeep Cherokee, his cowboy boots, which he hated, sunk deep into the soft mud, and he lost his balance. Before he could right himself, he was face down in a wet pool of sandy mud. His men held their laughter, turning away so he couldn't see the snickers on their faces.

He pulled himself up, wiped the mud off his face, and vented his anger at the two officers. "Stop standing around and look for some evidence," he screamed.

"Chief, it appears the victim died of natural causes," the young rookie stammered nervously. "We can't find any signs of a struggle or any wounds or bruises."

While the rookie fumbled with a small spiral notepad, the coroner paced impatiently.

"I've got other appointments as soon as my office opens," said the coroner, who was also the town's only family doctor. "I don't like to keep my breathing patients waiting."

The two officers, frustrated with their chief's unprofessional behavior, released the body to the coroner.

"I think you need to get some help for your problem," Davis said, taking the chief aside as he had many times before. "You're scaring that young officer."

Brad Davis had been working in Springs River for over twenty years, turning down the Chief of Police position when it opened up, and was happy the town had hired an experienced detective from Los Angeles. He just wasn't prepared to work for a drunk. Still, he liked Philips, and they became close friends in a community that did not offer much of a social life.

"Go home," said Davis, "I'll write up the report. Come back to the office when you're sober."

* * * * *

Later that morning, Philips asked Davis into his office to discuss the case. Davis, unable to hide the frustration on his face, tossed him the file, which was labeled, *closed*.

"What's this? You've closed the case already?" Philips asked, as Davis stood up. "Sit. We need to talk about this and a few other things."

"What's to talk about?" Davis replied. "The guy died of natural causes. There was no evidence of foul play. He was as big as a house."

Philips was alert, sober, and ready to investigate last night's death. The quick conclusion that a thirty-five-year-old white male had died of natural causes made him uneasy, even if the victim was obese. Something was strange at the crime scene, and it wasn't his fall in the mud. He couldn't put his finger on it just yet, but he was determined to figure it out.

"How the fuck can someone so young die just like that?" he barked.

"Shit happens," Davis said nonchalantly. "This guy just had a load of crap dumped on him yesterday. It was his time to die. That's how it works. We all have a number…when it's up…it's up. Just give it a rest and close the file."

The look on Philips' face said he wasn't buying it.

"You do what you gotta do," Davis said, throwing his hands up in the air in disgust. "As far as I'm concerned, he died of natural causes. Case closed."

"My gut," Philips said, massaging his temples, "tells me we missed something out there."

"Headache?" Davis asked with a sarcastic grin, changing the subject.

"What do you think?"

"I think you need to get some help before that poison kills you."

"I can stop whenever I want to," Philips said. "I'm just not ready. The pain . . . is still there."

Davis stood up and left. Philips memories drifted in as he stared at a picture of his wife and daughter on the corner of his desk.

Robert Philips, a washed up detective put out to pasture in the Town of Springs River sixty-five miles southwest of Las Vegas, was their new chief of police. Having been implicated in a Los Angeles police scandal, he had hoped that the calm surroundings of Springs River would slow down his drinking. In addition to the disgrace that affected over forty officers found guilty of planting evidence to convict known criminals, Philips' close relationship with most of the officers involved had the rat squad ripping his life apart. To them, he was guilty by association, and his promising career was over. Even though he was found completely innocent, he had become a pariah; the cloud that remained over his head put him behind a desk and out of the field. With his wife and daughter dead and now his career seemingly finished, his drinking had escalated to the point where he arrived at work drunk almost every day. He had become bitter and angry with everyone.

He looked at the now tainted picture of the woman he was married to for fifteen years. She was a simple, loving woman, who tolerated the hours and moods of a Los Angeles detective. Even though he missed most of the family life he so wanted due to the irregular hours of murder investigations, he loved his wife Alice and his daughter Stephanie.

He was a moral man at heart, even though the job had hardened his soul. He had always prided himself on doing the right thing. When Alice had become pregnant after one night of an emotional escape, going beyond the casual platonic relationship he was happy they had, he did without hesitation the only thing a responsible man would do: he married her. While he had never been married before Alice, he always felt an abyss deep inside his soul about a past life he had once experienced. However, he had no memories of such a life. He just rationalized that God was filling this void by giving him a daughter.

When his wife and daughter had been killed in a car accident, he was convinced those feelings he kept locked deep inside foretold the future. He went into a deep depression, crawling inside a bottle. He became obsessed and bitter that his detective skills did not catch the clues he should have seen to prevent the accident from happening.

When the job opened up for police chief in Springs River, he decided the desert would be a good place to dry out and start a new life. His prostate cancer was in remission, and minimizing his stress was, according to his doctor, his top priority. The desert air, being secluded from the memories of his wife and daughter, the quiet town he was in charge of—all gave him the opportunity to drown his sorrows in private.

The town's residents, mostly retired couples desiring a simple life, along with mineral hot springs, golf courses, five star restaurants, and outlet stores, made Springs River a perfect setting to be the chief of police. The adjustment from big city crime to the mundane job of giving tickets to speeders who drove through his town was hard to make at first, but he soon learned to relax, take up golf, and read. Last night's crime was the first he had encountered that didn't involve a dispute over a parking space or someone playing golf too slowly.

His thoughts returned to the present. He pictured the way they had found the body inside the car. It didn't make sense to him. If the victim had died of natural causes, why was he covered in mud? His shoes were ruined. He must have been outside his car when he died. If the death occurred somewhere else, at least four strong men would have been needed to lift the three hundred pound dead body. He speculated that the death had occurred somewhere else and that these mystery men had positioned Allan Vincent back inside his car. However, if his theory was correct, why was there only one set of tire tracks at the scene? He had to go back out there.

He told Officer Davis that he was going over to the coroner's office and would be back around 3:00 p.m. to relieve him. His partner had a golf time at 3:30 p.m., and Philips did not want him to miss it. The unsolved crimes in Springs River could always wait.

He had a hunch that needed more massaging before he officially closed this file. He hoped the coroner had concluded his autopsy so he might have some additional clues.

CHAPTER THREE

Chief Philips was grateful that the rain had stopped and the skies
had cleared the following morning. He did not want to deal with
the mess created by a desert rainstorm. It was a crisp, bitter cold
morning, which froze the previous day's moist desert floor, making
the sand a hard, slick mess. He carried in his pockets several
plastic sandwich bags, Spring River crime scene supplies and a
black permanent marker. With his evidence toolbox in hand, he
was ready to look for clues that his men might have missed early
yesterday morning. Something just didn't make sense to him. *Why
would a man, whose car worked perfectly, stop in the middle of
nowhere and walk out into a desert storm?* Phillips mumbled.

The blackness of the morning when they found the body
had not revealed an old shack a hundred yards from the highway.
Footprints heading in that direction were perfectly molded into the
frozen clay. They could have been Vincent's, since they were
almost twelve inches below the surface—a sure sign of someone
carrying excessive weight. With a chisel and hammer, he carved
out one of the footprints, placing it in the trunk of his police car to
compare later with Vincent's shoes that were at the coroner's
office.

The trail led toward the old weathered shack, which might
mean the victim sought help before he died.

"How would he have known a house was out there?"
Philips mumbled aloud. "It was too dark."

Maybe these aren't his footprints, he thought.

He scowled.

As he followed the trail of footprints, he noticed that the
clay closer to the shack had changed both in color and in

consistency. He held up the evidence bag of the mud from around the car and the mud near the cabin. They were distinctly different. He would have to check Vincent's shoes to see if there were two samples of mud, which would confirm that he had come to the cabin.

At first, he hadn't noticed the clues, but then it hit him. Why weren't there footprints leading back to the car where Vincent's body was found? He squinted. Something just didn't make sense. The only impression going back to Vincent's car was a smooth wake, as if a small boat had carried the body back. It was possible that someone had dragged the body back to the car, but the smooth impression was too small for Vincent's body size.

"Now you're thinking crazy, Philips," he scolded himself. "Get a fucking grip, and do your job."

The building, by all appearances, had been abandoned for years. The porch light's exposed wires dangled unconnected from the light fixture.

"Did Vincent find this place by sheer luck?" he wondered, his brow furrowed.

There were no visible signs that anyone was living there or had lived there for some time. He dusted for prints, spraying a light powder over the doorknob and a portion of the door where a hand might have pushed it open. He found some prints and pulled them off with clear tape. He used his camera to take additional shots of the prints, just in case his first attempt failed.

After he had put on his rubber surgical gloves, he tried to open the door, twisting the knob. It easily opened to his touch. Inside was an empty shell—no furnishings of any kind.

Someone must have moved out long ago and took everything, he thought.

Once he was fully inside, the door gently swung closed. The short hairs on the back of his neck perked up, his internal alarm system ringing in his head as his heart pounded. He assured himself the wind had closed the door. The room became quiet, drowning out the swirling winds that had begun to stir up the sand outside. It was so quiet he tried the door to let in some sounds. It was locked. Even though the doorknob turned, the door would not move. It was sealed tight. His legs began to shake as his trembling hand reached for his gun.

He backed away from the door and drew his gun, ready to

shoot off the lock and escape. Before he could take action, his
body had become paralyzed. He felt a cold force blanket his body.
He wasn't in any pain. He knew someone was in the room with
him, and he tried to call out. His lips moved, but there was no
sound.

With his heart pounding, he felt a tingling sensation over
his entire body. He could feel thousands of hands lightly caressing
his body all at once making his muscles twitch with little spasms.
It felt good, healing, and relaxing. Then he felt the sensation go
inside his body, warming him. For a moment, panic consumed
him, his muscles clenched, his stomach filling with acid. Then, it
stopped and he became tranquil, more relaxed than he had ever felt
in his life. He could hear distant voices calling out to him. But
they were not voices; they were thoughts filling his head. He
heard his wife and daughter calling his name, but wondered if he
was hallucinating. Then those voices were overtaken by the din of
a large hall full of voices. Slowly, imperceptibly, his mind drifted
back to the shack and the present moment. Was he drunk, after
all? Had he lost his mind from so much alcohol abuse?

"No," said a soft, gentle voice.

"Who are you?" he said as his voice returned.

There was no response.

And just like that, he was alone again. Exhausted and
baffled, he glanced at his watch: only one minute had passed. The
door automatically swung open from a gust of wind, and sand
scattered across the floor. He picked up his evidence box and
made his way back to his car, his heart pounding out of control.
He wondered how he would explain what had just happened. He
knew no one would believe him. Everyone would just assume he
had been drinking again.

CHAPTER FOUR

Robert Philips sat on the cold examination table, in his dressing gown. He was waiting for the doctor to begin his six-month checkup. He hated this part of his illness, always dreading hearing the words from his doctor: *the cancer has returned.*

Today, he had even more on his mind. What had happened to him yesterday in the old shack had stirred up dreams he could not explain. He dreamt of people he had never known and places he had never been to, all of which seemed familiar somehow. A chateau, a woman and two small children, an angry mob shouting obscenities at them in French, the images in his dream evoked a strange sense of déjà vu. The woman in the dream had red hair and fair skin. His wife Alice, his first and only, had had dark black hair and olive skin. In the dream, he understood the language, which seemed odd since he didn't speak a word of French. He knew this had been a dream, and a strange one at that, but he couldn't get over how real it had seemed. He heard a light knock on his door.

"Come in," he said warily.

Dr. Abraham, a slight, East Indian who rarely smiled, entered the small examination room. Philips always wondered if the good doctor had been teased in his youth or if his seriousness stemmed from all the years of treating patients with terminal diseases. Regardless, he trusted his doctor with his life. If it hadn't been for Dr. Abraham's early detection and the radical radiation treatments he recommended, Philips knew he would be dead today.

But today, Dr. Abraham seemed more serious than normal. He wore a troubled expression, causing Philips' heart to sink and the bile in his stomach to rise.

"Don't spare me," Philips blurted out, his eyes riveted on the Doctor's expression.

"I am," Dr. Abraham began, still studying his report, "confused."

The silence was palpable.

"At first," the doctor continued with his East Indian lilt, "I thought the laboratory made a mistake. But they analyzed the blood work again, and the results came back the same."

"My cancer's back?" Philips said, his voice cracking, his face draining of color.

"No," the doctor said, astonished, "it is totally gone."

"Gone?"

"Yes, as if you never had cancer. I cannot explain it. Nothing like this has ever happened to any of my patients. Inside your body, your molecules communicate with each other. And, in your case, they had always said you had cancer—until now. It is as if your body received a new message telling every communication center inside you that you do not have this disease. We have drugs that can fool cancer genes, but what has happened to you is totally amazing, light-years beyond the capabilities of modern medicine. While I don't believe in miracles," he continued, smiling and pointing toward the ceiling, "something or someone likes you very much."

"This is a good thing?" Philips, puzzled, asked as the blood flowed back into his face.

"A very good thing. You are cured. I will want to monitor you for the next two years, but, by all accounts, your cancer is nonexistent. Go have a normal life and do not worry." The doctor for the first time grinned, giving his patient a warm hug before leaving.

* * * * *

After a long, forty-five minute drive back to Springs River, Philips decided to stop by the only house of worship the small retirement community had. The non-denominational building was used by the town's large Jewish and Christian communities.

Inside, a rough, unpolished brass crucifix made by a local sculptor dominated the center of the building. Adjacent to the cross was an oversized mahogany cabinet that housed the Torah. Each symbol could be tastefully covered when not in use.

Philips was amazed how two diverse religious traditions could coexist in one house of God. Throughout the years, certain holidays had been enjoyed by everyone, bringing together what seemed like God's original plan for the world.

As police chief, Philips rarely spent any time in church. He was the reticent fourth cog in a weekly golf game with Rabbi Stein, Pastor Holcomb, and Father O'Conner. They enjoyed their time with him, using it to help him find salvation in the torment he carried around each day, preaching God's wisdom as they ruined his concentration and his game and took his money as he consistently lost to them.

Today, for the first time since his wife and daughter died, he needed to be alone before God. He knelt down in a pew near the front and opened his Bible, discovering a picture of his wife and daughter. He once believed God existed. He even accepted that there were good in all human beings, but now he was depressed, drunk every night and angry with God.

"God, you're still a bastard," he whispered. "You've done it again. I don't understand why you've continued to keep me alive— *me*! Why did you take Alice and Stephanie, the two most innocent and sweetest people?"

He covered his eyes and wept, unaware that Father O'Conner had sat down next to him.

Father O'Conner placed his hand on Philips' shoulder, startling him.

"Robert, what's the matter?" he asked a faint Irish accent floating out with each word.

Father O'Conner was an immigrant from Northern Ireland. He had given up on his country, no longer willing to waste his efforts trying to stop a bloody revolution that knew no end. The deep lines on his face wrinkled as he looked at Philips, still sobbing.

"God's doing it again," Philips said softly. He looked up at the priest, his eyes swollen with tears.

"What has he done this time, my son?" Father O'Conner asked.

"He took my cancer away and allowed me to live."

"That's not a good thing?"

"No. He should have saved Alice and Stephanie. I'm not worthy of his forgiveness. And please don't tell me he has a purpose for me. All I know is that he must own a large share of all the liquor made, because I'm his biggest customer."

"Do you really believe that?" Father O'Conner said. "We've discussed this before that God does things we might not understand or accept. But everything that happens has a purpose and a logical reason, a reason that will become clear when your life ends and you meet God. Then, you'll be with your Alice and Stephanie. Right now, he has a job for you; look for the signs. You have a purpose in this world, so don't waste it."

Father O'Conner stood up, pausing for a moment. "Are you ready to take confession?"

Philips nodded.

Inside the confessional, he continued to cry as he let go of the bottled up emotions that were trapped inside him. He struggled, trying to explain about the voice, he had heard, and what had happened inside the shack. Father O'Conner didn't seem too surprised.

"If the voice was God's or one of his angel's, then a true miracle happened out there in the desert," the priest whispered through the mesh screen that separated them. "God works in mysterious ways, and this just might be one of them. If God's calling on you, you need to have a clear head so you can fully understand his message."

"You've been trying to get me to stop drinking for a long time," Philips said, his voicing growing in volume as he stood up. "I thought you were really listening to me, but you're just using this as an opportunity to—"

He left in a rage, stopping just short of saying something he knew he would regret later.

"Robert!" Father O'Conner called out.

Philips was already gone, speeding away in his car.

CHAPTER FIVE

Katie O'Riley, "Covert Meeting Planner Extraordinaire," had
brought together an elite group of terrorists on short notice,
accommodating their demands, all for a price. Her secluded
island, built like a five-star resort, had welcomed the worst of the
terrorist organizations for the last ten years. With the holy war
against the United States and its allies running out of ammo, she
filled a niche for a new breed of terrorist.

An ex-IRA soldier, Katie was the most sought-after
international weapons broker. She hated the bloodshed that she
perpetuated, and she hated herself for the role she played in
fostering a world bent on destroying itself. She was only in it for
the money. She was by partisan walking the fine line between
good and evil. While she counted her profits, hundreds of radical
factions in small, underdeveloped countries were becoming as
powerful as the corrupt armies they attacked, all because of her.

At first glance, Katie looked like a sweet Irish woman. She
stood a slender five feet, seven inches and had fair skin and long,
bright red hair that tumbled over her shoulders. Dainty freckles
dotted her nose and cheeks. Her outer appearance masked the rage
that welled inside her, a rage aimed squarely at the British
government.

Her ability to organize and bring important people together
was being tested. She had prayed that she wouldn't succeed this
time. She wanted out. But, like so many of her criminal activities,
opting out was not an option.

Nevertheless, the meeting would go on as scheduled. And she
sensed that its objective, if met, would send shockwaves
throughout the civilized world. She also understood that, after the

dust settled, she would be the most wanted criminal in the world, assuming there would be anyone left to punish her.

She promised herself this would be her last.

The meeting, though shrouded in mystery, was unprecedented in both scope and urgency. Three terrorist groups, each ruthless but largely unheralded outside their respective countries, planned to combine forces and strike decisively and swiftly against the US and its allies. Bin Laden's attack on America would pale in comparison. This time, the survivors, instead of uniting, would turn on each other.

Katie glanced at the three men waiting to be taken to their rooms. Impeccably dressed, articulate, and sophisticated, they did not look like cutthroat killers. They spoke flawless English. And they carried themselves with all the charm and refinement of Western businessmen.

It was the first time the leaders from the Irish Liberation Movement, the Arab United Front, and the Asian Freedom Fighters had met at her island. Though dapper and polite, they were clearly eager, while impatient, to even discuss the operation.

"This will make the Attack on America seem small by comparison," said Shawn Miller, the leader of the Irish Liberation Movement.

A chill ran down Katie's spine. She blushed as Miller gave her an icy stare.

Miller, dressed in a pinstriped suit, turned his back to Katie. The most wanted criminal in Great Britain, he had managed to remain elusive while, in the name of liberty, ruthlessly bringing death and destruction to anyone that got in his way. For the last decade, he had dreamt of uniting several terrorist groups and creating one military force to, in his words, "finally take the world back from the oil barons, the dictators, and the greedy CEO's that controlled their respective governments."

With Allan Vincent's Pulsar XR-36, Miller could kill two birds with one death ray, uniting the terrorists *and* giving them something with which to destroy their enemies.

Hamir Farad, head of the United Arab Front, loosened his silk tie and approached Katie.

"What you've done here…," he said, holding her hand and bringing it to his lips… "Will make you a saint in the eyes of every freedom fighter."

Katie forced a smile. *Freedom fighter my ass,* she thought.

All of you are nothing more than a need breed of Mafia.

Farad scared her the most. He was merciless with everyone, including those in his own party who disagreed with him. His pattern of destruction was simple: ignite all sides, take advantage of existing fears and prejudices, and perpetuate the cycle of violence. The UAF never claimed responsibility for their acts, which, to the organization's delight, often left Israel the primary suspect. Always blame the Jews—nobody trusts them anyway.

Farad did not have faith in anyone—let alone Shawn Miller. But he liked Miller's long-range philosophy and agreed for a time to let him organize the groups. Over the last four months, Farad had secured the allegiance of ten fanatical Arab groups, bringing together over a million mercenaries and escaped criminals.

Less was known about Lon Kim, leader of the Asian Freedom Fighters. He was quiet, with a look of patience bordering on relentlessness. Katie sensed he would cut her throat without changing his expression. An unknown commodity, Kim, like Farad, never claimed responsibility for the acts of terrorism he sponsored. His armies of killers were spread throughout Asia, blending in with the local infrastructure and going unnoticed as they planted bombs, assassinated politicians, and disrupted corporations. They acted like Muslim terrorists, but had no religious affiliation. His Army enjoyed killing, as well as getting paid for doing so.

With plenty of old money at his disposal, Kim had little difficulty paying his army of mercenaries and terrorists, which numbered close to 50,000. His group was well organized and could, with the speed and ease of an e-mail, carry out all of his orders.

The three men had met two months earlier in France, where they floated into Paris undetected. They stayed at a five-star hotel on the banks of the Seine River and conducted a meeting that, thanks to one of O'Riley's most trusted spies, could be recounted in detail. Katie had the video of the Paris meeting, which she had reviewed before the three men had arrived.

CHAPTER SIX

TWO MONTHS EARLIER IN PARIS

Shawn Miller arrived wearing a three-piece, navy blue pinstriped suit, accented with a white shirt and bright red tie. He sat at the head of the table, his smile warm and inviting.

"Gentlemen, write this day down, for it will be a day that we will celebrate for years to come. In two months, the world as we now know it will no longer exist. For the first time in modern history, or, for that matter, in the history of the world, people will be in charge and in control of their own destinies, with a little help from us."

Lon Kim raised his hand, not for permission to speak but to interrupt Miller.

"Who from the group will be in charge once we destroy our enemies?" he asked.

"We will be the new leaders," Miller responded.

Farad grinned as he listened to their conversation, slowly massaging his beard. "Are you planning on being the new world leader, Mr. Miller?"

"No. We will all share responsibility by forming the Council of Three, which will keep control over our new world order," Miller said. "Together, the three of us will be the richest people in the world, controlling most of its wealth and resources. We'll have enough weapons and followers to police the world and keep everyone in line."

Miller continued, "The Pulsar XR-36 is the most destructive weapon ever created. It can, vaporize a hundred men with one push of the trigger. Imagine what we could do with a weapon like this. Our Armies would be invincible."

Lon Kim apparently troubled at what he was hearing, stood up and paced.

"Who will have control of this weapon?" Kim asked. "What will stop us from using it on each other, eliminating the Council of Three and making it a Council of One?"

"We'll each have an equal supply," Miller said with a boyish grin. "It's called balance of power. It worked during the Cold War and no one went nuclear."

Lon Kim stared at Miller, his eyes little slits of mistrust. "I expect we will all receive our weapons at the same time? Correct?" he asked sternly.

Miller bit his lower lip, noticeable disturbed by Kim's lack of trust. "Trust me. You have nothing to worry about."

* * * * *

A month after the three men met, their plans began to come together easier than anyone had expected. Farad's ideals were accepted, especially the destruction of Israel and its Jewish occupiers. As easily as Hitler united Germany, Farad united the Arab nations. The small groups that resisted were dealt with severely, which instilled fear in anyone who dared to go against the new leader of the Arab world. His strength came from 125,000 fighting men and over a million supporters around the world.

Kim found it even easier to build his army. The economies in Asia had stumbled dramatically, causing massive unemployment, and poverty levels were on the rise. His army and his followers were ready to bring down their most hated enemy: Japan.

Miller, meanwhile, was not as lucky as his other partners were. His following, while strong, was not as large. But he was pleased with his army because it was made up almost entirely of men from British, French, and US Special Forces. They were cloaked throughout Ireland, Great Britain, and Europe, ready for rapid mobilization.

* * * * *

Jacob was conducting one of his many morning briefings, which today proved to be more adversarial than normal.

"If we act now with a swift and powerful hand and kill the Council of Three," Ian, his oldest son, said, "the terrorists will go back to being disorganized and ineffective."

"We will, my son, but not right now," said Jacob, unable to control his shaking hand or the weakness that was rapidly consuming his body. "Our timing has to be perfect and dramatic. If we just eliminate another unknown terrorist group, the world will dismiss it and not take notice. They need to believe that if terrorism is not completely stopped by all of them and all weapons of mass destruction eliminated forever, the world will be destroyed by us. They must fear us and understand negotiation of any sort will not be tolerated."

He handed out a list of the executions he wanted his children to carry out within the next two months.

"The timing has to be perfect," he said, "without any deviations. Is that understood?"

CHAPTER SEVEN

Katie's island off the southern tip of Chile was uncharted, perfect for clandestine meetings. She considered herself a facilitator, something like a matchmaker. Not for the sake of love, of course, but for the furthering of her own obsession: to see bloated and unresponsive governments suffer. Her clientele were infamous. And wealthy.

As for tomorrow's meeting, she had already begun to have second thoughts. For the first time in modern history, the Third World would move up the power ladder, bringing to their knees the bullies that had kept much of humanity starving and poor for too long. A worldwide revolution was underway, and the Council of Three held the key to its success, providing the XR-36 lived up to all its hype.

Through paid informants within the Department of Justice, Katie had learned that United Weapons Systems was about to be closed down and that Vincent, its owner and CEO, would be arrested. Thus, the stakes would be high when Miller, Farad, and Kim met.

The island had its own landing field and private, secluded pier. And Katie rarely knew her clients' mode of arrival, much less their itinerary, ahead of time. When a date was decided upon, she allowed a seven-day window to prepare for her guests. Some came very early to enjoy her hospitality and the amenities of her island, while others arrived just at the last minute. Right now, the only person missing was Vincent.

Twenty contemporary ranch houses sat along the water's edge, each the same size, and none more impressive than the other. Each house, decorated in a different ethnic theme, boasted four thousand square feet and could easily accommodate ten people. A visit to the island came with a heavy price tag, which Katie had no problem charging and her clients had no problem paying.

As was tradition for all of Katie's clients, the Council of Three's meeting had begun the night before with a lavish dinner party, prepared by two of the finest chefs in the world. The reception was lavishly displayed with chafing dishes filled with shrimp scampi, lobster, and crab legs. Caviar and the best Champagne were being passed around the room as the council of three tried to become comfortable.

For dinner roast boar, wild turkey, and pheasant topped the menu. And dozens of bottles of Bordeaux and French Cabernet towered over a steaming assortment of vegetables, yams, oysters, fresh fruits, and side dishes, each of which could easily have graced the cover of a gourmet magazine. The fine bone china used could be found at any head of state's dinner party, and the extra large wine glasses provided the added touch: a forum for the exquisite bouquet of wine.

Katie O'Riley had become a supporter of the terrorist movement long ago, forced into this occupation by the British government.

She had been born in Wexlee, Ireland, five kilometers south of Killyberg of the Don Negal bay, where her father, the town mayor, watched over the close-knit, crime-free community of farmers and craftsmen without the aid of a police department. Like she often did, Katie drifted back to her innocence.

"If you wake up to the morning sun, my little angel, and let its rays light up your face," her father began, "nothing bad will happen to you that day."

Katie's ninth birthday began like so many other mornings in Wexlee. Sitting on the back porch and cupping with both hands a warm mug of hot chocolate, she positioned her wicker chair due east to await her morning blessing.

"Katie," her father continued playfully, "give your mother a good morning kiss and then paste one on my cheek."

"After sunrise," she protested, giggling. "I don't want to not feel God kissing my cheek first."

"Oh, I see," her father teased. "God won out again."

The air was moist from the dew that fell from the tall pines that draped the back perimeter of their property, and the tile roof glistened in the morning light. The ocean behind her radiated an orange glow as the sun climbed the horizon.

Her mother sat on her pine rocker under a dim porch light, working on her needlepoint tablecloth, rocking to a tune only she could hear.

Her father, John O'Riley, stood on the porch, his stocky frame silhouetted against the morning glow. His thick, black hair and bushy mustache gave him a rugged look that set him apart from the other men in town, most of whom sported clean- shaven faces and cropped short haircuts.

John sat down to read the newspaper, as usual, but stopped short. As though on alert, he raised his head, sniffing the air and squinting at the horizon.

"Daddy," Katie called out, "what's wrong?"

"I'm not sure. Something doesn't seem right this morning."

"The sun's coming up. What could be wrong?"

"Maybe it's just my imagination," he said unconvincingly.

Barely audible at first, a thunderous roar soon overwhelmed them. Katie's cup of hot chocolate fell, shattering on the porch's wood planks. She cried as the warm, sweet brew emptied between the floorboards. Her mother jumped up as if she knew what was about to happen, dropping her tablecloth on the porch. Her father ordered both of them into the house as he scrambled to get his shotgun.

Three British military trucks and one jeep sped toward them, their engines roaring. Soldiers pointed their rifles at her father. From inside the house, Katie could hear the soldier in charge and her father shouting at each other.

"John O'Riley," the young lieutenant shouted in a high-pitched, nasally voice, and "you're under arrest for conspiring against the British Government."

"I'm the mayor of this town," her father said in disbelief. "There must be some mistake. I...like all of our citizens are peace loving people."

"I have my orders," the young lieutenant shouted. "Please cooperate, and no one will get hurt."

Realizing he would have to talk to this man's superior to

clear up the matter, John rested his shotgun against his wife's rocking chair.

Just then, Katie's mother opened the back door.

"John, what's happening?"

The shotgun slipped off the chair and crashed on the porch, misfiring from the concussion. Katie's father bent over to pick it up before it could go off again.

"Gun!" a nervous soldier in one of the trucks shouted.

The soldiers started shooting, shattering the windows and puncturing the walls with a hail of bullets. As Katie's parents tried to protect themselves from the flying shards of glass and splintered wood that too, was mistaken for aggression. Katie covered her head as the soldiers intensified the barrage. As the firing died down, she could hear the muffled moans of her parents as they writhed on the porch floorboards, riddled with bullets.

"Cease fire!" the young lieutenant shouted.

Katie peeked out the window, reeling back as one last shard fell from the window and shattered on the frame.

"Shit!" the young lieutenant blurted out, rifling through his orders. "Damn, he was not the one to supposed to be arrested...just questioned. Bloody hell. I've really screwed up this time."

Katie lifted her head higher and for the first time saw her parents lying face down, pools of blood spreading from their twisted bodies, now motionless. She held her hand tightly on her mouth, trying to muffle her cries.

"We had no choice, sir," a sergeant major nearby said. "We thought he was going to kill you. That's how we all saw it, sir."

The rest of the men nodded in agreement.

"That's not how it happened!" the young lieutenant snapped.

"Sir, that's the way I'm going to write it up in my report, and I suggest you do the same."

"Whatever you say, Sergeant," the young lieutenant said numbly.

He started back toward his jeep and then dropped to one knee and vomited.

Katie huddled against what was left of the kitchen wall and sobbed quietly. She could hear the sergeant major barking orders to two of his men.

"Go find the mayor's daughter," the sergeant major said. "We don't need any witnesses."

The sergeant major walked casually over to the lieutenant and kept him occupied while his men searched for the little girl.

Katie heard footsteps on the porch and crawled toward the living room. She looked back and saw two soldiers drag her parents inside the kitchen. One of the soldiers had a big red can and began pouring liquid over them and all over the kitchen.

Katie's eyes widened as the soldier tossed a match on her father's body. In an instant, both her father and mother were engulfed in flames. The fire began to spread toward her, forcing her toward the front door.

"She's headed out the front!" a soldier screamed.

Katie bolted toward the swath of pines, her long, red hair streaming behind her and pulling at her scalp. The first explosion seemed distant as the speeding bullet whizzed by her ear. The next one seemed closer, and for a moment, she thought she was hit. Her side burned as if a hot iron had scorched her skin. She didn't miss a step and was into the woods before another shot could be fired.

She slipped into the bough of a large pine tree and paused to catch her breath. She could feel a burning pain in her side, where there was a large hole in her blouse. She lifted the material up, fearing for the worst. The bullet had missed entering her body by a millimeter. She sighed and thanked God for protecting her. But, then she realized that God did not really protect her, he had just made her an orphan. For the first time in her life, she felt a foreboding hatred toward the God her parents had taught her to love.

She knew the woods, her childhood haunt, better than anyone. She forced herself to hold still, her heart pounding in her chest, until the soldiers gave up looking for her.

She left the tree and watched as the soldiers returned to her house, their silhouettes framed against the bright red flames that engulfed her house and lit up the morning sky.

"I'll never forget this day," she whispered, shivering in the forest. "I'll make them pay."

* * * * *

Katie's guests were arriving for their dinner party. She greeted them cordially. She offered them cocktails, knowing that dinner would be mostly silent unless she decided to do the talking. The three men never talked business until their official meeting started. They remained relaxed around Katie and engaged in light banter. They kept close to their bodyguards, giving them orders as if they were valets.

They always came dressed in black tie, a uniform that kept them on equal terms. Power was so important for each of them.

Before dinner started, the conversation centered on Allan Vincent. Why hadn't he arrived? Katie tried to assure them that he had no scheduled time of arrival and would be at the meeting tomorrow.

The tension in the room was thick. Everything rested on this new weapon, and the three men would have preferred to have Vincent with them at dinner.

"See where that bastard is hiding out," Katie whispered to Michael, her foreman. "If he's not here in the morning, we might have a bloody gunfight on our hands. And we'll be the victims!"

"Yes, Miss O'Riley," he replied.

Michael phoned Vincent's office and then tried his mobile, but he was nowhere to be found. He decided to wait until later to inform his boss of the problem.

The dinner took an hour and a half. After the last dessert was served, along with the traditional shot of fifty-year-old brandy, the three men toasted to the success of tomorrow morning's meeting and retired to their guesthouses.

As the three men and their assistants began to settle into their respective houses, their rooms, claustrophobically quiet, began to vibrate. The air in each filled with a light cold mist that crept through every crack.

The guards drew their guns and checked the windows but found nothing. Then each house went silent, the men frozen where they stood. A voice echoed inside their heads, and then a thousand other voices, the voices of their victims, joined in. Finally, the voices of the dead faded, and the one voice began to speak.

"Your plans, though intricate, will never see the light of day," Ian intoned. *"No one will ever know your designs. You have been judged by us and condemned to die without mercy."*

Farad tried to speak, but all he could do was hear his own thoughts. Miller and Kim could hear him also and began to scream their protests at the intruder who held them captive.

Release us now, bastard, Farad demanded, his rage vibrated inside his partners' minds. *You do not know who you are dealing with!*

Farad was surprised he could sense Miller and Kim, even though they were not in the room with him.

Miller yelled profanities, and Kim remained silent, as if he had accepted his fate from such a powerful force. A blinding light filled each room, and their thoughts disappeared into a cold, black void, while their bodies lay motionless.

* * * * *

David met Ian outside, laughing about how dramatic his brother had been.

"It's all in the technique, brother," Ian said. "All in the technique."

As they sucked back the stale air that had penetrated the three guesthouses, they went to find Rebecca and see how she had done with Katie.

Moments earlier, Katie had felt something strange in the air. Her instincts were very keen, but she dismissed it as just her nerves acting up, since this was going to be her last time helping this group, or any group.

Since she had taken up her quest, she had made no time for men or romance. Anger and hate had consumed her, leaving no room for the pleasures that life might have offered her. She promised herself that, once this meeting concluded, she would return to her parents' home that she had rebuilt a few years ago, begin to watch the sunrises once more, and try to heal her troubled soul.

By 11:30 p.m., she was in her room, getting ready for bed. She had to get up at 5:30 the next morning to make sure everything was ready for the meeting.

The noise from her kitchen staff seemed louder than usual. Dishes clanked. Pots and pans rang noisily. Mixed with her servants' singing, it sounded like a badly out of tune jam session.

When she closed her bedroom door to muffle the sounds, they surprisingly disappeared entirely. At the same time, her dimly lit lamp suddenly glowed brightly.

She sensed someone was in the room and looked toward her nightstand, where she stored her Beretta. But she couldn't move. She tried to scream, but all she could hear were the screams inside her head. A cold chill filled her body, draining her energy.

Her fears subsided and she began to relax. It was similar to the feelings she had had as a child while watching the sunrise with her parents. A quiet calm came over her, and she thought she could hear her father calling out her name. His voice was soon drowned out by a throng of voices. There was a bright flash of light, and then everything went dark.

The staff working in the kitchen jumped when a power surge turned on all the appliances that were idle. They could see the three guesthouses glowing out the kitchen window. Then nothing. The staff dismissed the events as some sort of electrical problem.

＊ ＊ ＊ ＊ ＊

Katie rarely had to be woken up, but she wouldn't budge. Her alarm had been buzzing for several minutes. Her maid, after knocking on her door repeatedly, finally entered the room and walked slowly over to her bed. Carefully, she shook her mistress' shoulder, but she didn't stir. She tried again a little harder, and Katie came awake, startled.

"Miss Katie," the maid said nervously. "You'll be late for your meeting."

"Oh yes, the meeting."

Katie looked puzzled. Just then, her foreman came rushing into the room.

"They're all dead," he said, obviously in shock.

"Who's dead?" she asked calmly.

"All of them!" he said. "Your guests for the meeting. Allan Vincent. They're all dead."

"When did *Vincent* arrive?" she asked, puzzled.

"He never did. He died on his way to his plane."

"Give me a minute to dress," Katie said, seemingly lost in thought and uninterested in the news. "Then show me what you're talking about."

She was still thinking about her dream: the chateau and her husband and two children.

"It was so real," she whispered. "Was it just a dream?"

In each of the guesthouses, the men lay peacefully on their beds, with no indication of foul play. Their bodyguards were also dead. Again, no obvious trauma.

"Dig some graves by the orchard and bury them before the day is over," she said, still transfixed by her dream. "And take photos of this. We might need them later on."

As she walked back to the house, she took her foreman aside.

"Get my plane ready. I'm going home."

CHAPTER EIGHT

"Why is she still alive?" Ian barked, cinching his rope belt tight around his yellowing robe.

"My choice," Rebecca replied harshly, shaking her finger wildly at her brother. "Why do you care?"

"Father's orders were explicit," he shouted back, his face red with rage.

"As the eldest and the one in charge, I have a certain amount of discretion during our assignments. If I feel other actions will further our goals, then Father requires me to implement them."

Ian looked over at his brother David, who sat quietly.

"Father will not like you changing his orders," he said, looking back at his sister.

"I'm not like you," she said, shrugging. "When I end a life, I do so peacefully. And, further, I don't play games with my subjects," she said waving a finger at her brother. "This time, since I knew of our ultimate goal, I chose to let Katie live."

"Was that the same logic you followed when you took away Robert Philips' cancer?"

Rebecca rolled her eyes, frustrated that she had found herself in another meaningless argument with her brother.

"Ian, you've never been able to see the big picture," she said. "All you're capable of doing is taking life. While I, like our mother, can differentiate between taking a life during a mission and saving a life that needs saving."

"I'll never understand you and don't want to," he said, disappearing into the dark night air.

She had already tuned him out. In eight weeks, her assignment would be completed and she would be headed home. She was happy they had chosen the United Nations as their stage to make their statement to the world. She was prepared to do whatever was necessary to cleanse the world without destroying it.

* * * * *

Katie couldn't understand why she had decided to return to her childhood home. She had terrible memories of the place, and she could still remember her parents' deaths vividly.

She tried to rekindle her hatred for the British government, but for the first time felt compassion instead. Her quest for vengeance had been transformed into a yearning for peace. Something that night on her island changed her.

How?

She wasn't sure. All she knew was that something was pushing her gently toward a destination that she, before the dream, had never known existed.

When she arrived in Wexlee, she was dismayed at how much it had changed. Her birthplace had been ravaged by the IRA's cancerous "Religious War."

"You're the spitting image of your mother," said Father O'Brien, now in his seventies, as he hugged her tightly.

"My mother had a special quality," she said, wiping her eyes. "One that I hope God will bestow on me, if He'll forgive my sins."

"God forgives all his children, Katie," Father O'Brien said, holding her tight, "if they commit to the Holy Word and ask for forgiveness."

"I'm ready, Father," Katie said, looking deep into his eyes. "I'm so tired. I just hope I can move on before the pain takes my soul to hell."

"You're home now."

* * * * *

Before settling into her parents' rebuilt home, she stopped at the post office to mail away the photographs of the three terrorists that died on her island. She walked into the small office in a daze; she had become a messenger for the voice in her head. She did not know or understand the meaning of her actions, but she followed them without question.

The voice?

It must be God, she thought, *telling me to undo the wrongs I have committed.*

She wrote a simple note to go with each set of photos:

You're next.

She sent the packages out, each one addressed to a different terrorist organization, addresses she had in her client files. She hoped some of the letters would end up in the hands of law officials as well.

The voice continued to speak to her, repeating, *"Relief will soon consume you. Relief will soon consume you."*

CHAPTER NINE

Robert tried to sleep, disturbed by voices that continued to echo in his head. They were not loud or physically disturbing. He just couldn't sleep. Instead, he spent his night's wide-awake, still absorbing the good news from Dr. Abraham, still waiting for the voices of his wife and daughter to return.

He kept going over his experience at the abandoned shack. The light, the dead quiet, the sensation of being massaged by a thousand hands, none of it made any sense to him.

"Could that shack hold the secret of divine miracles?" he wondered aloud.

He was convinced that Allan Vincent had been in the cabin before or at the time, he died, and he was certain that a higher power had destroyed one life and saved another. He kept dissecting it repeatedly. Why was he saved and another human being put to death? Who was this Vincent guy?

He tossed and turned in bed, working out the clues in his mind, unable to find a connection. By 6:30 in the morning, he was up and out the door. He was gripped with the need to find some answers and knew that he needed to start understanding that Allan Vincent was. He hoped there was a trail, something to make sense out of what had happened inside the shack.

Rain returned with a vengeance to Springs River, triggering rare flash flood warnings all over the county. That afternoon, Philips was notified that the shack he had dubbed "The Divine Miracle Sanctuary" had been swept away by a river of mud. When the raging waters finally subsided, nothing remained to prove that the shack had ever existed. He was now forced to keep to himself whatever story he might have wanted to share about his miracle. He pondered the irony of the flash floods, the first ever recorded in the county.

At his office, he tapped into the FBI database and located Allan Vincent's home address. He had lived in a new suburb fifteen miles due east of the Las Vegas Strip. What was once desert had now mushroomed into a typical American bedroom community. He was amazed by how sprawling the once small transient town had become.

Since his investigation was unofficial, he lied to the local authorities in order to get access to Vincent's house. And since he was the lead investigator into Allan Vincent's death, the Board of Directors allowed him some access to Vincent's office.

Even after spending two hours at the victim's home under the supervision of Vincent's personal attorney, nothing meaningful turned up. Frustrated, Philips wondered if he would find the same result at United Weapons Systems.

You old fart. You don't even know what you're looking for, he thought. *Something just has to turn up at his office,* he assured himself.

* * * * *

"Everything was destroyed," Katie's foreman on Sunrise Island said between gulps of air. "The servants' quarters are the only buildings left standing. A fire, one so hot, that nothing remains but ashes."

Katie was silent, paralyzed by his words. *How could this happen? Every building had a state-of-the-art sprinkler system.*

The voices had become less frequent, which brought an emptiness she did not enjoy. They acted like a drug: when they stopped, her bitterness returned.

She did not want hateful thoughts controlling her again, so she resumed her family's morning ritual, except now she read the newspaper like her father before her, scanning the articles while watching the sunrise. She had been home just a week when the voices returned.

CHAPTER TEN

Before Robert had left Springs River, he received a fax from a friend at the FBI, which was proving to be very useful. He learned that Vincent had been the CEO of a company that designed state-of-the-art weapons, more like designer guns, created from the specifications of his clients.

Had an illegal weapons deal gone sour? Vincent had been dealing with some fanatical customers, selling guns to countries with factions that hated the United States.

The FBI had known for some time that a big order was coming down the pipeline. They were not too concerned with the sale of the M-16, FAL rifle, AK-47, or RPG-7 grenade launchers that worried the Bureau. It was a new weapon that Vincent's company had been working for the United States military. Information on the weapon itself was sketchy at best. The Bureau knew its code name, Pulsar XR-36, but little was known of its design or function.

Philips read the long list of countries Vincent allegedly sold weapons to, most of which had known ties to terrorist groups.

"What the fuck happened to our country's commitment to destroying these terrorist groups?" he grumbled aloud. "Are we back to square one?"

It appeared the FBI was getting ready to shut down United Weapons Systems. Perhaps Vincent's clients panicked and opted to erase any trail that might lead the authorities to them. But, Philips wondered, did they get the secret weapon?

He was frustrated. He needed answers and had no clue how to link this to Vincent's death out on the desert. The fax listed the senators and congressmen who supported United Weapons Systems, but their names had been blacked out. He wondered if Vincent's friends in the government knew about his impending arrest.

"Is that why he was killed and not me?" he wondered aloud. "Maybe it was a deal gone sour, and my cancer being eliminated had nothing to do with the shack and his death. But *how* did they kill him? Shit, maybe a new biological virus!"

He folded the fax and placed it in his jacket pocket. He had a puzzled look on his face as he remembered his miracle in the same place where Vincent had died.

As he got out of his SUV, the enormous size of United Weapons Systems overwhelmed him. He was asked to wait in the lavishly decorated reception area until Vincent's secretary was off the phone. The lobby was decorated with awards and what he thought was propaganda, giving the impression that military weapons, the toys of grown men, the destroyers of life, were as wholesome as apple pie and the American way of doing business.

He glanced at the *Los Angeles Times* on the coffee table and noticed the headline above the fold: "Three terrorist leaders die mysteriously on uncharted island."

Below the headline, a mug shot of Katie O'Riley sent chills down his spine. Her face was eerily familiar, but he couldn't place where or how he might have met her. The black and white photo didn't do her justice; still, Philips felt his heart skip at the sight of her.

He jotted down her name and decided to dust off his old files and see where he might have met or seen this striking woman.

"Hello," someone said, startling him.

He looked up and saw a short, stocky woman wearing a black dress and dark hose. Caked on makeup and silky, jet-black hair gave her a Gothic look. She introduced herself as Mr. Vincent's secretary.

"I was told you think Mr. Vincent was murdered?" she said, patting her red nose with a tissue. "I hope you're wrong. He was such a wonderful man to work for, and everyone around here loved him."

A little over the top, Philips told himself. *Liar.*

She directed him down a long corridor decorated with awards and photos of Vincent with presidents, prime ministers, and other officials from around the world. Vincent's office was larger than Philips had imagined. Of course, anything was larger than his cubbyhole. He looked around but didn't know where to begin.

The desk drawers were all locked, as were the file cabinets. The secretary sat down on a large leather couch and watched him intently. She sat upright, with her hands resting on her thighs.

"Can these drawers be opened?" he asked pleasantly.

"Not unless you have a search warrant," she said, her demeanor turning ice cold.

"What about these file cabinets?" Philips asked sheepishly, trying out his boyish grin that had always worked on his wife.

She scowled.

"What are you hiding?" he asked, hoping for a reaction.

"We're on contract with the government and everything in these offices is highly confidential," she said matter-of- fact, turning her nose up as her lips pressed together. "As you can see, there is nothing here to help your investigation, and it's time for you to go."

He noticed Vincent's calendar on the corner of his desk and thumbed to the day he had died.

"That's not for your viewing," she snapped.

He ignored her. There was nothing noted on that day, but he noticed the letters "K.O." on the next day.

"Thanks for your time," he said, heading for the door.

In the elevator, he remembered the newspaper headline.

"KO, KO," he repeated to himself. "Knock out? No. It's gotta be something . . . Katie. Katie O'Riley?"

CHAPTER ELEVEN

The sentry shivered. The full moon illuminated his path as he kicked the sand, bored. He hated patrolling the perimeter while his comrades slept in warm bunkers.

"We're in the middle of nowhere," he complained aloud. "No one knows we even exist."

The desert night was quiet as it had been every night since they had come into Syria under the protection of President Bashar al-Asad. He waved to his brother fifty yards away. But his brother, dancing to the music that was coming out of his Walkman, didn't notice. Amir made his turn toward the entrance to the quarters where the rest of his comrades slept. Their snoring was as loud as the machine shop his father owned in Pakistan. He sighed sadly, wishing he were home and resting quietly in his bed. He kicked the metal door, hoping to disturb someone so they could share his boredom.

Hidden in cement bunkers sixty miles west of Damascus, Hamir Farad's army waited for orders to mobilize against Israel. The orders had been expected earlier that day; however, word from their leader never came, nor had the new weapon they had been promised. The soldiers had become restless, anxious to rid themselves of the Jews who did not belong in their homeland.

The night wind slowly swept across the desert, kicking up swirling mounds of sand. The skies were clear like every night, thousand of stars shining in the black sky. The wind whistled through the cement bunkers, playing a meditative song that lulled the soldiers to sleep. The sentries shuffled through the compound in a relaxed mood, knowing they were protected by the vast desert sand dunes.

Amir's brother did not notice the change as he surveyed the compound while listening to his music, his headphones tightly affixed to his ears. He looked across the perimeter and saw his brother waving his arms. He waved back, confused at the erratic movements his sibling was making. He pressed the stop button on his Walkman, a gift he had bought himself his last semester at Yale. With his headphones draped around his neck, he cupped his hands to call out to his brother.

His lips moved, but nothing came out. The silence was frightening. It was then that he saw the wave of sand approaching the compound. His brother was still standing, motionless, frozen in time. The sand rolled over him like a fog bank. Before he could react, he, too, was engulfed in the sandy mist.

He found the sensation paralyzing and at the same time peaceful. Voices filled his head, banging loudly to get out. Then came the pain. First, it felt like a headache, then it started to rip at the nerve endings inside his skull. Unable to move, his arms glued to his sides, he could not apply any pressure to his temples to relieve his anguish. Then, suddenly, a blinding light flashed before everything went dark.

The mist seeped quietly through the cracks and crevices within the bunkers, extinguishing all life in a matter of seconds. Five thousand men and women died in their sleep. No signs of foul play. No signs of aggression from an enemy.

Across the globe, terrorist armies in Asia and Northern Ireland perished in similar fashion that night.

* * * * *

Ian, corralling the vapors for use in the next job, smiled at how smoothly he had completed his assignment. The ubiquitous nature of his campaign, the fact that he struck seemingly everywhere at once, impressed his sister, who just shook her head in wonderment.

Several weather-monitoring stations worldwide reported three isolated storms in Syria, Asia, and Northern Ireland. The storms appeared on-screen for just forty-five seconds before disappearing. And officials could offer no rational, let alone scientific, explanation.

* * * * *

The United Nations called an emergency meeting the following morning, which every member nation attended. Speculation inside the UN's General Assembly focused on the possibility of a power play by some radical terrorist faction. Was there an internal purge? More important still, did some fanatical group have at its disposal a new biological weapon?

While it appeared to be a good thing, ridding the world of madmen and fanatics, not knowing who was responsible left world leaders terrified and confused. Every investigative agency from the free world was put on alert and assigned the tasks of finding and then destroying the group responsible.

Religious people of all faiths feared that God was sending a message, and panic spread like wildfire. No one could possibly know that the world had only just begun to undergo a radical transformation, one that, when complete, would forever alter life on Earth.

CHAPTER TWELEVE

While the world watched as their Muslim leaders denied any involvement in the mass murders, the UN argued. Some member countries that had been accused in the past of harboring and supporting terrorist activities were now frightened. Others, primarily Iran, Syria, Jordan and Saudi Arabia, suspected the United States and Israel were behind the mass killings.

The US, meanwhile, snubbed its nose at the UN, holding a secret meeting at Camp David with Great Britain and Israel. Peace talks had ceased, and the tension in the Middle East rivaled that of the Six Day War.

* * * * *

"Idiots!" President Hopkins growled under his breath, slamming his fist down onto the table.

Already burdened by a weak economy and unfavorable press, the president now had to contend with conspiracy theories from the Middle East. The legacy from George W. Bush did not help matters. Countries from the Middle East accused the US of building weapons of mass destruction aimed at another war on terrorism.

Hopkins' own track record of covert operations, assassinations, and illegal arms sales further eroded his credibility. If causing distrust was the killers' intent, they were succeeding. Hopkins' staff was being ripped apart; his military chiefs hid behind their loyal followers.

The president appeared uneasy and impatient, setting the

tone for the meeting.

"Gentlemen," he began, "unless your people have come up with some idea of who is killing off the scum of the world and how they are doing it, we are powerless to defend ourselves, especially from what the world thinks of the three of us."

"We've been accused of so many things for so long that it just rolls off our backs," Abraham Levy, the Israeli prime minister, responded. "You know our stand on terrorism: we retaliate with equal or stronger force. That's how we've survived and will continue to survive. These men that were killed, they were our enemies. So let's not worry what the world thinks. Let's find this group and give them a medal, maybe even a parade."

"I don't feel bad for the dead terrorists," the president said, "but in a free world, we cannot tolerate a group of fanatics taking the law into their own hands, especially with some sort of biological weapon. We could be next?"

Allan Smith, the prime minister of Great Britain, stood up and began to pace, his hands locked behind his back as he addressed the two men.

"Interpol and her majesty's Secret Service can't find any clues or informants that know what's going on," he said. "Our best biologists and covert operatives have all hit a dead end. We know it's not a new strain of anthrax. And we've ruled out the most obvious, botulism. It could be a new strain of mycoplasma. If it is, we're all in trouble. If history has taught us anything, it's that crazed fanatics will go to any length to achieve their objectives. The Nazis demonstrated the relentlessness of this pathology. Someone out there has developed a biological weapon that far exceeds any of our experiments. Right now, I believe we're powerless until we figure out what we're dealing with."

"Maybe these people are on our side and we should offer them our support," Hopkins said. "Well, do any of you have any suggestions?"

Smith exchanged glances with Levy, and Hopkins got the sense that the two of them knew something he didn't.

"Right now, all we have is the note and photographs we intercepted, which we now know were sent by Katie O'Riley," Smith said. "What happened in Syria, Asia, and Northern Ireland must be connected to the deaths on Sunrise Island."

"How did you figure that out?" Hopkins asked, puzzled.

"It's speculation. We first determined where the letters were mailed from. We were lucky she used a post office that had a security camera. We've had eyes on her for a long time. She was there the day the packages went out, so, with her connection to these men, we concluded she was involved."

"Our religious fanatics claim it is the beginning of Armageddon," Levy said, visibly annoyed with Smith's haughty tone. "They believe that the world is going to be destroyed if we don't go back to seeking God's forgiveness."

"Maybe you should make peace with the Palestinians," Smith said sarcastically. "I'm sure neither of you can remember what started your fighting."

"Who are you to talk about making peace?" Levy steamed, his brow furrowed. "How long have you been fighting with the IRA? We could be next. These fanatics could look at our policies as terrorism."

"Then stop what you're doing immediately," Smith said, "and show the world you're a peaceful country."

"It's not that easy," Levy said, trying to control his anger. "We can't trust the Palestinians. If we give them an opportunity, they will do everything in their power to destroy us. Hamas is stronger than ever since Bush was president and uncontrollable. We'll just have to let God decide who is right and who is wrong."

"Shit," Hopkins said. "This isn't getting us anywhere. When we don't have logical answers we're supposed to, without question, have God lead the way. If we can't find any trace of chemicals on any of the victims, maybe it's not biological but something else."

"We're checking it out," Levy said, regaining his composure. "But so far we've hit a stone wall."

"Don't you think it's strange that Bashar survived this?" the president asked. "Could he have created a biological poison that we don't know about? The Syrian president is not one to be trusted."

"Anything's possible with that crazy bastard," Smith replied.

"Let's get our people on this immediately," Hopkins concluded, "before we're next."

* * * * *

"Father, have we made our point yet?" Rebecca asked.

"Not yet," he told her. "Until we destroy the primary contributors, what we need to accomplish won't be realized in the short time we have left."

"We need some messengers to spread our wishes," she said. "Unless we have more supporters who will preach the new beginning, we might fail again."

"Just get your job done before it's too late."

"I'm sorry, Father. I just feel a different approach is warranted, or we won't be able to save the world in time."

"It's time for me to show myself to the world without going through my intermediaries," her father replied. "Go out and complete the remaining assignments. Everything has to be completed before I speak to the world."

"I'll get everything done," she said, "Don't worry."

"I do worry about your judgment lately. What happened in the shack with Philips?"

"I was tired and late in cleaning up the area when he arrived and surprised me," she said, uncomfortable with deceiving her father. "He was dying from cancer, and I felt my intervention wouldn't hurt our mission. We might be able to use him later on."

"I think he could be trouble. He's already investigating what happened to Vincent and will soon discover that Katie O'Riley is connected to your little project. This can't happen anymore."

"It won't," she said, trying to block her thoughts. "I'll stick to our plans from this point on."

She kissed his cheek and was gone before he could respond.

"She's just like you," he said, smiling at his wife Esther.

As usual, she remained silent and just smiled back before returning to her computer monitor.

CHAPTER THIRTEEN

Three days had passed, and the world still had no answers. With no workable clues and only speculation, fear took over. The international police forces searched for answers but came up with dead ends. No one had come forward with demands, nor had anyone claimed responsibility. The waiting game fed the fear. Large numbers of fanatics looked away from God for answers, and prejudice and hate had begun to dictate the actions once again of a troubled world.

* * * * *

Dr. William Kensington, a British coroner working for Interpol, adjusted the microphone attached to the front of his light blue surgical scrubs. He snapped on a pair of sterile latex gloves and proceeded to read the chart of the first victim that had died in the Syrian Desert.

His initial dictation was routine: "Case Number 1-10000. Name unknown, Arab descent, male, fully developed, estimated age nineteen."

He had not found any signs of trauma after taking X-rays, CAT scans, multiple photographs, and a blood analysis. He stared at the CAT scan. Something troubled him. He opened one of his many reference books, turned to what a normal brain looked like, and compared it to his corpse's brain picture.

He continued his autopsies on all the remaining victims, finding a similar pattern. His final words into his tape recorder upset him: "Cause of death unknown."

Dr. Kensington had no choice but to report his findings. And he knew he would not be believed. He had conducted, and repeated, all the tests. He knew that even after a person dies, the brain, like an old battery, has some electrical charge left. He had received the bodies within twenty-four hours of their deaths, but each brain was totally drained of any electrical current. In fact, the CAT scan revealed that the brains had been wiped clean, drained of any sign that they had ever functioned.

At his medical briefing, the authorities sat in amazement. Some scientists argued, some yelled he was nuts. All he could do was suggest they examine the bodies themselves. He didn't want to believe his findings and would appreciate someone giving the world a more logical answer.

* * * * *

The US public still devoured irresponsibly reported news, despite the gravity of the situation. Talk shows spotlighted Jewish, Christian and Muslim fundamentalists, who talked about God's retribution. And every cable news station gave precious airtime to conspiracy theorists, who warned of alien invaders. With the world paralyzed by fear, the media, like a vulture circling a dying animal, honed in on the weak and vulnerable, all the while reaping a profit and great ratings. Reporters were even calling the deaths "the Vampire Murders."

The one man getting most of the publicity was the leading expert on molecular signal circuits: Dr. Robert Fishburn. He told the press he had the only theory on how the terrorists might have died. He predicted that sometime in the near future scientists would be able to imprint and store a dead person's molecular electrical signal circuits and reinsert them inside a clone of the departed individual. The copy, the twin, the double would have essentially the same characteristics and memories.

He was sure that some advanced race from another planet was experimenting on our scum. He couldn't explain logically why aliens from another world would want to clone our worst specimens except perhaps to create a powerful army of madmen.

His research was speculative and unproven, but, because it was based on the coroner's reports, it had some merit.

"Maybe in a hundred years we'll have the technology," he

told reporters. "But now it's just impossible, pure science fiction."

There were two intriguing correlations between Fishburn's theories and Dr. Kensington's reports. First, none of the dead bodies showed signs that they had ever had any brain wave electrical movement. The brain tissues on all the bodies after dissecting them appeared untainted, as though years of activity and memories had been erased. They were comparable to the brains of newborns and fetuses. Dr. Kensington's findings were substantiated by the leading scientists around the world. Secondly, all the victims' facial expressions had been peaceful. None had any signs of fear or terror that they were about to die. No one wanted to think about it, but whoever had killed these people had the power to render them helpless.

CHAPTER FOURTEEN

Interpol, frustrated by a lack of clues, continued their surveillance of Katie O'Riley. Since she had been dealing with the three terrorist leaders and had sent out the packages of photos, she was their chief suspect. They were unsure how she had possession of the photos, but were confident they would find out soon enough.

The FBI and Department of Justice had launched a major investigation into the death of Allan Vincent. Since he had been under investigation before he died, his recent weapon sales order had been traced to the three terrorists who died on Sunrise Island.

Robert Philips was written off as a suspect. He was a washed-out detective who had nothing to offer their investigation. The FBI had run a brief background check and had come up with nothing important to warrant wasting time watching him.

Each day, more and more suspected terrorist and fanatical leaders died of unexplained causes. The first lead was discovered on the ninth day after an autopsy of fifty Arab and Israeli right-wing groups came in.

"We hadn't picked up this residue before," William Kensington advised. "The substance unfortunately is not on any of our known chemical or biochemical charts. I'm not even sure if this was what killed any of them. But, they all had the same residue and it was a least some kind of direction."

He moved away from the rows of cold, stiff bodies, slowly loosening his surgical mask as he spoke. A sheet covering one of the dead victims got caught on his apron and, as he turned, he dragged it with him, exposing a grayish-blue corpse that had the top of its skull cut off.

"Oops," he said sheepishly, holding back a smirk as he watched Captain Fellows' facial muscles twist in disgust.

Without skipping a beat, he walked toward the row of twenty large jars containing the brains of the victims. He pranced around his lab, totally engrossed in his garden of death.

"If this substance killed all these terrorists and we don't know anything about it," he said, "I'm hesitant to predict that we can come up with an antidote."

"We'll find the killers," Inspector Fellows of Interpol barked, upset that this entire ordeal had produced no answers. "You solve this problem, and do it fast. We might be running out of time if the killers decide to try their poison on the good guys."

"I can only do what I can, Inspector," he complained, upset at the suggestion that he was not doing an adequate job. "I'm limited by our current findings."

He turned his back and went to his microscope, ignoring Inspector Fellows and leaving him to converse with the hollow skulls that filled his laboratory.

Sergeant O'Conner burst into the room, flushed from his run down the steps to the morgue.

"O'Riley's applied for a visa to France and bought an airline ticket," he said, sucking in air to catch his breath. "She's scheduled to leave for Paris the day after tomorrow,"

"Paris?" he said animatedly. "What's in Paris?"

"It's been for quite some time the hub of secret terrorist conferences," Kensington interrupted sarcastically.

"Alert the French authorities, and be sure to X-Ray all her baggage," Inspector Fellows ordered.

* * * * *

Ruth had not seen her father this upset in a long time, but what Jacob and his family were doing was affecting her father's plans. She knew if Jacob and his family succeeded in curtailing or even ending terrorism, it would be all over for her father and her two brothers. Their movement survived on hate and without it, they would have no followers.

She sat down, weak from all their hiding these last ten

years.

"Father, maybe it's over," she said. "It's been so long, the fighting, the killing, and where has it gotten us?"

She saw the rage in her father's eyes, knowing she had hurt him with her disrespect for his mission.

"I need that weapon before Jacob destroys it and ruins everything for us," he told his two sons, ignoring Ruth.

"If he's killing the terrorists," Saul, his older son, told him, "then we should kill the politicians he wants to protect."

"We need to be more dramatic. I have a better plan to make it appear like Jacob and his family is targeting the innocent now. The world is not ready to hear from us just yet. He looked at his three children, his eyes menacing and cold. "Don't do anything until I give you the go ahead. Is that clear?"

Saul just nodded, his eyes closed tight. His brother had a blank stare, looking off in the distance.

* * * * *

Ten hours later inside the Sports Arena in San Diego, California, fifteen thousand people were convened at the United Christian Fellowship. They never had a chance to leave for their march. All were found murdered. Again, investigators could not find a cause. At the opposite end of the country at the Jacob Javits Convention Center in Manhattan, ten thousand Jews were found in the same condition: lying peacefully, their bodies drained of life.

* * * * *

The free world could tolerate the mass killings of known murderers, but now the attention had turned to the innocent. President Hopkins had put the United States military and every unit of the National Guard on alert. An enemy had once again invaded the most powerful country in the world and had done it without leaving a trace and without the knowledge of the CIA.

* * * * *

"You stupid fools," he lashed out at them. "I told you not do anything, and you did the opposite."

"But father, they were not innocent," Cain, his younger son, whined. "They were going to protest against war, terrorism, everything we stand for."

"You're both idiots," he screamed as he slapped them hard on the backs of their heads.

"Father," his daughter Ruth interrupted, "maybe they really didn't do that badly. If the world believes Jacob has now turned his attention to randomly killing anyone, then it's possible they might not be that cooperative when he makes his demands."

"I hope you're right," he said. "We're running out of time, and I need that weapon built and ready for us."

He hugged his children before he gave them their injections, since rest was needed now.

CHAPTER FIFTEEN

The voice jolted Philips, who had been daydreaming as he drove the boring desert road back to Springs River. He kept seeing the chateau in France— the family in the dream—that kept recurring these last few days.

"Chateau Rose," he muttered. "I've got to go there," he whispered as if in a trance.

He slammed his foot on the brakes, veering onto the shoulder, a trail of sand spewing in his wake. The loose, soft shoulder had made his car fishtail before he skidded to an abrupt halt.

"Find her," the female voice said. *"She will help you understand."*

"Find who?" he shouted.

"You'll know. Trust your instincts."

He shook violently as the voice went silent. His body heaved; the seizure-like movements were uncontrollable, as if brought on by a drug. His skin felt clammy and cold, and his neck became stiff, bringing on a headache unlike any he had ever had before. He wondered if the cancer had returned. Maybe it was something he had gotten from the shack the other night.

In a few minutes, the headache subsided, and his skin returned to its normal warmth. He continued driving, wanting to get back to his office to pursue a few ideas. He turned the radio up loud to help drown out any further invasion of his mind by a force he did not understand . . . yet. Before he pulled his car back onto the highway, he noted in his Blackberry to get his passport and a ticket to Paris.

In five minutes, he was back on the road when a special

news report came on the radio:

"The number of victims is increasing around the world," a reporter said. "The killers of terrorists are now killing men and women with no known terrorist ties. The foundations that hold humanity together are being destroyed by a power that has its own rules and justice."

Nothing surprised Philips anymore, especially after the recent deaths in San Diego and Manhattan. Five OPEC leaders were the latest victims. Even more shocking: the Israeli and British prime ministers died earlier that day after leaving a secret summit at Camp David. President Hopkins was flying to the UN to address the assembly.

* * * * *

"Father, are you sure we need to continue to rid the world of these people?" Rebecca asked sorrowfully.

"We have to stick to our plan," Jacob said, looking sad and tired. "Soon the world will know that we have not killed the innocent and will put their trust in us."

"It's just not going smoothly," she said.

"If we are to return the world to a more simple time, one that is free of madmen and fanatics, then we're doing the right thing," he said. "These men were living dual lives. They would have never stopped instigating terrorism and would hamper what we need to do. I've lost too many of my children to the selfish and unmerited greed the world has come to know. It will soon be over, and only the truly righteous will survive."

"What if they don't believe us and resist? Aren't we acting like the people we're killing?"

"This time, they won't have a choice. The warnings we're sending are going to be clear enough, and, by the time I speak, they will force the changes I want."

"I hope so, Father," she sighed, looking for support from her mother. "I surely hope so."

Her mother just stared at her monitor.

Rebecca, the wisest of all Jacob's children, had taken on too much of the responsibility of seeing that her father's wishes were carried out to initiate The Cleansing. She hated that Genesis was the council's alternative, but she'd carry out her father's wishes as best she could.

Unlike her brothers, she never made the decision to take a life while in a highly emotional state. Her brothers were a different story. Sadly, she could not control their actions and could only watch in disgust.

The youngest brother was the most rebellious, always playing with his victims first, watching with pleasure the fear in their eyes, knowing they were about to die and not be able to prevent what was happening. Her other brother liked to make the deaths appear as accidents. He especially liked car crashes that involved property.

She complained, but her father reminded her that the outcome was the same, regardless of the method used.

"Who are you to say that your way is the most humane one to end a life?" he asked. "Doesn't death with a reason placate the survivors, unlike your methods, which leave them wondering why? I've never been able to figure out the best way for a human to die. So don't be so hard on your brothers."

She knew he was right. She just couldn't stomach all the unnecessary pain her brothers were inflicting. She checked the remaining lists and divided them up for the three of them.

CHAPTER SIXTEEN

Miguel Ortiz, president of the World Peace Organization, a facade for his real business, sat comfortably on the couch in his office while talking with his two partners.

"This is a marvelous opportunity," he said. "The balance of power has shifted. A small window has opened up. Let's seize the moment, gentlemen."

"I agree," Albert Mitchell, Chairman of the WPO board of directors said. "With Allan Vincent now out of the picture, United Weapons is ripe for a takeover," Mitchell, nervously decided, puffing on his pipe.

"Owning this new pulsating assault rifle," Ortiz began, "will give us the corner on the world weapons market and the respect we rightly deserve."

"I can get our foot in the door," Rudy Glickman, deputy director at the Department of Justice, interrupted. "Our shell company we established three years ago now owns forty-three percent of UWS. The FCC, DOJ, and FBI haven't connected the dots yet. And, with so many other holding companies involved, by the time they find the true owners, it will be too late. The DOJ doesn't want to take over this company and be involved with the political fallout for the next decade. A few of the board of directors are primed to sell their shares, and in a couple of days, we should own over fifty percent."

Ortiz stood up, trying to tuck his shirt in his pants over his enlarged midsection, the result of too much eating.

"Good," he said. "The opportunity is right in front of us.

We're all going to be very rich."

"Once the DOJ sees that the company is still controlled by its stockholders, and assuming the new board of directors doesn't let the business falter, the Department of Defense will want to continue with their contracts," Rudy said, seemingly afraid to speak his mind. "We just have to be careful. Let's err on the side of caution for a time."

Ortiz wasn't shocked that Allan Vincent had been murdered. He was disappointed he had not done the job himself after putting out the contract to have him killed.

The World Peace Organization continued as a front for his drug trafficking business that needed weapons from Vincent's company. Vincent had brushed off Ortiz' desire to buy weapons, as if his money was not clean enough.

Ortiz had expected, after opening his home to this stranger, favorable treatment from his new friend and business associate. Instead, he was insulted. Vincent's excuse that he was retiring and that Ortiz would have to deal with the new board of directors disappointed him. Ortiz knew that the illegal sale of weapons was Vincent's solo program and that no board of directors that took over his company would violate the federal law regarding weapons sales to known drug lords.

After the news of Vincent's death, Ortiz immediately wired five million dollars to an offshore account for one of his paid assassins. To his surprise, the assassin returned the money, saying he had not done the job.

Ortiz didn't care who had done it; he was just happy that the company could now be his.

* * * * *

"Ortiz and Mitchell will be trouble for us," Jacob told his children. "I want David and Ian to handle this next assignment. We'll make an example of these men. The world will be better off without them."

"Father," Rebecca countered, "we can't get inside everyone's mind, or we'll have to kill the whole planet."

"These men have to be taken out of the picture, or they will take over where Vincent left off," her father answered. "It's not just the pulsating weapons I'm concern about. If someone like

Ortiz finds out about their other experiments, we could be doomed along with everyone else. We have no choice. Just see that it's done."

I'll do your bidding, she thought, *but under my terms.*

"I love when she thinks I can't read her thoughts," Jacob said, laughing, after she left.

CHAPTER SEVENTEEN

Robert Philips was relieved to be home. He immediately poured himself a tall glass of scotch. He leaned back in his recliner situated near the large picture window in his living room. He loved his bird's-eye view of the desert foliage that lined his property. He lived simply. His house was modestly furnished with the remnants of the home he once had with his wife and daughter. His first thought was that he needed to get his windows cleaned; the heavy rain had stained the panes with the red sand that surrounded his home.

As he peered out the window, the effects of the rain that had encased his home in mud triggered a horrible flashback. It was happening again, the same feelings he had on the day his wife and daughter were killed by a drunk driver.

Alice, his wife of fifteen years, and Stephanie, his fourteen-year-old daughter, were on their way home from a ballet recital. He had to miss Stephanie's performance because a murder case he had been working on had taken a positive turn. Like always, his family took a backseat to his job. This case needed his immediate attention. "Another excuse," he told himself as he slowly sipped his scotch. He knew it could have waited until morning, especially since he had just pulled a twelve-hour shift.

He played his last words to Alice over and over in his head, as he did almost every night before passing out drunk.

"I'm sorry. Please tell Stephanie I love her, and wish her good luck for me."

"This is her final performance," Alice had said, barely able to control her anger. "She was so looking forward to showing off for you, you selfish bastard."

He was never one to feel remorse or guilt for his actions;

this event took exception. That horrible night was the last time he let work affect his life. Now it was the bottle, his friend and companion.

The night they died, "Desert Storm" had captivated the attention of most Americans. He was left to mourn for his loved ones alone, while military families anxiously prayed for their sons and daughters to return home safely. He wept for his loss that was chiseled deep inside his soul.

He remembered being head to head with a suspected murderer when his captain came into the interrogation room. The anguish on Captain Ryan's face immediately told him something horrible had happened. He got up and walked toward the door. Everyone in the room could hear the tragic words. Philips began breathing heavy, his face drained of color as he tried to comprehend the gravity of what he had just been told.

The suspect he had been questioning interjected a sarcastic remark about his family, which triggered Phillips' fury. He lashed into this criminal as if he were a punching bag, rendering him unconscious.

He never stopped torturing himself for not driving that night, convinced he could have prevented the crash. After their deaths, his work had become substandard, his mood toward criminals too assertive, and his drinking too intense. The Los Angeles police force was losing one of their best detectives to depression and alcohol. Refusing to go to any anger management counseling or a twelve-step program, he watched his career take a nosedive. While it mattered to his Captain, it didn't matter to him.

If it hadn't been for his close friend Jasper Billings, who worked for the CIA, he might have retired and died somewhere in a dark alley, a homeless drunk. When the chief of police position came available in Springs River, Jasper convinced him that the opportunity to be away from his memories would be the best therapy for him. Except for his friend Brad Davis, and right hand at the police department, the small retirement community never knew their new chief was a drunk.

Holding the picture of Alice and Stephanie tightly in his hand, his glass of scotch in the other, he cried as usual, tears adding more stains to the photo. It was a snapshot of his wife and daughter tickling him on the beach close to the Santa Monica pier. The few real moments he had spent with them seemed to be captured in this single picture.

"I'm so sorry," he sobbed. "It should have been me. I should have been there to protect you."

His body trembled uncontrollably, and he spilled his drink on his pant leg and the picture. Like most nights, he slept in his recliner in his dirty clothes, the photo on his lap and an empty bottle of scotch on the floor by the side of his chair.

This night his dream was not of the accident or of the life, he once had with Alice and Stephanie. This time it was a large home outside a small village. Everyone seemed to be speaking French, which in his dream he understood. Then he was looking at what appeared to be a chateau, a woman with red hair, and two small children. This time there were no angry crowds shouting, just a bright light exploding inside the house. It was as if he could see through the walls of the house. The woman and children were screaming as some invisible force was pounding their bodies against the floor. He tried to run, but his feet were frozen, affixed to the ground. He tried and tried to pull himself free, his heart pounding as he heard the screams reach a fever pitch and then go silent. He knew he had failed and had lost someone important. But he still had no clue about that family.

It was 3:30 in the morning when he felt the cold chill overtake his sleep and wake him. This time he knew he was not dreaming, even though his eyes remained closed. It was happening again, the same feeling he had gotten in the shack.

"Robert, we need to talk," the voice inside his head said.

He could not talk with sounds; he heard his thoughts respond, *who's there?*

"That's not important now," the female voice said. *"We need you to carry a message to the United Nations in four weeks."*

A message? Who are you? he repeated.

The voice inside his head was soft, with an air of tiredness. *"Let's just say for now that I'm your conscience and everyone else's conscience."*

He sat there, confused and scared, wondering if this was the first sign that he was going mad. He had heard that some people begin to hear voices in their forties, right before they get diagnosed as full-blown crazy.

"You're not going crazy, Robert."

You can read my thoughts?

"Not just yours. Everyone's. We need you to bring a message to the United Nations in four weeks."

On his lap, he found a white sheet of paper, its sides singed as if it had been pulled from a fire before it was destroyed. He stared at the paper, taking a moment to read it. He held it up in the air as if someone were right in front of him.

They'll never believe me, he told her. And I'm not one of your people. In fact, I'd like to arrest all of you and bring you to justice.

"You'll understand our mission very soon, and I will expect a change of heart from you. The key to the world's survival rests on your shoulders."

I'm not sure the United Nations will even give me an audience, let alone believe that I have a message about all these killings.

"You'll have to find a way to make them believe you," she told him. *"Find a way. Or it will be too late."*

Too late for what? he tried to scream.

"Go to France first. You'll get some answers there that will renew your faith and give you purpose."

She was gone and so was the quietness he had felt in the shack the night his cancer was cured.

He looked at his watch; it was 3:31.

Only a minute has passed, he thought. *It felt like hours. I must be going mad?*

He was unable to sleep. His mind raced.

"How the fuck am I going to even get an audience with the United Nations assembly?" he asked aloud. "What does France have to do with all of this? Does this voice have anything to do with these dreams?"

He spent the next four hours downloading all the information he could find regarding schizophrenia, dreams about a past life, telepathy, fanatical terrorist groups, and divine miracles. He had no clue as to what had been going on these last few weeks, but his gut told him to investigate more before he could commit to getting involved. With the alcohol impairing his judgment, he did not want to trust the voice and remained skeptical about what she'd had to say.

He found his passport and was delighted it was still current. Then he remembered he had planned to surprise Alice with a trip to Europe, which triggered another bout of depression.

He booked his ticket to Paris for the next day at 8:00 in the morning. A rental car was reserved to get him to a small village seventy-five kilometers outside of Paris. All he knew was that the Chateau Rose that he pictured in his dream was outside a small village called Rene.

He had almost forgotten he had a job, his mind pre-occupied with the voice and his dream. He was on the phone, his one bag in his hand, as he called Brad Davis at the police station.

"Brad, I'm taking some needed time off," he said. "It's personal. I'll be gone a few weeks to France on vacation. You know, the one I had promised Alice before she died. It should be quiet, and being acting chief shouldn't interfere with your golf game."

"Are you all right?" Davis asked. "You sound different."

"I am," he said. "I need some time alone. I'll keep you posted."

He didn't like lying to his friend, but if he told him the truth, he would have suggested he go instead to the Betty Ford Clinic in Rancho Mirage, California instead. He hung up the phone and carried his bag out front, where a taxi waited, blasting its horn.

CHAPTER EIGHTEEN

For the first time in two weeks, the "Vampire Aliens" had suspended their brutal killings. It made the world more agitated, waiting for the next slaughter. World powers, terrorists and every religious faction were helpless against a power they could not see or find.

Selected teams of scientists had begun analyzing a residue found at three of the crime scenes. Laboratories in the United States, Germany, Japan, and Russia had put their top scientists on the project. The substance was not poisonous in nature. The confusing part was that it had human DNA properties. While this discovery was an important clue, the DNA did not match up on any worldwide database. In fact, it had DNA components that were not part of present day human DNA. This only exacerbated the fear and rumors within the scientific communities.

The light, powdery composition felt like sandpaper to the touch. However, the dead bodies showed no signs of skin trauma. The DNA from the powder, though human, was off the charts. Scientists were keeping quiet about their findings, but they were now thinking some alien force was visiting Earth.

For the first time, countries agreed to cooperate and exchange information daily via the Internet, whether productive or not. Then another set of special analysts were given the accumulated data with the sole purpose of unlocking the mystery behind the killings.

Military forces were put on alert and being prepared to fight a new type of chemical war, one which, admittedly, no one knew how to combat. A new anthrax vaccine was administered to all military and government personnel around the world. Generals hated having to speculate on how to fight an enemy that had an invisible weapon. Their choices left them guessing and their men scared.

Forensic experts were attempting to establish some type of sketch or profile of the type of person or persons that could be responsible for the murders. But what they initially came up with didn't make sense to the professionals who had to search for them. The profile of the killers that forensic experts came up with fit every religious fanatic on the face of the Earth, from Christians to Jews, from Hindus to Muslims. This haphazard description triggered a new wave of hate crimes. The media, favoring sensationalism over hard news, labeled the events "the Secret Holocaust."

Attacks upon minorities, mostly blacks, were reported throughout the United States. Orthodox Jews in New York and around the world were attacked. Right wing Christian groups were persecuted. Arab countries stepped up their attacks against Israel. And hardcore Zionists reacted with large-scale violence against any Arab strongholds near Israel.

Genocide spread across Southeast Asia, with monks and religious extremists bearing the full brunt. The world was beginning to self-destruct, not from war, but from hatred and fear.

The last four weeks had awakened the world to a terror everyone feared, but no one dreamt could ever happen. World leaders groped for solutions that were not available, and the average citizen wanted to know if God was punishing them. NATO stepped in to halt the worldwide vigilantism. Man's fear of the unknown, the black hell that was infecting the globe, had finally exploded into chaos and anarchy.

Was this the goal of the terrorists? Had they handed humanity the match to light the fuse that would destroy civilization?

United Nations members could not control what was happening in their countries and knew, as history had taught them, that fear and prejudice could kill millions of people. And now this virus of hate and fear, had infected the most dangerous vehicle created: the electronic highway.

The world economy had slowed down. Stock exchanges around the globe had started to crash, further inflaming the hatred that held the world hostage. More and more workers were not reporting to work because of fear.

The excuses didn't matter. It was obvious. Depression had begun to sink in. People began to view life a little more preciously, and work was not a high priority.

Attendance at places of worship had tripled. Heavily armed guards were hired to protect the innocent who wanted to ask for God's forgiveness. For the first time, Christians, Jews, and Muslims worshiped together, squeezing shoulder-to-shoulder, chanting any and all prayers they could remember.

Man's dormant virus that had been in remission and medicated by his religious beliefs had begun to consume his mind. The answers he always found in God no longer held water. In fact, the loving God he had worshiped turned out to be a vengeful killer, randomly executing innocent people. Religious leaders had a hard time justifying what had been happening around the world as God's will, and were as bewildered as their parishioners.

Then, unexpectedly, something happened amazing happened. News broadcasts around the world were interrupted with a short, concise message: *Tonight, terrorist leaders and those who harbor them have been eliminated in Columbia, China, Kenya and Libya. This is a warning to everyone who supports terrorism. More deaths will occur unless the world begins to control terrorism. In four weeks, you'll hear from our messengers at the United Nations. In the meantime, we'll be watching. Prove to us you can manage your civilizations and live peacefully or you will be destroyed. You can't hide from us.*

Within minutes after the message disappeared from the screens, the news announcers confirmed the predicted terrorist deaths. The world was in shock. The religious communities were convinced Armageddon had begun, that those who did not repent and show God the support he deserved would perish.

PART II
TRANSMUTATION

CHAPTER NINETEEN

The residue found on the bodies around the world had proven to be a dead end. All the scientists came to the same conclusion: the substance had not killed any of the terrorists. They did agree that it was more similar to a life form than a synthetic agent.
Unfortunately, for the world, there were still no answers only what the scientists labeled "unknown DNA." Some scientists speculated that it was possible that a human could carry a poison and by contact release the poison without being noticed. It was only a theory, with too many holes in it for anyone to be definitive about what had been killing the thousands of men and women around the world.

They continued analyzing what little evidence they had, but their tests proved inconclusive. Since they had no other answers, they speculated that one of the countries that had chemical weapons capabilities either leaked data to a terrorist nation or had the technology stolen.

Some scientists began to look into Dr. Fishburn's theories and study the possibility of downloading a dying person's molecules and storing them for future use. They already knew that a human could be cloned. It had been done, producing a twin from the DNA used. But that's where it stopped. The cloned human had unique characteristics, totally separate from the donor.

Only a few scientists worked on this new theory, while the rest continued looking for a biological agent that had caused the deaths. There were twelve known countries that had biological weapons facilities: China, Taiwan, North Korea, Iraq, Syria, Egypt,

Iran, Cuba, Israel, Russia, Japan, and the United States. They all
made their research available to see if a connection could be found.

The Automatic Chemical Agent Alarm systems, the GID-3
IMS, were deployed at all the locations where the deaths had
occurred. If there were a chemical still out there, this unit would
detect it. The M21 Remote Sensing Chemical Agent Alarm
(RSCAAL) was positioned in strategic areas to warn world leaders
of any impending danger. The UN received a unit in preparation
for the upcoming assembly.

Each member of the assembly was fitted with protective
gear in case of an attack. Reporters and spectators were warned
that they could attend the meeting at their own risk.

With most people believing only the wicked would die, the
room promised to sell out. The media and religious leaders had
been given most of the passes to attend the session.

As the United Nations Assembly prepared, the military
continued searching for answers. Samples continued to be taken
from every area where the mass murders kept happening.

CHAPTER TWENTY

Katie O'Riley arrived in Paris confused and bewildered by the voices in her head. She had gotten to France a day before Philips was to arrive. Her bright red hair was pulled back in a ponytail. She lacked makeup, wore denim jeans, and went unrecognized as she passed through customs. If it hadn't been for the computer flagging her name, Interpol never would have known she had entered the country. She was used to being followed, so she scanned the airport. She noticed at least fifteen agents talking into their microphones conspicuously. She winked at one of the men, causing him to blush and immediately put his lips to his lapel.

"We've been compromised," he whispered.

She giggled as she hailed a taxi.

Her pale, soft skin, spotted with freckles, and her deep blue eyes made men turn their heads. Carrying only one bag, which she had taken on the plane, she was able to avoid the long, crowded baggage lines. She jumped into the taxi and told the driver to take her to the J.W. Marriott. She was mystified by her dreams, dreams that painted an enchanting picture of the French landscape and a beautiful home called Chateau Rose in the small village of Rene outside of Paris.

Unconcerned that she had been spotted by Interpol she relaxed for the short taxi ride to the hotel. On her flight, she had not been able to relax. The voices filled her head, keeping her awake and restless. At times, she thought she heard her mother and father talking to her, unleashing old emotions and anger.

"Their deaths were a mistake," the female voice said.

She sat up straight in her seat. Her mind seemed to be communicating with her visitor.

A mistake? she asked. *You were not there; I was! Who are you, and why am I doing all of this?*

"*Tomorrow you will have some answers. You will meet another who will guide you on a new path. We need your help. Without it, the world as you know it will come to an end.*"

But, she thought, frustrated, *why me?*

Then the voice was gone, and she was again alone. On her lap, she found a piece of paper. How it had gotten there, she hadn't a clue. She was shocked at what it said.

"That'll be forty-five Euros, please," the taxi driver shouted to wake her up.

"We're here already?" she asked, stretching her arms above her head. "You speak excellent English," she said unaware that he had spoken to her in French.

Inside her hotel room, she unpacked, took a shower, and dressed for dinner. Before she went to the hotel restaurant, she stopped at the concierge to arrange for a rental car for the next day and to get directions to the village of Rene. The man was confused by her questions about a Chateau Rose.

"I know that village very well," the young man said. "It has an interesting history. Chateau Rose is a legend that has to do with a family of witches that terrorized the people of the town, until one day they, along with their home, were destroyed in a fire."

He stared, making her feel uncomfortable. He looked at her as though he knew her.

"Does the town have information on this family?" she asked.

"It's a tourist attraction and a Mecca for religious fanatics who feel what happened in 1746 was a sign from God."

"You said they were a family of witches?"

"A husband and wife and two small children."

"Thank you," she said, the color draining from her face. "You've been very helpful."

What does this have to do with what happened on my island? She wondered what else she would uncover tomorrow and who she might meet if the voice was correct.

Dinner was quick and uneventful until she noticed a pair of familiar faces: Inspector Fellows and his sidekick, Sergeant O'Conner. They tried to remain unnoticed in a dark corner of the dining room. But the waiter brought them two beers, compliments of the lady waving at them from across the restaurant.

Fellows got up and approached Katie, pulling a chair out and without an invitation sat down.

"O'Riley," he began, "we know you had something to do with the deaths of your terrorist friends."

"If you're so confident, inspector, why haven't you arrested me?" she replied softly, her arrogant smile embarrassing the inspector.

"We will soon enough. You'll make a mistake, and then we'll lock you up and throw away the key."

"Enjoy your beers," she said, getting up defiantly and throwing his beer in his face. "I'm tired and going to sleep."

Inspector Fellows, his eyes wide with disgust, sat there, the foaming beer clinging to his lips and chin. He cussed and then glared at his partner, who had almost fallen off his bar stool from laughing.

"That bitch will be history soon enough," he mumbled as he tried to dry off his face and jacket.

Katie hated Fellows because he was the lead detective who had investigated her parents' deaths. His one-sided investigation backed up the stories of the British military, and no one served time. Being Irish, she knew how the British felt about her country and people. Fellows had concluded that her father had attacked the soldiers first and that they acted in self-defense. As far as Katie was concerned, Fellows was just as guilty as the soldiers who murdered her parents.

Sleep was not very restful. The dream returned but this time with more intensity. She was being attacked by an invisible force, and when she resisted, the beatings became worse. Her two small children watched helplessly as she was tossed against the walls of their living room, bouncing off of pictures and cabinets. The pain in her dream felt real; when she woke, she saw bruises on her legs and arms. She returned to her sleep only to be caught up in the same horrible fight that was about to take her life.

Then her husband burst through the front door, holding a pitchfork and stabbing at the air, hoping to connect with something solid to save his wife. As he fought with his invisible enemy, another force grabbed his children and in one quick movement, as they appeared to levitate in mid-air, snapped their necks, dropping them like rag dolls to the floor.

Katie tried to scream, but nothing came out. She rushed over to help her children, when their attacker lifted her up and flung her across the room. Before her husband could react, she was impaled on his weapon, in shock at what had just happened. She watched, terrified, as her husband began to turn blue. His throat was being squeezed, becoming more and more constricted, as the life was being drained out of him.

She tried to tell him she loved him. He seemed to understand as their eyes locked. The flash of light was so bright she was not sure if it was part of the dream or the lightning that was exploding outside her window. She was awake, trembling, exhausted from the nightmare.

She hadn't experienced anything this intense since the day her parents were killed and she hid in the forest that bordered her home. She wondered if she was going mad, if she was descending into a void of pain from which she wouldn't be able to escape. Rationally, it made no sense to her. She had been dreaming about an episode in the local folklore, unproven and unsubstantiated tales that made for scary stories to tell small children, to build fear and prejudice into their souls.

These last few weeks had upset her life more than she had imagined, and now she was going to a small village outside of Paris, searching for something or someone.

The light on her phone blinked, indicating she had a message. Still trembling and sweating, she pressed the lighted button and heard that her rental car would be ready for pickup at noon. She was afraid to go back to sleep and called room service to bring her a pot of strong coffee and some pancakes and eggs.

CHAPTER TWENTY-ONE

The flight attendant announced that the plane would be landing at Charles de Gaulle airport in twenty minutes. Her words, not much more than static, startled Philips, who had been sifting through documents, news clippings, and files. While he had no more answers about what had been happening to him, he knew one thing for sure: he was not going crazy. Everything was real, and everything was being manipulated by something genuine and frightening.

He knew there was an explanation, and his instincts told him he was getting close to finding it. He had once been a well-respected criminal detective. Today, he promised himself that he would clean up his act. He just wasn't sure what the voice inside his head had to do with all of this. If the voice was right, France was going to reveal some answers. But, what kind of answers? Were the mass murders of terrorists at all connected to his voices, to the messages he was receiving? "Shit," he whispered. "Why me?" He continued to ponder his situation.

He believed that, in some instances, vigilante justice was warranted, especially when the system breaks down. What scared him was that he had compassion for what they were doing and at the same time fear and disgust for the absolute power, they wielded.

He had brought just a small carry-on bag, which contained all that he needed for the few days he planned to be in France: a few sets of clean underwear, socks, one pair of comfortable jeans, two flannel shirts, a windbreaker, and his fully broken-in cowboy boots, which would for sure distinguish him as a tourist from the

Wild West. He spotted his reflection as he walked toward the
Hertz counter to pick up his car; a John Wayne look-alike he was
not.

"Sit-ups, definitely," he whispered. "Maybe cut back on the
fried foods and more exercise."

He grinned sheepishly, knowing it would not happen, at
least not now, maybe after he solved this investigation.

The directions to his hotel on Avenue des Champs Elysées
seemed simple enough. But the signs were foreign to him, and the
racecar drivers who called the French roadways their home were
crazy and suicidal.

He almost missed the sign directing him to Porte-de-la-
Chapelle. But, after embracing the merits of offensive driving, he
cut across three lanes at eight-five kilometers per hour, the most
exhilarating feeling he had experienced in a long time. A few
cowboy hoots and high fives to himself later, he was at his exit,
Porte Maillot, and following the sign, that was directing him
toward the Arc de Triomphe. He circled the Arc a few times,
unable to get off without killing himself and a few other people.
But, after saying a quick prayer and closing his eyes, he found
himself on Champs Elysées Avenue, from where he coasted into
J.W. Marriott's driveway. He felt his pants to see if he needed to
buy some more underwear: nothing moist, just nervous sweat. The
bellhop just shrugged his shoulders.

* * * * *

Checking into the hotel went smoothly; he tipped the bellhop and
had his bag sent to his room. He needed a drink and some
information on where the village of Rene was located. And what
of Chateau Rose? The concierge gave him a puzzled look as he
asked for information. Philips had heard how rude the French
could be toward Americans, but just smiled patiently and waited
for some answers.

"I'm sorry if I seem rude," the young man said. "I just find
it fascinating that in less than a day I have been asked twice about
this village and the legendary Chateau Rose. Are you on some
historical tour?"

"No," Philips said, his brow furrowed. "What's so strange
about it?"

"I've worked here four years and have never had a single
inquiry about that village, let alone the Chateau. Now, in less than

twenty-four hours, a beautiful woman wants a rental car and directions. And now you."

"Do you know the name of the woman you spoke to?" Philips asked politely.

"I don't think I can tell you that," he said apologetically. "Hotel policy, you understand. But," he continued with a wink, "if you need a drink right now, you might find her on your own."

"Thank you. You've been a great help."

As he walked toward the piano bar, he passed Sephora's, Europe's largest perfume shop. Several boxes of Chanel, Alice's favorite perfume, were displayed in the window. His eyes became moist; he wished he could go inside and buy her what she loved so much.

The piano bar was dimly lit. The dark mahogany bar and paneled wall did not make the room any brighter. The bartender was dressed in dark green knickers and a puffy white shirt opened at the collar. He nodded at Philips as he walked in and, extending his hand, pointed to an open barstool. The room had a smell of mold that seemed to match the age of the furniture and fixtures. At first, the bar seemed deserted of patrons. Then he noticed a secluded corner of the small room, where a woman sat nursing a Bloody Mary.

Philips wasn't sure if it was her. Her hair was covered by a knit hat, which she had pulled down over her ears. She was staring down at her napkin, lost in thought, so identification was impossible at that moment. He took in a deep breath and briskly advanced to her table.

As their eyes met, the air seemed to stop circulating from the ceiling fans, the room frozen in an eerie silence. Feelings of deja vu captured both of them. They were fixated on each other, trying to place a name with the face, searching the deepest depths of their memories for some clue.

Philips holding his Campari and orange juice resumed walking over to her table. She smiled, inviting him to approach. He had seen that smile before, but the image was too fuzzy for his tired brain to remember.

He extended his hand, which she took without hesitation. Her cool touch sent familiar chills throughout his body, which only made his frustration more unbearable. She seemed to have the same confused expression, as her puzzled expression raised her cheeks, wrinkling her nose and at the same time compacting her adorable freckles.

"I'm Robert Philips from the United States," he said.

"I'm Katie O'Riley from Ireland," she replied, her Irish accent adding an exotic zest to her looks.

He just stood there, his mouth open and his eyes wide with surprise.

"Are you all right, Mr. Philips?"

"I've wanted to meet you," he said. "I think we have a lot in common."

He went on to explain in detail what had been happening to him since the day Allan Vincent had died.

After five minutes, Katie just sat there, dumbfounded that there was someone else who had been experiencing the voices and the mysterious deaths. They compared their dreams of the violent deaths in the chateau, wondering what it all meant. They agreed to travel together to the village of Rene to seek out answers in a place that they both swore they had never been to.

An hour later, they were on their way to discover the secret of the Chateau Rose and what it meant in their dreams, unaware that they were being followed. Inspector Fellows and Sergeant O'Conner kept their distance, hoping to uncover some sinister plot.

CHAPTER TWENTY-TWO

President Hopkins sat behind his desk in the Oval Office. He was holding an emergency meeting with William Thomas, CIA director, Gail Smith, FBI director, and Neil Conway, director of the Department of Justice. James Turner, his chief of staff, sat beside the president's desk, eager to help his boss.

"We have a shit-load of questions," the president shouted, "and no answers. We're all at risk of being blackmailed by these terrorists."

Exhaustion showed on his face. He had not been getting much sleep, putting out one fire and then another while, his administration fell apart. What he didn't need now was another unsolvable problem.

"Apparently Robert Philips and Katie O'Riley know each other," Director Smith reported. "They met in Paris earlier today, acting like they were long lost friends."

Smith's deep, commanding voice did not fit the petite frame she covered under a business suit two sizes too large. Everything about her seemed out of proportion. Her long blonde hair, which tumbled down to the middle of her back, was shaped in front in a Dutch girl cut.

Her background was what had gotten her appointed by the president. She had been a tough attorney general for the state of New York for five years and before that a narcotics detective in Brooklyn. She took no shit from anyone, especially men.

"What's the background on both of them?" William Thomas asked. "Where have they met before?"

Thomas respected Gail and had always fantasized about how she would be in bed. He loved white women who were tough and serious. He had found them to be more exhilarating sexually than the submissive types.

Thomas had been a CIA operative for fifteen years before becoming the first black director of the CIA. He had a reputation for being ruthless, especially with those who pissed him off. If he liked someone, then the punishment was quick and as painless as possible. Rumor had it that during the Gulf War one of his men panicked and couldn't pull the trigger on a terrorist. The man's inaction resulted in two unnecessary deaths. Thomas had never lost a man on a mission before, and he expressed his feelings by snapping the weak operative's neck with his large hands. That mission was so covert that it never officially happened, and the three dead men were never accounted for.

"That's the strange thing," Gail said. "According to our databases, these two have never met. What we do know is that O'Riley was involved with Allan Vincent. And Vincent was found dead near Springs River, Nevada, where Detective Philips is the new chief of police. That's our only connection, and it's pretty weak."

"Why, if he's the head honcho there, does he go by detective?" the president interrupted. His question caught Gail by surprise and seemed irrelevant to her, which she expressed with a scowl.

"It's a small town," Director Conway said. "And he acts as a one-man show with an experienced deputy and a new officer fresh from the academy. He has never dropped his title that he had when he worked for the Los Angeles police force. He was at one time a well-respected homicide detective until his life fell apart after his family was killed by a drunk driver. Mister President I can look further into this matter if you'd like, but it's irrelevant to the subject at hand, sir," he said patronizingly.

Only Neil could talk to the president that way. He was an ex-attorney and federal judge, had resigned from his plush job on the Eleventh District Appeals Court as a favor to his longtime friend, President Hopkins. Hopkins and Conway were former college buddies, and when the president asked his friend to be part of his staff, he could not refuse.

Before Hopkins had become president, Conway represented him in a criminal case in which he was accused of having sex with an under-aged girl. She was a call girl that looked over twenty-one, and someone had illegally bugged his hotel room. Neil, being a ruthless shark and able to call up some favors, had the matter dismissed when the girl, along with any proof that the incident had ever happened, disappeared.

President Hopkins trusted no one but Conway.

Hopkins just rolled his eyes in disgust. "Then what's the connection between the two of them?" President Hopkins asked. "And what the hell does it have to do with the message we're going to get in thirty days?"

Hopkins had a volatile temper. He got elected because he was a good politician. But as a leader of the most powerful country in the world, he was bull-headed, stubborn and basically inept.

"What we've gathered so far is that Vincent died as mysteriously as the three terrorist leaders who died on O'Riley's Sunrise Island," Thomas told them. "O'Riley survived whatever killed these men. I'm not sure if Philips had contact with this group, but our investigation revealed that one day he had cancer and the next, I mean after Vincent died, the cancer was gone. I mean totally gone, as if it never existed."

"This whole thing gets crazier and crazier as each day passes," Gail interrupted. "Thousands of people dead from unknown causes and now a fucking miracle. What's next, little green men from 'The Planet of Peace' here to bring some order to our screwed-up world?"

"Is it possible that they have the antidote?" the president asked, totally ignoring Gail's remarks.

"We're not even sure if there *is* an antidote," Thomas said. "We don't even know what's killing all these people, least of all, or what kind of antidote is needed."

"I'm terrified that we're trying to fight an enemy that we don't even know exists," President Hopkins said. "We don't even know how powerful they might be. Right now, it's beyond anything we've ever encountered, and we're in a position of weakness that could humble us as a superpower. If we don't find a solution fast, our economy and society could be in ruins."

The president's staff stared at each other in disbelief.

"I think," Director Smith began, "we have no choice at this point but to let Philips and O'Riley play out their cards. Maybe then we might find some answers."

"I agree," the president said. "Let's keep monitoring their movements."

"Both their phones are being monitored by NSA and in Paris their rooms have been bugged," Director Thomas said confidently. "If they sneeze in the wrong way, we'll know about it. Inspector Fellows from Interpol is watching them and has agreed to keep us aware of their activities."

"I want to be briefed daily, if not hourly," the president said.

CHAPTER TWENTY-THREE

The long ride to the village of Rene was extremely relaxing for the two of them. The rolling green hills dotted with cattle and small cottages seemed very peaceful. The blue sky was filled with bright white puffy clouds, like the landscape of a French painter. They passed bikers and tractor-driving farmers, and for the first time in Robert's life, he was not annoyed by the delays.

The closeness they immediately felt for one another didn't seem to surprise them. Robert unguardedly opened up and talked more to Katie than he had ever talked to anyone, even Alice. In his relationship with his wife, he had hid his feelings, thinking she needed protection from the horror and danger he faced each day on the job. Katie, however, unleashed something inside him that he didn't even know he had. But, as it spilled out, it felt familiar somehow.

"Robert, are you all right?" Katie asked.

"I'm fine. I was just thinking how comfortable I am with you despite the fact that this is our first time together."

"I have to say I'm also amazed at how relaxed and comfortable I am with you. I usually don't talk to men, unless it's for business. And that's a whole different me."

"Can we talk about these dreams we're having?" he asked sheepishly.

"Yes, fine. Me first," Katie volunteered, a sheepish grin on her face. "They started for me the day after my encounter with the bright light and voices on my island. The dreams keep getting more intense the more I'm contacted by what I think is a woman's voice or maybe thoughts. I'm just not sure."

She told him about each dream, especially the one from the previous night. When he described the dreams he had been having, they both were in shock. With the exception of the different viewpoint they had, everything was the same. They appeared to be describing the same events, only from their viewpoint. It was as if they were there, inside their dreams together. Katie just stared at Robert. "That's impossible? Right?

Robert just shrugged his shoulders. It's a little spooky for me to even think about it."

Then she told him about the folklore that the young concierge had mentioned, how the family that occupied Chateau Rose had mysteriously disappeared. Robert became disturbed when Katie described the violent ending in her dream. It was as if he had lived that scene sometime before. But he hadn't had the same dream as of yet, which further compounded his confusion.

At a fork in the road, a sign pointed west to the Chateau Rose monument. Symbols indicated lodging and food were available in Rene, four kilometers south.

"Let's go to the monument first and check it out," Robert suggested. "I'll buy you dinner in town before we head back."

"That'll be great," she replied, taking a brush from her purse and stroking her silky red hair. She turned toward Robert and smiled, sending chills over his entire body.

I've felt that smile before, he told himself as he stared blankly at her.

Much to their disappointment, Chateau Rose had been destroyed in 1746 the night Madame and Monsieur Rose and their two children, accused witches, demons of sorts, disappeared. The only structure standing on the property was a small chapel that appeared to have a dual function. Along with being a house of worship, it was also a small museum and information center recapping the history of the chateau and its family.

Katie read aloud from the brochure the hotel concierge had given her. It explained that forty-seven years after the property was destroyed by fire, the villagers constructed a small chapel to ward off any demons Satan had left behind.

Before the chapel was completed, townspeople and workers began to disappear mysteriously. Ten reported disappearances were recorded between 1746 and 1793 before the chapel was officially opened.

"If I were a betting man," Robert mused, "I'd wager that the ten disappearances were probably people who just moved away from the nut cases that controlled the village. It's just too convenient that a building can ward off the Devil. It sounds more like a marketing ploy for the town."

Katie looked at him, shrugged her shoulders, and humored his musings. She did come from a community that believed in the Devil and understood how fear could control a small village like Rene. The Church used the Devil to control the weak, which she had never really worried about.

They parked close to the chapel, unsure if it was open or if anyone was inside to direct them to the chateau. The building looked more like a rustic cottage than a chapel. The high-pitched roof was in need of repair, and thick ivy covered the red brick walls. The thick-paned windows were dirty from years of neglect, and the large wooden door at the entrance was warped and cracked from year-round exposure to the harsh weather conditions.

Katie noticed the white smoke gently rising from the chimney, pointing it out to Robert, confident that someone was inside.

"I thought we had come to a dead end," Katie said, smiling. "Maybe someone inside can shed some light on all of this?"

Inside the chapel, a small sign read: *Candles to keep the demons away. Two Euros per candle, please.*

A thick velvet rope and a closed sign separated the information booth from the rest of the chapel. Not taking the warning seriously, Robert stepped over the barrier to look for some information or directions to the chateau monument.

An elderly, feeble-looking woman in her nineties slowly came out from the pews, taking small steps without lifting her feet. She shuffled like she had sandpaper for soles. She held onto a squeaky walker as she struggled forward, aiming herself toward her desk and chair that had a thick, fluffy pillow for her bony bottom.

"The chapel will be open as soon as I get to my desk," she said, her voice quavering.

Robert, frustrated by her progress in inches, was ready to help her.

"I can take care of myself," she said in English, as though she had read his mind. "Please be patient."

Her walker continued to scrape the concrete floor, sending chills up his spine.

"Would you like me to officially open the chapel?" he asked, unable to endure the sound any longer.

"Thank you, young man," she said as she organized her desk, her hands shaking. "That will be a big help."

Katie walked up to the desk and dropped several Euros in a jar that bore the cross. The woman, unable to control her head from shaking, slowly looked up to hand her a packet. Then all of a sudden, the old woman gasped. Fear filled her eyes as she stared in disbelief at Katie. She clutched her chest as the blood drained from her face.

"Are you all right?" Katie cried out, frightened. "Robert, come here."

"What's wrong?" he asked, turning quickly to see the old woman on the verge of passing out.

When the woman's old eyes focused on Robert, she let go a louder moan and then went limp. Her head and body fell forward and caught the top of her desk. Robert reacted fast and caught her before she could fall toward the cold concrete floor. Katie saw a restroom sign and rushed over to get some cold compresses to help revive the poor old woman.

Katie applied the cold, wet paper towels to the back of the woman's neck. Robert was ready to lay her down and apply some CPR when she began to stir, moaning in French. Katie seemed to understand, but the woman was too incoherent.

Finally, after ten minutes, she sat up, still breathing heavy, her face light gray like the statues in the chapel.

"Madame and Monsieur Rose, you've returned!" she screamed, horrified. "God save us all."

She passed out again, but this time for good. She was dead, her eyes bulging, her mouth frozen from the last words she uttered, locked in a fit of terror.

They carried her into the chapel, placed her frail body in one of the pews, and decided they would call the authorities when they found a phone.

While Katie searched the outside, Robert walked toward the back of the chapel, past the rosewood seats. The faded wood had been neglected for years, its rough surface marred with tiny splinters caused by parishioners who, for centuries, must have sat enthusiastically praying, believing what they were doing would keep their town safe from the Satan.

Robert rushed past a giant cross and a pulpit covered with cobwebs. Both had not seen a priest in many years. He found a small room that appeared to be the living quarters of the caretaker. One small window provided the only source of light, except for an oil lamp that rested on a night stand by the side of a small cot, which was covered with a beautiful, multicolored frayed quilt that must have been made long ago.

The room was very clean and neatly kept. A bookcase covered an entire wall near a table she used for eating and reading. She must have been rushed that morning since her breakfast dishes were still on the table. Her Bible sat open, marked with a blue velvet ribbon.

Disappointed that there was no phone in her room, Robert turned to leave when an odd-looking book on a shelf caught his eye. Slipping around the small eating table, he dislodged the bookend that was holding up the book, causing it to fall toward the ground. He tried to catch it, embarrassed by his clumsiness and the possibility that someone might see his intrusion into the dead woman's living quarters. The book he was reaching for skidded across the floor, stopping under her bed. He picked up the other books that had fallen and replaced them exactly in their original positions.

Afraid that the rest of the room could come tumbling down around him, he scurried over to the bed and on one knee felt for the book. His hand bumped into a box of some sort, which he pulled out. To his amazement, the box looked familiar. He thought it was impossible, since the antique must have been a hundred and fifty years old. Placing the box on the cot, he fumbled around for the book until he was successful. It was an old diary that was worn and battered, its cloth cover, a faded purple. Sewn on top in red needlepoint were the words *Journal Particulier Chateau Rose.*

A small key fell from the journal, bouncing on the small throw rug. He guessed it was for the box he had found. Inserting it gently, he was able to unlock the frail coffer. Inside were some loose papers, old newspaper clippings, a tiny rag doll, and a blue and red cow pull toy. A chill swept over his body as he stared at the contents; he knew what they all meant. He quickly closed the top, locked it, and walked briskly outside, carrying the journal and box in his arms.

"Are you okay?" Katie asked. "You look like you just saw a ghost."

"I'll explain later. Let me put these things in the car."

"Why don't we go into town and let someone know what happened?" Katie said sorrowfully.

"What's the rush? She's not going anywhere. Let's look around and see if we can figure out why this place has been in our dreams."

Katie had begun to walk up a grassy knoll toward the monument when Robert noticed the wind kicking up in an isolated area fifty yards to the left. Strangely, the air was calm around them. The swirling dirt had a certain graceful rhythm, a sort of dance of many feet, choreographed and purposeful.

He shrugged his shoulders, already used to the many strange occurrences that had followed him these last few weeks. He closed the trunk and jogged up the path, catching Katie before she made it to the monument.

They walked slowly, cautious with every step. Both of them felt a sensation come up from the ground through their feet. The ground became warm. The deep grass curled around their shoes as if hugging long lost friends. They glanced at each other, realizing something familiar was happening to them.

Katie grabbed his hand, squeezing it tightly, steadying herself as they reached the foundation of where Chateau Rose had once stood. She released his hand and began pacing around as if she were inside a home she had once occupied. For a moment, she just stared, her eyes fixed on an imaginary painting that hung on a wall. Then she spun around, circling slowly, taking in every morsel of memory. She took ten paces forward, toward what she estimated had been the living room, and then fell to her knees, crying. He rushed over and kneeled down, putting his arms around her. She looked up into his eyes; he could see the sadness of something from her past.

"I died here," she said softly. Her whisper floated off her tongue, raising the hairs on the back of his neck.

"What do you mean you died here?" he asked.

"In my dream, I died here the night our home was destroyed."

"Our home?"

"It was you in my dream. You held me right before the light flashed: the moment when I died."

Holding her tight, his eyes fixed on hers, he understood. He was now feeling what she was feeling. He remembered the invisible enemy he had fought, Katie impaled on his pitchfork. And he remembered his two children, their necks broken, lying in a corner dead, a doll squeezed tightly in his daughter's hand, a toy propped up against his son's head.

"What does all this mean?" he mumbled. *Did the stuff in the box belong to my children?* he thought.

Katie stood up, extending her hand to Robert. "Let's go into town and sort this entire thing out. I'm really in need of a stiff drink right now."

"That sounds perfect," he replied, taking her hand and leading her back to the car. His mood had turned melancholy as he walked deep in thought. He didn't notice the dust storm still swirling fifty yards on a knoll to their left.

* * * * *

"They've returned," Ruth said in a panic. "I saw them die that day."

"It's possible the harvesting happened in time," Dável remarked intriguingly, his face contorted in the most bizarre expression she had ever seen. "What I don't understand is how they could be together again. It just doesn't happen."

"What are we going to do?"

"Nothing at this time. The new owners at United Weapons Systems must manufacture what we need to defeat Jacob first. Then we can deal with Katherine and Robert once again."

"What about the inspector and the sergeant that have been following them?" she asked, trying to stifle a cough as her body continued to weaken. "They could be trouble for us."

"I'll deal with them," he said, hiding his grief at her deteriorating health, "and anyone else who tries to prevent us from finally succeeding with our mission. This time, we won't fail, and you'll be healthy once again."

* * * * *

Hidden high on a hill, elbows resting on the grass, Inspector Fellows was befuddled.

"Strange goings on with those two," he remarked, pressing his binoculars tight against his eyes.

"Sir, let me look," the sergeant asked, grabbing the strap and accidentally jerking his boss' head to the side.

"Idiot, just wait," the inspector said, trying to refocus. "She's acting very strangely, like she just saw a ghost. I wonder what would happen if they just turned up dead out here, so I could go home to my family."

"Give me the word," O'Conner said, fondling his gun, "and the pleasure will be all mine."

"Maybe an accident on the road," the inspector replied menacingly, his eyes red with rage. "I despise O'Riley and would love an excuse to see the life drain from her body."

They watched helplessly, not knowing what their next move would be. Inspector Fellows rose slowly, brushing off the dirt and grass that stuck to his jacket and pants. He handed the binoculars to his assistant.

"Here, you watch them for a while," he said. "I have to take a piss."

He stumbled back, tripping on a boulder and falling down hard, his breath knocked out of him. Looking up from a prone position, he crawled backwards, dragging his rear on the dirt. His face knotted in terror as he saw his partner hanging in midair, his feet jerking wildly as the life drained from his body. O'Connor's eyes were blood red as the tiny vessels began to burst from a lack of oxygen. An invisible vise squeezed his esophagus like a can of soda. The inspector heard a pop as the cartilage cracked inside the sergeant's neck. The inspector, frozen with fear, didn't move. He watched helplessly as sergeant O'Conner dropped like a limp dishrag to the ground.

Fellows felt his bladder release as he was lifted up by, what felt like, two powerful hands that were squeezing tightly around his neck. Then, everything went dark, his neck snapped and his body slammed to the ground falling next to sergeant O'Conner.

* * * * *

Robert peered over the top of the car, startled by a popping sound that seemed to come from atop a small hill overlooking the meadow between them. He couldn't focus clearly, because the sun's afternoon rays were directly in his eyes, but he figured it was just another illusion in a day of surprises.

"Is there something wrong?" Katie asked.

"No, nothing. Just my imagination getting me spooked again."

CHAPTER TWENTY-FOUR

Miguel Ortiz anxiously sat in his living room as he watched the preliminary reports each TV network aired.

"Who the fuck are they?" he shouted. "Someone's killing my customers."

Albert Mitchell, Chairman of the Board at United Weapon Systems, seemed lost as he stared blankly at the TV screen. He sat in a recliner drinking a cold beer, stuffing pretzels into his mouth, and getting more pieces of pretzel on his lap than in his mouth, an orifice Ortiz had adequately named the toilet bowl.

Ortiz gave him a disgusted look as Mitchell's beer spilled on his clean white Berber carpet.

"I wonder what your home looks like," he grumbled, stopping himself from wasting any more breath on the slob, he called his partner.

"Do we really want to buy United Weapons Systems after what happened to their last CEO?" Mitchell asked, belching. "What if this group's demands are for real?"

"You're a slob, Albert," Ortiz said, shaking his head. "I'm not worried. The world believes we're the good guys and Vincent wasn't. We'll set in motion a wonderful campaign that will show us developing peaceful solutions to the world's weapon problems. When things quiet down, we'll market our wares to the highest bidder."

"What if this group finds out about us and what we're planning to do?"

"How? I've got the most sophisticated security systems and scanning devices money can buy. No one or any group of madmen can penetrate my fortress."

"Well, I have the papers with me today for your signature. They've agreed to your terms, and if you sign them today, you'll be the new CEO tomorrow with seventy percent ownership of United Weapons Systems."

"Let's do it before they get cold feet."

Within twelve hours, the deal had been executed. United Weapons Systems, Inc. had been sold to Ortiz. Mitchell gave him a thumbs-up sign as he cradled the phone on his shoulder.

"It's yours," he said, hanging up after Glickman told him it was official.

* * * * *

In the conference room of United Weapons Systems, Rudy Glickman, the deputy director of the Department of Justice, had just fired all the board of directors. He was gathering up his papers when a short man walked in and asked nervously to speak to him. His hair was cut close to his scalp, with the bangs held in place by some type of hair gel. His plaid short-sleeve shirt, two sizes too small, made the sleeves point up around his skinny biceps, and his pant cuffs rode high on his ankles, exposing the white socks he was wearing. The uniform of the typical geek.

"What can I do for you, uh, Mr. Barry?" Glickman asked, squinting at the nametag draped over his overstuffed pocket protector.

"Yes, I'm Stanley Barry, chief operations director here at UWP. I wanted to see about a meeting with the new owners. I wasn't able to tell Mr. Vincent about our new discovery that could revolutionize war."

He now had Glickman's attention.

"Nobody knows of this new development?" Rudy inquired. "I don't like people who lie to me."

"No, sir," he stuttered. "Mr. Vincent died before I could tell him. I'm the only one, except for you that will know about our new product."

He nervously tapped his pen on the table before Glickman grabbed it from him.

"What new discovery are you talking about? I didn't see anything mentioned in any of the paperwork we reviewed before making our bid."

"Our orders in development have always been to keep all new discoveries confidential," he said, "until we bring them to the attention of the CEO. Mr. Vincent, we all suspected hid strategic information about new weapons development from the United States for his own selfish gains. We've all suspected for some time that he was selling weapons to terrorists, but we're just scientists trying to make a living. It's just a job for us. So, I just assumed the new owners would expect the same from my department."

"You did well, Stanley," Glickman said. "I want a full report on this delivered to me by tomorrow. And remember: the same rules still apply."

* * * * *

"You're so stubborn, Father," Rebecca said, exasperated. "Maybe waiting thirty days isn't going to do us any good. We need to show our power now. If we use Katie and Robert to convey a serious demand before your speech, the world will then be ready for us when you address them. United Weapons Systems can't be allowed to go on."

"What do you have in mind?" Jacob said, unfolding his arms.

"I want Katie and Robert to deliver a warning that will show the world our strength. That we're deadly serious about our demands."

Her father grinned at her. "They're not ready to come aboard just yet. They're just finding out their connection to each other. If they learn too much too soon, it could overload their circuits and cause more harm than good."

"We have no choice, unless we destroy the source of the new weapon. This weapon can expose us and leave the world ripe for Dável. We're close to capturing him and his family, but if he gets hold of the Pulsar XR-36 and finds out about the RX-666 at United Weapons Systems, we'll become the hunted and won't be able to stop him."

"Be cautious and take it slow with Katie and Robert," he said, his hands shaking from the weakness that was consuming his body. "Don't reveal everything right away, just enough to make them believe that what we're trying to do is the best thing."

CHAPTER TWENTY-FIVE

The local constable in the town of Rene was saddened by the news
of Teresa Asnar's death. Robert Philips introduced Katie and him,
and told the constable they had come up from Paris for the day.
He tried to act concerned about her death as he explained that he
found Teresa lying on the floor when they arrived at the chapel.
Robert was not a good liar. He could see the constable raise his
eyebrows. He continued with his account and estimated how long
she had been dead. He showed his credentials, discussing his
background as a Los Angeles police detective. From his
experience, he explained, she had been dead a few hours before
they arrived. He knew it was a lie, but it would be too difficult for
them to prove him wrong.

    "I'll get our medical examiner out to the chapel
immediately," he said. "We don't want other tourists to find her
and panic. That mysterious site has such a scary past."

    "Why was she up there all alone at her age?" Katie
inquired.

    "She's lived up there all her life, like her ancestors. The
Asnar's were the caretakers of the chateau and remained there all
these years watching over their masters' property. Teresa was the
last of them, so now there will be no one to maintain the chapel or
the monument."

    "May I ask you a few questions about the history of that
place?" Robert asked politely. "Unless, under the circumstances,
this is not a good time. . ."

    "Death is part of life," the constable replied. "And life goes on. I'd be happy to tell you what I know; just let me call the people who'll bring Teresa back to town."

Katie was already looking at some reference books stacked in no particular order on a small table that had other information about the village. She found it interesting that a specific book had been written about the chateau and the Rose family. If what she had read was true, the family that occupied the estate was the first and only family to have ever lived there. There was no information on how they accumulated their money or how they earned a living, which apparently planted the seeds for plenty of rumors while they were alive.

As someone who had grown up in a close-knit community, Katie knew that loners, people who stood out from the rest of the community, sparked fear in the imagination of the ignorant, leading to panic and then blame when things went wrong. She understood that a bad season for a local crop, or a mysterious death among the town's cattle, would immediately be blamed on the village's most misunderstood person, or in this case, the Rose family. Apparently, there had been a series of murders in villages around the area, leaving a horrible trail that pointed, according to the villagers, to the Devil. As she read on, she came upon a photo of a painting of the Rose family. Her breathing stopped, and her eyes just froze.

"Robert, come here!" she said, pointing to the photo. "Look!"

He turned white.

"Shit. It's you and me, or two fabulous look-alikes."

"That's what scared the old lady. She thought we had returned."

Katie slammed the book closed, looking very guilty. Her face flushed bright red, and she turned away from the constable.

"Let's get out of here and head back to Paris," she said. "I don't think we're ready to ask the local people or even the constable, for a welcome home party, just yet."

The constable was still on the phone, arranging to meet his friend, the medical examiner, at the tavern later that night. Katie whispered they had to go and thanked him for his help. They were both out the door and didn't notice his empty wave, or the disappointment he showed as they rushed out.

As soon as he hung up the phone, he immediately grabbed

the book Katie had been looking at and was shocked when he got to the photo. He called his friend at Interpol, Inspector Lefebvre, in Paris and told him the story.

"Pierre, your imagination is running away with you," Lefebvre scolded him. "The Rose family is a fable, something we were told as children to keep us well behaved and out of trouble."

"You have the book, check it out yourself. What if the tale is true and they've returned? Maybe they have something to do with what's been happening around the world."

"I'll check it out, but even if they look similar, it doesn't mean anything. Remember, we're working with paintings over three hundred years ago. It's just a silly coincidence, so calm down and get a hold of yourself."

"Just check it out and call me."

Inspector Lefebvre liked his friend but understood, after living twenty years in a town that believed this fable of witches to be true, he had lost his perspective. He was impressed, however, that his friend had retained the foresight to write down their vehicle license number, which he punched into his computer and traced to Philips' hotel in Paris.

"This is a ridiculous waste of time," he muttered to himself after hanging up. "But for an old friend, I'll send him the bill for the drinks I'll have while on this assignment."

* * * * *

A few hours later, Inspector Lefebvre received a fax from the constable, which he found very disturbing. The deaths of Inspector Fellows and Sergeant O'Conner at the Chateau's monument had now made his uninteresting investigation more interesting. Maybe these two tourists had something to do with their deaths, and maybe not. Regardless, there was only one set of fresh tire tracks near the chateau. He felt they must know something about the three deaths that had occurred while they were there. How he was going to approach them was something he had not yet figured out, but he would in the next hour.

He was connecting to the Interpol database and then to the FBI's, which he believed would give him enough information to question his two suspects.

CHAPTER TWENTY-SIX

Katie was quiet during the ride back to their hotel. Leaning her head against the window, her eyes fixed on the fast-passing countryside; the dark green rolling hills and the pastures blanketed with cows grazing under the afternoon sun reminded her of her home back in Ireland.

So many coincidences rambled through her head: the similar dreams with Robert, the voice, the message to come to France, the memories at the chateau, the death of Allan Vincent, and now the picture of the two of them in a painting that had been completed in the eighteenth century.

She trembled as the realization set in that she might have had a past life that was filled with tragedy. Once again, the dark clouds of death hung, suspended over her head, waiting to inflict a new and unknown pain upon her.

Her recent dream, in which her two children were violently murdered by a power she could not stop, had to have meant something. She'd had the same feelings the day her parents were murdered by the British soldiers. Her eyes were swollen with tears; again, she was helpless and scared.

What's next? she thought. *Am I to lose someone else close to me?*

"That's not going to happen," the familiar female voice said. *"You've had your share of loss. Now it's time for you to get back what you deserve. Have faith."*

Katie looked over at Robert, aware that he had not heard the voice.

"I need to know what's happening to us," she spoke inside her mind, trying hard to communicate with the voice, *"and what*

all of this means at the chateau."

"Tonight in Robert's room, you'll be given some answers." The voice faded and was gone as quickly as it appeared.

"Robert, I was just told we'll get a message tonight in your room. Let's have room service and wait."

"Was it the female voice?" he asked. "She spoke to you? Why not me?"

"I don't have an answer," she said, "but if it's that important to you," she said testy. "Ask her tonight."

"I've got something to show you that I took from the old lady's room. I hope you're prepared for another big shock."

"There's nothing that could surprise me more than what's already happened."

"Don't count on it," he replied.

CHAPTER TWENTY-SEVEN

They separated for the first time since their first meeting down in the piano bar. Katie wanted a little time to freshen up and get into some clean clothes. She agreed to allow Robert to order their dinner, her intuition telling her he would know what she liked.

He ordered dinner with room service, plus a couple of French cabernets he hoped she would enjoy. Why he ordered her rack of lamb with a salad of sliced tomatoes, cucumbers, and asparagus tips, he had no clue. He just sensed she would like it.

They had only met earlier that day, but to him it seemed that they had been together a lifetime. He sat on his bed, holding the box and journal he had taken from Teresa's room. Nervously, he began to thumb through the journal.

The first entry was dated August 6, 1727. The handwriting was difficult to read, but he was able to discern that Katherine and Robert Rose bought the chateau on that date. It had remained vacant for over thirty years, prior to their purchase. The original owners had died before moving in. The chateau was in need of much repair, which, as he read on, was completed by May of 1732.

It appeared the Roses were very much in love and were distraught that they could not conceive, since building a family was something they both wanted and needed. Just as they gave up hope of having any children, Katherine became pregnant with their daughter Nicole, who was born September 17, 1736. Then two years later on the same day, their son Robert, II. was born. That coincidence was the beginning of the terrible rumors that plagued the entire Rose household, including their servants. The townspeople accused them of being followers of the Devil and practitioners of witchcraft. Elderly spinsters and widows in the village convinced everyone that they were unholy and possessed by Satan. The more Robert and Katherine distanced themselves from the villagers and their nasty rumors and hateful eyes, the more the town believed they were hiding their witchcraft ways. Nicole and Robert II, learned to be best friends because neighbor children were not allowed to set foot on the property for fear that they would be eaten nor have some horrible spell cast upon them.

Philips put the journal down, his heart racing. He knew this story as if he had lived it.

He took a deep breath and went back to his reading, trying to digest what was described next. In 1746, just six months before the Roses disappeared and their home was destroyed, other mysterious disappearances began occurring across the countryside. The village of Rene was the last to be affected. Villagers maintained that the Devil and his witches were kidnapping children and fertile women to build an army of evil.

The day that Robert and Katherine disappeared, the townspeople stood high on a hill overlooking the chateau and watched in amazement as the house burned down, cheering that God had come to their rescue. As if to confirm their suspicions, since that day no children or women had disappeared from the village. Forty-six years later, they built the chapel in homage to their miracle and their devotion to prayer. They also hoped it would keep the Roses and the Devil from ever returning. The villagers felt the property caretakers were diseased, believing that their exposure to the family of witches had corrupted them and would not allow them access to the town. The Asnars received food and supplies and some gold in exchange for watching over the property, not mingling with the townspeople, and later operating the chapel.

Teresa Asnars' great-great-grandmother had made an entry two days after her employers disappeared in the flames:

The white flash of light after the rumbling ceased brought a quiet that was not from this Earth. Like Jesus during the resurrection, the four of them floated into the heavens to be with God.

"This sounds like what happened at the shack, except no bodies floated away," Philips mumbled. "I'm so fucking confused and wish this mumbo jumbo would find another soul to torture."

A knock on the door startled him, and he jumped up off the bed. Katie stood in the doorway, her hair brushed straight down. She wore a cotton sundress that clung to her perfectly shaped curves.

Robert was mesmerized.

"Are you going to invite me in?" she teased. "Or are you trying to use your X-ray vision to burn a hole in my dress?"

"Excuse me," he stammered. "That was impolite. You just look so beautiful."

He couldn't stop focusing on her body, the way her dress clung to her, gently caressing every inch of her figure and revealing that she was not wearing any undergarments. As she turned, she caught him off guard again. She was amused as he attempted to look away.

He invited her to sit in the fluffy white cotton armchair near the window. The wine had arrived first per his request, and he poured her a glass, which she passionately accepted.

"I'm impressed," she said, holding her glass up in a toast. "You know my favorite wine."

"It was easy," he said, returning the toast. "I just ordered my favorite."

Katie noticed the box and journal on his bed. Her curiosity piqued, she reached across the bed and drew the box closer to her chair. Robert handed her the key and watched her reaction as she gingerly opened the top. As if surprised by a jack-in-the-box, she brought her hands to her mouth in startled amazement.

"It's Nicole's doll," she whispered. "Oh my God, little Robert's pull toy you made him."

"Why did you say those names?" Robert asked, stunned. "And why do you believe I built that toy?"

"While I was taking a shower," she said, suddenly choking back tears, "I saw them and you and their toys."

Robert walked toward her, extending his hand to bring her to the couch. She accepted his offer willingly and sat in the corner of the love seat, her legs folded comfortably under her body.

"I feel there is a higher reason that we've been set up to meet as we did. Then to have the same experiences that we've had at these precise moments has me baffled," Robert said, gazing into her eyes. "I still don't know why, but after reading Teresa's journal about the Chateau Rose, I'm beginning to believe we've been together in another life."

"I came to that conclusion earlier out at the monument," she said warmly. "What's taken you so long?" she teased.

He felt guilty for being so attracted toward Katie and wondered how that would affect his memory of Alice and his daughter Stephanie. Just then, the room went silent, something they both knew about, and then the voice came.

"It's been quite a day for both of you," she said, her voice more relaxed than at previous times. *"We've exposed you to a lot of facts and memories that need some explanations, and tonight you'll receive a brief introduction before your formal indoctrination begins."*

Indoctrination? Robert thought. *What training are you talking about? I haven't agreed to help you or your cause!*

The voice became stern. *"You will once you realize your purpose in all of this and how your help will save the world from destruction."*

CHAPTER TWENTY-EIGHT

Hidden in a dark cave high in the Arizona desert, a madman's daughter questioned her father's logic.

"Father, can you really trust Ortiz?" she asked. "He might turn the weapon around and kill us once it's completed."

"He's not that smart," her father replied. "And with his greed for power, he'll want us as a friend, rather than a foe. Once we get control of the weapon, we'll have one week to come out of hiding and make our move. I'll destroy Ortiz and his partners and any evidence that the weapon ever existed. Our days of running and hiding will finally be over. Katie and Robert will finally be in our camp, making us complete and ready to take our rightful place in the world.

He wrapped his arms around her, squeezing her tightly. And, he held back tears of happiness that in three weeks their hiding would finally be over.

"Now it's time for you to rest and take your serum," he told her as he pushed the cold fluid inside her vein.

His two sons received their injection first and were   quietly asleep on their cots at the far end of the cave. Once she was asleep, he injected himself, ready for his rest that would take the better part of five days.

The carved-out space he had made in the red clay hills in Arizona provided the perfect hiding place. The hunters' detection equipment, Esther's tracking device, could not read their body temperatures as they rested deep within the thick soil composition.

CHAPTER TWENTY-NINE

Ortiz was at United Weapons Systems early the morning after his communication with his new invisible friend. He was known at the company as Mr. Samuel Diaz, the newly appointed CEO. Since there had never been any photographs taken of Ortiz, his new identity was easy to pull off.

He met with Stanley Barry after Rudy had told him about their conversation. Barry was more than eager to begin his work and liked that he would remain autonomous, reporting only to Ortiz, or as he knew him to be, Mr. Diaz.

Trying to understand what this new weapon was capable of doing confused Ortiz, since Stanley had his own language and code names for everything he talked about.

"Stan, my friend," he said, putting his arm around the geeks shoulder, "can you talk in layman's terms before I kick the living shit out of you?"

"Ouch," he cried. His high, irritating voice was like fingernails on a chalkboard. "Don't get violent, man."

"Don't tell me what to do, asshole. Just explain to me what you're building and how it will work, understand?"

Ortiz' eyes were cold and hard, and when they met Stanley's, the nerdy scientist wet his pants.

After about an hour, Ortiz was amazed by what Barry was trying to create. The Pulsar RX-666, the Destroyer, was to be the ultimate weapon. While allowing an army to become invisible, it could destroy up to 100,000 or more men without harming property. Ortiz realized that if this weapon worked, he could be more powerful than he had ever imagined.

"Speeding up the body's molecules can make a person seem invisible?" he asked.

"Yes, in theory only. We've tested it on animals, and it worked perfectly, except," he said, hesitating, "for one major flaw."

"What flaw?"

"When we attempted to return each animal's body back to its normal molecular state, we couldn't slow down the speed of their molecules, which caused an intense friction, something like what you see on reentry by the space shuttle into our atmosphere. What we had was a fireball of charred fur and melted bones. But," he said nervously, "the weapon still works without using the cloaking mechanism. Once I get the flaws out, then the Destroyer will become the ultimate weapon."

"Can it be modified so it can be tested on humans?"

"That's what I'm working on. I'm getting close. It just needs a little tweaking of the equations."

"I want this project worked twenty-four seven, and I want it up and running successfully in three weeks."

"I'm not sure we can work that fast—"

"You bet your sweet ass you can, or you're going to be the first human we test!"

Ortiz just stared at Barry, his chiseled facial muscles bulging as the excitement of what was going to happen swept over him.

Maybe my new friend has his molecules trapped and can't come back, he thought. *Maybe my new friend won't be so arrogant when I have this new weapon?*

* * * * *

Inside the situation room, President Hopkins rubbed his bloodshot eyes as he leaned back in his chair. It was obvious to his advisors that he was not sleeping well. The worry and frustration etched on his face told a sad story about a weak president engulfed in a world crisis.

"Why wasn't I kept in the loop about the secret experiments the military was conducting with United Weapon Systems?" he shouted, slamming his fist against the conference table.

General Armstrong was the first to speak. His deep voice resonated inside the room as he spoke in a monotone, his eyes focused on a spot on the wall.

"Sir, the military has been conducting experiments without Oval office's knowledge or that of the Congress for over a hundred years. If we are to remain strong and one-step ahead of our enemies, we can't be hung up in the committee bullshit that goes on in this town. 9/11 is a good example of us being caught with our pants down. We began to step up our experiments on new weapons and covert military warfare that was the new game in town."

Hopkins sat dumbfounded.

"Are you telling me," he began, his face beet red, "that our military no longer takes orders from its commander and chief?"

"Sir, we've always gone through the proper channels with our experiments. You will need to confer with your staff. We've followed established protocols." Armstrong, his disdain written on his face, finally turned his head and looked at Hopkins.

The rest of the Joint Chiefs of Staff sat speechless. Admiral Dawkins, a long-time friend of Armstrong, supported his friend's attitude, while General Miller of the Air Force and General Stevens from the Marines remained silent, knowing that the general always took an arrogant, aggressive stance toward the president and his staff. They knew Armstrong was an ambitious military man who believed that the White House should be run by men like him and not political wimps like Hopkins.

Hopkins' eyes narrowed, and his lips were pressed tightly together.

"Could it be that your supposedly secret experiments have been leaked to our enemies?" the president lashed out at Armstrong and they are using it right now wiping out their competition?

"That's impossible. We don't have and won't have something of this magnitude built for the next fifty or so years. All I know is that Allan Vincent had a prototype of the Pulsar XR-36 that he was taking out of the country the night he died. I have to assume his killers have it."

"Well, someone or some group has it. It's obvious that you've lost control of your weapon and really don't have a rat-ass idea of what's really happening," the president said, looking lost.

"And they're using it to restructure the balance of power. If you and your experts don't find a way to stop them, we'll be kissing their asses right after their UN presentation."

Stephen Daily, the Secretary of Defense, rose and began pacing around the room.

General Armstrong looked around, looking for any support, but heads began to drop, his colleagues, one by one, staring down at the table. Everyone knew how Daily operated. Someone would be nailed to the Cross.

"Anyone ready to land on their sword and take one for our country?" Daily asked.

No one volunteered.

President Hopkins was relieved that Daily had taken charge of the meeting. He usually deferred matters of this nature, the real dirty work, to him anyway. However, in this case, Hopkins knew he couldn't resolve the issue at hand.

"I didn't think so," Daily remarked, his tone indignant, his contemptuous attitude making even his boss uncomfortable.

"We've made mistakes before and will take our losses," General Armstrong asserted. "But don't insult us with your Boy Scout attitude that you can solve this problem."

"General, you're the only one sitting here without his tail between his legs," Daily said. "And I can guess you would like to take your anger out on someone other than me."   "You're a mind reader, Mr. Daily," the general said, smiling. "However, my anger will be better served by destroying the weapon Vincent's killers have before anyone else gets hold of it."

"I think we're all missing an important point here," Neil Conway of the Department of Justice said, interrupting the macho war dance between the two men. "How do we explain the way they are killing everyone without any sign of trauma? The General's description of the weapon vaporizes the enemy. That's not what's been happening. We might have two powerful weapons we're dealing with."

"We don't have that answer just yet," General Armstrong said, "but we will once we find them and destroy them."

"We don't know how the weapon works," Conway said, incredulous. "And we don't know how they have solved some critical problems our scientists can't. How the fuck are we going to combat that without jeopardizing our own safety? They hold all the cards right now, and I for one don't want to piss them off after seeing what they are capable of doing."

"The FBI thinks they've tracked down the weapon source," Daily replied, "and, as we speak, are ready to capture the people responsible."

"My department is in charge of all actions of that nature," Conway said. "Why wasn't I informed?"

"Because your department might have some leaks," Daily said, "and I didn't want to jeopardize our plans."

"That's bullshit, and you know it," Conway shouted. "Unless I'm under suspicion. It sounds more like a power play by you and President Hopkins to boost your failing administration's ratings."

"You're out of line," Daily said. "We made our decision for the good of this country, whether you believe it or not."

"Now that I know what you're up to, I expect to be kept in the loop," Conway countered. "I'll deal with the leaks. Is that clear?"

"Perfectly," Daily responded contemptuously. "Tomorrow at noon, we're amassing a joint effort with the military and FBI to close down United Weapons Systems and arrest the new board of directors and their scientists. We believe that they have been selling weapons to terrorist groups worldwide and that the mysterious death of Allan Vincent was the direct result of this group's cover-up. Once we analyze their databases, we are hopeful we'll find the answers to our weapon problem and then be able to launch a full military operation and destroy this vigilante group."

"What if you're wrong and United Weapons was not that advanced?" Conway asked. "You're going to piss off a lot of powerful people and put us all in danger. I'm voicing my objections to this action at this time until we are sure that Vincent's company even created the weapon this group has."

"Maybe he has a point," the president said. "What harm would it do to find out if they even have the capabilities at this time for such a weapon?"

"Whether they do or they don't, this company has new owners that we believe are getting ready to start up where Vincent left off, supplying weapons to our enemies," General Armstrong said. "We have no choice but to stay on course and execute our plan for tomorrow."

"The operation is a go for tomorrow at noon, gentlemen," Chief of Staff Turner concluded, speaking for the first time since the meeting started. "There'll be no deviation from our original plan."

The president and Stephen Daily left the room for the Oval Office, while Turner finalized the minute details. The Joint Chiefs departed for the Pentagon, leaving Neil Conway alone in the conference room, dumbfounded.

* * * * *

Later that day, Conway set up a meeting with Bradley Young, a friend at the National Security Agency. He knew if anyone could be trusted, Bradley was the man.

"Have we gotten any more data from the weather satellites regarding those unexplained dust storms?" Conway asked.

"We've got the data, but it's not easy to decipher. What we're seeing isn't possible. Most weather patterns start up from some atmospheric condition. These anomalies just began in one spot and remained concentrated in the same area until the victims were murdered."

"You're talking like this thing is human," Conway said nervously, afraid of what he was about to be told.

Bradley pointed to a spot on the photograph that was of the desert in Syria.

"Our photographs, as you can see, are pretty clear," he said. "See this? If I didn't know better, I'd say it's the outline of a person moving so fast that he or she leaves this trail of dust. But what's strange is that coming from this person is a vapor of some sort that is being pushed forward toward its designated target."

"How could your camera pick that up?"

"It's similar to how lights from a distant city seem to flicker as you look at them. Even though you can't see a light bulb flicker up close, it really is flickering, but very fast. Same thing here," he paused. "In the absence of any other explanation, let's just say this is human. Look at the outline here, as the sand storm overtakes the compound. If I'm a betting man, that's one person doing all that damage."

"What could allow a human to do something like this?"

"That's the problem. There's nothing on our planet that's

been created that could pull this off. In fact, we know that United Weapons Systems has been working on a way to speed up human molecules, thinking they could someday create an invisible soldier. But their data suggests that their experiments on animals have so far been unsuccessful."

"Are you suggesting this technology is from another planet?" Conway asked, amused.

"Unless you have a better answer, I like mine," Bradley nodded, raising his hand in a Vulcan, *Live Long and Prosper* gesture.

Conway didn't buy the little green men theory but was worried that tomorrow's assault could prove regrettably dangerous.

"I hope the president knows what he's in for," he muttered.

CHAPTER THIRTY

It was an overcast day at the Vatican. Black clouds hovered over the home of the pope and his cardinals. The health of Pope John had been deteriorating for the last year and a half, and before the killings had begun, a search for a replacement had been underway. For the first time, an American-born cardinal was the number one candidate. A more liberal church was needed and the American Cardinal was the perfect candidate.

Cardinal Richman was sixty-six years old, sporting a healthy and fit appearance. Unlike previous pontiffs, he was an active man who exercised and played golf. He was the total opposite of what Catholics expected in the Holy Father; nevertheless, his popularity and ideology answered the prayers of the modern Christian world.

Cardinal Richman had devoted his life to helping others. It did not matter what creed the person belonged to, so long as that person believed in God and his teachings. He was the Mother Teresa of priests, respected and loved around the world by almost every religious leader. Where he stood out from the other Cardinals is that he saw God as more of ideal, rather than something that was realistic and infinite. He believed that the word God was just that and that all human beings have the ability to be good and to be evil. He did not acknowledge that God created all the good in the world, nor did he acknowledge that God created the evil that existed. He knows that if he is to succeed as Pope and unite all Christians, he would have to bring about a new thought process about God for Christians and the divine role God must play in the world so all people can live with love in their hearts.

He spoke eight different languages, which, for an American priest, was unusual. He used his gift and his saintly personality to negotiate with terrorists and dictators after diplomats had failed. He had a unique way of being able to look at other people's beliefs and extract the "good teachings" and accept their point of view, while negotiating for peace.

He was saddened that during the last twenty years a belief in God had been slowly replaced with a belief in material things and acts of pleasure that were prohibited by the church. If one individual could unite the world and bring it back to God's teachings, Cardinal Richman was that man. His radical beliefs scared some of the more conservative cardinals, especially his arch rival, Cardinal Gironde. While Richman preached pluralism, Cardinal Gironde wanted the Catholic Church to lead the world. Jesus was the only God to worship and everyone else was going to be damned to hell.

Cardinal Richman's most famous speech, heard around the world, described one day when all human beings, men and women, would be free to follow God's original teachings. The hardcore fundamentalists from the Jewish, Islamic, and Christian traditions called his words blasphemous and condemned him as a religious leader. He responded in the only way he knew.

"God did not create our world so we could fight with each other," he patiently explained. "His teachings are clear in the Torah, Koran, and the Bible. God chose special prophets since the beginning with Abraham to spread his powerful word, but man's greed for power and lust for war, has misinterpreted the Holy Word. One day, God will return, not with the Messiah we all hope for, but with his judgment that will set straight his teachings."

The world was ready for a man like Cardinal Richman. The hate and continued fighting in the name of God had become tiresome to the majority of people around the world. And large numbers of Jews, Muslims, Hindus, Christians, and people from all other peaceful religions supported his ideas.

The legislative body of the Holy City had been divided as to who should be Pope John's replacement. Prejudice was not excluded from the religious leaders who controlled the world's largest flock of devoted Christians. The thought of an American priest becoming the next Pope was difficult for some of the Holy Father's cardinals to stomach. The worst of politics were at play in the Holy City, and a few of the highest ranking leaders within the Vatican were seeing to it that Cardinal Richman would never become the next leader of the Christian world.

The meeting with Pope John had gone well, even though most of the communication took place with his number one cardinal, Pierre Gironde, who was leading the fight to make the next Holy Father a European, as the tradition had been for centuries.

"We have an important assignment for you," Cardinal Gironde said unemotional. "You need you to talk to a Robert Philips and his priest. They believe that some form of miracle happened out in their desert called Las Vegas. They are claiming that God eliminated Mr. Philips of his cancer inside a broken down shack. The Priest believes it's a pure miracle," he said in Italian, hoping to confuse his rival. "See if the location should be analyzed to determine if the church should make it a Holy Monument to God," Gironde said patronizingly.

Without hesitation, Cardinal Richman responded, his Italian more fluent than Gironde's. "Your Italian is coming along very well, Pierre," he said, adding in French, "You could have addressed me in French to make it easier on yourself."

Gironde blushed, noticeably embarrassed. "I want your findings completed and back to me in two weeks," he ordered. "The world has been too focused on all these killings as an act of God's anger, and I don't want this fabricated miracle to further complicate matters. What you report back to us will determine your standing within the Holy City. We don't need a Pope who alarms the world with unfounded miracles, do we?"

"I'll report the truth and only the truth. If a miracle happened out there, the world needs to know," he replied, smiling at Cardinal Gironde as he knelt in front of Pope John. He kissed the Pope's ring before leaving.

* * * * *

Later that day, Cardinal Richman was on a plane for the United States. His first stop: Las Vegas, to interview Robert Philips' doctor. He knew he would need the patient's permission to review his medical records; nevertheless, his first order of business was a preliminary investigation with the doctor and then a quick inspection of the place where the miracle was said to have occurred.

Cardinal Richman traveled in civilian clothes to avoid attracting attention. He traveled with a bodyguard that had come highly recommended from the Emperor of Japan who, even though he was a Buddhist, liked Cardinal Richman and wanted his best man to protect him.

Standing five feet, six inches, the bodyguard didn't look the part of the highest ranking martial arts expert in all of Japan. He was highly skilled in everything from Karate to Aikido, and he was well-versed in weapons use. This small man was the most proficient killing machine Japan had to offer.

At first, the cardinal protested. It was against his beliefs to defend himself by killing another. The emperor assured him that his man was fully instructed in using his skills to protect him and not kill any would-be assassins. The way of the pure martial artist was passivity; death of an opponent was the last alternative, the emperor told him.

"The world cannot afford to lose a great man like you," the emperor said in Japanese.

Cardinal Richman responded in the only language his friend understood, thanking him for his concern and love, and accepting graciously this human gift who would become over the years more than just a bodyguard, but a close friend and companion.

Hirshumi Kubota looked older than forty-seven. Over the last few years, he had finally learned to speak and understand English, not fluently, but well enough to be able to communicate with the cardinal and his American friends. No one knew their true relationship, believing instead that Kubota was his valet, ready to assist him with any project.

It took just a few years, but Hirshumi began relaxing around the cardinal, learning to tell jokes, keeping them both in stitches with his often silly facial expressions as he stretched his brain to find the words to express himself. The flight was to be a long one, and like always on long journeys, the cardinal took out his travel game of Scrabble, which had always proved to be an hysterical pastime for the both of them as they argued about the new vocabulary Hirshumi would create while phonetically pronouncing the words he wanted to use. The cardinal knew how blessed he was to have such a good friend and travel companion.

* * * * *

"Father, we have a problem and it's getting out of hand," Rebecca complained. "President Hopkins has ordered the takeover of United Weapons Systems tomorrow and the arrest of Miguel Ortiz and all the scientists at that company. If it happens, we will lose our opportunity to capture our enemy and his family."

"I think you're right," Jacob said, worried. "But we have a bigger problem. If the United States and this president get hold of this new technology before we have the opportunity to destroy it, the world will have finally signed its death warrant."

"What do you want us to do?" she asked, afraid of what his answer might be.

"Put the fear of God into all of them. Have your brothers handle it at United Weapons Systems, and you handle it with the president."

Rebecca seemed annoyed as she spoke. "I'm not going to kill anyone this time. These are not terrorists or totally bad men. I'm not comfortable that my brothers see things that way. Please speak to them so a more serious problem doesn't grow from our actions."

"I'll have a talk with them. You just visit the president, and then go to Katie and Robert and begin your work."

CHAPTER THIRTY-ONE

Relaxing in his bed, President Hopkins opened a file that needed his attention. Without warning, the lights began to flicker in the bedroom, and then the entire room glowed in a bright white light. His body started to tremble as fear blanketed him.

He tried to call out to his Secret Service men that were positioned outside his door but couldn't speak. The last thing he heard before the voice started talking to him was his guard banging violently on the door, unable to come to his assistance.

"I don't think taking over United Weapons Systems will make us happy," the voice said to him.

"Who are you, and what do you want with me?" Hopkins asked, surprised he was telepathically communicating with the feminine voice.

"You will find out in five days, when our messengers reveal a warning to all of you. Don't disappoint us. You've seen what we're capable of and believe me we won't hesitate making an example of the President of the United States. Stop tomorrow's raid." Her thoughts were menacing, sending chills over his entire body.

"How do you know about our operation tomorrow? Who told you?"

"Your thoughts. We can read your thoughts and everyone else's. Call off tomorrow's operation, or you'll feel our power."

The bright light faded and the room returned to its normal state. The Secret Service men burst into the room, their guns at the ready, startling the president.

"Are you all right, sir?" the first agent asked.

"Yes, there's no problem."

"But, sir, we..."

"You can go back to your post now," he said, waving them off.

He sucked down his drink in one gulp, wondering what had just happened. He picked up his phone and got Turner on the line.

"I want the Joint Chiefs, Director Smith, Conway, and Thomas in the situation room in one hour," he ordered, his tone serious.

Deep down in the darkest depths of his soul, Hopkins was a coward. He made decisions that affected his country and his administration slowly, usually delegating the difficult ones to his staff and speech writers. However, every move he had ever taken in his political life had been based on getting him elected and not based on what was good for the American people.

Now he was faced with a major dilemma that required his and only his deliberation. He believed he had just communicated with God or one of his angels. He imagined how Moses felt when he spoke to God and led his people out of Egypt to the Promised Land. Hopkins just wasn't sure what he was doing or where he was leading his country.

He opened his Bible, looking for answers. As he read, he was sure that it was God who had just spoken to him, possibly choosing him to be the new world leader.

* * * * *

President Hopkins surveyed the situation room; all his military advisors were dressed in full uniform, as they waited for their Commander and Chief to start the meeting. His staff was not as formal. Their tired faces showed disgust for being awakened at this hour. Unlike his normal staff meetings, which encouraged light banter and jovial discussion, this gathering had no one smiling.

"I'm scrubbing the operation at United Weapons Systems," Hopkins said, nervously playing with a cocktail napkin, trying to shape it into some origami figure that would bring some laughter to this solemn group.

"That's nuts, sir," General Armstrong said, his face bright

red. "If we don't go through with it, a dangerous weapon could be sold to one of our enemies. We'll become vulnerable to every country that might want to bring us to our knees. Shit sir, my gut tells me that one of our enemies already has this weapon and it eliminating their competition first before they blackmail us and force us to bow down to them."

"I was told we have to stop the operation," the president said, "or we'll be punished."

They all looked at him as if he were crazy.

"Who told you?" General Armstrong asked.

"A voice, just a little over an hour ago," the president replied, his hands together as if he were praying. "She spoke to me."

"Were you drinking?" the general asked.

"I believe the person who spoke to me is the same one who has been killing all the terrorists around the world. Until I have better information, we'll comply with her request."

"We can't do this, Mr. President," the general said. "You're exposing our troops around the world to attacks by our enemies, and I can't permit that to happen. What if she's a terrorist and the one that already has this weapon?"

"Are you going to disobey my orders?" the president shouted. His anger and assertiveness shocked the others.

The other men supported the general, expressing that they, too, would refuse to follow the president's orders. They all got up to leave, while President Hopkins staff sat in shock.

"If you disobey my orders," the president said, "I will see that each of you is put in front of a court-martial board today and brought up on charges of mutiny and treason."

They stopped, surprised at Hopkins continued hostility, and retook their seats to listen to what he had to say.

Turner touched the president's arm, getting ready to speak. Hopkins pushed his hand away, "I'll handle this. You just sit and listen."

Turner relented.

"Thank you," the president said, taking in a deep breath. "Let's see if cooler heads can prevail and we can come up with another solution."

President Hopkins spent the next hour telling them about what had happened in his bedroom and the ultimatum he was given.

"She could read my mind, which didn't leave me any alternative but to comply. She was able to seal my room and prevent my guards from entering. If she has this much power, I think we need to listen, at least for a while until we figure out who or what we're dealing with."

"How do you think she can read your mind?" Admiral Dawkins asked guardedly.

"I don't know, but it was strange communicating telepathically with her. She did tell me she would be revealing a messenger to all of us in five days. Maybe by then our experts will have some concrete answers. We don't have much time."

Hopkins stood up and ended the meeting. He was out the door, followed by his staff, before any more questions could be raised.

The Joint Chiefs just sat there, staring at each other, wondering what their next move should be. General Armstrong was the first to speak.

"We can't allow this man to affect our national security," the general said. "It's obvious to me that President Hopkins is mentally impaired. He's hearing voices for Christ's sake! I love this country and my men who have devoted their lives to securing peace around the world. I will not sit idly by and watch their sacrifices wasted."

"I agree," Admiral Hawkins said. "We can't let a sick president ruin our country, especially considering the problems we're facing."

"It would take the Congress to back us up, which I don't think would be too likely under the present circumstances," General Armstrong responded sarcastically. "We might have to act on our own."

"If you're wrong," General Miller of the Air Force began, "it could throw this country into the biggest upheaval it has ever known. Maybe we should wait and see what will happen in five days. I cannot support what this coup you're planning on doing at this time."

General Armstrong, his eyes little pools of lava, his face beet red, pointed his handgun at General Miller's head.

"If you're not with us," General Armstrong shouted, "then you are a traitor. And you know what we do to traitors."

"You're nuts, General. You've always wanted to run this country, and you're using this as an excuse to make your move."

"We can't wait for Congress," General Armstrong continued to shout, pointing his gun at the others. "It will be too late. This administration put us in this weak position in the first place. I propose we relieve the president of his duties and put our military in charge. Are there any others who want out?"

"You're asking us to take over our government," General Stevens said, horrified. "That's a coup, and I'm not ready to end my career or be in front of a firing squad until I know for sure what these people really want. A war is won with patience, even if we concede one battle we can still win the war."

Before General Armstrong could threaten the general, the room began to shudder. It vibrated with such force that the coffee mugs that were still filled with their hot liquid toppled and fell to the floor. The fluorescent ceiling bulbs flickered. The men were still focused on General Armstrong when a bright flash of light blinded their eyes. Their bodies became frozen. The general's gun dropped from his hand, as he stood still, unable to move.

"I'm sorry you have objected to my demands," Rebecca said sternly. *"Justice must be done."*

"Who the hell are you?" General Armstrong responded with his thoughts, shocked he could speak telepathically.

"An example will have to be made to whoever doesn't follow your president's orders."

Everyone trembled except Armstrong, unable to take action.

"Not all of us condone Armstrong's methods." General Miller tried to reason.

"You weak asshole," General Armstrong scowled. *"What kind of a leader are you?"*

Admiral Dawkins agreed with General Armstrong's thoughts, expressing his support. *"We need to be united."*

"The two of you have made a grave mistake," the female voice said. *"I do not have time for your inflated egos."*

A flash of light blinded them. Then the room went dark. It was over in a second. General Armstrong and Admiral Hawkins lay dead on the floor. General Miller, speechless, trembled so hard he fell to the floor weeping. General Stevens seemed unmoved. He felt for a pulse on the two bodies and shook his head, signaling that they were dead.

"Call the medics," Stevens said, sticking his head out the door. "We've got two men down."

* * * * *

Sitting in the Oval Office thirty minutes later, General Stevens briefed the president and James Turner.

"Yes, sir, just like that," he told the president. "The voice was strong and without emotion. She sounded young, with a cruelty of someone who had experience in matters of execution."

"Were you paralyzed with just your thoughts?" President Hopkins asked.

"I couldn't move, but I was alert to the voice. What was very strange was that in the far reaches of my mind I could hear what sounded like crowds of voices calling out to me."

"Armstrong and Dawkins will be replaced in the morning," the president said. He folded his arms behind his head and spun his chair around to stare out his office window. "God have mercy on anyone else who decides to piss them off."

* * * * *

President Hopkins addressed the nation the next day. He sadly explained the deaths of two of his military advisors. He was direct and to the point, warning that this group was unmerciful. They could, without notice, hold court and punish those who failed to comply with their demands.

President Hopkins announced that a messenger was coming in five days to talk to the world.

The press, meanwhile, did not report the president's message the way he had intended. The headlines read: "Coup averted."

CHAPTER THIRTY-TWO

Katie and Robert were dozing on the love seat, the two dead
bottles of French Cabernet lying empty on the coffee table.
Nurturing the special connection between them, they had passed
out after four hours of eating and drinking.

Robert was the first to wake up, disgusted at how he felt.
His head pounded. His stale breath almost knocked him out before
he could scrub away the dead bacteria that had found refuge on his
tongue and gums. He turned on the television, looking for an
American news channel. From the bathroom, he heard a
newscaster talking hysterically about the deaths at the White
House.

"Late last night, during an emergency meeting between the
president and the Joint Chiefs, the terrorist group we now fear
killed two of this country's military leaders, General Armstrong
and Admiral Dawkins," the newscaster hysterically reported.
"Armstrong and Dawkins were great leaders, respected by all
Americans. Spared by the terrorists were General Stevens and
General Miller, who witnessed the killings. The facts are sketchy.
The White House is blaming the terrorists, but this reporter
wonders if a coup had been thwarted by President Hopkins?"

The reporter, already choked up, continued, "The president
stated earlier today that it was the group who had been murdering
terrorists around the globe and has an ultimatum for all of us.
Apparently, a messenger will appear in five days to tell us what the
demands will be.

"The bizarre facts surrounding these latest killings are
vague, and few details have emerged. The president maintains that
the group is very powerful and can read the minds of its enemies.

We all know how faith based the president has always been in decisions and in interpreting the Constitution. I was about to doubt the president's states, except that in an earlier interview, General Miller and General Stevens confirmed the president's statements. We'll update you as soon as we have more information."

Robert looked at Katie; he scowled when he realized that they were going to be the messengers. He was pissed that this group could arbitrarily murder people, something he did not want to be associated with. He woke up Katie and told her what he had just heard.

Just then, the room was bathed in a bright white light, paralyzing the two of them.

"*I'm sorry I'm late,*" the young voice said, "*but I had some important business to attend to before we got started.*"

"*I just heard what your important business was,*" Robert tried to shout. "*Unprovoked murder is something I cannot condone under any circumstances.*"

"*You'll understand in due time that our actions are just.*"

"*Who's made you the judge, jury and executioner?*" Katie interrupted.

"*If you're the good guys and want our help, the killings will have to stop,*" Robert demanded.

"*I can't promise that*" she said. "*However, when you understand who we are and what our reasons are, I'll consider your request.*"

First, do you have a name? Robert asked. *I want to know who I'm dealing with.*

"*Rebecca,*" she said softly. She spoke as though she hadn't uttered her own name in a long time. "*My name is Rebecca.*"

Rebecca? Robert asked, not waiting for a reply. *Are there others like you? How many of you are part of this group?*

Katie squeezed his hand, whispering for him to slow down.

"*Just my father, Jacob, my mother, Esther, and my two brothers, Ian and David.*"

You've got biblical names. Are you a religious faction believing that God is leading you to save the world? Robert's words had again become rapid, not leaving room for her to answer.

"*Robert, slow down and let her talk,*" Katie chastised him. "*I'm sure she'll tell us everything we need to know in due time.*"

"*Listen to Katie,*" Rebecca replied with a softer tone. "*I've got a lot to tell you, and if you interrogate me, we'll never get done."*

Rebecca allowed them to get comfortable on the couch.

"Today your life will forever be changed. You'll question your existing beliefs and teachings that have been instilled deep within you since the day you were born. What will surface are your fears that you've buried deep within your soul."

Rebecca could see the bewilderment on their faces. Against her better judgment, she abruptly started the procedure.

"You'll feel a cold sensation that will at first irritate your lungs as you breathe. Don't fight it; it will ease up in a matter of seconds." Before they could react, the process had started.

They both shook their heads, holding each other's hands tightly. Robert appeared more nervous than Katie. A blanket of sweat covered his body. The perspiration cascaded down his cheeks, and his neck became sticky, as he squirmed closer to Katie's cool, relaxed body.

A cold mist flowed like a wind-blown fog, gushing from Rebecca's mouth. Their bodies heaved only once, then settled into a relaxed posture. Their heads slumped forward, stopping after two gentle spring-like jerks. Then their heads lifted in slow motion and locked, their mouths opened wide.

They were awake, though paralyzed in a coma-like state, able to hear and see their surroundings, but unable to react. They became engulfed in the most beautiful rainbow of colors, floating about on an imaginary carpet of air. As they expanded their lungs, taking in the heavy mist, the air felt warm and bitter as it passed through their nostrils, entering the liquid highway of life that flowed through their body.

Then, the room exploded with a bright white light, making it hard to focus. They felt like they were moving at a high rate of speed, as a cool wind caressed their faces, lifting Katie's silky red hair as if each strand were a ribbon tied to a circulating fan. Then everything stopped, and they were in a room with two curved dentist chairs.

Before they could blink, they were floating into the chairs. Two icy cold probes came down from the ceiling and gently pushed inside each of their ears. The static was extremely high pitched, vibrating hard against their eardrums, the pain unbearable. It stopped abruptly as a hologram of a city populated with people filled their heads. What they started to see amazed them, as the smiles returned to their faces.

The process took almost eight hours, and when they were done, they were back in the hotel room, exhausted. As they dozed off to sleep, they finally knew why they had been brought together. Locked in each other's arms, they fell soundly asleep.

CHAPTER THIRTY-THREE

Katie rolled over, her head still lying on Robert's outstretched arm. At first, she thought she had been dreaming. The utopian world she witnessed seemed so surreal.

Inside her mind, she still wanted to fight the brainwashing, the propaganda, as well as the lies about her existence and how the world she knew and loved had really come about, but after yesterday, all bets were off. Everything she knew and believed, everything she put her faith into, all the things she had been taught in school, in church, and from her parents had somehow been a twisted lie. She wanted to believe it had not been intentional, just manipulated by religious men that had the good intentions to care for their people. However, the world she trusted it seems had been duped through a beautifully laid out series of misinformation campaigns that began when man first started believing that there was a creator, some divine being that had all the answers. Her frustration was overwhelming; her mind could not block out the indoctrination by Rebecca's people. While she wanted this decision to be hers, it was obvious the power they had over her was becoming too much to fight. She felt her old life slipping away.

Growing up, there had always been plenty of alien theories and conspiracies, none of which had ever been proven. *Just like our religious heritage,* she thought. But now that she had been made aware, shown proof, she could understood the manipulated words inside her bible. Still, she was afraid to let go of a life that had been comfortable in favor of a new one that looked into a vast void, a black hole of uncertainty. The safety of faith was now gone for her. No more was ignorance bliss. Knowledge was very scary.

Seeing Earth yesterday flash in front of her like some orderly choreographed documentary seemed too impossible, a convenient time machine used to verify what history had recorded. The biggest shocker for her was that evolution, as she knew it, had never happened. At least not the way scientists had theorized. And stories in the Bible were nothing more than fabrications, setups to lead a maturing race in a preconceived direction for the selfish purpose of Rebecca's people.

Rebecca told Robert and her to refer to their new friends as "The Family." Unfortunately, for Robert, the one-sided onrush of information seemed too methodical and too easily programmed, completing a puzzle that was too new for either of them to comprehend.

Unlike Robert, Katie wanted to believe, but just couldn't fully let go of her faith, the spirituality that her parents so lovingly gave her.

Even though Rebecca and her family had God-like power, and she was asked to accept that tens of thousands of years ago a group of space travelers, called creators, came to Earth's solar system to save their own race. They had contracted an incurable virus that was wiping out their planet. If they hadn't brought their sick and dying to Earth's solar system, they would have become extinct.

Their Supreme Council had made the decision to find the right planets that could allow their dying to incubate with the hope of ridding the sick of the virus. Once they were cleansed, they had hoped to find a cure for their disease.

The scientific advances on Pallas had allowed their planet, to evolve to where they could extrapolate, before a death, the electrical sensor circuits of the brain and at the same time maintain the essence of a person until a suitable body was found. Body shells were picked at random, unless the family had cloned a loved one they wanted back. Katie had cringed at the sight of seeing what she thought was the soul being vacuumed out of a body and stored in an incubator for later use. This could explain the visions people had seen over the centuries of the soul rising up and traveling to the heavens to be with God.

It was a shock to Katie that Mars had been the first planet the creators inhabited. It was a flourishing planet filled with humanoids that for ten earth centuries worked to harvest the cure they needed to save Palas. What kept troubling Katie was the eventual problem the Creators had had on Mars. She had seen how Mars was a flourishing planet, green, with the deepest blue oceans. Millions of people lived in normal cities like the ones found today on Earth. Then, during her indoctrination and without an explanation, the planet became barren, bleached of life, a red desert that had no signs it had ever been inhabited by human life. Did the creators become angry with the people of Mars and destroy the planet? It was a question that she needed answered, but Rebecca just pushed on, unwilling to address the Mars situation.

What she witnessed next was the genesis of Earth. Hundreds of thousands of humanoids, maybe from Palas or maybe from Mars, Katie was not told, were placed around the globe with animals from other galaxies to sustain life and to flourish until they were to be harvested.

Katie's mouth was dry as gauze. She wanted to pinch herself and wake from this confusing dream. She cringed, sliding her fingers over the sticky perspiration that clung to her arms. She slumped deep into the armchair, gazing out the window at a waking Paris.

"What are we?" she whispered softly, not wanting to wake Robert.

She closed her eyes again, seeing Rebecca's planet once more. What she had been shown appeared similar to Earth. The only difference, a big one to Rebecca's people, was that Earth contained damaging radiation in its atmosphere that shortened the life expectancy of their people. Mars had been a more perfect planet being further from the Sun's radiation. Again, *why* filled her mind, but still Rebecca would not provide answers.

The creator's experiments had a very short incubation period. If they didn't succeed in a timely fashion, their ill would just die, far away from their families and home.

On Pallas, as opposed to Earth, Pallasians lived for thousands of years. When the virus started killing their people, it dished out a slow and painful death that lasted what felt like a lifetime. The radiation properties of Earth helped kill the virus within the time frame the scientists needed, something like Chemotherapy on Earth, before they would have to return Pallas.

Katie's head filled with all the information, which confused her, yet gave her some relief. She still couldn't fathom the lie about God and religion.

After two thousand years, the experiment had ended, the virus had been fully eradicated from Pallas, and the Supreme Council had no more use for Earth. Rebecca's family was now responsible for monitoring and watching Earth's development. The Family had been coming back to visit for over seven thousand years, and this visit, Katie had been told, could destroy Earth, just like Mars had been destroyed. Rebecca and her father did not want to destroy Earth, they had grown fond of the people and the planet, but the Family's Supreme Council wanted Earth destroyed if Jacob and Rebecca failed to get every country to destroy their weapons of mass destruction.

A cold shiver rushed over Katie's body, thinking about everything that was swimming inside her head. She didn't know the role the family had for her and Robert and wondered why they had been picked.

* * * * *

Robert began to stir, stretching his arms and yawning with a roar.

"You're up early after such a grueling day," he said, smiling at Katie.

"How can you be so relaxed about all of this?"

"I'm not totally sure I believe any of it. We were drugged and had no choice but to listen for eight hours to their half truths. I don't know what went into my body, but it was some very powerful stuff. My head is still spinning. They could have given us mind-altering drugs to make us believe them. We're being manipulated. I just don't know yet why or what for."

"But . . . it seemed so real," she replied, puzzled. "I spent this morning seeing everything over and over again. I'm a nervous wreck."

"Hallucinations generally do that," he said, popping out of bed. "Ask any resident of a mental institution."

"Have you even considered that what they told us could be true?"

"That's my problem," he sighed. "I want to fight it, to get back the beliefs I once had. But what they did to me yesterday has changed all of that. I was having a problem before them believing there was a God anyway. I'm just not sure what they are preaching is the whole truth."

"Maybe they didn't do anything to us except allow us to see the truth we've always suspected. You can't tell me that, having seen the horror the world can inflict on itself, you've never questioned the existence of God, well, the one we believed we knew."

"It so hard for me to accept their bull-shit, even if it seem too good to be true. I'll be fine. It's just taking me time to digest what Rebecca put us through."

He leaned down and gave her a kiss on the forehead.

"I see the two of you have some questions about yesterday?" Rebecca interrupted them.

That's an understatement, Robert lashed out heatedly. He was surprised how easily his telepathic abilities had improved.

I can hear you, Katie said excitedly as she looked at Robert.

"You will both discover more powers as you become more comfortable and accepting."

Powers? Robert asked confused.

"Today you're going to unleash your Molecular Sensing Circuits and use them like you've never used them before."

Molecular Sensing Circuits? Robert thought, letting out his frustration and upsetting Katie in the process. *What the fuck is that?*

Before we go much further, Katie interrupted, *I have a lot of questions that I want answered first.*

"Then let's get started," Rebecca replied.

"First, can we talk normally?" Robert asked. "I'm uncomfortable with this means of communication."

"Yes, that will be fine. But you'll have to get used to using your telepathic abilities so your brain can exercise adequately and grow to cultivate your new strengths."

"Why can't we see you?" Robert asked, his tone serious. He didn't notice Katie scowl as he continued controlling the conversation.

"Our metabolic rate is much faster than yours. If we slow down to materialize, then we'll become entrapped where we are, and we'll die at an accelerated rate. We can materialize for short periods, but we then need to hibernate and recharge our circuits."

"Then how were you able to sustain your people here on Earth?" Katie asked.

"We only needed fifty to seventy years for them to incubate before we harvested what we needed."

"That's my problem with all of this," Robert shouted. "If what you tell us is true, then we've just been an experiment that, as I understand it, has no further use to your planet or your Supreme Council."

"That's partially true. Once we cured our planet of the virus, the harvesting was no longer needed. There have been times throughout your history when we still harvested some good specimens to enhance our species. My father was put in charge of monitoring Earth and to make sure your growth and development did not interfere with the safety of our planet."

"Is that what happened on Mars?" Katie asked.

"Uh," Rebecca paused, "Mars was a problem that needed to be terminated before it could spread throughout the universe."

"What problem?" Robert probed. The detective was at work interrogating a witness.

"I'm not authorized to tell you at this time," she replied coldly.

"Has it something to do with what is going to happen to Earth?" Robert asked.

"Let's just say that in due time you'll understand, but for now Mars is not going to be discussed."

"Can you explain our dreams and the Chateau Rose and what we have to do with that place?" Katie begged. "And Robert," she continued, pinching his arm, "this time don't interrupt."

"Ouch," he complained. "What was that for?"

"Your rudeness," she said with a grin. "Rebecca, please answer my question."

"That will also come later. Right now we have to move on to what's important."

Katie felt like screaming, dejected that her questions were being ignored. Robert, meanwhile, sensed that Rebecca was not going to answer all their questions. Disappointed, he motioned for her to move on.

"Then let's get to why you need our help," he said.

For the next hour, Rebecca discussed United Weapons

Systems, Allan Vincent, and the terrorists. She told them that the Supreme Council was concerned that Earth had developed a weapon that would allow humans to increase their molecular state and become invisible. Humans had progressed faster than expected and, being the infants that they were, they were not ready for the responsibility associated with that technology.

She told them that, unless the world agreed to eliminate all weapons of mass destruction, including the technology of United Weapons Systems, Earth itself would be targeted for destruction in ten years. Once the decision was made, there would be no way to stop the Council's Army that was on their way to wipe out all life on Earth.

To their shock and dismay, Rebecca told them the Council had already deployed their fleet of destroyers to evaluate Earth before the annihilation would take place. In order to save Earth, Robert and Katie's first assignment was to go to the United Nations in four days and present the world with the family's ultimatum. Otherwise, the killings would continue until their demands were met. Robert tried to reason with Rebecca, explaining that the United Nations did not respond well to threats, especially ultimatums that were coming from what they would believe were terrorists.

Katie tried to convince Rebecca that the major religions around the world would not take their word that God was a space alien and that the thousands of years of believing, the thousands of years of killing in the name of their God would not take lightly to what she and her father had to say. She tried to tell her that cultures were built upon the belief that God was on their side and the millions of people who have had to die in sacrifice so that Christianity, Judaism and Islam could hold power over their part of the world would have a whole lot of people upset. Now, to have every human told that they were created not in God's image, but in the image of visitors from outer space and that thousands of years ago Man was just a farming project to help save another planet would get some strong resistance.

Rebecca snickered at Katie's attempt to reason with her. "It boils down to what story will be believed. If Earth fights us and makes no attempt to change after our message is given, then my family will be forced to leave and allow the Supreme Council's Army to deal with your ignorance. It's up to the two of you to be

as convincing as possible at the UN. The world will see the power
we have through the two of you. If Man believed that Jesus could
do what was written about him without any concrete evidence,
then what we will show the world in four days will make a lot of
believers that our Family is a power God and can either save
mankind or destroy it. The choice will be up to your world leaders
at the United Nations. It now time for you and Robert to head
back to New York and prepare our message."
Before either Robert or Katie could object, Rebecca was gone.

* * * * *

Inspector Lefebvre sat inside the white Renault police van, wiping
the perspiration from his eyes as the temperature in Paris climbed
to a humid 85 degrees. He grumbled, as usual, that his department
was too cheap to provide their vehicles with air conditioners,
exposing their state-of-the-art surveillance equipment to the worst
weather conditions.

He cursed, adjusting the camera as he panned the room. He
was unable to find the third person Philips and Katie were talking
with. He heard their voices but could only see his two suspects.
He banged the screen a few times, hoping to remove a blur that
appeared on the upper left corner of his monitor. He thought the
heat had begun to affect his equipment as he watched the hazy
image move around the room.

He did not know what to make of their discussion. He had
heard many theories in his lifetime about how Earth was created,
but what he was listening to amazed him. With everything that
had been happening around the world lately, he wondered how
much truth there was in what The Family had told them about
Earth's creation. He decided to follow them to Manhattan to listen
as they addressed the UN.

CHAPTER THIRTY-FOUR

Robert hated talking to reporters, after so many horrible experiences dealing with the Los Angeles media during his tumultuous days with the LAPD. He had sworn off talking with anyone from the press. Against his better judgment, he called a press conference to tell the world about The Family's ultimatum. He spared no detail.

Rebecca had convinced him to also warn the world that another series of deaths would be occurring unless he was granted time to speak in front of the United Nations General Assembly. Acting like a fortune-teller, he relayed the day and location of each execution.

The immediate reaction from the members at the General Assembly was negative. They had never allowed a terrorist or a messenger from a terrorist group to speak before them. He was refused a forum to speak.

When his predictions of death happened, right down to the exact time and location, the members of the security council reluctantly agreed to let him speak.

* * * * *

Katie and Robert arrived at Kennedy International the day before the speech. Katie's bright red hair hung loose around her shoulders, partially covering one side of her face. She wore a floral print dress that bounced loosely over her firm yet soft, curvaceous body.

Robert wore olive khaki slacks, a light blue oxford button-down shirt, and blue-green, two-tone deck shoes. Customs was ready to accept the two of them. They were treated with caution. The Customs agents seemed nervous; they acted very strange.

As they walked to catch a taxi, Katie seemed to float on a cushion of air as her dress and body moved like a well-choreographed dance. Men turned their heads at her natural beauty. Robert felt a twinge of jealousy stab at his heart, not understanding where it was coming from.

Katie took the initiative and flagged down a taxi.

"Please take us to the Plaza Hotel in Manhattan," she told the driver, her Irish lilt and stunning beauty mesmerizing him.

For a New York cabby, he was tongue-tied.

They giggled at Inspector Lefebure's clumsy attempts, a la Peter Sellers, to follow them. They sat back and relaxed for the sixty-minute drive from Long Island. The stop-and-go traffic on the Long Island Expressway lulled Robert to sleep within minutes, and Katie stared out the window deep in thought.

She had not been able to relax on the flight. The voices filled her head, keeping her awake and restless. At times, she thought she heard her mother and father talking to her, unleashing the anger that dwelled deep within her.

"That'll be fifty-five dollars please," the taxi driver shouted to wake them up.

"We're here already?" she said, stretching her arms above her head and then tapping Robert on the shoulder to arouse him.

She slipped the taxi driver a sixty and told him to keep the change. She was surprised there was no thank-you, but remembered this was New York.

She had never been to Manhattan before. Standing outside the hotel entrance, she was overwhelmed by the concrete towers that shot up toward the heavens. She tilted her head until her neck ached. Robert saw her stumbling backward into the busy street. He grabbed her before she backed into an oncoming bus whose driver had been honking his horn and gesturing violently at her crazy behavior.

"This is not the Irish countryside," Robert scolded her as he wrapped his arm around her and escorted her toward the entrance. "Manhattan's a jungle, with predators ready to have you for dinner. Be more alert."

Over a hundred demonstrators had lined the streets around the hotel. They held up signs that read "Murderers" and "Anti-Christ" and even "Savior." One sign actually made them laugh: "May the Force be with you."

Robert kept Katie by his side and away from the shouting crowds, his arm wrapped tightly around her waist. He moved quickly, pushing outreached hands and cameras away as he entered the hotel, Katie in tow.

Once inside, they were surrounded by television crews. Reporters pushed at each other as they shoved their microphones at the famous couple. Katie cringed at the thought of talking to the media.

"I don't want to talk to them," she whispered to Robert. "After so many years avoiding notoriety, I'm just not ready for this."

Robert took charge, pushing his way through the throng to the front desk. The persistence of one reporter made him angry. The reporter was a tall, youthful looking man from Newsday. Robert read his name tag: Andrew. He seemed nice and not as pushy as the other reporters, but it didn't matter to Robert. He stopped abruptly and turned toward the parasites he hated. With a quick gesture of his hand, the cameramen dropped their cameras and the reporters watched helplessly as their microphones were pulled from their hands and fell to the lobby's soft carpet. He left the reporter named Andrew alone and watched him madly record the events that had just happened in his small spiral notebook.

Robert tried to contain his surprise about his new found power, his facial expression stern. "You've seen our power," Robert said, his eyes smoldering. "Don't irritate me! I'm very tired from my long flight. Later, I'll let this reporter," he patted him on his shoulder, "Andrew, interview us. If he wants to share it with all of you then see him later. Tomorrow everything will become clear. In the meantime, I suggest you restrain yourselves from exaggerating what you've witnessed today."

For the first time, he felt his power.

"Do I make myself perfectly clear?" he said firmly.

He promptly turned, holding Katie's hand tightly, and moved toward a sign that said check-in. He read Andrew's mind and told him telepathically to meet at their room in two hours. He smiled as the reporter's eyes bulged with surprise and wonderment.

They were staying on the thirty-fifth floor and faced Central Park. They had been given a two-bedroom suite with a large living room and a bar. They decided to have dinner in their room with the hope of avoiding having to talk to anyone until the next day.

* * * * *

Two hours later, there was a soft knock on their door. Standing like a tall tree, the handsome six-foot-five reporter came into their room. Robert and Katie spent only thirty minutes with him, which was enough since he managed to fill his notebook with enough information to help Newsday break its own circulation record.

When he returned to the lobby, Andrew said nothing to the media throng. He briskly pushed his way outside, jumped on his bike, and peddled off towards Newsday.

* * * * *

"Why did you let that cute reporter interview us?"

"I was able to read his mind, and he seemed like a very brave man. He was reporting the news at the base of the Twin Towers when one of them collapsed. He was injured and refused help, staying on the scene for eighteen hours. I just felt he and his family deserved another good break."

"Robert, you're still amazing me," she said, drawing him close. "I almost thought you didn't have a heart."

CHAPTER THIRTY-FIVE

"Have we gotten any information about what this message is going to be tomorrow?" the president Hopkins asked.

"None of our sources know what's happening," James Turner replied, rubbing his hands together nervously. "After these recent deaths, we've been asked to arrest O'Riley and Detective Philips and hold them as conspirators, until things can get sorted out."

"That makes no sense," the president said. "They've shown us their power, and until someone can give me an explanation and a way to defend ourselves, I'm not going to piss them off at this time. Tomorrow we'll find out what they want, and then we can formulate a plan."

He searched the Oval Office, hoping the woman's voice would return to give him another sign.

"Have you had any more voices visit you at night?" Director Smith interrupted, her trenchant remark quieting the room.

"You don't believe me, do you?" the president shot back defensively. "Weren't the deaths of Armstrong and Dawkins proof enough for you? Miller and Stevens confirmed the voice. I know what I heard and what I was told. The generals didn't listen, and they were punished."

"I'm not comfortable with the leader of the free world hearing voices, or at least broadcasting it," she said. "You have many enemies that would love to use that to harm your administration."

The air in the room was stale. The tension among the president's most valued staff had begun to show. He could sense their distrust.

"My administration was hurting long before all of the killings. I know who my enemies are," he said, pausing to look directly at Smith and Thomas. "I'll deal with my enemies after we're done with these terrorists. We all have to work together. I want to know before tomorrow what this detective is going to talk about. Bug his hotel room if you must, but get me some answers."

"I guess we have no choice at this point, but to let detective Phillips speak and hear what he has to say," Director Smith conceded. "Maybe then we might find some solutions."

She tried to fix her makeup, which was smeared by the pouring beads of sweat that dripped down her cheeks. She had a perspiration problem that needed medical attention. She never thought it was a problem, though, in the masculine world in which she worked, how she looked at all times had different rules for her.

"I agree," the president said. "Let's keep monitoring their movements."

* * * * *

Inspector Bernard Lefebvre checked into the same hotel as his two suspects. Until recently, he had not believed his friend's hysterical accusations about Robert and Katie, how the devil had returned to the village of Rene and the Chateau Rose. But he was beginning to change his mind.

The package his friend had sent was waiting for him in his room when he arrived. It was the only reference book available that contained portraits of the Rose family. He had never believed the legend or that the Devil occupied that property. But after studying the color portrait of Robert and Katherine Rose, he noticed a striking resemblance. He knew an explanation was out there; he just didn't have one yet.

CHAPTER THIRTY-SIX

While unpacking, Katie could not believe how familiar everything felt. She had not had much time to figure out her attraction toward Robert. It was not just his appearance, but also the goose bumps he created when he touched her hand. It had been a long time since she had felt comfortable around a man; however, Robert exuded a captivating charisma. She was a big believer in fate and that a soul mate waited for her somewhere in her lifetime. *This man*, she told herself, *might be that person.*

After freshening up in her room, she went out to the living room, a little nervous, but ready to continue exploring the commonality between the Chateau Rose and a past life that each day became more familiar.

Robert greeted her with a light kiss on the cheek and directed her to the love seat near the big picture window that overlooked Central Park. He was dressed in jeans, a red and blue striped polo shirt, and loafers with no socks.

She smiled at his effort to suck in his stomach, as he attempted to hide his spare tire. He had shaved and sprayed on her favorite cologne, Obsession, which she thought he overdid a little. But she was enjoying his effort to please her.

She had changed her clothes and was wearing tan Capri pants and a sleeveless black blouse. Her hair was brushed down, falling naturally around her shoulders, the bright red hues contrasting with her beautiful, fair-colored face. Most of her freckles converged at the bridge of her nose, thinning out as they spread down her cheeks. Her long, slender calves were exposed as she sensually crossed them, allowing the cuff of her pants to ride further up her leg. The top button on her blouse was undone, maybe by choice, he thought, revealing enough cleavage to be tasteful without overstating her intentions for their meeting.

Her beauty captivated him, and her smiling eyes lit up her face. She just sat there, not speaking, waiting for him to make the first move.

A peaceful silence descended on them. Instead of the cold, loud city echoing up the hotel's concrete walls, they heard a lone seagull cry out in the distance, letting them know it had found safety, something they both longed for.

Robert kept looking deep into her eyes, being drawn into the depths of her soul, understanding that she was his shelter. His heart finally felt at peace. And his eyes became glassy as he began to speak.

"Rebecca doesn't have to tell me what I'm feeling at this moment," he said. "I can't explain it or comprehend it. But our dreams . . . it was us, that family, with two beautiful children. I'm remembering our love, what we shared before our life was taken away from us by an evil force that had and still has something to do with The Family."

"I felt that evil force the other day at the chateau, trying to interfere with my warm feeling, but couldn't accept it then," she said, crying softly and moving toward him. "I too believe we are the couple in our dreams."

They embraced, and it was as if they had never been apart. They were home. Together again like it was yesterday.

They talked about their lives, the good and the bad, the pain and joy that they had felt while drifting apart for all those years. It was still unclear how their souls came together again; they hoped Rebecca could explain it to them.

Robert had finally lost the tension in his facial muscles. His voice had become more relaxed and softer.

"Then it's done," he said. "It seems we're going to be partners for a while on an interesting journey—"

He was interrupted by a knock at the door. Their food had arrived. They spent the rest of the night eating, laughing, and crying about both the family they had lost in this lifetime and their past lifetime and their second chance at happiness.

For the first time in many years, Robert felt a physical urge he had not had since his wife died. Katie seemed to sense it, too.

They kissed as they walked back toward his bed. What they experienced was not sexual, but rather an emotional release that had been stored up for a long time.

* * * * *

Waking after a few hours of blissful sleep, Robert got up to go to the bathroom, still savoring the pleasures he had forgotten ever existed. He looked in the mirror and sobbed.

"Forgive me," he whispered. "I'll always love you, Alice, but now I'm returning to a love I had before you and Stephanie."

He folded the picture of Alice and Stephanie and inserted it back inside his wallet. He no longer needed alcohol to soothe his bruised heart.

He returned to the bed and watched as Katie slept blissfully. The moonlight through the window bathed her naked body in a shimmering glow. He thought about how beautiful she was and how this first encounter had made him feel. At times during their lovemaking, it had seemed familiar, and at other moments, it had not. Like a powerful magnet, she drew him closer to her, and he gave into his feelings, refusing to put barriers in front of him like he had done so many times before in his life.

"Are you going to just stare at me or do you have something else in mind?" she whispered, startling him.

He was taken instantly back to the Chateau, remembering her wit, and the loving mother she was to their children. He started crying uncontrollably. After taking in a few deep breaths, he smiled through the tears, his face flushed. He bent down and softly began kissing her neck, then her eyes, moving slowly down her body, kissing her inner thighs until she grabbed his hair tight.

"I want you inside me," she whispered, biting her lower lip and almost drawing blood.

For the next hour, he remained inside her, moving ever so slowly, washing over her like the rising tide. He lost count of how many times her body quivered with an orgasm, each one more powerful than the last. Her uncontrolled internal squeezing kept him preoccupied as the pleasures of the sexual act filled his body with mini-explosions of release.

CHAPTER THIRTY-SEVEN

The humid, sultry air crept ever so slowly, like a fog of dry ice that danced across a stage. It seeped through his mansion on the Columbian coast southeast of Cartagena, crawling up Miguel Ortiz's body with its slimy coating. A clammy, hot layer of sweat began to soak his silk shirt, making him irritable as he prepared for the upcoming news coverage of the United Nations General Assembly meeting.

Fearless on the surface, Miguel Ortiz felt uneasy today as reports came in that three of his drug associates in the jungles of Columbia had succumbed to the same mysterious forces that had been plaguing the world the last three weeks.

Ortiz had never been controlled by superstition. But he could no longer ignore the signs. He had doubled his security and had available for himself and his guests protective gear in case the unknown chemical found its way to his mansion.

The morning continued to get worse. An infestation of rodents had been found in his food pantry. And cockroaches swarmed inside his cupboards, between the crevices of his stove, and atop breads and the pastries he had brought in for his party later that morning. Two of his maids and his head chef were nervously spraying poison to rid the house of the infestation, while crying out to God to forgive them for the sins they had committed. Ortiz did not believe that there was a God so malicious that he would be playing such a sick game with him today. He just hoped his guests would be comfortable, and ready to open their checkbooks, while they watched Robert Phillips' message.

Ortiz anticipated that his new company, United Weapons Systems would make him enormous profits. He was the only one interested in how Robert Phillips, a powerless man, could affect his world of greed, drugs, and now weapons. He had hired one of his assassins to show the world that no man or group can hide from the power of a true terrorist, but he too had turned up dead.

He kept rushing about the house, shouting profanities at his servants to stop worrying about God's wrath and begin worrying more about what he might do to them if today did not go exactly as planned. As he settled into his study, swirling dark black clouds appeared out of nowhere. They hung directly over his estate, blacking out the sun. For a moment, even the rodents and cockroaches paused, sensing that something terrible was about to happen.

The women had arrived first, as was the normal order of business. He had made it a practice to screen the entertainment for his guests by himself, making sure each handpicked female was dressed and groomed appropriately and ready to perform with enthusiasm.

Madame Talvera knew the likes and dislikes of her number one patron and had never failed to satisfy his requests. As usual, she had dressed her girls in sheer crepe sundresses that were kept fastened by small hidden ribbons of Velcro. The thinness of their outer garments left nothing to the imagination, and they could be opened from the front with a light tug by an excited partner.

The five young olive-skinned women, slim in build with large bosoms and firm, accentuated butts, lined up in a straight line and faced Miguel, waiting for their orders. His silent gesture with his hand was their signal to let their flowered dresses glide off their silky smooth bodies and float gently down toward the carpet, falling silently to the floor. Then they were ready for their inspection by the man who would be paying them to be very good to his guests.

Ortiz rose slowly, marching like a general to inspect his troops. He was a controlling man, but he had a gentle heart toward the people who pleased him. People who knew him tried to avoid triggering his uncontrolled temper. The girls knew they had to please him and not show any signs of displeasure.

The first girl could have been no more that eighteen or

nineteen years old, her breasts firm, her nipples protruding straight toward their inspector as if at attention. His eyes remained fixed on her, watching for any sign of resistance or fear, as he began to caress and probe her body.

He unzipped his pants, gently placing her hand inside, feeling her cool fingertips against his hard erection. She didn't smile at first, until his finger moved slowly between her thighs. She bit her lip. Her breathing increased. Then her mouth parted as her tongue sensually glided over her dark red lips in a circular movement. Her eyes remained closed. And with a submissive moan, all the while stroking him with her perfectly manicured nails, she made his knees buckle.

He smiled, giving her his approval, and proceeded to inspect the remaining ladies-in-waiting. He had never had to turn away any of Madame Talvera's girls. Nor had he ever tired of having the power to satisfy his sexual urges with the most proficient actresses he had ever known.

In the hour that it took to complete his perverted little fantasy, he and the girls had become covered in a rancid, foul coat of slimy sweat. He sent them off to shower and get prepared for his guests that would be arriving in two hours, and he retreated to his bedroom to take his third shower of the morning.

Never had weather so stressed his four, ten-ton air conditioners, which were designed to keep his home a cool sixty-five degrees, a temperature needed to preserve the fifty original Van Gogh's that decorated his house.

* * * * *

Albert Mitchell was the first to arrive, carrying his oversized briefcase full of weapons brochures.

"Rudy's waiting by the phone to process the orders for shipping today," he told Ortiz, who seemed more agitated than usual.

"That's good," he replied, his gaze distant as he peered out his window at the blackness that blanketed his home.

"Are you all right?"

"No, not really," he said pensively. "My house has never been infested with rodents or cockroaches before. My superstitious servants are ready to bolt out the door. They say the sun was taken away from us as a sign that today someone is going to die a horrible death."

"It's just a coincidence," Mitchell tried to assure him. "It's been more humid and warmer than usual, which would explain why the rodents and cockroaches came inside looking for food and water. The dark clouds are just that. Your property has just been hit with a small isolated weather pattern. You're not so important that a god would single you out on this day. Your help has you spooked. Take a tranquilizer and relax for a few hours. I promise everything will be all right."

"Greet our guests when they arrive," Ortiz said, "and have the girls entertain them until I get downstairs."

He got up and made his way up the spiral staircase to his bedroom, where the young eighteen year old he first inspected was waiting for him.

CHAPTER THIRTY-EIGHT

Robert awoke early, nervous and apprehensive about what he was going to say and how he was going to portray himself as the messenger for The Family, who for now held him emotionally captive. As Katie slept soundly, he stared out the window, looking down at Central Park as the morning sun filtered through the forest of tall buildings that bordered the park.

He had not slept soundly, reviewing over and over the message in his head that he was going to give to the UN in six hours. The last few weeks had turned his life upside down. He felt changed forever. He would never look at life, or God, the same.

Initially, he had doubted what Rebecca told them: that Earth had first been inhabited by the sick from Pallas, and that humans were the direct descendants of these alien space travelers. But the unknown had become clearer, giving him answers that made more sense than those provided by his religion. His faith had now been replaced with logical truths from strangers. What intrigued him was that Jacob had formed the foundations of all the religions over eight thousand years ago.

He remembered that during his indoctrination Rebecca said something had happened a few thousand years after the original harvesting began. That all only the male species had developed an abnormal genetic compound on Mars, which increased their testosterone levels so much that they had become uncontrollably aggressive and war-like. It was as if the genetic mixture had been tampered with, but all protocols had been followed and it was just written off as an anomaly that the atmosphere on Mars had created.

Robert at first thought this was women's liberation propaganda. But now he understood that The Family was serious.

It seemed that females were not affected by this genetic irregularity. Unlike on Pallas, females had became the weaker sex, in strength only, controlled by an angry animal that could kill without conscience or regret. As man became stronger, religions developed, as they interpreted the word of God, religion fell victim to man's greed for power and control. Robert wondered if the world would be in so much trouble if females had written and interpreted God's word. He shrugged his shoulders as he kept recalling the events inside his head.

Rebecca had told them that a cleansing on Mars had almost worked at the beginning. Earth might have become a peaceful planet with the remaining humans sent from Mars, if it hadn't been for a small, powerful group of males that had infiltrated into the exodus program and spread across the globe, bringing death and destruction to anyone who stood in their way.

Rebecca's father, therefore, had a dilemma. His mission was failing. This was going to be his last visit to Earth to rid the planet of the worst of the male species and to let his new improved cleansing compound take charge to save the world.

This was the point where Robert had difficulty accepting everything he had seen on their mystical journey. Something was missing. There were holes in the explanation about the Mars failure. Until he could fill in the gaps, he would not fully commit to helping Jacob and Rebecca.

The coffee he had prepared by the wet bar was ready; its aroma evoked fond memories of the warm coffee and donuts he and his partner used to consume as they wrote up their case reports. As he passed the large mirror that was affixed to the living room wall, something strange caught his eye. He inched closer, surprised at what he was seeing.

His face had become thinner, the dark circles under his eyes were gone, and the deep lines that used to show his age and torment had been replaced by the smooth skin he remembered he'd had in his twenties. His salt and pepper hair had become thicker and darker, and his receding hairline had disappeared. He opened his robe and was impressed that his stomach, or as he called it, his spare tire, was gone. In its place was a flat washboard torso that he had once had in his youth.

"Can I look, too?" Katie called out coyly.

"Get over here!" he said excitedly. "I think you'll like what you see."

"If it's what I felt last night," she teased, "I know I'll like it."

"It's not that," he said, madly waving his arm. "Just get over here!"

She jumped out of bed naked, bouncing as she stepped closer to Robert and the mirror.

"Well, I'll be," she said, savoring her image in the mirror. "I had forgotten that body ever existed," she said surprised at what she was looking at. "What's happening to us?"

"I'm not sure, but I think it has to do with the vapor we inhaled yesterday. Since then we have developed special abilities we did not have before."

"Well, I like what it did," she said, hugging Robert tightly.

"I'm beginning to feel stronger and more aware of things. I'm changing, and I don't know why or where it's taking me."

"Rebecca needs to tell us more about what's happening and fill in the blanks before we go too much further," she said, slipping on her robe and pouring herself a hot cup of coffee. She sat down on the couch, her feet curled under her, holding the warm cup with both hands and basking in the aroma. "She told us that there would be no turning back. I just hope we know what we've gotten ourselves into."

Robert cinched his robe and sat next to her.

"I believe the key to all of this is what happened on Mars," he said. "They're not telling us the whole story of what really happened before they inhabited Earth. A big piece of the puzzle is missing, and until we have it, we won't know what Rebecca and her family's intentions are for all of us."

He spent the next hour rehearsing his speech, asking for suggestions on how to improve it. The message was clear and very powerful. It just made him extremely uncomfortable being a potential instrument of death. He suspected the world might not believe or listen to his ultimatum, and he feared the consequences.

CHAPTER THIRTY-EIGHT

The United Nations General Assembly convened three hours before Robert Phillips scheduled speech. They all agreed that they would not tolerate any form of blackmail or intimidation from this group.

"It's important that we stick together and remain united in our stance," the president said.

As brave as they all appeared, the room was charged with nervous emotions as each member contemplated what was at stake and pondered the group's power.

* * * * *

A police escort drove Robert from his hotel. Their sirens rang, echoing off the skyscrapers that enclosed downtown. Katie had been taken in a separate car at Detective Phillips suggestion.

Supporters and detractors lined the route to the UN. As he glanced out the window of the Lincoln Towne Car Robert let his mind drift. His glossy stare seemed oblivious to the supporters that were cheering his arrival, and the agitated groups that protested as his vehicle sped by. The heavy police barricades barely held the spectators back, some hoping to touch a part of a man they believed was sent by God to save the world and others eager to rip him apart.

He lifted his head out of the car as it came to a halt and felt the warmth of the morning sun filtering through a thin blanket of polluted air that hung over the city. A gentle breeze had stirred up the trash left behind by last night's street people, New York's forgotten. The demands from reporters tossing questions at him seemed distant as he thought of his speech and tried to imagine how the world would react.

He walked briskly, thinking of what both he and Katie had been told this morning by Rebecca.

He could not relax about what he would be initiating another series of murders, and that this time the world would be witnessing the power of The Family. Katie was going to be in charge of illustrating the results, her body used as a projection unit. Frustrated and powerless, he had reluctantly agreed, hopeful Rebecca could be trusted to carry out her part.

There had been times in his past that he had wished for swift justice for murderers and rapists. He had always wondered how it would feel to become the judge, jury, and executioner, and today he would find out. *Beware of what you wish for, Robert,* he told himself. Participating in this form of justice was not making him feel as good as he had thought it would.

As he walked through the lobby toward the General Assembly chamber, his wing-tipped shoes clip-clopped, announcing his arrival. A UN security guard opened the large wooden doors and announced in a loud baritone voice that Robert Phillips was ready to enter the room. He passed faces that stared at him with no emotion, just cold, hard looks at a man who had intruded on their home turf. He smiled nervously, adjusting his tie, something he hadn't worn since Alice and Stephanie's funeral. He hated ties and being dressed up he kept pulling at his collar, which felt like it was strangling him. He tried to control a twitch that made his right cheek and eye move uncontrollably as he approached the podium. At that moment he wished whatever magic Rebecca had put into his body would curtail his nerves, but at the moment, his face kept twitching.

As he panned the group, he was convinced that they were not ready to accept his words or the instructions he was about to give them. Their faces seemed innocent to him, not yet fully grasping what was about to happen. *If I were in their shoes, I wouldn't accept what I was about to say either,* he tormented himself.

As he started to speak, he read the fear in their eyes. He was a stranger, a foreigner come to change their lives. Their body language told the story. Most of them had their arms crossed, as well as their mouths pinched tight. All their eyes were fixed in a stern stare. A few just looked away, afraid that if their eyes met his, an evil spell would be cast over them.

He wondered how these leaders, who were assigned the job of managing the world and keeping it safe, truly functioned. The fear and contemptuous behavior, the xenophobic looks, all explained why the world, even in this supposedly modern age, remained stratified and stale.

Without hesitation, the words that he had been instructed to speak flowed from his lips. It was his voice that made the speech come alive, but another force controlled its content.

* * * * *

"It's time, Father," she said. "I think the two I've picked will accomplish what you want. Can we rethink what you're going to do in twenty-five days?"

"It's not negotiable, sweet daughter. Your twin brother, if he were still here, would be proud of you and what you've become. This time, I must give the final message."

"I don't like your solution. It doesn't make sense after all that you've accomplished here on Earth."

"I'm too old and tired to continue. I should have turned all of this over to you and your brothers long ago. Let's be silent and see how Robert Philips does."

* * * * *

Ortiz smiled as his guests enjoyed their ladies. The men were oblivious to the sixty inch TV screen that featured Robert Phillips' face up close and personal. Mitchell pushed his young woman away as he gulped down his beer and stuffed a fistful of pretzels into his mouth.

The girl, worried she was doing something wrong, had a frightened look on her face. She looked over at Ortiz and, noticing his displeasure, shrugged her shoulders. She tried to continue to arouse her partner, but was rejected again and could feel how limp her client had become. She realized her partner was more interested in watching TV than receiving pleasure. She forcefully unzipped his pants, keeping her head on his lap so she would not block his view of the TV, and with the gentleness of licking an ice cream cone, did her job.

Ortiz and Mitchell watched Robert walk up to the podium to address the world leaders. Mitchell had a worried look on his face, oblivious to what was going on in his lap. His lips compressed inquisitively after he stuffed another handful of pretzels into his mouth, the crumbs landing in the silky black hair that moved slowly up and down on his lap.

* * * * *

Robert Phillips looked around—his papers neatly positioned on the podium—panned his audience. He was a total nervous wreck. He noticed Katie standing at the back door holding her thumb up, signaling him she was ready.

"Gentlemen," he began, taking a deep breath, "today marks a new beginning for mankind, a day all of us have dreamt about at one time or another, but have yet to experience. Our world as we know it is on the verge of collapse, the victim of greed, corruption, and callous self-interest."

He paused to take a sip of water. His hand shook, spilling some water on his notes.

"I am here to bring you a message from The Family," he continued. "You've witnessed what they can do at will. They can read our minds. They know our every thought. And they will rid our world of evil."

He paused once more, looking at his audience for any sign that they understood or were listening. They just stared back at him, hanging on his next sentence.

"The Family, as they want to be known, are among us, watching and doling out a type of justice we are not used to, but one we have long needed. Travesties are nothing new to our planet, and as history will attest, we have not learned from our mistakes. We've allowed businesses and countries around the world to manufacture weapons of mass destruction, which, if not destroyed immediately, will change the balance of good and evil. It is time for us to unite and oversee the removal of all these weapons. Not one country can do it alone. You work as one unit or you will perish as one unit."

The air had become stale. The assembly members squirmed in their chairs as the first of the demands reached their ears. Some wanted to speak, to address the ridiculous demands he had made, but Robert instinctively raised his hand, hushing the members as he continued to talk.

"If, in twenty-five days, these demands have not been met, there will be more deaths until the world is cleansed of its filth."

Several representatives jumped up, yelling in foreign tongues, waving their fingers at Robert. He did not need an interpreter to understand their disapproval. Reporters, meanwhile, shouted out questions. And the chamber became a cacophony of sounds, frenzied and out of control.

Robert raised his arms above his head and slowly lowered them, hushing the room. A new power had been found as he attempted to control the situation with his mind.

"They want to give all of you and the world that's watching an example of their power and justice," Robert shouted. "Take heed of their warning. They are serious and will without hesitation punish anyone who does not comply with their demands. They believe actions speak louder than words . . ."

Robert hesitated, knowing what was next. The bitter bile that had coated his throat almost made him gag.

"So please turn your attention to the screen behind me," he continued, "and witness what will continue to happen if you don't begin, immediately after this meeting ends, to appease The Family."

Coming out of Katie's eyes was a projection of Miguel Ortiz and Albert Mitchell sitting in Ortiz' living room. In the background and unaware of what was going on were three men totally enthralled with the women Ortiz had provided for them.

Robert looked up and greeted them: "Gentlemen, welcome to the General Assembly. Prepare to be judged for your crimes."

Miguel was shocked; he sat up straight, looking around for the cameras that must be taping him.

"Where the fuck is this coming from?" he shouted to Mitchell, twisting his head left to right, then behind him, panic registered in his eyes.

"I haven't the foggiest idea," Mitchell screamed, tossing the young girl to the floor, his moist hardness peaking out at the bottom of the screen.

Not sure what they were watching, the General Assembly and spectators started to laugh at the comical scene unfolding. Roberts' cold, hard stare quickly quieted the room. His harsh look left no doubt that what was coming next was not a laughing matter.

"It's not important where we are. You've been judged by The Family and will pay for your crimes today."

The assembly began to stir, unsure what was going to happen next. The projection on the screen had split in half. One side showed a replay of the last two weeks, detailing everything Ortiz and Mitchell had been planning. The other portion of the screen showed their live reactions to what was happening. The two well-respected men were being exposed for their illegal behavior, from drug sales to weapons deals.

"This is a lie," Ortiz said, standing up. "You've doctored what we've been doing and planted false evidence to discredit our wonderful contributions to the United States and the world."

Their covert actions, their evil thoughts, all were paraded on the screen.

Mitchell gagged on his pretzels as his homosexual attraction to Ortiz became public knowledge. Ortiz looked at him with disgust, turning bright red from the possible association between him and his partner. He swore at Mitchell, promising he'd deal with him and his sexual orientation later.

"That's not important or why you're being judged today," Robert said. "You've both been found guilty of selling death around the world. Ortiz, with your drug dealings and all the lives you've destroyed, with your ability to expand your sick and evil ways toward more killings, you've been sentenced to die today. The world will be your witnesses as we watch you pay for your crimes. The rest of the criminals that don't repent will face their judgment shortly. And Mitchell, for aiding this man and feeding your pockets with the blood money of those you've helped become addicted to your drugs, and for being a co-conspirator in Ortiz's plan to sell weapons of mass destruction to terrorists around the world, you are also sentenced to death."

"Who the fuck do you think you are?" Ortiz shouted. "This is not a court of law. You've invaded my home with an illegal wire tap. You'll be hearing from my lawyers."

He and Mitchell rushed to put on their protective hazmat suits as Robert continued to talk, his melodic voice floating like musical notes on deaf ears. Ortiz, placing his protective headgear on, brimmed with satisfaction that he had outsmarted The Family.

"It's the new justice," Robert said, undeterred, "and you

will pay by their divine justice."

The other three men had become aware of what was happening, and the young women realized that they were being watched. The women got dressed and sat shaking nervously, their hysterical cries echoing in the room as the terror of the moment sunk in.

"Today, only Ortiz and Mitchell will die," Robert said, his eyes wide with anger. "The rest of you are to go back to your countries, where you must spread the word of our power and rid yourselves of any weapons or thoughts you have of bringing terror to innocent people. You'll be next, if you don't take us seriously."

Everyone watched as a bright light exploded on the screen. When the spots in everyone's eyes subsided and they could see clearly, the audience gasped. Ortiz and Mitchell were lying peacefully on his carpet, dead. The other three men, their mouths agape, sat in shock. The five young women were screaming at the sight of the dead men, trembling uncontrollably, and two of them threw up the lunch they had eaten earlier. As they heaved the contents of their stomachs onto the white Berber carpet, cockroaches flowed from their mouths. The others in Ortiz's room joined them, induced by the foul smell and hideous sight.

Ortiz' and Mitchell's bodies lay peacefully; their orange jumpsuits with their fishbowl helmets had not provided the protection they needed. Inside, their faces were contorted, and the rats that had been in the house earlier were now inside their helmets squealing to get out. The rodents, in their panic, gnawed at the dead men's faces, eating away at their skin with the futile hope that they could escape.

Shouts of terror filled the chambers, and words like "murderers" and "killers" were hurled at Robert and Katie.

Without acknowledging the accusations, Robert continued his speech, again quieting the room as he had done before.

"The following will need to be accomplished before our deadline," Robert said, pushing his mouth close to the microphone so his words could be heard. "First, all weapons of mass destruction will be dismantled and destroyed. Just so there is no misunderstanding, we mean *everything,* including chemical and biological weapons. Second, all Third World countries will be brought up to the standards of economic health that the four major powers are experiencing. This includes all native peoples of all countries that have been made an impoverished class. Third, there will be one world court that will judge and convict any violators of this new order."

Robert paused to watch his audience's reaction. *They're listening*, he thought, panning the chamber. *I wonder if they really believe me?*

"They must or they all will suffer," Rebecca's familiar voice startled him.

"And, if they don't, are you going to destroy the world?"

"Not the whole world. Only the people who still care to destroy your civilization."

Robert saw everyone watching his lips move without making any sounds. He caught his breath and returned to his notes.

"They can't be deceived," he shouted, trying to be heard above the chaos on the floor. "All your brain waves can be heard! They will know before you act if you are going to comply with their demands. This is their final ultimatum. There will no room for negotiations."

He folded his speech, inserted it into his inside jacket pocket, and said, "Twenty-five days. They'll be watching and listening."

The police had grabbed Katie when he finished his speech, which surprised him, and then roughly removed him from the podium, bending his arms and attempting to place handcuffs around his wrists.

At the precise moment when Katie and Robert were in custody, the room became silent, everyone staring at the words on the projection screen:

Don't attempt to harm our messengers, or you will experience our anger once again.

The policemen that were holding both of them were now frozen, paralyzed in their tracks. Other officers drew their guns. They too were stopped by an invisible force, their guns falling uselessly and skidding along the marble floors.

Katie and Robert walked slowly out the door toward the car that was waiting to take them back to their hotel. A sense of power consumed them as they watched the tormented eyes that followed them.

The crowds that lined the hallway and outside walkway

were in shock, not knowing what to do or how to react to what they had just witnessed. A few fell to their knees praying, others yelled profanities, and some just cried.

One spectator who held a sign that read *You're the Anti-Christ* threw a rock. To everyone's amazement, the rock just bounced off an invisible barrier that surrounded the two of them.

"What's next?" Katie asked, looking at Robert as the car door closed and they sped away toward their hotel.

"I'm not sure," he replied, confused. "But I'll bet we'll know soon enough."

* * * * *

Rudy Glickman sat in shock at the conference room table at United Weapons Systems, along with the new board of directors.

"That could have been me lying there," he muttered, trembling uncontrollably, wondering if The Family even knew of his connection to Ortiz and Mitchell.

The rest of the board members just looked at each other. A sense of helplessness marked their first day on the job.

CHAPTER THIRTY-NINE

"We're not going to be blackmailed by terrorists," President
Hopkins shouted. "The Taliban tried, the Islamic terrorists tried,
al-Qaida tried. And, we won't change now. They've committed
murder right in front of the world and expect us to condone those
actions?"

"Mr. President, we might not have a choice if this group
does have the ability to monitor our thoughts," Chief of Staff
Turner said, trying to calm Hopkins down. "They're killing the bad
guys, something we should have done ten years ago."

"That's bullshit," the president screamed.

He looked around the room, recalling the voice's visit last
night, nervously wondering if she was listening. While Hopkins
acted tough, it only masked his fear that these Gods were going to
judge him and his presidency and take punitive action against him
unless he acted strong.

"We've been bugged before," the president continued.
"Let's get our people sweeping offices, vehicles, restrooms, and
every crevice where a listening device could be planted. I want
every cavity searched, if necessary, including the asses of everyone
that works in my administration."

"If we're to meet their demands," Secretary of Defense
Stephen Daily said, "we need to begin mobilizing our troops to
supervise the dismantling of our weapons around the world.
Twenty-five days is not leaving us much time."

"First, you need to calm down, Mr. President," Turner
added. "Right now, we don't know the true power of these people,
and until we do, we need to be careful how we talk and think."

Hopkins looked at his friend and threw his hands up in the air. The president felt his skin become clammy and cold.

"Get our surveillance planes in the air," he said, resigned, "and keep me posted on the actions of our allies and enemies."

He ended the meeting to retire to his residence.

I'm not going to comply that easily, he thought. *We'll pacify them, but I will not jeopardize this country's security.* He was a good politician and knew how to manipulate the special interest groups that had put him in office; he felt he could handle these terrorist blackmailers.

In his bedroom, he sat in his favorite armchair with his feet relaxed on an ottoman. Before he could get settled, the lights began to flicker as they had once before. He dropped his glass of bourbon, frightened that his mind had been read and God's angel was coming to kill him.

"I don't think you should take us that lightly," the female voice said sternly. *"We expect the United States to lead the way and set the example for the world."*

Hopkins responded, his voice cracking. "We don't negotiate with terrorists."

"We are not terrorists. The Family is angry at how his world has turned out. Don't make a foolish mistake, or you'll suffer like everyone else who does not comply with our demands."

The lights went back to their normal power, and President Hopkins sat in his chair breathing rapidly as a cold sweat soaked his body.

CHAPTER FORTY

The newspapers featured headlines and articles that analyzed the events at the UN. Television stations preempted all regular programming to hash out and second-guess what everyone had witnessed just a few hours earlier.

Religious groups called the demands for the dismantling of all weapons God's will. They mounted a media campaign to get as many people as possible back into the fold and to show God that they wanted to be saved, cleansed of their sins.

Not everyone assumed this was a heavenly sign to repent. Scientists had been searching for logical answers since the first unexplained deaths. However, all the evidence was pointing to an alien invasion.

Maybe Epiurus, a Greek philosopher 23 centuries ago truly understood that Earth did not exist all alone. Since then scientists having the Hubble's eye sight have estimated that there are 370 planets outside Earths solar system and they could possibly host a life form. Now, with NASA'S Spitzer Space Telescope, they can see 27,000 stars, light-years long and Earths solar system lies in the partial arm of the Orion Spur. These scientists have begun scurrying about believing their worst scenario that a more advanced species has come to Earth or a scarier possibility that they have returned to see how their experiment has turned out and they are pissed.

The military leaders around the globe, doing what they do best, started to coordinate their efforts with the intelligence agencies from every government, hoping to uncover some clues.

They knew now that their protective gear offered no defense against whatever chemical had killed those men. One thing Military men hated was an unfair fight, especially when it was directed against them. Ridding themselves of weapons was not an alternative and they were madly trying to figure out how to combat an enemy that appeared more powerful than them.

Only the three scientists at United Weapons Systems knew better. They had been working on a secret weapon, the RX-666. For years, experiments with cloaking abilities had failed, but United Weapons was very close to cracking the genetic code that would create an army of invisible soldiers, just like the terrorists they faced now.

Edgar Wilson, chief scientist at UWS, had cracked the code on laboratory animals. The experiment had worked, but the aftereffects were not worth the risk. With Vincent gone and with new owners he did not trust, he had to bury the invisible soldier project, the RX-666.

Wilson was proud of his creation. The idea was simple: speed up the metabolic rate to create the illusion of invisibility. Like an exploding bullet leaving the barrel of the gun, which the human eye cannot see, so would these soldiers explode around their enemies, moving at great speed, carrying out their mission and disappearing before anyone knew what had happened. The stumbling block: when the molecules slowed down, their tissues, like that of the tested animals, could not cool down fast enough, exposing raw bone and shredding the victim in short order. Unless each soldier agreed to a suicide mission, the project had some important bugs that needed to be worked out.

Wilson feared that Vincent had sold their data to this group of terrorists who had been able get the bugs out. It would surely explain what had been going on, apart from their ability to read minds and kill with such undetectable power. Such power was beyond the scope of his work.

* * * * *

"Father, everyone seems confused and scared," Rebecca said. "Do you think twenty-five days is going to be enough time?"

"It will have to be," he replied. "We're running out of time ourselves. The Supreme Council needs answers. There's no alternative left for us."

"Don't you think I can handle things after you're gone?"

"Yes, you can, but your hands will be full with other problems. It's important that this portion of our plan be completed on schedule."

"I'm just not sure they can accomplish what you want in your time frame."

"We can't make the same mistakes we've made before," he barked, startling her. "It's just going to have to happen, or Earth will suffer the same consequences as Mars."

"Yes, Father," she replied, upset with his tone.

CHAPTER FORTY-ONE

President Hopkins was elated at the news that the new mind-altering drug, C459, had passed all its trials and was ready to be implemented. The drug had been created to prevent captured soldiers from turning over strategic information during interrogation.

"This better work," President Hopkins told CIA Director Thomas. "Or we'll be the next victims of this group's justice."

"Your top staff has already been inoculated," Thomas said. "You're the last one."

The president rolled up his sleeve, praying he wasn't making a big mistake. His doctor wrapped elastic just under his bicep, gave him a soft rubber ball, and instructed him to squeeze the ball slowly. He found the vein, and with a slight prick, which made the president jump, he slowly pushed the solution into his body. Hopkins felt the warm fluid flow through his body and smiled.

"It's done?" he asked.

The doctor nodded and was asked to leave the room. Hopkins scanned the room as if he could spot the mysterious voice that had visited him the other day. He hoped the voice had not been listening.

"Now whatever we talk about will be stored in our minds as the opposite of what we mean," he said, confidently. "Hate will be love, deception will be cooperation. We can now plan how we'll destroy The Family."

"Sir," Thomas said, "it doesn't quite work like that. We're hoping that whoever is able to read our minds will not discover our real plans. This serum has been tested and has performed well during interrogations. We don't know how, or if it will work when someone reads our minds. Unfortunately, it's our only alternative if we want to find a way to destroy these fanatics."

"I hope you're right," the president said, "or we just signed our death warrants."

"Mr. President, what we do already know is that an energy force is transmitted each time during the flash of light. If at that moment they are at a weak point, then we might be able to use an energy surge and disable them as their leader addresses the UN. We've developed a stronger version of the stun gun that packs a more lethal shock. Our range is a hundred yards, giving us a safe distance from which to mount a surprise attack."

"You seem unsure of yourself."

"I am, sir. We still don't know anything about this group or their power, and what we're attempting could end in tragedy . . . for us."

"I'm not going to turn over our power to a group of blackmailing terrorists. I'd rather fight to my last breath than bow to a controlling force that will imprison us within their ruthless, dictatorial methods. We've been a free nation for over two hundred years, and I'm not going to be the one responsible for putting us back under the rule of a monarch."

"I hope you're right, Mr. President. I hope you're right."

Thomas wondered what had changed Hopkins' mind and then remembered that he was a politician and his soapbox antics were all part of his act. Tomorrow he could change again if he believed it would benefit him politically, even if it meant selling out the American people.

CHAPTER FORTY-TWO

With twenty-four days remaining, a pilgrimage was underway. Tens of thousands of apprehensive people flocked with sleeping bags, tents, and whatever they could carry to camp out in front of the UN, waiting to hear what they believed was the divine word of God. Christians, Muslims and Jews all walked together, talking and hoping that maybe for the first time more than one manipulative prophet would hear a message from God and it would finally be revealed the real message, the actual instructions God intended for everyone.

Vendors had already begun to stake out their territory, selling T-shirts, banners, handheld signs, even oversized gloves made of sponge with a single finger pointing toward the heavens and the slogan *God, You're Number One.*

The police had a circus on their hands, but at least the large crowds that blocked the streets and sidewalks were calm and under control. The mayor brought in five hundred portable toilets and truckloads of bottled water for the not-so-fortunate. Shelters provided meals, believing that what they had been doing for all these years was going to be rewarded by the Lord they swore to serve. If the crowds had known that their so-called God was going to be either captured or destroyed, a riot would have erupted, causing Manhattan to plummet to total collapse. But the New Yorkers were oblivious, showing hope for the first time in recent memory.

The president did not realize the enormity of what he was about to do and was having reservations after seeing all the people favoring The Family.

"Is it possible that this is God that I'm planning on destroying?" he muttered. "That God might be just a traveler from another planet?" He closed the Bible he had been reading, unable to find any answers.

* * * * *

"I think we should destroy the president and his staff," Ian said to his father.

"They mean no harm," Rebecca interrupted, her nasty look making Ian blush. "They're afraid and are doing what they feel will protect them. It's quite funny their new serum. Their thoughts are their thoughts, and we can read them. They can't fool us. We need to step back a little. Destroying them could turn the world against us."

Jacob looked at his two children and knew Rebecca was right.

"Let them have their fun," he said. "We'll proceed with our original plans."

* * * * *

"I think the president's too weak. Shit, we all know he will not follow through with what we need to do," FBI Director Smith said.

"I agree," Thomas said. "He's too religious, and if there's any indication this group comes close to making him believe they are associated with his God, he'll back down."

"We're taking a big risk and could end up like the general and admiral," DOJ Director Conway argued. "How do we know that what we're about to do is the right thing? This group has been cleansing the world of the men and women we have been trying to get rid of ourselves."

"Do you want to be under the control of this group? I sure as hell don't," Smith barked. "My people are in place and have been briefed."

"I'm with Gail," Thomas interrupted. "I don't care to be a slave to anyone, not now or in the future. We have no choice but to follow through with our plan, even if the president gets cold feet. You might not be fathoming the long range implications here. What if The Family is just a fanatical group of religious crazies that acquired a WMD...shit do you want to be another Iran? Hell I don't. I want to preserve the great life we have now."

CIA Director Thomas noticed the seductive wink Smith gave him, and his excitement bulged in his pants.

Conway, the director of the DOJ shook his head, his reluctance written on his face. "Has everyone in our departments been given the drug?" he asked nervously.

"We have two hundred and fifty of our most loyal and qualified people fully inoculated and standing by for the green light," FBI Director Smith advised.

"Well," Conway said, "for a woman, you've got bigger balls than I do. May God, if God exists, have mercy on all of us?"

Their secret meeting concluded, and Conway was the first to leave Smith's office. Thomas remained on the couch, staring hard enough to burn her clothes off her body.

"Have you undressed me yet?" she asked, locking the door. "I can't get any wetter than I am."

As she walked toward the couch, she kicked off her shoes, and in one swift motion her dress dropped to the carpet, revealing a well-toned body. Her small, firm breasts didn't move as she sprang toward him.

She was on her knees, loosening his pants, as his erection sprang out like a jack-in-the-box. She was like a little girl on top of a giant of a man, slipping him inside her and riding him as if he were a wild bronco. Her stamina could not outlast his, and she begged him to climax so she could rest her exhausted body.

"You're up to something," she said, collecting her breath. "I want to be in on it. My sources tell me you're planning something at UWS. Don't keep me out of the loop."

He looked surprised and caught off guard by her perceptive comment. He did not want to lie to her and piss her off.

"Let me get the groundwork started," he said, "and then I'll bring you in on what I'm planning. Something has been going on at United Weapons Systems that I don't have all the answers to, and I'm going to find out what it is. I think they've created a weapon that we might be able to use to defeat The Family."

CHAPTER FORTY-THREE

Robert reveled in the rush he had gotten from the power of his speech and surprisingly watching Ortiz die such a brutal death. He wasn't fully onboard the methods of The Family, but he did like the swift justice they performed. Something he had wanted to be able to do when he was an LAPD detective.

He took a deep breath and exhaled slowly. "I started out nervous; my knees would not stop shaking," he told Katie, who was sitting on the love seat in his room. "Then a powerful energy came over me. Did you see me quiet that room with just a wave of my arms?"

She tapped her hand on the couch, inviting him to sit next to her.

"I noticed," she said softly. "There were lights streaming out from your body. The aura kept changing colors as the intensity of what you were saying altered. I think I was the only one who could see it."

"Something's happening to me. I feel a transformation. The old Me is dying, and a new person is trying to emerge. It's as if all my life I've hid away this wonderful person who could have helped the world, and now, since meeting Rebecca's family, my true calling has come. I just don't know yet if I can kill without hesitation like Rebecca can."

"I've been feeling the same way," Katie said, relieved. "It started that night on my island, and it keeps getting stronger each day."

"I'm not sure what part we'll play in all of this," Robert said, struggling to find the right words. "But I've figured out, I'm sure of it, how I could feel the way I do for you so quickly. I'm positive we're soul mates. This is just how I've heard it happens when two people connect. I'm sure we have a cosmic history. It just feels wonderfully strange."

"It's also possible if you believe in reincarnation," Katie said, smiling and glassy-eyed.

"Do you believe this could have happened?"

She grabbed his arm and pulled him closer, kissing him on the cheek.

"I didn't before," she said. "But after the last few days and the dreams we've had, anything seems possible."

He didn't respond at first; he just looked at her, totally at a loss for words.

"I thought reincarnation had you come back as a goat or cow if you were human before," he said finally. "Are you saying I was a stud of a bull and you were a sexy cow in another life?"

Stifling a giggle, she tried to change the subject.

Wanting to change the subject she spoke. "Tell me about Alice," she said, rubbing the back of his neck with her cool fingertips. "How did you meet? What kind of a life did you have together? Unless it's too painful."

"No, it's time I spoke about it. I've never truly mourned her death or my daughter's. I've kept the pain bottled up inside and numbed myself with alcohol."

"Take it slow," she said, taking his hand in hers, "and stop whenever you feel uncomfortable."

"We knew each other twenty years. The first five we were just friends, going out occasionally to dinner or a movie. We never felt close enough to pursue a more serious relationship. But, we helped each other through some lonely weekends."

"I find it hard to believe that you didn't have your pick of women," she said, squeezing his hand. "You're too handsome to have a problem finding a date."

"That was not my problem in those days. I buried myself in my work, especially when I was training to be a cop. It seemed impossible to find time for a meaningful relationship. Alice was not the most beautiful woman, but she was a caring friend. And she accepted me and what little I had to give."

"That sounds so sad for both of you."

"It just got worse. Finally I got promoted to detective, and that night I celebrated with Alice."

"Wasn't that a good thing?"

"For Alice, yes. But not for me. That night, one thing led to another, and we had sex together for the first time. After keeping it platonic for five years, I let my feelings take me in a direction I never wanted to go with her. Six weeks later, she told me she was pregnant. At first, the news made me extremely mad at myself, but then a calm came over me. I was raised to do the right thing and take responsibility for my actions, so I offered to marry her and raise our child together. She didn't hesitate accepting. I found out later, after a year of marriage, that she had always loved me more than I had loved her."

"It sounds like you were forced into a marriage and child you didn't want."

"At first that was true, but Alice tolerated my bad moods and long hours and still made a warm and loving home for me. I grew to love her, not in the way I had always dreamt love would be, but I accepted my fate without complaint. I was never much of a father. I worked long hours and missed most of my daughter's childhood. I loved Stephanie, but my work never allowed me to really know her."

"You poor man," she said, trying to hide her tears.

"When they died in the car accident, I realized that night what a bastard I had been. I've been punishing myself ever since."

He let go and cried harder than he had ever cried before.

He took a deep breath and pulled Katie close. His moist eyes and warm smile projected his love for her. He kissed her passionately, holding her tightly, understanding for the first time how love was supposed to feel.

"I can't remember ever feeling so relieved," he said, gazing into her eyes. He sucked in a deep quivering breath. "Tell me about your life after your parents were murdered. You were nine? Who raised you?"

"I'm not sure I can tell you everything. All I remember is my parents being murdered on my ninth birthday. Next thing I know, I'm nineteen and fighting for the IRA."

"I understand. Just tell me what you can remember. I'm in no hurry."

She slid back into her corner on the couch, flipping her long red hair back away from her face. She had washed her makeup off, which revealed her natural beauty.

"I'm so lucky," he whispered

"Did you say something?" she asked.

"I'll tell you later."

"That day, on my ninth birthday after my parents were murdered, I ran away, fearing that the soldiers were right behind me carrying gasoline cans to set me on fire. Knowing the woods as I did, I hid for a while in an old hollowed-out pine tree, trying to stop crying so I wouldn't be found."

She was shaking. She rubbed her arms as if a terrible cold wind had penetrated her body.

Robert got up and brought her his LAPD sweatshirt, which she gladly pulled over her head. It was several sizes too large, and she looked like a little girl playing with her father's clothing.

"Thank you," she replied with a sad smile. "After a few hours, I don't remember how long, I took a trail to my aunt's house, where they took me in for just a short while."

"I wish I could have been there to protect you."

"There was nothing anybody could have done. I was lucky to have survived."

She stopped, lost in thought, and then looked up as if a light bulb had gone off in her head.

"I do remember one thing," she continued. "A few months after my parents were murdered, there was a trial conducted by the British military. They wanted to show the Irish people that they did not condone what had happened. The trial lasted just ten days, and the young lieutenant and his sergeant were found not guilty. The defense attorney argued that my father's shotgun had accidentally gone off, panicking the soldiers. Nothing was mentioned about their abusive attitude or that they had tried to kill me to eliminate any witnesses."

"Didn't it come out that they burned the evidence, trying to cover up their crime?"

"There were no witnesses, and the lieutenant denied any knowledge of a fire."

"But you were there. Didn't you testify?"

"During the trial, they threatened my life. And one night, men in ski masks came to my aunt's house looking for me. When my aunt surprised them, they killed her, leaving a warning note on her chest that the same would happen to me if I testified. I was lucky that I was not at home at that time. Then the IRA took me in and raised me. That's where I go blank."

Robert tried to jog her memory. "You became a soldier and then a broker of weapons until we met in Paris?"

"Something like that. As a teenager, I fought side by side with the IRA, blowing up cars, buildings, anything that would avenge the deaths of my parents and aunt."

The fire in her eyes made Robert uncomfortable.

"You still have a lot of hate locked up inside."

"I did up until that night on my island. Something happened. It's like all the contempt I had for the British was erased with the wave of a magic wand. I feel the pain and hate still inside me, but it's controlled."

"What made you leave the IRA and become a gun broker?"

"The leader of a fanatical faction of the IRA had fallen in love with me and wanted me out of the action in order to raise his children. His egotistical and chauvinistic attitude was a big turn off, so I left to get away from him. I loved him, but I couldn't see myself in a life with that type of a man."

"What happened to him?" Robert asked. "Is he still alive?"

"A few years ago, I got a report that he had been killed when one of the bombs he was transporting accidentally went off, killing him and two other IRA fighters. He had married and left a widow and five children. That could have been me."

"I'm glad it wasn't you," he said, drawing her close. "I'm happy we met when we did, and I want to pursue the feelings I'm having for you."

She put her head on his lap and looked up into his eyes.

"I want to pursue those feelings, too," she said.

He caressed her silky red hair, listening to her purr as she snuggled deeper, beckoning him to pull her closer. He leaned down and kissed her cheek.

She moved so she could look up at him, catching his eyes as he surveyed her body. She could feel his excitement, which matched hers, as he unbuttoned her blouse.

They spent the next two hours gently making love, only stopping to catch their breath when one of them reached climax. Afterward, as they lay in each other's arms, Rebecca's voice returned.

"You did very well yesterday. Your powers are progressing

nicely."

"Don't you believe in knocking?" he thought, pulling the covers up over them.

"Modesty doesn't exist on our planet; it's something humans created, believing God demanded it. We feel that the two of you have the most potential to accomplish what we have planned for our last mission. Today, you'll fully understand what your responsibilities are and what we expect from you."

"Why us and not someone else?" Robert thought, reaching for his robe and pulling himself out of bed.

"The two of you do not have the mutated DNA that has plagued your planet for centuries. You are our best choice to save Earth. We don't have much time left and need to have your transformation in place before my father speaks."

"We have so many questions that were not answered yesterday," Katie joined in. *"If we're to help, I think it only fair that we know everything."*

"That's a fair request, but you might not be able to handle it," she replied seriously. *"Yesterday, we gave you an overview. If you insist, I'll be more specific."*

"I've seen and done terrible things in my life," Katie thought. *"Nothing you could say would shock me."*

"I agree with Katie," Robert added. *"I want to know what this is all about."*

"Okay, but I must warn you that, once you find out, there will be no turning back. Death will be your only salvation, should you decide to reject your responsibilities."

Katie grabbed Robert's hand, turning her head.

"I love you," she said, a tear running down her cheek. "No matter what happens next."

"I love you, too," he replied, sitting back down and pulling her closer as they listened. "One thing before you go on. Can we not use telepathy for all of this? I can't concentrate completely on what you're saying. And if you want us to cooperate, please let us talk normally."

Katie sensed Rebecca was unsure of herself. She looked at Robert with a surprised expression, shrugging her shoulders.

"That's fair," Rebecca said. "You already know that my family is not from here."

"Where's your planet located?" Katie asked, challenging

Rebecca.

"Our home, let's say is further than you can comprehend. Over 27,000 light years, just outside what your scientists call the Milky Way. We are at the farthest reaches of the universe," Rebecca said, clearly uncomfortable with the question, "hidden away and protected from our enemies, with which we are constantly at war."

"Then why are you here? I sense it's not for altruistic reasons."

"Robert," Rebecca said, "your doubts frustrate me. You've believed in a God that requires faith in his existence, but now that we have shown you our powers, you question our motives."

"It's a big leap to put faith in something so powerful and angry," Robert replied.

"That's so untrue. Since man first believed in one god there has been so much killing and hate all in the name of a God that no one has ever seen. Now you are coming face-to-face with visitors that have godly powers and you deny us your respect. Our DNA structure is much more evolved than yours, allowing us powers that your civilization will never experience until certain things change. However, right now United Weapon Systems is developing a weapon that has the potential to see us and if we are not careful harm us."

"So just destroy it and be gone," Robert said impatiently.

Rebecca hesitated, uncomfortable showing their one weakness. "Yes we can destroy the weapon, but the ability to create it again is still there. That's why we need a transmutation to take place. This process will remove the mutated gene that makes Man seek war instead of peace. When the process is complete, then we can go home without destroying any more of your planet."

Katie shivered at Rebecca's words. "Transmutation? I don't like how that sounds," she said.

"Humans have yet to tap their true potential. Your mental powers are still fairly embryonic, and until they mature, centuries will pass before your world will know peace. My father is trying to correct a genetic flaw so the human race can mature on a peaceful path. Have you ever wondered why the Middle-East has been fighting for thousands of years? I'm sure you believe that no one today can remember what started the fighting, but it continues and will continue until there is a transmutation. No peace talks or treaties will work. They never have and never will."

"I'm confused," Robert said. "If we're just infants in our development, and if what you say is needed will happen in a few hundred years, what alternatives are you giving us?"

"You and Katie have the power to save the world," she said softly, almost whispering. "You've been chosen. Trust me."

"Why now?" Robert asked, crossing his arms. "We've had these problems for thousands of years."

"We've tried before and failed," Rebecca replied despondently. "Now my family has one last chance to complete our original mission. Or we will have to destroy Earth."

"That's pretty final?" Katie said solemnly.

"Yes. We've tried in the past to utilize humans to help in The Cleansing, but they failed, because the damaged DNA was too strong for them to fight off—"

"What damage are you talking about?" Robert interrupted.

"That's not something we're going to discuss today," she replied menacingly.

Robert had become angry. "You're asking us to follow you blindly, which I won't do."

"I'm not comfortable with telling you about this problem," Rebecca said.

"Neither are we," he said, his tone softening. "If we want to work as a team, we've got to be honest with each other."

"Fair enough," she said, pausing to find the right words. "Before Earth was selected to house our sick, Mars was the most suitable for our experiments. Our laboratories on the planet worked feverishly day and night, trying to find a cure. Our test subjects began to respond favorably to the clean atmosphere and low radiation effects from your sun. Understand that, for almost twenty thousand years, Mars flourished like Earth does today, with cities, people, oceans, hopes, and dreams. Because we could harvest the molecular circuits of our cured patients, we were able to bring them back to Pallas and set in motion the cure we so needed."

"What does that have to do with our problems here on Earth?" Robert asked.

"A group of unethical scientists and criminals escaped from Pallas and landed on Mars in between one of our return trips home for regeneration. They introduced a new strain of DNA that made our harvesting impossible. It took just a few hundred years and all of Mars was contaminated.

"Their leader had been one of our most respected molecular biologists. It took us a while to discover, but he had developed a serum that would allow his people to live productive lives without having to regenerate back on Pallas. They could last approximately eighty years and if they found a new host body go another eighty years and so on. Since our project was considered a failure, the Supreme Council ordered the destruction of the planet with the hopes that once and for all we would be rid of the fugitives."

"I'm getting the picture of what happened next," Robert said anxiously. "Does this man have a name?"

"Yes, and it might seem contrived under the circumstances," she replied cautiously.

"This is a great story already," Robert said. "What's one more surprise?"

"Dável Lucifer," she whispered, hoping they wouldn't hear her.

"The Devil?" Katie laughed.

"That's your interpretation. His name is D.A.V.E.L. Most of our names on our planet are similar to the names you find in your religious texts. His surname, Lucifer, is not a name per se; it's a description we give to certain criminals."

"Something's missing from all of this," Katie said. "I hope you're getting around to telling us."

"I will," she said, hesitating. "When we returned to Mars, we determined that Dável Lucifer and his flock of criminals had begun taking over the molecular sensor circuits of our people. By combining their molecular sensor circuits, brain waves, in layman's terms, with those of our cured community, the mixture mutated, turning our cured race into an uncontrollable warrior society. Fighting, killing, and corruption became the norm on Mars. Our only alternative was to destroy the planet before they evolved and became a threat to Pallas. Dável we believed was building an army to attack and gain control of Pallas."

"If Lucifer and his army of criminals were from Pallas," Robert asked, "shouldn't they have the same DNA as your cured race of Martians?"

"Our people, Pallasians, can't be away from our planet too long or our DNA begins to change, making us go mad. At the time they started taking over these healthy bodies, their DNA had mutated. The mixture was tainted."

"So if you destroyed every living thing on that planet, and now you're concerned about our future, I can only guess what happened," he said. "He wasn't destroyed, was he? He escaped and is here on Earth, right?"

"Dável was a brilliant scientist. He figured out how to harvest the worst of his followers and escape the destruction that was inevitable. He had a powerful ability to predict the future. He escaped with over ten thousand harvested brain wave impulses, including his children's and departed to Earth to hibernate until more suitable life forms were found."

"Are you going to tell us that he's the Devil of the Bible?" Katie asked.

"At first, Earth was not contaminated with the Devil's poison. That bought us enough time to inhabit your planet and find a cure for our virus. And then about seven thousand years ago, Dável and his followers came out of hibernation and infected your planet. My father had learned from his first mistake on Mars and had inoculated everyone with a cleansing vaccine that he hoped would counter any of Davil's poisoned DNA."

"What about Lucifer's poisoned DNA?" Robert asked.

"After two hundred and fifty Earth years, Lucifer and his followers spread out around the globe, infecting unique humans that seemed less resistant to my father's cleansing agent. They were grouped and targeted. We had no clue until it was too late."

"Are you telling us that our ancestors are Pallasians?" Robert demanded. "That they were compromised by these criminals you let escape Mars?"

"Yes. This is how prejudice and hate evolved on Earth. Lucifer's followers divided the world, creating barriers of hate and fear to gain power and money to feed their hunger."

"If what you say is true," Robert said, "then explain this cleansing agent your father created. Does it have anything to do with our mission?"

"When we returned to Earth and found that Dável had again invaded our most prized project, my father was distraught at another pending failure," Rebecca said, sounding tired. "He knew the Supreme Council would not tolerate that. At first, the Council decided to eliminate and destroy Earth since the virus no longer threatened our planet."

"Then," Katie hesitated, "you're here to destroy Earth?"

"No. Fortunately, my father is disobeying his orders and giving Earth one last chance to evolve. That's where you and Katie come into the picture. You're Earth's salvation."

"How can we do this," Robert asked, "when you and your family have failed for so long?"

"That's what will be explained to you shortly," she said, her voice cracking. "We just have to know if you're going to cooperate."

"So you've set in motion the destruction of all terrorists, no matter what side they might be on."

"That's right. Since Dável infected most of the leaders of the world, they were able to hold strategic, powerful positions in almost every country around the globe. They eventually began to control the religious structures that my father established. Lucifer's power was not omnipotent, though. With our help, some people became stronger than him. They were able to remove some of his followers' molecular sensor circuits and return them to our prison incubators. You call this an exorcism. Only a few enlightened people have had these powers. Unfortunately, there have never been enough of them, and evil has spread more quickly than we can control it."

"You want us to believe that murderers and criminals are descendants of Dável?" Robert asked, incredulous. "You've made all of this too easy and perfect. I feel like I'm being snowed by a great con-artist."

Katie pinched his hand to shut him up. He had never seen her look at him with such contempt before. His face turned red as he apologized to Rebecca.

"I expect you to have your doubts. What you've believed all your life has now been retold in a different way. I can't offer you proof to make you believe. But what proof did you have before, when you turned your faith over to an invisible God? If He's really there, why isn't he protecting you from my family and me? Much of what you've believed about God is true, although He's not the divine, omnipotent power you worshiped."

"You have a point," he acquiesced. "And you've been kicking the shit out of everyone who's pissed you off lately. The ball's in your court for now. How have you been able to kill so many people without leaving a trace?"

"I can't tell you that. I've got to go. We'll continue this at a later date."

She was gone before either of them could ask another question.

"Robert, you were rude," Katie scolded him. "I hope you haven't hurt her feelings."

"She's been murdering thousands of people. I don't think she has feelings or not the kind of feelings we have. I just think it all fits together a little too neatly."

"Unless you have a better explanation," Katie said, "what she said makes more sense to me than what I've been taught all these years. We've always had to believe with unquestionable faith that God existed. Now we have someone with powers we've never seen before telling us a different story."

CHAPTER FORTY-FOUR

Dável awoke from his five-day hibernation, his body stiff from lying in one position. He stretched his arms over his head, aligning up his vertebrae, the cracking sound his spine made echoed inside the damp, dark cave. His quarters were quiet. Ruth was still sleeping soundly, curled in a fetal position, her breathing deep and relaxed. He sighed, sad to see how frail she had become. Cain and Saul were busily working at their computers.

His heart was filled with sorrow, because he knew he had to wake Ruth and begin. He gently shook his daughter's shoulder. Her thin, emaciated body startled him. He knew she was getting weaker but did not realize it was happening so quickly. He knew they were all running out of time.

"Ruth, you need to take your shot," he said, "and get moving. This will be our last hope to find our place in this world. I regret ever bring you here."

Ruth tried to speak, her eyes fluttering open. "Father, I'm not sure I have the energy left to go on," she moaned, rolling over and pushing deeper into the clay soil that was her protection.

Dável bit his lower lip, pain etched on his face. He needed his daughter to remain stronger for just a little longer. If his plan worked this time, she'd have the new body that would sustain her life and complete his original plan. Unfortunately, Jacob and his family were making things difficult. He needed control of the Pulsar X-36 and RX-666 if he was to defeat his arch enemy.

Dável's two sons had already been up for hours surveying their area, making sure it was safe for them during their most vulnerable time.

"There are no scanning waves from Jacob and his family," Dável's youngest son advised. "They seem to be too busy monitoring the world."

Dável looked dismayed as he focused on the last vial of serum they had to maintain their invisible state. He seemed lost in thought.

"Jacob's too old to worry about," he said at last. "It's his daughter Rebecca and his two sons that I fear the most. Their power is too great. We have to keep avoiding them a little while longer until I get the weapon and the new bodies we'll need. Without it, the Council will be able to destroy us. We're the last of our group that can save this forsaken planet."

His voice trailed off as desperation filled his mind. He tried not to let his worries affect him. But he knew if they failed again and had not found four people who were not affected by Jacob's cleansing agent, then his plan to control Earth would be finished. If anyone could hold off the Council's army, Dável knew he was the one to do it. He needed the weapon and pure, un-cleansed human bodies for his family.

Saul, his second born, had not been listening to the conversation between his father and his younger brother Cain. He was concentrating on the updated reports their monitor had recorded during their hibernation.

"Father!" Cain interrupted his voice ringing with alarm. "You won't believe what happened while we were asleep!"

Dável shuffled over to the message on the computer screen. He could not believe what he read.

"Miguel Ortiz is dead?" he shouted in disbelief. His face

had turned beet red. "Jacob has to suffer. The world has to suffer, as well as his pain-in-the-ass family. Think!" he muttered to himself. "There's a solution to every problem. After seven thousand years, you can't lose now."

After completing the injections, he sent his sons on an assignment. Ruth stayed with her father.

* * * * *

"Jacob, come here and look at this," Esther called to her husband.

"Do you think that's them?" he said doubtfully.

"I'm sure of it. Look at this. This is the frequency his sons use to travel. I've lost Dável and Ruth, but this time I've got a fix on his sons. I'll take Ian and David with me. We'll have them before the day is over. Make sure you tell Rebecca to be alert. Dável is desperate and will do anything to harm us now, as well as Robert and Katie."

She folded her monitor and called the boys, readying them for their journey.

CHAPTER FORTY-FIVE

Robert and Katie walked through Central Park unnoticed at first.
They walked slowly, deep in thought. They observed the sparrows
singing and scurrying around from branch to branch. Squirrels
searched for food without fear of any of the strolling pedestrians.
Some propped themselves up, resting on their fat, bushy tails,
while others scampered up the tall, thick maple trees that sheltered
the park.

Hand in hand they walked. Sunshine filtered through the
trees that lined the path, casting shadows that danced a happy
ballet noticeable only to lovers strolling slowly arm in arm. Robert
thought that this was one of the happiest moments in his life as he
turned his head and smiled at Katie. She seemed lost in the
splendor of their surroundings. She had never looked so beautiful.

Men and women, young and old, sat on benches eating
their lunches, reading books or newspapers. They all looked up as
the two lovers passed. Some recognized who they were. They
became humble, avoiding eye contact as if an enemy had come
into their town to pillage and rape without cause. Others who had
no interest in what was going on around them went back to what
they had been doing.

Robert was the first to notice the looks. He offered a
pleasant smile, which was returned with contemptuous looks that
he had never received before.

"Are you noticing the hate and fear being directed at us?"
he nudged Katie, who seemed lost in thought.

"What?"

"Look around," he said. "What do you see?"

"I'm not sure what you want me to look at," she said.

"These people are scared of us," he whispered.

"These are New Yorkers. They're scared of everyone since the Twin Towers were destroyed. It's just your imagination, silly. Relax and enjoy the beauty of what the park has to offer us.

"Robert scowled. "Yes Pollyanna".

"Oh, Robert, stop looking for suspicious characters in this town. There are almost five million of them, and as they have shown the world, they are a very strong and unwavering people. Just enjoy yourself; you'll drive yourself mad if you don't. Manhattan has a beauty that, if you look hard enough, will hug you tight and make you fall in love with it."

"I'm not sure I'm ready for this town to embrace me just yet," he said, cautiously watching a band of young men walking toward them.

As they got closer, Robert, read their thoughts. The hairs on the back of his neck stood at attention. He made sure Katie was behind him. As if a show was about to begin, the people on the benches put down what they had been reading or eating, refolding the wrappers on their sandwiches, and watched a familiar scene unfold. Normally insensitive to violence, they all stood, ready to help. Robert was surprised and signaled them to sit down. His thoughts filled their heads, assuring them he and Katie could handle this problem.

The dozen boys, who appeared to be no more than eighteen years old, began to circle them, pinning them in the center of the circle.

"Boys, we don't want any trouble," Robert calmly said, watching each boy to see if any had drawn a weapon. "I suggest you keep moving and enjoy the park."

"This is our park, man," the leader said. "You have to pay to walk through our territory."

The leader's long hair was wrapped in a fishnet with a blue and white bandana tied tightly around his forehead. The boys looked like wannabe gang-bangers. Their "uniforms" of black and red ski parkas and baggy pants seemed to give them a special air of confidence.

"How much does it cost to travel in your beautiful park?" Katie asked sweetly, her smile captivating the leader.

"For your boyfriend," the leader said in a thick Brooklyn

accent, "his wallet and his watch. But, for you my sweet little bitch, something more romantic for me and the boys."

He grinned, exposing a gold tooth.

"If I'm to have any romantic frolics today," Katie said, "it will be with a man, not a bunch of snot-nosed boys."

"What are you doing?" Robert whispered in her ear.

Katie squeezed Robert's hand. "Not taking any shit from a group of boys who should be in school or home with their mommies," she said loud enough for all twelve of their potential attackers to hear.

"Bitch, I changed my mind," the leader said. "Romance is out and a severe beating before we fuck the life out of you will be what you'll get."

Dry, white spittle had begun to form around the sides of young boy's mouth. He waved his followers to attack, some holding metal rods, others spinning thick chains. He had drawn a gun, pointing it at Robert.

Robert seemed more nervous than Katie as they kept turning clockwise, their backs pressing against each other. The first boy lunged with his metal pipe, swinging it at Robert' head. Robert could see two other boys from the corner of his eye spinning their chains as they inched closer.

Katie prepared herself for the four that had drawn their knives and were approaching nervously. She could see that this was the first time they had attempted something like this. She assumed this was the boy's initiation into the gang.

As the thick chains spun faster and faster toward Robert, they had become invisible, except for the perfect circles they made as they whistled through the air. Katie offered the four young boys that approached a fearless smile.

Robert was first to take action. The two boys with the chains were first levitated about ten feet off the ground and slammed to the hard cement pathway, their chains wrapped tightly around their necks and torsos. The boy with the rod, watched helplessly as the rod jerked from his grasp and he fell to the ground screaming in pain. The rod he had been threatening Robert with, now protruded from his thigh, stuck deep into the concrete. The four youths pointing their knives at Katie stopped as their weapons were suspended a millimeter from their eyes. They backed away slowly.

The remaining young boys, who had not begun to attack, ran up a grassy knoll, straight into the arms of two policemen. The leader, in shock at what he had just witnessed, kept his gun pointed at Robert. As he drew the hammer back, the gun had started to point toward his own leg. It released a loud explosion, the boy's knee shattered.

The policemen approached with their weapons drawn.

"Are you folks all right?" one of the officers asked.

"We're fine," they said in unison, giggling at what had just happened and what they had just done.

"This is for all of you brave men and women who risked your lives ten years ago and who still continue to do your job," Katie said, surprising the officer with a hug.

"We'll need a statement from the two of you," the other officer said.

"That won't be necessary," Katie said, eyeing the boys. "I think these young hooligans have learned their lesson and won't be harassing anyone again. That's right," she said pointing her finger at all of them. All the boys nodding nervously as Katie and Robert continued their leisurely stroll through Central Park.

Katie looked at Robert and said, "I told you Manhattan has its own beauty that will embrace you."

Robert shook his head.

They returned to their hotel two hours later, after finishing their relaxing walk.

"That was exhilarating," Katie said, pouring herself a whiskey straight up. She downed it in one gulp and poured herself another shot.

"Did you know you could do that?" Robert asked.

"I've been drinking whiskey for a long time."

"No, that thing you did with the knives," he said, perturbed at her coyness.

"I knew what you meant, and the answer is 'No.' It just happened. I pictured the action I wanted, and then it happened. What about you?"

"The same thing, except I was felt a lot of anger at the egotism of the leader and what he said he would do to you. I felt like killing them, knowing that's what they had in mind for us."

"Why didn't you?" she said, surprised.

"I realized in that split second that we were not in any

danger, and that we had the power to kill them. I just couldn't do it. Having the power doesn't always justify picking the worst solution. It was easy to put the fear of God into them instead."

"Maybe that's why we've been picked," she said, taking his cold hand and blowing her warm breath on it. "Rebecca said we're the last hope for our world. It's possible she sees in us our undeveloped potential. I don't fully understand yet what this *cleansing* is all about; however, I do think we possess the goodness of the chemical that's been in our system for our two lifetimes."

"Very profound. However, I think you're being a little naive. We're still missing some pieces of the puzzle."

"Spoken like a true detective. You can doubt, while I believe. I'm sure we'll come together on this very shortly."

* * * * *

Katie and Robert tried to relax and watch the news, but watching themselves on TV made them uncomfortable. Reports of their actions in Central Park, which had been caught on video by a tourist, had made the afternoon news. For the first time, newscasters seemed lost for words, almost afraid to say the wrong thing, afraid to invoke the wrath of Katie and Robert.

"Your second test went well today," Rebecca said.

This time they knew she had been watching them and were not surprised by her interruption.

Another test? Robert thought.

"Yes. You will today understand our intentions and why we've picked you to save your world. You have seen the very powerful weapons we have that can destroy life. But today, you chose not to use those powers. I was hoping that Davil's poison had not affected you and needed confirmation. I am relieved I was correct."

"That was a pretty risky test to put us through, Katie scolded her. *We could have killed those young boys. I don't want any more tests like that.*

"You were perfectly safe. It was those boys who were in danger. But their lives were spared by the new messiahs."

New messiahs? Robert thought. *Are you crazy? Do you remember what this world did to the last one?*

"I do. He was my twin brother, who my father thought could ignite The Cleansing and usher in a new world."

Katie was shocked, her face drained of color. *"Are you telling us that Jesus was your brother?"*

"Yes, he died at the hands of Dável and his men, not the Jews or the Romans that history has portrayed as the villains."

"But he was born as a child in Bethlehem," Robert said.

"That's a great story. But that's not exactly how it happened. A baby was born that day under the bright star reported in the New Testament. But the baby was just that: an infant with pureness that was not affected by Dávil's poison. We, for almost thirteen years, hid him and his parents so my brother could enter this young boy's body and begin his mission on Earth."

"How could Dável harm your brother?" Katie wondered.

"During Jesus' trial, Dávil's people were the judge and jury. We got back too late to stop the foolishness, but we were able to harvest his brain impulses and bring it back to Pallas. We rushed to complete the process and there were witnesses. You know it as the resurrection."

"If you failed that time, with someone from your family, how in hell do you think we'll succeed?" Robert asked.

"We've had many failures and lost many members of our family in the struggle. We've sacrificed a lot, when it would have been just as easy to destroy Earth like we did Mars. Until you understand my father, you'll never understand how he feels towards everyone on Earth. They're like his children. He feels a strong need to protect and watch over them."

It sounds more like guilt for creating us and making such a mess of his experiment, Robert thought, losing his temper. *"Who else has been given this responsibility before us?"*

"There are too many to list today. It goes back to the beginning when humans first occupied Earth after Mars was destroyed. Mars was a simple culture that did not need a specific religion to control their actions. There was no good or evil until Dável entered the picture. People just took care of themselves and their communities. When Earth was populated the Supreme Council thought that dividing Earth in the same five tribes we had on Pallas would help combat what Dável had done on Mars. Each tribe had their own unique way of living a healthful and prosperous life that did not know of war or murder. My father was the overseer of the tribes, the commanders reporting directly to him." Robert interrupted Rebecca.

"Are you saying that another experiment by your Supreme Council failed?"

Rebecca sucked in a deep breath. *"We didn't fail. We just under estimated how powerful Dável had become. Over a few thousand years we tried to form religions to bring the tribes back to a more peaceful existence, but Dável and his followers infiltrated the leadership of the three major religions, corrupting them in such a manner that the Supreme Council's message to everyone on Earth was lost as well as misinterpreted. My father even sacrificed his son to help Earth and it failed. Over many centuries he kept trying, but failed."*

Katie stopped Rebecca. She needed some answers. Her head was spinning out of control. *"Who before me and Robert did you give your powers to?"*

Rebecca sighed. *"The list is too long. But here are a few humans we gave some of our powers to. We gave it to Moses, but he failed. Then, Mohammad, but he was too saturated with Dável's serum. We gave our powers to other promising religious leaders, but again they failed miserably. Some men who seemed to have promise just couldn't pull it off, and certain women were just burned as witches. It was probably because we never gave them the powers we have chosen to give the two of you. In due time, you'll discover your other powers and be able to see us without exposing us to the world."*

If you're so powerful, Katie wondered, *why couldn't you change the world by yourselves?*

"While we're powerful in most respects, we're still human and limited to what we can do with what little time we have on your planet. Before we leave, we believe you and Katie will have enough strength to change your world and prevent the Council's army from destroying your planet. I've been slowly transferring part of my DNA and my own stem cells into your bodies to make you strong and prevent you from being killed."

This doesn't make sense, Robert objected. *I've witnessed the power you have and your ability to control life and death. You saved my life, by removing my cancer, but decided to kill Allan Vincent. You have the power to do whatever you want, so why give it to us?*

"These are all good questions that in time will be answered. You'll have to trust that this benefits us both."

"We'll help you up to a point, Robert concluded. *"Mark my words, if I determine you've been lying to us, our deal is off. Are we in agreement?*

"I've got to go now. You'll have your instructions shortly for your next assignment."

As fast as she had abruptly invaded their minds, she was gone. Their ears rang softly in the quietness she had left behind.

"What have we gotten ourselves into?" Robert shuddered.

"I'm not sure," Katie said. "But it's obvious we really don't have much of a choice. If it involves being a party to more killings, I'm not sure I can handle it."

* * * * *

"Why didn't you tell them the whole truth?" Jacob scolded. "I don't think deceiving them will help us accomplish our mission."

"I was afraid that if I threw too much at them today before I got their commitment, we might lose them."

Rebecca could see her father was disappointed and dropped her head, embarrassed.

"Don't wait too long," Jacob said, gently squeezing her shoulder, "or we'll fail and have to go home in disgrace."

His wink told her he still had confidence in her abilities.

CHAPTER FORTY-SIX

"Something's still missing," Robert said reluctantly. "I feel like we're being used."

"Robert, can't you just trust," Katie said, holding his hand and looking feverishly into his eyes. "They've given us something important. If they didn't really need us, we wouldn't be sitting here today, together, discovering something we both lost a long time ago."

Robert slowly shook his head. "I hear you, but I still have to question it. I sense you're not very convinced at this moment, either."

Katie's face flushed red. She felt invaded by Robert.

"I don't think you can read my mind just yet," she said. "Or can you?"

"If I could, I wouldn't. I respect you too much. Understand, it's my nature to have reservations. In order for me to come fully on board, I'm going to have to look further at United Weapons Systems and try to get a handle on what's going on there. It seems like everything that's been happening these last few weeks can be traced to that company. There's something we're missing, and I've got to find out what it is. Everything *Rebecca and her father* have laid out for us just seems a little too tidy. I really feel like we're pawns in a wild game of chess with this Dável character."

* * * * *

"We have twenty-three days remaining," President Hopkins said, gulping down a glass of Scotch. "Are we ready?"

"As we speak, our people are fitting the UN assembly room with an impulse power grid," CIA Director Thomas explained. "We told the members we were hooking up a satellite feed. I didn't think they should be in the loop."

"Good call," Hopkins said, giving Thomas two thumbs up. "Where have O'Riley and Phillips been since his speech the other day?"

"They have been holed up in his hotel room, getting it on like long lost friends. They also took an interesting stroll through Central Park. I guess you haven't listened to the news today."

"Why haven't I been briefed?" the president scowled.

"I wasn't implying anything by my comment, sir. I thought your staff would have kept you up-to-date."

His sarcasm was lost on Hopkins, who was drifting.

"I want to meet with them," he said after a moment. "I've got a lot of questions that need answering. How long will it take to have Air Force One pick them up and bring them to the White House?"

"Turnaround time, say, three hours. Assuming they cooperate."

"Make it happen. Let them know I want a friendly meeting to understand what is needed by all of us before the head of *The Family* speaks."

"If they refuse?" he asked nervously. "Should I use force?"

"Use your people skills," President Hopkins snickered, "and just bring them here. I don't think, after what we saw at the UN, that force is an option you can afford to try out."

* * * * *

Katie and Robert had just finished their dinner, when someone banged loudly on the door.

"Who the hell is it?" Robert shouted as he opened the door abruptly. He saw Katie's disapproval and with both hands gestured he was sorry for the outburst.

Four Secret Service agents and CIA director William Thomas stood in the doorway, holding up their credentials.

Thomas, a six-foot-four, two hundred pound African-American, stared at Robert, looking him up and down. He noticed

Robert back away from the door, giving himself enough space to act defensively if necessary. Thomas had learned long ago to watch suspects closely. He thought Robert didn't look so powerful but recalled what he had done at the UN. He tried to smile, which for him was a foreign act. With his hand extended he spoke first.

"The president would like to meet with you," he said as he noticed Katie come toward the door. He scanned her body as he thought of her naked. His deep, baritone voice made her step back.

"I'm not sure we can do that at this time," Robert said.

Thomas stood facing Robert, his face drained of emotion. "It's imperative that you come with us. The president has already set in motion all your demands and now has questions he needs to address with you before he fully complies."

"Where does he want to meet?"

"The White House. Air Force One is at Kennedy ready to take you there immediately."

What do you think? Robert asked Katie, enjoying his telepathic abilities.

It can't hurt to find out what's on his mind, she smiled. The agents smiled back, thinking her smile was for them. She was enjoying that they could communicate privately, like two foreigners stuck in a country that did not understand their native language.

"We'll be downstairs in thirty minutes," Robert said, abruptly closing the door in their faces.

He grabbed Katie's hand, bringing it to his mouth.

"How does it feel to be in such demand?" he said, unable to keep a straight face.

"Scary. But I could get used to it."

* * * * *

They arrived at the White House two and a half hours later, finishing the last part of the journey from Regan International in a helicopter. Robert had always wanted to meet a president and stand on the carpeted presidential seal in the Oval Office. Katie was coming from a different place. She seemed genuinely impressed with the surroundings.

"Robert, isn't this fabulous being in the White House, especially the Oval Office?"

Robert gave Katie a condescending look.

"It would be impressive if I were meeting with a president I respected."

His thoughts lashed out like a dagger. He saw Katie's face turn red because she had just been put down by someone she trusted.

Shit. I'm sorry, he told her. *That didn't come out exactly the way it sounded in my brain.*

The president was dressed in blue jeans, snakeskin two-tone cowboy boots, and a blue polo shirt. He seemed relaxed, his mood bubbly, as he greeted his guests.

"I hope I haven't inconvenienced the two of you, but time is of the essence," he said, pointing to a couch for them to sit on. "Please, make yourselves comfortable. Can I get you anything to drink? Just name it. We have it, or if we don't, we'll get it for you."

"Can we get to the reason you dragged us here?" Robert asked. He had never liked this president because he reminded him so much of Bush. Unfortunately, it was easy for another Texan to live in the White House, even if he was a moron.

"Detective Phillips," the president began, somewhat taken aback, "I didn't bring you here to reprimand you. But I can speak for the rest of the world when I tell you how shocked we were by the brutal actions of *The Family*. If we're to comply in the drastic manner that your boss demands, we need to get some answers."

"Your answers will be coming in twenty-three days," Robert said, unmoved.

"I recently communicated with a female from *The Family*," the president fumbled, trying to use his political charm. "Did you know that?"

"No. That's none of my business. Did she give you any answers?"

"Well, no, not exactly," Hopkins stammered.

"Then it's obvious you're to wait until the designated time."

"Do you have any specific questions you'd like to ask us?" Katie asked, hoping to bring the temperature down a notch.

Hopkins shifted his chair toward Katie, acting relieved one of them wanted to speak civilly to him. "Well, thank you. For starters, who are these people?" the president asked, smiling at Katie. "And where do they come from?"

"We can't tell you that," Katie said sincerely. "You'll know that answer when our boss, as you put it, addresses the UN."

She noticed Director Thomas eyeing her in a very inappropriate manner. She found his thoughts disgusting. She eyed his large shoes, which must have been size fourteen, and returned his smile.

"Director Thomas, could you please get me a drink of water?" she asked in a sexy voice, as she patted her bosom.

Thomas rose from his chair and stumbled awkwardly, falling forward with his hands outstretched. He tried to break his fall on the coffee table, but his reactions were too slow, and his nose smashed hard on the table's pointed edge. His nose broke instantly, its cartilage popping on impact. His head bounced off the table and onto the floor as his body, like an uprooted sequoia, followed.

"What the fuck?" he wailed, noticing his shoelaces tied together.

"Next time, have better manners," Katie said. "Those nasty thoughts will get you into serious trouble someday."

The president didn't know what to do, except laugh, albeit somewhat uneasily, along with Robert and Katie. He tried to get the meeting back on track as Thomas, holding his bloody face, stormed out of the room.

Outside, Thomas was confused. He hadn't been thinking bad thoughts. The drug was reversing his signals.

"Shit," he said as a marine led him to the infirmary.

"Can you tell us what they want?" the president asked, trying to refocus. "And why are they asking all of us to become vulnerable to our enemies?"

"First, you'll never be left in a position of defenselessness," Katie assured him. "They promise to protect everyone from harm once the world is free of all destructive weapons. But before the world can live in peace, your weapons of mass destruction must be eliminated. Punishment for those who do not comply will be terrible."

She saw Robert's concerned look and hesitated.

"Second," she continued, "they want everyone to live in peace. They want all countries to have everything they need to fulfill their destinies and live happy and secure lives, free from starvation and poverty. Everyone will be given back their right to live in peace and freedom. If this does not come to pass, Earth will be destroyed. That's it in a nutshell."

President Hopkins stood abruptly and began pacing nervously.

"That a tall order in such a short time period," he said, "I don't understand how we can overcome centuries of poverty and starvation?"

"This country," Robert interrupted, "along with most of the free world, has more than enough surplus to end starvation. Drug companies don't have to become rich while impoverished people around the world die because they can't afford medicine. We just need to spread the wealth around and live in peace. You might call it Socialism, but *The Family* calls it survival of the human race."

Robert stood, signaling Katie that it was time to go.

"You have twenty-three days," he reminded Hopkins. "I hope you are taking this seriously! *The Family* means what they say: all who don't comply will be punished like the terrorists who have already met a bitter end. I've seen their wrath and don't wish it upon any of you."

Thomas, holding a bag of ice on his nose, returned to the meeting just as it was breaking up. His white shirt was stained with blood, which matched the fire in his eyes as he hatefully stared at Katie.

"You're thinking bad thoughts again," Katie teased. "Haven't you learned your lesson yet?"

Thomas looked down at his shoes and moved quickly toward the leather couch.

* * * * *

The return flight to Kennedy went by quickly. Robert seemed disturbed by their meeting.

"Did you sense something strange with their thoughts? Something just didn't seem right. I can't put my finger on it just yet. But I felt like we were surrounded by lies."

"I had the same feeling," Katie agreed. "Especially with that Thomas character. He gave me the creeps."

* * * * *

Two hours later, President Hopkins sat impatiently, waiting for the results of his surveillance from Director Thomas. The CIA director entered Hopkins' office, his face swollen and a white adhesive bandage covering his nose. His eyes were puffy and discolored. He looked like he had gone twelve rounds with Rocky Balboa.

"Did we get a good recording?" President Hopkins asked.

Thomas' anxiety reached a boiling point as he watched Hopkins fiddle with his paper clips. He looked at the pile of broken clips, wondering what the president's office would look like if he fed his nervous habit with pistachios instead. He tried to grin, but it was too painful to move his swollen cheekbones.

Thomas rose from his chair and inserted a videocassette into the VCR. He pulled a metal pointer from his jacket pocket and remained by the TV monitor.

"We caught something very interesting from our meeting," he said, pointing to a blurred image in the upper right corner of the screen. "Someone else was in the room with us."

The president squinted and leaned forward in his chair. "I don't see anything except a fuzzy blur."

"That's the image I'm talking about. It was cloaked to the naked eye, but not totally invisible to our cameras. If our intruder's metabolic rate is faster than ours, it's possible the camera, if sped up, could catch an image. What concerns me is that United Weapons Systems has been working on a serum to speed up the metabolic rate of animals. We contracted with them a while back to perfect it so it could be used safely on humans. Allan Vincent we already know was someone who could not be trusted. He would have sold his mother for a price. I just hope he didn't perfect the serum and sell it to this terrorist group."

"If that's a possibility," Hopkins asked, "can we get a warrant and search United Weapons Systems?"

"I'll get on it right after I finish explaining what I found on this video," Thomas said, holding his nose. "This individual was right here eavesdropping on us without us even knowing. See this faint outline by the window?"

President Hopkins showed his disappointment. He realized that *The Family* might not be looking to him to lead the new world. "Yes, it looks like a ghost."

Thomas watched his boss drift and tried to bring him back.

"To the camera it appears that way."

"What are you talking about?" President Hopkins shouted, looking like a man who just been brought back from a dream.

"The camera, sir! Remember, the ghost? Are you all right?"

Thomas' frustration had grown to contempt. He wished he could snap the president's neck and be rid of this idiot.

"It's the blur of a high-speed object coming across our lens," he said, exasperated.

"What does this all mean?" the president asked, trying to seem interested, staring out his window toward the White House lawn.

"Watch. We've sped up the camera a hundred times normal speed and the image gets clearer, while all of us become blurred. Now with it at five hundred times normal speed, we see a woman in a long, flowing robe. I believe this is one of the terrorists."

"Can we do this during the UN talk?"

"Yes."

Hopkins stood up and smiled. He paced slowly around the room, his hands clasped behind his back like a general planning a major offensive. "This is good, very, very good," he smirked.

* * * * *

Rebecca's mother seemed distant; something was on her mind.

"Maybe it's hopeless," she told her husband. "It's time to let go of our problems on Earth and return home. Failure will be accepted by the Council, and you can live out your remaining years teaching our youth."

"I have to see this through, whatever the cost," Jacob said. "I have faith that good will prevail. We can't leave without Dável anyway, especially if he gets control of this weapon. It could mean doom for Pallas and the Council's army."

He tried to touch her hand, but she pulled it away and returned to monitoring her screen.

CHAPTER FORTY-SEVEN

Robert felt more exhausted than Katie did. The day had proven more stressful than either of them had anticipated. Once inside their hotel room, he stripped off his clothing, making himself ready for a deep sleep. He prayed his rest would not be overrun by dreams.

Katie looked out the window and stared at the lights of Central Park as they flickered behind the gently swaying trees. A stream of red and white lights sped up and down the streets, Manhattan's metabolism shifting into nocturnal overdrive.

Then, driven by an unknown force, she began to undress, stopping by the side of the bed to look down at Robert. She felt blessed he was back in her life.

A cold chill suddenly came over her body. It seemed familiar; however, she could not feel Rebecca's presence in the room. She must just be tired and cold, she thought. She slipped under the covers, pushing her cold body up against his, waking him.

"You're freezing!" he said, pulling her to him. "Get closer and warm up."

She did not stop moving, and before he could object, she was on top of him, her arms tightly wrapped around the back of his neck.

"I thought you were tired."

She touched her finger to his lips, silencing him. Her eyes smiled as they became moist. She felt his excitement and slowly slipped him inside her as she lay snuggled tightly against his chest. She moved only her bottom, slowly, making sure she squeezed tightly with each up and down movement. This time, his climax came in a powerful rush, filling her with warmth that brought goose bumps to her entire body. It has been said that a woman knows the moment she conceives. Katie rolled over, a motherly smile on her face.

* * * * *

Rebecca watched over them, not wanting to wake them from their blissful sleep. She hesitated and then realized she had no choice. Their instruction had to continue today. The curtains opened as if they were on a motorized timer, signaling that Act Two was about to begin.

The bright light from the hazy sun beamed down across their faces, causing Robert to pull the bed sheets over his head. Katie stretched and smiled at the new day, happy that the love of her life had forgotten to close the curtains. She nudged him gently, rolling over and kissing his neck until he stirred.

"Why are you waking me so early?" he replied, his voice raspy and tired.

"If you hadn't left the curtains open, we would have missed this glorious new day."

"I didn't. I specifically remember closing them before we went to sleep, or before you seduced me."

"I opened them," Rebecca said. "It's time for some more instruction and for the two of you to find out a little more about our mission."

"Why haven't you leveled with us about who you really are?" Robert thought, wasting no time.

"I haven't lied. I intentionally haven't told you the whole truth. You don't have a problem with that, do you?"

"It's obvious that we're powerless against you, he responded. "So let's cut out the threats and intimidation and get on with what you have to tell us."

"I'm not here to bully either of you, but time is running out. I need you both to take this seriously before it's too late."

What do you mean? Katie asked nervously. Has your father changed his mind about helping us?

"Not exactly," Rebecca said, a hint of desperation in her voice. "We've been given advance warning by the Council that our troops are on the way. It seems the Council doesn't feel Earth will *change. Our track record on bringing Earth's immature nature to the level it should be after five-thousand years and they believe if humans haven't changed by now they will never change. For the Supreme Council it's easier to start over."*

"Then why all the rush to meet your demands?" Robert lashed out, forgetting to communicate telepathically. "Have all the recent deaths been unnecessary? What was the point if you've decided to kill all of us anyway?"

"My father feels there's still a chance the Earth can be saved. We have to continue with our plan and show the Council that Earth is not a threat. That's the urgency. If, before we leave to return home, Earth has not destroyed all its weapons and your world has not found a way to live under one government, one religious belief, then you will be doomed."

Robert stared at the ceiling, wishing he could look Rebecca in the eye and see if she was telling the truth. He trusted his instincts more than her threatening words.

Just then, a strange sensation enveloped him. He felt the same as he did that morning at the shack in the Nevada desert. The only difference this time was an electrical tingling that radiated through his body. Then, without warning, the tingling turned to irritating pinpricks. That sensation turned into hot friction and his skin began to burn. Then, suddenly, it was over, and Robert disappeared.

Katie's mouth hung opened. Shock and fear surged throughout her body. *Had he finally upset The Family?* she wondered. *Did they kill him?* Then she began shouting for Robert, turning, spinning rapidly, her heart pounding wildly, searching for a sign that the love of her life was not dead.

"Katie, I'm all right," he said, his voice shaking like he was talking from a meat locker. *"I'm here with Rebecca."*

"What happened?" she asked. *"How the hell did it happen?"*

He stopped talking telepathically, his voice soft and almost a whisper. "I'm not sure," he said. "When I became angry and wished I could see Rebecca face-to-face, it just happened."

The chattering of his teeth seemed to be subsiding, and he was warming up.

"Robert has advanced faster than normal," Rebecca interrupted. "I underestimated his powers. He is evolving with our

DNA beyond our wildest dreams."

"Katie, I'm going to be awhile. I have so many questions that now I think can get answered. I love you. I'll be back very soon."

CHAPTER FORTY-EIGHT

Robert seemed amazed. His expression somewhat comical, as he realized he had been able to step inside another dimension, or so it seemed, by just willing it. He stared, his eyes wide, mystified at the sight of the young woman he was face-to-face with. He saw her surprise, her bulging eyes, as his unexpected materialization startled her. He then realized the woman he was looking at was Rebecca.

He was astonished that she looked so human in all her features. She didn't have gray skin, but dark olive skin. She was not hairless, but had long, silky blonde hair. Her head was not large or pointed, but normal; she looked Middle Eastern. She was not in a space suit, but a light white robe wrapped with a blue and red belt. Her young body appeared to be no older than seventeen. He was taken aback at her age, wondering how a father would expose a daughter so young to the callous murders that had taken place around the globe.

His words fell out of his mouth awkwardly as he kept staring.

"You're not what I pictured you to be," Robert said.

"And what had you expected?" she replied cautiously.

"I thought you'd be a lot older. Maybe more like the aliens in movies."

Showing off her perfectly straight white teeth, she grinned at his silliness. "I'm older than you think, by a few thousand years, your time."

She had an interesting prettiness, but in a homely way. Her

countenance was not threatening. Robert felt welcomed. He finally realized that little green men with large bald heads and oval eyes would not be attending this meeting.

He began to rub his arms from the coldness of his surroundings. The transporting he had accomplished seemed to have given him a feverish chill. He saw he was no longer in the hotel room. At first, it looked like some type of laboratory, and then he understood he had entered their vessel. Flashing colored lights and oscillating screens musically filled his space.

"I thought you were in our hotel room, talking to us."

"Not this time. I have the ability to communicate with you from any place I choose."

"Is this your spaceship?" he asked. He tried to appear unruffled, but felt foolish and awkward.

Rebecca's eyes narrowed at his question. "It's something like that." Her tone was ambiguous.

"Where are we right now?"

She scowled, frustrated that his questions had begun to probe deeper than she or her father wanted him to go. "We're at the bottom of the Atlantic Ocean. It's close to what your scientists call the Bermuda Triangle."

Like an inquisitive child, he kept asking questions. "Why here and not on one of our deserts where other UFO sightings have been?"

Her face started to show the strain of his questions. "We've found this to be a safe place to hide our transporter while we conduct our business."

"How was I able to come over and see you?"

He observed that she seemed to enjoy that question, and for the first time he was able to look deep into his telepathic friend's face and see the soft, light green eyes that accented her olive skin beautifully.

"Our stem cells have made you and Katie's bodies stronger and free of your planet's diseases. While you're not immortal, you'll be able to live over nine times Earth's normal life expectancy. Your powers will allow you to control your pain and protect you from mortal harm. You'll feel immortal for at least the next seven hundred or so years. With this change, you now have our powers and the ability to enhance them as you learn to control your sensor circuits."

He seemed puzzled, and his facial muscles knotted. "We've become immortal? We can't die in any manner over the next seven hundred years?"

"Something like that. But you'll understand more as your indoctrination progresses."

"How's all this possible?"

"As my cells continue to attach to your own cells and multiply, powers that we have on Earth will become part of your normal evolving. What would have taken another two-hundred years, is happening much faster. Since we have similar DNA, your bodies will be changing each day, modifying your DNA structure to look like ours. The first major change came today. You've just been able to figure out how to speed up your molecules by using that part of your brain that had been idle all of your life. You're just touching the surface of what you're going to be able to do over the next few weeks."

"Will I be able to be precognitive, predict future events, and see the future to be better prepared for my new role?"

"I'm not sure what you're referring to. We can't predict the future, and I'll guess you won't be able to, either. You're okay with this?"

"Sure, I still don't understand what's happening. Have we been the first humans to be given these powers?"

She frowned, then hesitated before she answered him. "As scientists, we have periodically picked subjects, humans, for our experiments. We first introduced only our telepathic abilities, never giving them the stem cells that would transfer our powers. We still don't know fully what our cells will do once they completely integrate with your human cells. Maybe in a few years, you might be able to see into the future. Maybe you'll be more powerful than us? It's hard to predict."

"What other experiments have you performed on us?" Katie asked, disturbed by what she was hearing, stumbling across the metal floor. "I'm so uncomfortable knowing we've been guinea pigs for your nauseous and perverted experiments."

Robert smiled at her sloppy entrance as she tripped when she materialized.

"Greetings," he said, trying to mimic a Vulcan greeting, but failing because his fingers would not cooperate. "I'm glad you could find us. This is Rebecca, and she's explaining a lot of things."

Katie smiled sheepishly, giving her a wave of her hand. "Sorry for interrupting. Please continue."

"What I'll tell you next will make what you've just heard mild in comparison," Rebecca's voice turned robotic. "This is not going to be easy to comprehend. Nevertheless, here I go. During the early stages of Earth's development and a few thousand years after our research to find a cure for our virus, we had a population problem. We did not need as many harvested molecular sensor circuits, so we allowed your planet to multiply. As you already know, we did not know that Dável had begun to infect the DNA of your planet. During one of our regular visits to monitor Earth's progress, we found the drastic changes to your DNA and had to make a decision."

"To either destroy us," Katie interrupted, "or give us the false security that an all-powerful God existed?"

Katie's trusting personality had changed. She became upset and irrational while fighting off a dark side that was trying to take control.

Rebecca blushed. "Your world had turned barbaric from Dável's poison. The human race needed something to cling to in order to keep the good, the righteousness of our DNA, intact. We couldn't leave what we had created in such disarray. As my father covered your atmosphere with his cleansing molecules, he needed to have a way for your world to keep them active and counter Dávil's poison."

Robert seemed calm as he listened to her. "But, why all the lies? Why lead us down such untrue paths, making us believe in religious rules that really didn't exist? Be led by religious leaders that did not have our interests at heart."

"It wasn't a wrong path, or untrue. These rules were from our planet and had worked very well for all Pallasians. My father first spoke to a tribal leader named Abraham with the hope that he could become the leader of a peaceful way of life, believing in one God, with rules to live by. The sad thing for my father was that Dável's powers were greater than ours and man kept evolving using war and mistrust as a way of life on Earth."

Katie seemed puzzled. "So the stories in the Bible are true?"

Rebecca shrugged her shoulders. "Some of them are. However, with man's need to control, our rules were modified and misinterpreted to justify all the killings and conquering that took place. Your history is filled with campaigns that promoted mass murders all in the name of the same God my father tried to establish.

My father felt that your immature planet needed to believe in a God until all humanoids could learn to trust themselves and use their brains to their full potential. We now understand we were selfish and foolish in that belief, leading all of you down a path of impassioned disinformation."

"Now that you've recognized your mistakes," Katie asked, "you're expecting us to instantly change and find faith in ourselves, abandoning our faith in God?"

"If you look real deep at this so-called faith you're worrying about losing, it's a contradiction. Do the majority of the people on this planet really follow a true religious routine? Do the Jews, the Christians, the Muslims, or even the Hindus follow the exact teaching of their religion? If they did, your planet would not be in the serious turmoil it's in now. Jews and Arabs are trying to kill each other. Catholics and Protestants are trying to kill each other. It's also spread into governments around the world. The religious manifest we tried to instill on Earth has been a big failure. Do you want me to continue?"

They nodded their heads reluctantly.

Rebecca took in a deep breath. "Are all of your religious leaders honest and forthright? In some parts of your world, priests are raping nuns, molesting children, and acting like criminals under the auspices of following God's words. Women have no rights in the Islamic world. Do you really believe their religion was created to be that cruel to a human being or even human life? The craziest thing about all of this is that Jews, Christians and Muslims all recognize the same God. Dável's poison has to be eliminated. Even the two of you have lost this faith you're worrying about."

"Even though we sometimes question God's existence," Katie said, "I believe deep down in the darkest places of my heart I still believe a God exists. Even though we don't go to a house of worship or pray, we still worry if someday God will judge us for our sins."

Rebecca had become anxious and fiddled with the tassels at the end of the belt around her waist. "I guess that time is now," she shot back. "It's probably not how you imagined it to be. I told you before what our purpose was, but I left out some important pieces of information you'll need to help you bring order to your world. Our new cleansing agent will make the conversions easier."

"I don't like ultimatums," Robert said. "It's no way to get the cooperation you want. You're very naive to think that, after seven thousand years, you will be able to change a world's belief systems in less than a month."

"Our purpose here for the last seven thousand years has been to capture and bring Dável and his family back to our planet while at the same time save your planet."

"How do we know you're not the bad guys trying to trick us?" Robert asked.

"It's just faith in us or faith in Dável. You have to look deep inside your minds and souls and make that decision. If you had to follow our rules to exist up until now, then so be it. The alternative was not a pleasant one. We've transformed from scientists to bounty hunters. What's gotten in our way is how my father wants to handle our problem of saving Earth. He loves this planet and doesn't want to see it destroyed. He's trying everything in his power to prevent that from happening."

She'd become emotional. They noticed the strain she was under as her eyes welled up.

"I want to meet your father and the rest of your family," Robert said. "It appears we all have a personal stake in this problem of yours. I think it's time we spoke candidly, face-to-face."

As if on cue, two large silver doors slid open, releasing the air pressure that had filled the room. Robert and Katie felt their ears pop. Standing between the archway was an elderly man, his gray beard resting on his chest and his wrinkled face cut deep with lines of torment. His eyes were sad. He seemed like a troubled man. He adjusted his tattered robe, yellowed from age, and entered the chamber, steadying himself with a large metal staff.

Following immediately behind him was a younger-looking woman. Her silver hair and smooth, light-colored skin did not detract from the deep green eyes that shined like beacons of soft light, mesmerizing Robert and Katie.

After helping her father into his chair in the middle of the bridge of their ship, Rebecca gently kissed his cheek like any loving, obedient daughter would do. Her mother, who didn't need help, found her place to the left of her husband.

"Robert and Katie, meet my parents," she said nervously, knowing her father would be upset that she had brought them to their ship.

"I see that the two of you have discovered the powers we've bestowed upon you," he said, extending his shaking hand.

"I'm not sure yet if I can thank you for this gift," Robert replied, taking the old man's hand gently in his.

"You will, once you see what it will do for you. I understand Rebecca has told you of our problem with Dável and his family and about our army that's coming to pass judgment on Earth."

"Yes, she has. However, I have many more questions that need answering if we're going to be able to help." He tempered his tone down a few notches out of respect for Rebecca's old father. "Before I start, how should we address the two of you?"

"I'm Jacob, and this is my wife, Esther. We'll provide you with any answers you want to know. But, remember, don't ask a question if you can't handle the answer. Once you've been exposed to your new powers and new way of looking at your world, your life will drastically change. My suggestion is to trust our judgment and follow our directions. It's the safest and fastest way."

"I can't do that. Your track record these last seven thousand years has not been very impressive if what you've shown us is true."

Jacob's smile was gone. He stared coldly at Robert. "Are you sure of that?" he said harshly. "What's your first question?"

"Why did you choose to fool the world about God and his existence?"

"We did not attempt to fool anyone. The signs we left got misinterpreted. Your species fears the unknown, and without logical answers, you often turn to faith. It was you humans, not we, who created the term God. We just kept adding to it with the hope that my cleansing compound would take hold and counter Dável's poison."

"Are you telling us that the stories, the written word, they were all created by us?" Robert asked, puzzled.

"That's right. With your mutated DNA from Dável, certain men took power at crucial times in your history. And with the knowledge these men had about human nature, they were able to create religions that suited their selfish ambitions. Dável's followers, fully versed in our laws and rituals, twisted our practices to better control the masses."

Robert kept pacing and rubbing his arms as the cold air began to return to his body. He wished that Katie would ask some questions. But she just sat there in silence. Robert realized she would be no help, so he continued.

"Tell us about this mutated DNA we all have," he said.

Jacob in a soft deep voice spoke. "After we cured our planet of the virus that was destroying us, Earth became infected with Dável's mutated DNA." Jacob seemed lost in thought. "I'm getting ahead of myself. Let me back up a little. Dável was one of our most brilliant biochemists but, after turning to a life of crime, became an enemy of our world. He was serving time for his crimes when he escaped from one of our prisons on Pallas. After his breakout, he commandeered one of our transporters, taking with him over ten thousand criminal supporters. They settled on Mars, disrupting our harvesting experiments. Then he and his followers escaped to Earth before we destroyed Mars. He created a serum that he and his family could use to sustain their lives on Earth and hid it from our detection equipment. The rest of his followers immediately found bodies to occupy and, with their mutated DNA, altered the course of history on Earth. As your DNA evolved, your species slowly began to stray from the goodness and compassion that the original inhabitants were designed to emulate."

"But," Katie interrupted, "why persist in letting us believe in God and Heaven?"

"It was not a trick or a deception. Everything originally written in your holy works was true if followed properly. The words and thoughts I had laid out were supposed to trigger the cleansing agent and remove Dável's poison from the world. As you will discover, the brain is a powerful organ and can ignite the right chemical hormones to maintain perfect health. What I had hoped is that by reading the Bible, Koran, and the Torah, it would trigger my cleansing agent. Unfortunately, it wasn't strong enough. The humans that had evolved since our first harvesting program over seven thousand years ago had become weak and easily influenced, absorbing Dável's mutant molecular sensor circuits, making *The Cleansing* work only on a small portion of Earth's inhabitants. The remaining humans that were not affected by *The Cleansing* were easily affected by Dável's poison, causing, as you know, the tragedies that your world has witnessed for thousands of years."

Jacob seemed tired. His eyes began to close as he spoke.

"So why do you feel *The Cleansing* will work now?" Robert asked sorrowfully.

Jacob's head fell forward as he dozed off for a second. The snap of his chin hitting his chest woke him abruptly. He asked Robert to repeat his question. Once he heard it again, he seemed to get his second wind. He rubbed his hand across his forehead as he prepared to respond.

"I've come with a stronger cleansing antidote," he said, "and a new message that should trigger the brain to make the changes that you need."

"A new message?" Robert inquired. "I'm not sure I quite follow you."

"The words in your ancient holy works were designed to stimulate your brain waves and provide enough energy to counter Dável's poison. That approach was a feeble attempt and only in some cases controlled the poison. Now I believe my new message will stimulate the brain sensor circuits that will destroy Dável's mutant DNA like your chemotherapy killing cancer cells."

"How can words affect anything that is part of our DNA?" Katie asked.

"Try to remember how you feel when you witness a sunrise. Your body tingles, your spirit is lifted, and you have an overall satisfying feeling, which causes your mind to send a cleansing chemical throughout your body. That's how my new message will work, only much stronger and with a longer-lasting effect. The words will act like antibodies gobbling up the mutated DNA."

"How can we get everyone to read or hear your new message?" Katie asked.

"That's our second problem. First, we have to deal with our number one concern, or our efforts will be in vain. United Weapons Systems has a way to find and destroy us. They just don't know about it yet. They've had in their database the plans for a new weapon, the RX-666. That's why we've been eliminating all people that have been connected to this company. I'm sure Dável is attempting to get hold of this weapon before we can destroy it. He's a desperate man with very limited time left before he has to take a human form. He needs to accomplish this feat and control the RX-666. If this happens, he'll get a new lease on life and be a danger to all Pallasians."

"Can he just take any human body he chooses?" Robert asked.

Jacob took a deep breath, struggling to sit up straight. "Yes, but he's been looking for someone that has not been affected by my cleansing."

Rebecca came over to help her father, but he waved her off, telling her he was fine.

"Is there someone like that on Earth?" Katie asked anxiously.

Jacob looked deep into Robert' eyes, causing him to squirm uncomfortably where he had been standing.

"You and Katie," he said peacefully. "Dável almost got hold of your bodies once before . . ."

Katie's eyes grew wide. "That day at Chateau Rose," she said, her voice rising as tears flowed down her cheeks. "*That* was Dável, with someone else. Why haven't we been affected by your cleansing or Dável's poison?"

"We're not totally sure," Jacob shrugged. "Your DNA seems to be immune."

"And the other person with Dável was who?"

"That other person was his daughter, Ruth," Rebecca said.

"Was she the one who killed my two children?"

Katie fell to the deck, kneeling, her hands covering her face as she sobbed. She suddenly felt more pain than the day her parents were killed.

Robert rushed over to aid her, putting his arms around her heaving body as her cries became louder and louder. He looked up at Jacob, who had not shown any emotion during their conversation.

"What does all of this mean?" Robert asked. "Have we been reincarnated?"

"No, it's more complicated than that," Jacob answered, afraid to tell them more. "I'm not sure the two of you can take much more of this."

"Don't stop now," Robert pleaded. "Leaving us in limbo would be too much torture for anyone to bear."

Jacob signaled to Rebecca to explain, since she was the one responsible for what happened that day. She seemed uncomfortable with his request but obeyed her father.

"We had been trailing Dável and his daughter for ten hours," she explained, "and came upon him as he was about to take over your bodies. Then to Dável's surprise, his daughter, in a fit of rage, threw Katherine, impaling her on your pitchfork and causing irreversible damage to the body she needed to occupy. Dável couldn't allow his daughter to be alone after he occupied a body, so he turned his anger on you and tried to kill you. He could not complete his job before we found him. And, in a moment of weakness, I let them get away. I wanted to save Katie's and your brain waves, your molecular sensor circuits. That was the worst mistake I ever made. I let my emotions affect my judgment and my mission."

Robert said. "Is this molecular senor circuits something new, or does our scientific community know about this?"

Rebecca felt she was now getting somewhere. She smiled at his curious question. "Yes," she said, "some of your scientists know about this; but they're just in the theory stages of understanding the power of the brain and its capabilities. Most humans are still infants in terms of their development. What our scientists have learned to do is to capture the entire molecular electrons of a dying person and re-implant them in a new body shell, thus preserving the old life and giving it a new life. When the new humanoid form reaches around five or six years of age, the memories and knowledge of the old life begin to come alive. Are you two following me?"

"No," Robert said, shaking his head. "Not really."

"Katie, how about you?"

"I got lost when you said molecular electrons. All I could visualize were these little Pac-Men munching on my body as they traveled throughout my arteries."

"Let me try to simplify it a bit. On Pallas, we use ninety-five percent of our brains. Humans on Earth only use around five. Within that five percent, humans allow their aggression to be the biggest controlling force. Now that the two of you have our molecular electrons mixing with your cells, your use of your brains will keep increasing and providing you with expanded powers, like your experience in Central Park and how the two of you got here today."

"I've read somewhere, I can't recall where, that we use more of our brains than you're explaining to us," Katie said.

Rebecca hadn't anticipated that question and looked toward her father for some help. She saw him nod and sighed with relief.

"Your scientists don't really know how to properly measure brain waves," Jacob explained. "In fact, your medical community doesn't even understand mental illness, that it can be cured not with drugs but with teaching the brain to grow and expand. That's something that will be eliminated on your planet, if you and Katie help us."

Robert smiled. "Is that how some people have been able to make objects move by just thinking about it?"

Rebecca liked Robert's question and smiled at him, pushing her long flowing hair out of her face, causing it to whip around and drop down her back. "Crudely," she said, "but yes. The reason that humans on your planet can't progress is that Dável's poison has stunted your way of thinking. It has bred hate, prejudice, and greed. And it has blocked your true potential. It takes more energy to express anger than it does to express love. The brain can't grow positively when hate and mistrust are the controlling factors."

"That's why you want *The Cleansing* to take effect?" Katie asked.

"Yes. Once this planet is rid of Dável's poison and is totally cleansed, then your world will begin to grow and prosper. You'll learn to control your molecular sensing circuits and cure any diseases inside your bodies without the use of a doctor or drugs. You'll learn how to reverse your aging process and live longer and happier lives."

"Then how did you allow your virus to almost destroy your planet?" Robert interrupted.

Rebecca didn't seem rattled by his question. "We learned all of this during the time the virus was killing our people. We needed your solar system and the radiation from your sun to help rid us of the disease."

She slumped from fatigue.

"Why did you save us," Katie asked, attempting to distract

her from her pain, "instead of capturing Dável that day at the chateau?"

"I had been monitoring the two of you and found that you and your two children were what we considered unique humanoids. You were pure and sacred, without any flaws from Dável's original poison and without any side effects from our original cleansing. I had to save your molecular electrons, otherwise this phenomenon would have been lost forever. Dável had made a mistake with his anger. I couldn't. Though I regretted it early on, I now know it was the right decision."

"Why couldn't you have saved our children first?" Katie asked sadly.

"They were already dead when I entered your home. Once that happens, the brain waves, the electrons, are lost forever. I was devastated, and after safely harvesting what I needed, I destroyed your home and left evidence of your death that you both just discovered during your visit to France."

"But that's not the whole story," Robert said, "is it?"

"No, there's more. Once we begin the harvesting process, all molecular sensor circuits are labeled and given a number for future retrieval after they've been purified and are ready for another body to occupy. Your brain waves never made it back to our planet. There was a malfunction with the incubator, which is rare but has happened a few times before. After a harvest, the molecules are purified, and memories are either erased or kept intact. They're then placed in an incubator with a future date of placement. The unit malfunctioned."

"You're losing me," Katie said.

"We had been experimenting with cloning and harvesting to create an identical life form exactly like the one that died, one with the same traits, memories, and looks. The malfunction caused your sensor circuits to combine with your DNA, and when the incubator time clock placed you in the twentieth century, it created a perfect duplication of Katherine and Robert Rose. Your memories of your past life together were never erased, and after I found you on this trip and examined the two of you that night in the shack and on the island, I was surprised that your purity had remained intact and had even grown stronger."

Robert spoke his tone more gentle. "If we're so pure as you say, then how could we have done such horrible things in our lives? I don't get your logic."

Rebecca smiled, looking at her father for some help. He waved her on to continue explaining everything to them. "Do you really feel deep inside your heart that you are a bad person? Do you have a deep rooted hate that could lead you to murder someone without justifiable cause? It's just not there?"

Katie looked at Robert. Words were not spoken. The tears in both their eyes told the story. The message was clear: they had been reunited and given another chance to love once again and build a family.

"I'm not going to lose you again, Robert," she said defiantly, giving Jacob a stern look. "What do we have to do to save our world?"

Rebecca tugged at her hair, not knowing how to tell her some other disturbing news.

"Katie," she said, "there's something else you need to know: you're pregnant with a daughter."

"I'm going to be a father?" Robert shouted. The joy of the news lit up his face; his smile stretched from ear to ear.

"Are you sure?" Katie asked, puzzled that anyone could know so quickly. Then, abruptly, sadness fell over her as she pondered the news and the danger that lay ahead for the three of them.

"The three of you will have something close to immortality," Rebecca said. "And if we all fail, you'll be brought back to Pallas to live out your lives in peace, free from worry. I owe you that much."

For the first time, Esther looked up from her monitor, distraught.

"Dável has just set in motion a near-catastrophe that for now is being blamed on us," Esther said. "He just attempted to start a nuclear war. Then he stopped it, giving the world a twisted message about who he is and how *we're* the enemy. If he starts to stir up man's fear and mistrust again, it might overpower our new cleansing agent."

Robert was angry as he spoke. "I want this animal and his family; it's now personal."

"I've seen this before," Esther said, "when I lost my son, Rebecca's twin. He's trying to distract us. He knows our weaknesses. He's a convincing demagogue. Our only hope is that he doesn't know yet how powerful Robert and Katie have become. If anyone can destroy this family, these two can."

She spoke as though they were in another room.

"Don't ignore us," Robert said. "Talk to us. We're in this all the way and you need our help. But, I need to think about all of this and get us some help. We've got to go now."

Katie got up from the deck, crossed her arms, and blinked her eyes a few times. Robert looked over, smiling. Rebecca and her parents laughed.

"What are you doing?" Robert asked, embarrassed for her.

"I want to go now," Katie said nervously. "Shit, I forgot how I got here."

Robert smiled and held back laughter as she kept blinking her eyes with her arms crossed in front of her.

"I thought I could just do like they did on *I Dream of Jeanie* and be back in my hotel room," she said.

She was getting ready to cry, when Robert touched her arm.

"Don't be silly," he said. "Take my hand and watch."

They were back in their room at the hotel.

Robert, lost in deep thought, let go of Katie's hand.

"I want to practice using my molecular sensor circuits and see how far I can go with it," he said.

"Can I practice with you?" she pouted.

CHAPTER FORTY-NINE

Katie appeared refreshed and rested after the dramatic exchange of words that had upset her so much yesterday on Rebecca's command vessel. It had taken Robert almost all evening to calm her down as she ranted about the possibility of losing everything she loved once again.

Robert didn't seem too upset and thought he understood what was needed from him to help facilitate the changes the world needed and get ready for the Council's army. He wasn't too sure how much power they had given him and felt he needed to test his abilities before jumping in blindly as a messenger. They both got up early and at Robert' suggestion started to experiment with their powers.

Robert seemed to be able to control his mind easier than Katie could. They spent the next two hours moving objects around the room. Levitation seemed too easy. Katie was shocked when Robert cut himself with a knife and the wound healed itself in an instant. He seemed surprised and pleased at his powers. Katie's eyes almost popped out of their sockets when he took his index finger, yanked it back, and broke it at the knuckle. The loud popping sound made her cringe.

"Are you nuts?" she screamed. "Shouldn't you have taken this test a little slower before you maimed your body?"

Robert, his face drained of color, held his finger tightly.

"Possibly," he grimaced, noticeably in a lot of pain. "Quiet," he said waving his broken finger at her. "Let me concentrate, this really hurts a lot."

He put his free hand out, signaling her to stop talking. She noticed he was in deep concentration.

"This hurts like hell," he whimpered softly.

She couldn't believe her eyes as she watched his finger straighten and go back into place. The finger started to move slowly from the back of his hand until he could move it as if nothing had happened.

He was smiling, and the color had returned to his skin.

"How does it feel?"

"Fine. The pain is gone. I want to try something else and this time I'll try to keep the pain away."

He took off his shoes and socks.

Katie knew instantly what he was about to do. "Oh, I can't watch this," she said, cringing as he kicked the leg of the coffee table with his bare toes.

He broke all five toes. While he was sure he could heal his toes, the initial pain he felt could not be controlled or eliminated. He limped over to the couch and in a matter of seconds was able to walk on his foot as if nothing had happened.

"This is great, except for the initial pain. I'll work on that. Now do me one last favor—"

Katie raised both arms in the air turning her back to him and walking away. "I can't be part of your crazy experiment," she complained. "I don't understand this macho attempt to give me the heebie-jeebies. Haven't you done enough to prove your healing powers?"

"This one will be easy. I'm going to turn my back and you're going to try to hit me with that ashtray. Don't be a wimp. Try your hardest."

She hesitated, but his incessant put-downs got the best of her. She slowly tiptoed behind him and swung the ashtray as hard and as fast as she could toward his head. Just inches before smashing his skull, her arm stopped and bounced off an invisible barrier.

He turned with the broadest smile.

"It's amazing," he said, "I can feel my brain sending impulses throughout my body. It's as if my brain can sense pending danger. This power is exhilarating. Let's get you started. You need to practice."

Katie seemed to fight her powers, not wanting to experience the rush of pain she had seen on Robert' face.

However, after a few hours of taking small steps, she was able to accomplish what Robert had done earlier.

"It's amazing," she said, "We *do* have the powers they said we would have—"

Someone banged on their door, startling them.

"We want to be left alone!" Katie shouted harshly.

"My name is Cardinal Richman," a voice shouted back. "I need to speak to you. It's of the utmost importance."

He sounded desperate.

Katie looked at Robert and shrugged her shoulders, passing the decision over to him.

"Just a minute," Robert called out. First, the President. Now a famous Cardinal? Let's see what he wants to talk about. Maybe he's realized he's out of a job and would like to work for us?" Robert smirked.

"That's cute," she said. "It's nice to see you still have your sense of humor."

"I didn't mean it that way. This is like getting a visit from Mother Theresa. This guy is the real McCoy. He's what sainthood is all about; at least what we once believed it was all about. I think, depending on how he deals with the new reality, he could be a good ally to have.

"Good idea," she whispered. "I'm still not sure how I can break this news to the world anyway."

Adjusting her silk blouse, Katie brushed her hair back away from her eyes. Robert attempted to pat down a few cowlicks caused by his new method of travel, tucked in his shirt, and reached for the door.

The cardinal was dressed in his formal red and black robe and his red skullcap. A beautiful gold crucifix was draped around his neck, and he held the cross nervously in his hand. He looked tired. Standing behind him was a short, stocky Japanese man, who bowed. Robert and Katie just stared at the submissive man.

"Excuse me for being rude," the cardinal said. "This is my friend and personal assistant, Hirshumi Kubota. I call him Harry. It's a lot easier."

Katie pushed Robert aside. "Nice to meet both of you. Please, come in."

"Harry will wait outside in the hallway. He's very protective of me."

"I read about him," Robert said, amazed at Harry's small stature. "Is he as good as they say he is?"

"I'm not sure. He hasn't had an opportunity to show me, thank God. I do know he's a lousy chess player, and has an interesting way of playing scrabble, but he makes me laugh during times when it's difficult to laugh."

The cardinal looked older in person than he appeared on TV, where Robert had seen him. They could see the stress of years of hard work embedded on his face. The deep lines on his face, if they could speak, would have told a story of a life of sacrifice and pain.

Robert knew that the cardinal was on the pope's short list to become the first American spiritual leader of Catholics around the world.

Cardinal Richman's voice was low and deep as he spoke. Katie and Robert were captivated by the gentle way his words flowed from his mouth.

"The world feels that God has come down to Earth," he intoned, "and that you are his new messengers to preach a new salvation. Now, with the recent travesties that have befallen all our people, it's obvious that God or someone is angry and we need to repent before He destroys the world once again."

"I'm not sure how I should reply," Robert replied, turning to Katie. "We are messengers of sorts, but we're not being directed by God. We have a message that affects everyone on our planet without regard to race or religion. In a nutshell, every man, woman, and child will perish if we do not get the world to change as *The Family* has demanded."

"Do you think you're being a little too patronizing to him?" Katie scowled at Robert.

Robert continued to smile as he responded to her, *"I'm doing what I think is right!"* His harsh tone cut deep as Katie tried to control her composure. *"If you feel you can speak to him better, be my guest."*

"I'm very uncomfortable speaking with him, she replied. He's a great man and one of the few on Earth who is honest and good." She continued to force a smile as they communicated privately in front of the cardinal

Robert's expression seemed to mellow a bit. *"I'll be careful. I feel the same way you do."*

"You two can communicate without speaking," he said, his curiosity piqued. "I've always believed that a higher being could read our minds. That's how some of our prophets have spoken to God. I'm confused by your insinuation that the higher being that has communicated to the world might not be God. Are you saying God is really a person or something else?"

"It's something like that, Your Excellency," Katie said, stepping in front of Robert. "It seems that the God we believed loved us gave us disinformation in our civilization's infant stages, and now He's back to help straighten out our crazy world."

"Are you saying that there is no God as we have come to believe?" the cardinal asked, his expression puzzled, "and this family created our religious beliefs as we know them?"

"Something like that, Cardinal," Katie said, feeling guilty for trying to dismantle his faith.

Cardinal Richman staggered over to the couch and flopped down in disbelief. "I'm going to have to digest all of this. It's blasphemy to think something like this. I'm an open-minded person and have for decades tried to understand the inconsistencies of God and the cruelty committed around the world. But I have a job to do, which I believe in. I need to hear more about all of this so I can try to remain open to what you're saying."

Robert and Katie looked at each other, shocked that the cardinal was so open to such a heretical idea.

"We can't tell you at this time what we know," Robert said, "However, your faith will be tested like it's never been tested before."

Cardinal Richman closed his eyes appearing lost in thought. Then he slowly opened his eyes and spoke. "If we've been wrong in our beliefs," the cardinal smiled, "then the world needs to know. If *The Family* has a better message for us, then how bad can it be to know the truth? I'm just confused. They've committed a lot of murders. Is this group really someone we can trust?"

"*The Family* isn't responsible for any of the recent killings of the innocent," Robert responded. "There's someone else out there making *The Family* appear to be the perpetrators."

"It sounds like the classic case of good and evil fighting for Man's soul. God and Satan have always been fighting. Nevertheless, this is serious, which I'm sure you already know. I'd like to help if there's room on your team."

"We don't know everything yet," Robert said, "but before our twenty-three days are up, we should have all the answers. Can you assemble all the religious leaders that would be as open as you to meet with us, let's say, in four days?"

"I'll see what I can do. I have to first talk to the Pope and the Vatican cardinals before I can get involved."

"It will have to be with everyone or we won't meet," Robert said seriously. "No disrespect, your Grace, but what we have to accomplish will require everyone's cooperation. I believe that having the religious leaders getting their flocks to cooperate and listen with open minds will be better than trying to get our political leaders to listen…at least honestly."

They spent the next two hours going over everything they knew, telling Cardinal Richman about The Cleansing and about Dável and his family. They spent quite a lot of time explaining about *The Family*. Both Robert and Katie were impressed that the cardinal wasn't that upset about God and the disinformation the world had believed for centuries. He seemed to be adjusting well to the new information.

Cardinal Richman stood up, kissed both their hands, and left their room. They were astonished at his actions. Being treated like royalty by a man who was the closest thing to God either of them had ever known, it just didn't seem right.

Katie had a puzzled look on her face as she closed the door. "Do you think we did the right thing, considering we still don't really know what our role will be?"

"It will have to do for now. We'll need the world's religious leaders supporting us, or we might have riots in every country like we've never seen before. I'm not sure people will ever be ready to give up their various faiths. We'll just have to find a way to show them that a different kind of God really exists and loves all his children. We're on team now and we need everyone on board."

* * * * *

Father, I am not sure Robert and Katie will be able to carrying out the hardest part of their assignment. We are putting them in the position to be a vengeful God. Acting like the Judge, Jury and Executioner might be too hard for them to swallow.

Jacob gently caressed his daughter's cheek. "They will see that there is no other alternative."

CHAPTER FIFTY

Unable to sleep, Katie stood on the balcony, watching the pink rays of the morning sunrise reflect off the Manhattan skyscrapers. Street sweepers prepared for another day of tourists, and the worker bees that came from their underground hives swarmed the streets toward their flowers to gather their honey before returning home.

"You're up early," Robert called out, his voice raspy.

"I couldn't sleep. I'm having a problem dealing with all of this. Don't misunderstand. I'm happy we've found each other and that we're going to have a baby. It's just that my life feels like it's been disassembled. I have to mentally reconstruct my life with a new belief system…it's overwhelming. Everything's moving way too fast: the killings, you and me back together from another life, and now the awareness that we were a harvesting project by a race of possible crazies."

"Don't you think 'crazies' is a little too strong a description?" Robert debated, wondering if this was what happened to women in their first trimester of pregnancy.

"Think about it," she said, her voice rising. "What are we? A farmer's property, like cattle breed and fattened up for slaughter. I'm carrying more property for them. I'm not sure I like who they are or what they want us to do for them."

He tried to calm her down. "If what they say is true, we have little choice, especially if this Dável character is still out there. The alternative doesn't seem very appealing."

"All that we've known and believed," she said wretchedly,

"has been turned upside down and crushed like a can of soda ready for the recycling bin."

Robert had a pensive look as he started to speak. "Let's really think about it. What we've heard so far is not so unbelievable. We had faith that God existed. And by all indications, what we believed was somewhat true. These people are just not as divine as we had hoped."

"I'm confused. What you're saying does not make sense."

"What we had learned from the Bible was partially what Jacob wanted us to believe; just some of the facts we were taught were manipulated to control us. I've always had the fear that God might not exist and that an afterlife might not be waiting for me."

He could see she was not fully buying his logical interpretation of what their indoctrination had provided thus far. She was still distraught.

"During each of their visits to Earth," Robert continued, "they did attempt to correct their problems. If they are as human as they say they are, then they're fallible also. Look how Rebecca allowed her emotions to save us and let Dável escape. God is supposed to be logical not emotional…right? All they wanted was for all of us to be a peaceful, caring, and loving race. That's not too much to ask, even if it was for a selfish purpose."

"It's just too mind-boggling to accept," Katie said, wiping her eyes with her sleeve, "especially in the short time frame they're giving us to adjust and become their messengers. I'm not ready to see myself as a prophet after all that I've done in my life."

"I'm really worried about having our powers for almost seven hundred years," Robert said, trying to lighten the mood. "That's a long time to be with one person. I'm concerned I might get bored with all of your bad habits."

Her eyes narrowed.

"I'm just joking."

A faint smile started to form.

"Now that's a horrible thought," she replied with a laugh. "This puts a new slant on living happily ever after."

Katie stopped crying and nestled her head against his chest. For the first time, he felt the little girl who missed her parents as she pushed deep against his body. He understood for the first time her pain and felt compassion for her inner turmoil.

A few minutes passed before they both felt a cold chill fill the room.

"*Good morning, Rebecca,*" Robert thought.

"*Good morning to both of you. Are you ready for the next part of your training?*"

"*Do we have a choice if we are to save this planet?*" Robert replied, his tone a little sarcastic.

"*You do. This is the last opportunity both of you have to back off from becoming part of the cure Earth needs in order to survive. However, the alternative will be a lot worse. That's not a threat. It's a fact.*"

"*I guess we're in your hands now,*" Katie replied, her enthusiasm gone.

"*Get ready. We're leaving in five minutes,*" Rebecca ordered.

* * * * *

CIA director Thomas sat alone in his study. He loved this private place he had created. The dark wooden panel walls of myrtle had been imported from Italy. His desk dwarfed him. It was an oversized French provincial desk, with a trim of carved occult friezes guarded by wooden gargoyles protruding from each corner.

Something about the last few days bothered him, especially the apparent concern *The Family* had with United Weapons Systems. His strong analytical skills led him to believe that something at UWS had them scared. *What is it?* he thought.

With the president depressed by the near devastation that had shaken the world and that there were now competing families with similar powers trying to control the world, Thomas knew he had a golden opportunity for himself.

"That's it!" he shouted, reading the report. "They're afraid of these weapons. But, if they're all-powerful, why can't they destroy them and be done with it?" He finally understood that their powers had some limitations.

He booked an early flight to Nevada for the next morning. Then he sat back, a devilish grin on his face.

CHAPTER FIFTY-ONE

Cardinal Richman waited patiently for his audience with the Pope. The waiting area was cold and dark; for the first time since being appointed a cardinal, he had been required to wait where common folk waited for an audience with the Holy Father. His surroundings were not very spiritual. In fact, he noticed how depressing this musty room felt. He speculated that Cardinal Gironde had to have had a hand in what he was being asked to endure.

He was apprehensive, unsure of what the response would be from Pope John and his cardinals. Even if they believed him about this new theory of God, he knew from past experience that truth does not always lead the way to enlightenment with the Catholic Church. Control was their mission of the masses and any indication that the structure of the church, it's rules, it's beliefs, even the written *Word* by God had been misinterpreted would destroy the Christian religion forever.

Cardinal Richman had for most of his life been devoted to the work of God, helping all he encountered, find salvation in an abusive world. His new understanding of God would not change much of what the Church had been teaching, but it would make the Christian world more accountable for their actions during their short time on Earth. Not having a better place to go after death would truly change how one lived during their life-time.

"Only a very few move on to another chance," he muttered to himself, feeling the cold, damp air race through his body as he continued to wait.

The new facts about God and his existence or nonexistence kept circling inside his head as he tried to picture the world accepting a new theology. He had grown up in New York and was educated at the finest universities around the world. He kept an open mind to things and had always suspected that the writings and teachings of the Church and other faiths had been slanted to promote each religion's own agenda. He wondered what harm it could cause if the teachings of God were pure and good and only one religious order was needed to live in peace.

As a child growing up in the Bronx, he had found it easy to follow a path of respect and love for his fellow man. He had stood out among the other young boys in his neighborhood that fought harshly for their survival while he avoided the dark side of life. He chose compassion and understanding for the pain his friends and neighbors felt while they struggled against a world that by all appearances was intentionally keeping them impoverished and suffering.

The gangs that controlled his streets never seemed bothered by his warm and compassionate personality. He never passed judgment or preached to them to change. He, then, and now, seemed to understand that God had given all his children the right to be who they wanted to be; he was just there to comfort them when they fell off their path and needed a new corridor to enter. He hoped today would be the same. He had a new roadway that could help the world, and he needed the support of his church to begin the process.

His hands were moist from the perspiration that covered his body. He repeated in his head the words he would be speaking to the religious leaders of the Christian world. He wanted to expose a new truth that should to be told to a waiting world. He was fearful that, for the first time in his life, he might be labeled as a traitor to God and the Christian way. He remembered how the ancient world did not accept Jesus and was afraid he would get the same reception.

Lost in thought, he was startled by the squeaky sound the large wooden doors made as they slowly opened.

"His Excellency is ready to see you," the guard said in Latin.

The cardinal stood, adjusting his robe, then froze as an old man's voice filled his head.

"You will help lead the world to the truth," Jacob said. *"Have faith that what I'm attempting to do in twenty-two days will*

bring salvation to your world. Support my messengers. They will need your help to succeed."

The voice was gone too quickly. He wanted to communicate, to say something, but he reasoned it was not his time yet. The long walk down the marble corridor allowed him enough time to digest what had just happened.

* * * * *

The meeting took almost four hours and did not go well. In another age, Cardinal Richman would have been burned at the stake.

"What if we were meant to have only one religion as the original plan?" he asked the court of Cardinals. "What if all the hate and differences could be abolished with one form of religious practice?"

The Pope was first to answer, his voice quivering and his hands shaking from the multiple sclerosis that was eating away at his frail body. "Why would God come back now to disrupt our lives," he asked, "showing us all the death that has transpired these last few weeks?"

"I don't have that answer yet, but he spoke to me right before our meeting. I ask you to look back at the other times God sent us his messages. They always came during turning points in our history, when life needed a new direction."

Cardinal Richman looked around the chamber. His colleagues had their heads bowed in disrespect.

"Why would he talk to you and not me?" the Pope protested. "I am the Holy Father, the leader of His Church."

Richman answered in a calm voice. "Why has he for so many centuries spoken to his children, making miracles that previous Popes were not privy to? He wants peace for all of us. He wants one family, in one united world that is not divided by power, greed, or hate. We have to eliminate all our barriers. Prejudice must stop. We are one planet and one human race. If there are other civilizations in other solar systems, in other universes, then we need to all be united as one people."

"Are you now professing that you have actually spoken to God today?" Cardinal Pierre Gironde shouted at him. "We sent you out on a mission to see if a miracle had occurred in the Nevada desert, and you've come back telling us you've spoken to God? What proof do you have? Or have you eaten too much desert cactus?"

"I... " He fumbled for the right words, unsure how to explain what had happened to him. He knew he sounded irrational, but the voice had been real. "I heard a voice, and it gave me a message that made sense to me. All I ask each of you is to search your heart for the proof that our old God exists and that what we've believed for centuries is still valid in today's world. Our church and the other temples of this world are unable to convince a troubled world that God's original teachings are valid today. Who here has spoken to God? Who here can prove his faith is real?"

"What you're trying to make us believe is that everything the Church has stood for is a lie," the Pope said angrily, pounding his cane hard against the marble floor.

"Everything is not a lie, your Grace. We've just misinterpreted the signs. If *The Family* helped form our religions and the stories and rules that have helped us live as best we can in our harsh world, then it behooves us to have open minds and learn the actual truth. If we've been living a lie or have strayed from the path God wanted us to follow, then we owe it to our followers and the world to change."

The men who were there to judge Cardinal Richman were locked in a frozen silence. Cardinal Gironde had too much power for them to go against his wishes. Cardinal Richman knew it was over; he had lost the support from the only family he had known most of his adult life. The Pope stood up, helped by a guard. He turned his back on Cardinal Richman. The other cardinals followed the lead of the Holy Father.

With a bounce in his step, Cardinal Richman marched out. "I'm on my own now," he said in a soft whisper. "I just hope the world will listen."

"Go back to New York and seek out Robert and Katie," Jacob told him. *"They need your help, like I do. The world as you know is about to change. Those who accept my terms will be saved and those who do not will suffer severe consequences."*

His eyes welled up as he realized God was addressing him. "When can I speak to you?" he pleaded. "I have so many questions and doubts." He did not notice the guard shaking his head.

"Soon. We'll all have a talk, and all will be revealed."

The voice was gone again. This time he felt happy that he was going to be part of a new world.

He turned his head and his eyes welled up; he was sad that his supportive family now considered him a madman. *A new family is needed,* he thought as he pulled out his cell phone to call some old friends.

* * * *

The Pope settled into his chair, adjusting the cushions he now needed to support his frail body. Even though his head rocked to each side from his disease, his face showed no emotion as he prepared to deliver the verdict on his longtime friend and potential successor.

"Cardinal Richman cannot be allowed to preach his new gospel," the Pope said sadly. "We have to stop him, even discredit his authority. The Vatican must be the only church recognized by God. It must be at all costs."

Cardinal Gironde tried to assure Pope John. "The Christian world will not believe him. Without our support, he will look like an old fool who has gone mad."

"I don't want him to be able to have an audience," the Pope said. "His words are blasphemy and an insult to the Church and to God. See to it that he's watched. Do whatever it takes to keep him silent."

"Anything your holiness?"

The Pope did not hesitate with his response. "Yes, anything. I love our church to have it destroyed by Cardinal Richman."

"Yes, your Grace," Cardinal Gironde obeyed. "It will be done."

CHAPTER FIFTY-TWO

Katie and Robert, now familiar with how their orientation worked, took their positions on the curved lounges that molded perfectly to their bodies. Like before, the probes softly positioned themselves inside their ear canals.

The room instantly changed from stark white to the crystal clear outdoors. They were traveling somewhere near a mountain range covered with a carpet of pine trees tipped with snow. As the scenery sped by more rapidly, it began to feel like a simulator ride at an amusement park.

The ride was over as quickly as it had started. The destination this time was unfamiliar. The straps came undone and a door opened, revealing a large room with two chairs. They seemed to glide, not walk, toward their seats, and, without a thought, sat down. Another set of ear probes lowered from above them, and their training began.

It was Esther's voice they heard this time. "We're pleased with how quickly the two of you have adapted to your new powers. Your ability to master and control what's happening to you will be the difference between success and failure. You will begin to become stronger each day as your Granule cells, tiny neurons in the cerebellum connect with your Purkinje cells. This growth process will allow your electric circuits to move faster than any computer on earth, providing you with the agility and coordination you'll need to control all that are around you."

Esther was wearing a red robe, her long white hair draped down in front of her chest. Her icy stare reminded Robert of how he acted when interrogating a criminal.

Robert stared back defiantly. "Why the serious attitude?"

"I'm sorry," she said, surprised. "It's just that the subject matter I'm going to talk to you about is very frustrating."

"You sound hopeless," Katie said. "It can't be that bad! Can it?"

Esther took a deep breath. "I hope not. Let's begin. Today we're going to discuss Dável and how we are going to stop him."

"I get the feeling Katie and I are going to have to do this on our own," Robert said. "You're scared, aren't you?"

"Yes and no," she said evasively. "Right now, we know we're getting close to capturing Dável's two sons. That will make finding Dável and his daughter easier. However, it will also make him more dangerous, something like a wounded animal trying to survive. While his powers have weakened, we cannot take be too over confident or he will, like he's done for thousands of years win out."

"What if Dável gets the weapon?" Robert asked heatedly. "You do have an alternate plan, don't you?"

"Sort of. Dável's daughter and two sons are the most dangerous as they grow weaker. The serum that keeps them regenerated on Earth is almost gone. Once we capture his sons, we believe Dável will become more irrational and make mistakes. Then we'll be ready for him."

"I've seen what he can do when he's angry," Robert said heatedly. "I've seen him kill hundreds of thousands of innocent people and destroy cities around the globe. I think your plan sucks. You're going at it in a piss-poor manner."

"It's all we've got!" she said her tone more serious. "I understand your anger at us and how hopeless it all sounds. But, it will be you and Katie that will bring Dável down as you get stronger. The two of you don't have any weaknesses, other than your anger, which we hope to help you control. Dável can figure out weaknesses in an adversary and believe me if he doesn't already know about yours Robert, he will shortly."

"I'm sorry," he said sincerely. "I'm not used to fighting a criminal like Dável without some logical plan. My anger was nothing personal. It's just a bad habit, you're right, that needs controlling."

"I'm sorry, too. I'm getting weaker because my time is running out here. I'm just as frustrated. Dável could succeed after we're gone, and we won't be around to help."

"Not if I can help it," he told her. "If you give me a little
latitude, I think we can draw him out and close the trap, but it will
take a little luck and some help from a friend. What I need is more
information on the weapon that Dável is trying to get, so I can
figure out a way to neutralize it."

"First, you have to understand better how we function here
on Earth. If he gets control of the RX-666, we will surely be
destroyed, along with our brain impulses. It will be as if we had
never existed."

She spent the next few hours explaining each and every
vulnerability they had, trusting Robert and Katie would never turn
this information around to harm them or anyone on Pallis.

Robert was most interested in how Dável had developed his
serum and how he and his family needed time to rest, hidden
beneath the Earth's surface. For *The Family*, the caves posed a
problem. But Robert knew about some new infrared cameras that
could see through anything. He was certain Dável and his family
would not be able to hide from him.

Ester just nodded, trying to show some interest in what
Robert had to say, but she had an agenda and needed to get back to
it.

"Jacob is confident that his new cleansing compound will work,
and once we capture Dável and his family, we will be able to rid
your world of hate and prejudice and the wars that come along
with it all."

Katie could no longer remain silent and interrupted Robert
and Esther.

"Then why did you push me to become pregnant? Am I to lose
another child to this animal if your trap doesn't work?" Esther
bowed her head unable to respond.

"I think you're getting too emotional about all of this,"
Rebecca said, entering the room.

"Emotional! Damn right I'm emotional. Have we been your
bait these last two times you tried to trap Dável?" she accused her.

Rebecca was sitting opposite to her mother, lost in silence.

Katie's eyes were fiery red, as she glanced at both Ester and
Rebecca. "You don't have to say anything. I know the answer by
the look on your faces. We're your bait, your sacrificial lambs, to
capture this evil man. Tell me one thing: were we created to be
this pure human you've told us about? Raised like cattle, just to be

sacrificed? Destined to die an unpleasant death each time you failed?"

Rebecca tried to respond. "I know how you must be feeling—"

"No, you don't. We're the ones at risk, not you. You've disrupted our lives. You've destroyed what little faith we once had in our lives. You have the option to go home and live out your lives. No matter what happens after you leave, we're stuck with the mess you've left us."

"I promise you," Rebecca stuttered, "this time you and Robert will have the power to destroy Dável and his family."

Robert had been listening to their conversation, and he, too, was upset. Their hearts ached as they watched Rebecca weep, releasing years of pent-up frustrations and guilt. Even though she was thousands of years old by comparison, she was, by her planet's clock, still a teenager.

Katie looked at Esther surprised she did not show any maternal emotion toward her daughter and when it was obvious that Rebecca was not going to be comforted, she walked over to her and brought her into her arms. She let her cry. She rocked her slowly back and forth, caressing her long blonde hair and patting her back gently, like a mother holding her child to ease her pain.

They both cried.

Esther had been watching this unfold. She was lost as a mother. It had been a long time since she had even touched her daughter, let alone embraced her.

As he watched them cry, Robert remembered that horrible day at the chateau when he had rocked his dying wife as Dável squeezed the air out of him.

"Ladies," he said, "we need to get back to the business at hand. I don't want to repeat our past mistakes."

He tried to smile, but his mind was on business, detective business. He saw the relief on Esther's face, sensing she, too, wanted to return to the training.

Katie released Rebecca, who surprised her with a kiss on the cheek. She knew a bond had been born that day, that moment, between the two of them.

Robert, like a general motivating his troops, summarized the problem they faced. "Here's our dilemma. The Council's army has been deployed. They're scheduled to arrive in ten years and can't be contacted. Aborting their mission is not viable. When they reach our solar system, they will scan the entire surface to verify that The Cleansing has worked. If they feel the threat is gone, then they will return home. Do I have it right?"

"Yes, you do," Esther answered.

"What if ten years has not been enough time?" Katie asked. "If we can prove we've made positive progress, won't that matter?"

"No. The army is made up of fifty thousand robots that have been programmed with two options: destroy Earth or return home."

"We're just two people," Robert said, "who you're leaving with a mission you couldn't accomplish in seven thousand years. What makes you believe we'll be able to do this in such a short time?"

"The Cleansing will work this time," Esther said awkwardly. "That's why we must capture Dável."

"It sounds like he's a true threat to your people and your army!" Robert said harshly. *Maybe he's our salvation to survive,* he told himself. *The alternative seems logical.* He realized he was able to block his thoughts from them because they didn't show surprise at what he was thinking.

"There's no solution but the one we've told you. If Dável wins, you won't be able to control his power and you'll wish our army had destroyed you." Esther seemed drained and anxious to leave. "Let Rebecca continue with your instruction. What you'll learn today will make you the most powerful native humans to have ever occupied the Earth."

PART III
GOD'S LOOKING GLASS

CHAPTER FIFTY-THREE

Rebecca released her hand from Katie's and directed her back to the examination chairs. One last hug initiated by her new friend, and Katie was back in her chair, ready to resume her training.

The probes were reinserted, and the show inside their heads began again. This time, it was Jacob who narrated.

Pallas, which by all appearances seemed serene. It appeared like Earth. The oceans were of the darkest blue, as white foaming waves crashed against the whitest beaches. The mountains, carpeted with the greenest pine trees, were capped with cotton balls of snow. Their farmlands were evenly divided. Each acre alternated between green and gold like a quilt that covered the flat countryside. The forests and mountains that surrounded the farms, formed the most picturesque mixture of colors and patterns.

Their citizens were not the distorted alien's science fiction books or movies had made them out to be. Robert was surprised they looked like normal human beings. They walked like humans and even laughed like humans, which made Katie grin as she was reminded of her home in Ireland. They did appear to be more relaxed. They dressed in long, flowing robes, which were tie-dyed and embroidered with symbols. The symbols resembled the brands one might find on the backside of a cow.

Their homes were a mixture of tall apartment buildings and small houses. Each building was different. A mixture of Cape Cod, early Californian, and large Victorian-styled houses were laid out in an orderly fashion. The apartment buildings were a mixture of brownstones and modernly laid out complexes. There were no cars. Instead, they used transporters: people movers intricately woven throughout the city, which transported the people to their destinations. Some Pallasians seemed to move from place to place, similar to how Robert and Katie had learned.

Everything appeared utopian. Children played and laughed. All ethnic groups interrelated happily with each other. The Pallasians seemed to live in harmony with each other and their planet.

Robert sensed something was out of place but couldn't put his finger on it just yet. He wondered if they were only being shown the good. He did not believe a paradise like this really existed, even if they were an advanced race.

Not knowing for sure if he could ask questions, he attempted anyway. "Is your planet all so perfect: no crime, no violence, or even poverty? Who are the elites, and who are the workers who makes everything function in your world?"

"Good question," Jacob responded. "We once had violence and poverty. Our heritage has its dark side, too. But we're proud that we've evolved into who we are."

"Are there no prisons anymore like the one that housed Dável?" Robert asked, still doubtful.

"We had prisons before we learned about The Cleansing and how it would help rehabilitate and enhance our lives. We had made a promise to all Pallasians that by giving up hate, they would forever be protected by the council."

"What about Dável? Why didn't you use The Cleansing on him?"

"Dável and his family escaped well before this stage in our evolution process had been perfected. We do have one problem. If we stay off our planet too long and remain in the high molecular state required to sustain our invisibility, we slowly go insane. Dável was one of our finest scientists, but he also committed our worst crime: murder. The thousands of years he's been away from his home have driven him mad; he has a severe form of schizophrenia. His insanity has led to some of Earth's worst tragedies.

"When he broke out of prison, he took with him an experimental drug that he had created. This drug could sustain our people for long periods of time away from our planet while we explored other worlds. It was in its final testing stages and held such promise for us. We had hoped to find a way to monitor the planets we had performed our experiments on for longer periods of time. When he vanished, our hopes vanished with him. It gave him a great advantage over us. He knew our time on Mars and Earth was restricted, and he used that gap of time to breed evil. He's been a fox, avoiding detection for thousands of years. He's able to mask his energy signature, avoiding capture during our visits. You're folklore about the devil and good versus evil comes from different periods of time on Earth when we were there and when we departed and Dável surfaced."

Robert felt frustrated as he spoke. "What powers have you given us so we can deal with Dável if he's this powerful?"

Jacob stroked his beard as his eyes narrowed. "We've given you our molecular sensing cells. This transformation of your DNA is rapidly changing your entire molecular structure. You are also gaining an ability to initiate two important things: sustaining life or eliminating it. You won't be limited like we are in finding and destroying Dável. Very shortly, you and Katie will become what your planet would call superhuman. Almost indestructible."

Robert, his brow furrowed, seemed confused at what Jacob had told him. "What do you mean, *almost?*" he said intentionally avoiding talking about his ability over life and death.

Jacob took a deep breath before he continued, closing his eyes tightly, searching for the right words. "The Council's army has a weapon that can destroy the two of you. It's our only fail-safe defense in case you turn against us."

Robert's face turned white. "So we're still your little experiment. You've created a weapon to defeat your enemy. If I read between the lines, our usefulness will be over once Dável is destroyed. Maybe we should deal with Dável and protect our planet."

"That would be foolish. He's been looking for the right body to occupy and live out his life in human form. His madness as best as we can guess has gotten worse, affecting his ability to be rational. He does not want partners; in fact, he wants your body and Katie's."

Jacob's words did not impress Robert. Everything was moving way too fast, not giving him time to think of a logical solution.

"It's obvious to me why you need our help," he said. "I'm

just not confident that, after you complete your assignment and head home with Dável and his family, we'll all be safe from your army that's on its way."

Robert felt lost, alone with his survival instincts. He pictured a future in ten years where he and Katie would be fighting alone, unprotected from a power he was yet to understand and an Army bent on his destruction.

"We'll be leaving you with The Cleansing in place. I'm sure it will work this time. We'll start with the affected religious leaders, then the politicians, and finally with the corporate leaders that control your world's economy."

"Why them?"

"I thought Rebecca had told you about this problem," he said, giving his daughter a scornful look. "Only the males on your planet were affected by Dável's poison. It mutated inside every male and combined with my cleansing compound. It created the aggressive and hostile makeup that has formed your genetic signature. Have you been blind to the fact that the worst travesties on your planet have been caused by men, leaders that proclaim they act in the people's best interest?"

"I've never looked at history that way," Robert said, shrugging his shoulders.

"Believe it," he scolded. "I've been trying to eradicate this problem for a very long time and feel I've found a way. I've never given up, nor will I give up before I leave Earth for good. It's you who have to believe and use your new powers to bring peace and harmony to your ailing planet either with an olive branch or an iron fist. I'm sorry for all of this, but this is how it's got to be. Your choices will be difficult, but necessary."

His patience had been stretched by Robert's constant objective behavior. He knew if his new messenger did not begin to see things subjectively, remaining outside of his emotions with his thinking; he would never be able to make the important decisions needed to save his world. People either change or they don't. He knew Robert would be able to figure out who's lying, but unsure if he when push came to shove allow his powers to destroy all those who stand in the way for peace.

Jacob gave a disdainful look at Rebecca as if she had made a mistake by choosing this man to help them.

"What about us females?" Katie asked curiously,

attempting to direct the already heated conversation.

Rebecca had remained silent during her father's instruction and just shrugged her shoulders when Katie asked her question.

Jacob seemed pleased with her question. He turned his attention away from Robert toward Katie, giving her a warm smile. "For some unknown reason, the genetic makeup in females was not affected by Dável's poison, keeping your gender less aggressive and less hostile."

"I think these differences screwed up the world," Katie teased, elbowing Robert in the ribs for his obnoxious behavior. "What will your cleansing do?"

"It will help everyone find the meaning of life. My previous attempts failed when my words were intentionally misinterpreted by the greed of your self-proclaimed religious leaders, who used the situation to control the masses."

"Couldn't you have changed the mistakes at the beginning?" she asked.

"I did many times. The great flood, for example. I thought it would cleanse the Earth. But Dável and his followers were able to hibernate and protect themselves from the oceans that covered the Earth. As religion began to take hold, the two tribes split. And they've been fighting ever since. Moses was another mistake. As he marched out of Egypt with his people, he made a wrong turn on the desert,
missing the location I had told him about and ending up in a land that had no potential for peace and tranquility. After each attempt to cleanse Earth, Dável appeared while we were gone and infiltrated the highest positions in all the strong countries."

"But not all mankind was like Dável?" Katie asked.

"You're right. The Cleansing did work with some men, leading them on a path of righteousness and peace. For example, some of your native peoples around the world adapted to The Cleansing, discovered life's great truths, and went on to become the purest people Earth ever produced. Sadly, Dável and his corrupt army of criminals dominated the American Indians, the Eskimos, the Incas, and the Mayans, and destroyed cultures that had been affected positively by my cleansing."

Jacob looked exhausted and sad.

"Just a few more questions," Katie pleaded. "If what you say is true, that some races were cleansed, then how can you explain their violent histories?"

"History has been twisted and manipulated by the men who recorded it. Lies that are magnified bring fear into people's hearts, and these groups are easily motivated to kill. Lies have a way of sounding more true that truth itself. Hitler found this out during his Holocaust. Men are weak and scared. Fear creates prejudice and hate. The new cleansing will eliminate that."

"But won't that make all of us weak and vulnerable to our enemies? What happens if we don't have the genetic composition to defend ourselves?"

"The Cleansing doesn't remove that part of your genetic code. Using your strength as a last resort is far different than being aggressive and creating lies and situations to promote greed and power. As your bodies begin to mature, you will automatically sense the powerful control you have. You will eventually be able to make whatever choices you want, either with love in your heart, showing compassion for your fellow human beings or with indifference letting go with a furor and rage you've never experienced before. However, right now you do not have a choice or earth will be destroyed," said Jacob with an air of finality that made Robert and Katie squirm.

"How can you talk out of both sides of your mouth?" Robert said unable to control his anger. "Every other word out of you is either optimistic or pessimistic. It can't be both ways if we're going to destroy Dável's stranglehold on Earth."

"I'm not, and I don't have to explain my actions to you! It's not just destroying Dável that will solve Earth's problems. It might take hundreds of thousands, maybe millions of deaths to rid the Earth of this problem if my Cleansing doesn't fully work. It's new. It's untested and it's my last hope to save your planet," said Jacob, his voice quivering as his energy had become drained.

Rebecca stepped in front of her father, facing him with a scolding look. "It seems that you two men are ready to prove that we females need to solve Earth's problems." Then she turned to face Robert, giving him an equally strong reprimand. "I know how fearful you are, Robert. And, Father, I know how important it is to you to succeed. But arguing is not going to move us forward. Remember, we have a short time frame to work from. Our time is almost up here and we can't waste any time bickering about any of this."

Jacob stood up, shaking uncontrollably. Holding his metal staff tightly in his hand, he shuffled out of the room with Esther holding his other arm.

"I'm sorry," Robert said worriedly. "I just don't have a clue how in just twenty-two days we're supposed to accomplish everything your father expects."

"We started before you and Katie got involved," Rebecca told him.

"That's why you've been killing all these terrorists and their leaders," Robert concluded. "How many are left on this planet?"

"We believe three thousand of the strongest have survived and are still hiding out. We've already neutralized the prototype weapon, but feel that Dável is close to obtaining the data to re-create it, as well as the RX-666. This is why our time here is running short. We have to stop them before they continue to infect your planet. We need to find the data at United Weapons Systems before Dável gets his hands on it."

"Can we get down to details on how Katie and me are going to pull all of this off?"

"That's the last phase of your training. You'll be given the power to initiate The Cleansing and approximately ten years to complete your job."

"You've told us we have ten years. Why?" he asked.

"That's how long it will take the Council's army to arrive and scan your planet. Our battleships move slower than our smaller, more efficient transporters. If they don't find the necessary improvements, then you'll be destroyed."

"Wouldn't it be better for all of us to figure out how to fight these robots than proceed on a wild goose chase?"

"That would be foolish, because you will never know they're out there until it's too late. You need to activate the Cleansing and fight to save your planet."

On their laps appeared a book no larger than a Bible. The title in gold leaf letters read *The Pallasian Covenant.*

As they read the first few pages, the same mist they had breathed in the other day filled their lungs. Its sweet smell warmed their bodies as they understood for the first time the true purpose to being alive.

CHAPTER FIFTY-FOUR

Rudy Glickman the deputy director of the DOJ had no clue why CIA Director William Thomas had set up a meeting with him at United Weapons Systems. He wasn't sure if Thomas knew of his involvement with Ortiz and Mitchell or just wanted to know how the DOJ's investigation was going. To avoid seeming like he had something to hide, he agreed to meet with him.

After the deaths of his partners, Glickman had been trying to sell off his interest at United Weapons Systems and had distanced himself as far as he could from what he thought was a deathtrap. But he had found no takers. Rudy had been drinking heavily and started hearing voices soon after Robert Phillip's speech. He dismissed them as normal side effects of his drunken binges.

It was happening again, but this time the voice was singular and demonic.

"Complete the project, and I will give you the power you and your friends dreamed about."

The deep voice sounded so real inside his head. He looked around nervously as he reached inside his desk drawer for his bottle of bourbon. The booze didn't help. He was still alone.

"If you don't cooperate, you will suffer like Ortiz and Mitchell did, only worse. I won't make it quick for you like The Family did."

Now Rudy was shaking nervously, trying to light his cigarette. He felt something icy cold touch his trembling hand. His skin had become red feeling like it had rested on dry ice for an hour.

"Relax, Rudy. I'm not going to hurt you."

He had hoped he was dreaming or making the noises in his

head during his spells of paranoia. The alcohol and drugs he had been consuming since his partners' deaths clouded any sane judgment he might have had left inside his pathetic, terrified body. He sat nervously behind Allan Vincent's old oak desk, his eyes wide, rubbing the top of his left hand, his raw skin peeling off from his nervous scratching.

His hands kept shaking as he tried to pop some aspirin to relieve his massive headache. The floor-to-ceiling mirror that faced him showed the reflection of a stranger. He could not believe how he had aged. Afraid to go home, he had hidden away from everyone. He took his earned sick leave and vacation time that he had accumulated at the DOJ hoping he could make all his bad mistakes go away unnoticed. He had buried himself at United Weapons Systems—the only owner left at an albatross that his depressed mind convinced him would be his tomb.

His face was moist from sweat, and his scalp dripped as perspiration soaked his wavy hair. Five partially smoked cigarettes filled his ashtray as he inserted another one into his mouth.

Before he could take a another drag, he began to choke, not from breathing in the poison he'd been inhaling into his lungs the last few days, but from a vise-like grip around his neck. Two invisible hands pressed hard against his throat. He could not see who was trying to kill him, but he could feel his starving lungs ache as the air he needed was blocked.

Gasping in convulsive heaves, he frantically reached to remove the clamps that tried to take his life away. He could see the dark circles around his eyes in the mirror as his body thrashed wildly in his chair. He knew, as he slowly submitted to his fate, that he was about to die. As if his attacker sensed the limit of what his body could take, he felt his assailant slowly ease up on him, allowing the flow of air to enter his starving lungs.

Wheezing uncontrollably, and gasping for precious breath, Rudy jumped up from his chair only to stumble and fall helplessly to the carpet, coughing, then vomiting the remains of his nearly-empty stomach on the carpet. Unable to find the strength to get up, he rolled onto his back, his eyes searching the office for his invisible killer. His chair began to rock. The leather had an impression of a large, undetectable body. It rocked slowly, like a mother soothing her crying child. But in this case, he knew it was death ready to rock him to the permanent hell he deserved.

"Who the hell are you?" he shouted, his voice coarse, the fire in his throat burning his bruised vocal cords. His eyes frantically focused on the mold the invisible body had made on his chair.

"You can't see me," the voice echoed in his head, *"but I'm as real a nightmare as you could ever imagine."*

"You can't be real," Rudy cried.

"Oh, but I am," he said unsympathetically. *"Your meeting today with William Thomas is important to me, and I have some orders for you to carry out."*

"I can't help you," he said, "I'm sick."

He felt the grip again around his throat and raised his arms in surrender. "What do you want me to do?" he wheezed.

"Very good, and don't disappoint me. I'll be watching your every move and listening to your every thought."

It only took fifteen minutes of instruction before he knew what was expected of him. He was already a traitor to his government; he knew that. But now he was being asked to help someone he could not see build a weapon that could destroy the world, or at the very least put a madman in charge of it.

Glickman could not believe what he was being asked to do—for all he knew the voice was a figment of his imagination. He looked at his neck in the mirror and saw the bruises—the finger marks were real. He took another drink and lit up yet another cigarette, trembling and unable to get it lit, helplessly watching the match fall to the carpet.

"If this is not my imagination, then what is it?" he muttered nervously, attempting again to light the cigarette between his lips.

Director Thomas arrived thirty minutes later, accompanied by two of his agents. He signaled them to wait outside as he met with Rudy.

William Thomas, a giant of a man, instantly intimidated Glickman as he walked toward the couch at the far end of the office and sat down.

"You look like shit," the director said, barely interested. "Been in a fight? Those are some pretty bad bruise marks around your neck."

"Just having a bad day," *Lots of them since Ortiz and Mitchell died,* he thought.

He tried to straighten out the wrinkles on his slacks and

jacket before he sat down across from Thomas, but his wobbly hands were useless.

"I'll get right to the point. I know what you, Ortiz, and Mitchell had been up to. With them gone now, I'm going to be your new partner."

He watched Rudy squirm.

"You saw what happened to the two of them," Rudy said, his voice quivering. Then he began to feel the invisible hand squeeze his throat a little tighter. "Why would you risk it?"

Before Thomas could answer, Rudy added, "I'm just giving you some friendly advice. I'd be happy having you as my partner."

"Good. United Weapons Systems has developed a Photon Oscillating Rapid Firing Rifle that I want: the Pulsar XR-36. I believe it can help us defeat The Family. After what happened the other day, the world is ready for some leaders to step up to the plate and hit a home run for them. I'm that man. Are you with me?"

His intimidating stare had Rudy nodding halfheartedly. Thomas was skeptical about how easy it was going.

"I need to meet with the scientists who have created the weapon and see if we can modify its use," Thomas said, puffing on his cigar, his feet resting comfortably on the coffee table.

"When do you want to meet with them?" Rudy said shrugging his shoulders.

Thomas showed his impatience. "How about now? I'm on a short time schedule."

Dável interrupted them. *"Before you get ahead of yourselves, there will be modifications, but to my specifications."* He laughed at Thomas, who searched the room for the voice.

"You bastard, Glickman. You've had this room bugged."

"Don't blame this poor wretched soul. He was just following my orders."

"I don't know who the hell you are, but no one threatens me. Show yourself, you coward, so I can deal with you."

Rudy was laughing.

"What are you laughing at?" Thomas scowled.

"You shouldn't show such disrespect. I'm not as merciful as The Family."

His threatening tone echoed inside Thomas's head, causing him to grab his ears in a useless attempt to block out the angry voice.

"I'm not scared," he said defiantly. "Someone who feels he needs to hide and is not bold enough to face me can't be that tough."

Before he could continue, he was lifted off the couch and tossed across the room, landing against the wall mirror and cracking it as he fell to the floor.

"Oops. Now you have seven years bad luck," he taunted him. *"But that's only if I let you live that long."*

He squeezed Thomas' throat.

"Uncle!" he cried out. "I give up."

Thomas had faced death many times while serving his country and realized this was just a new enemy that under the present circumstances could be an asset to him.

"I'm sorry for my behavior. It's just who I am," he said fearlessly.

"Good. I think we can become friends. You have the same goals I have. I hope the two of you will accept me as your new partner. Here's what I expect you to do. You will need to have everything completed in twenty days or else our partnership will be terminated. And you can imagine what termination means."

His laugh echoed until it disappeared.

"Is he gone?" Rudy asked, holding his bottle of Burdon tightly against his chest.

"You're useless, Glickman. Just get me to the lab. I'll get the job done, but with a little contingency to surprise my new friend."

CHAPTER FIFTY-FIVE

Cardinal Richman stood up his arms spread wide to greet his longtime friend, Rabbi Feldman. It was more than just a "guy hug". They were like brothers.

Rabbi Feldman was the leader of the World Jewish Movement. Their goal: abolish hate and prejudice around the world. The deli on Broadway near West 116th Street was out of the way on Manhattan's upper Westside across from Columbia University. Cardinal Richman had picked this restaurant that he had frequented regularly because of its proximity to his favorite church in Morningside Park. It allowed him the pleasure of mingling with the locals, who considered this part of the city suburbia.

"Shalom," Richman said, whispering in his friend's ear and then planting a kiss on his cheek.

"Your accent, my friend, is very good. Maybe you should think of becoming a rabbi like Jesus was," he said, laughing like he always did during their get-togethers.

"That might not be too far from the truth,"
he replied with a troubled expression.

Rabbi Feldman was extremely attuned to body language and facial expressions and he immediately noticed that his friend seemed upset. "You look peculiarly distraught today, my friend. What's on your mind?"

"You're not going to believe what I have to tell you, so please keep an open mind."

"After the last few weeks and what I heard the other day from this Dável person, my mind is open to anything you might have to say."

Their table was off in a corner, away from the other patrons who hurriedly chewed on sandwiches and engaged in light, rapid conversations before they had to return to work or the university.

Cardinal Richman nervously panned the restaurant looking for a distraction. "Oh, to be young again, Abraham," the cardinal mused. "To have the world and all its glory waiting to be plucked like ripe apples from a tree. The sweet taste of life! What I wouldn't give to have that back again for this tired old body."

The Rabbi grinned at his friend's digressions. "You're way past a midlife crisis, and they still haven't invented a pill to reverse the aging process."

"I know, I know, but it's nice to dream, right?"

"So tell this tired old man what's bothering you."

* * * * *

Five tables away from them sat two stocky men of European descent, their clothing atypical of the local scene. What made them stand out were the long trench coats they wore on a day that didn't have a cloud in the sky. If the cardinal had been a suspicious man, he would have noticed how out of place they were. His companion Kubota, who was sitting a few tables away, was always suspicious and did notice.

"It's confirmed," the man facing the cardinal said into his watch. "He's meeting with Rabbi Feldman, and from what we can hear, he's about to tell him what he told the Pope. Should we stop him now?"

He toyed nervously with his medallion, which bore the seal of the *Guardians of the Cross*, the Vatican's secret police.

"Wait," the captain replied. "Let's first see what response he gets. Maybe no one will believe him, and he'll be alone fighting his windmills. With this Dável coming out of the woodwork, we might not have as big of a problem as we thought."

* * * * *

Showing no surprise, Rabbi Feldman looked skeptically at his friend as he listened to the Cardinal's message.

"That's an interesting presumption. But it's just another notion about how we all started. We've been searching for answers for over six thousand years, and I still don't know for sure what God's plan is for all of us."

"I'm not crazy or that old yet that I'm losing my faculties. How can you explain what's been happening around the world?"

"I don't have an answer, but I don't believe it's something godly. We've seen how nations have developed weapons of mass destruction. Why shouldn't I believe that Star Trek is real? Understand, I'm not sad that some of my enemies have met their maker a little sooner than they expected. I don't condone murder in any fashion or for any reason. But if the international court had tried them, they would have been sent to prison for life. So what's the harm if another form of justice is ridding us of the scum of the Earth?"

"We've known for some time that there's only one God," Cardinal Richman said. "What if the messages, the signs we received thousands of years ago, were misinterpreted? What if they were manipulated for selfish reasons? Doesn't it seem strange that Jews, Christians, and Muslims have all believed in or at least recognized the same God? We all recognize Abraham as the father of monotheism. They've just interpreted his word so drastically different that our world has not seen peace since the dawn of organized religion."

"I've stopped wondering long ago. I'm like you, a doubter, but I still do my job for the weak souls that need my encouragement."

"I met with Robert Phillips and Katie O'Riley, The Family's two messengers, and heard their story. I believe that the God we thought was God came from another planet and we've been misinformed all these years."

"I'd love to see how you're going to sell this new bill of goods to the world," the rabbi teased. "Next you're going to tell me that there's no life after death and the kingdom of heaven is not waiting for us."

"First, we have more to learn about The Family. Maybe then those answers can be resolved."

"I hope so for your crusade. Without life after death, I don't believe you'll get many followers to take your side."

"Let me arrange a meeting with a few of our colleagues for tomorrow. We'll meet with Phillips and O'Riley and see what they have to say. Can we meet back here, say around six o'clock tomorrow night?"

"I'll humor you because we go back a few years, but I won't support what you want to do, at least not at this time."

"We've known each other fifty-four years. Just trust me on this; I'm not crazy."

* * * * *

"Abe, you seem troubled. A bad day today?" Mrs. Feldman asked her husband.

"A good friend is in some trouble that I won't be able to help him with."

"That's not like you to not help a friend," she said. "It must be serious."

"It is, my dear. But, don't worry yourself, I'll work it out."

While sipping a glass of wine, he read the Torah. He began to doze, something he did like clockwork every night around ten. He was suddenly startled awake. He thought he was imagining it, but the voice got louder. He looked around his study and turned the lamp switch up another click to brighten the room. He saw no one. Then the voice filled his head.

"Cardinal Richman is correct and needs your support," the young female voice said.

"Who's speaking to me?" the rabbi asked nervously.

"I'm the one who's been ridding your world of the scum you spoke of tonight when you met with the cardinal."

"How did you know that? You must have been at a table where you could eavesdrop," he said. *She must think I'm an old fool,* he told himself.

"I don't think you're an old fool," she said, *"I just need you to believe what the cardinal has to say and help him preach the new word."*

"How did you know what I was thinking?" he said, puzzled.

"It's what I can do. So meet tomorrow with your friends and become part of The Pallasian Covenant."

"Are you this *meshuggina,* Dável?" he asked.

"No. Dável has told the world lies and will soon be punished. My father and I are the only authority you will need to obey."

"Who are you?" he called out, but the voice was gone.

"Abe, are you all right?" his wife called from the kitchen. "I hear you talking to yourself again."

"I'm fine!" he shouted ecstatically. "I'm really fine for the first time in a long time!"

CHAPTER FIFTY-SIX

"I don't like knowing that I can end a life if the solution suits me," Robert said. "In all my years as a cop, I never had to draw my gun, let alone kill anyone."

She laid her hand on his and used her other hand to massage his fingers and palm.

"We do have a big responsibility," she said, "and can't allow our old morals of right and wrong affect our judgment, or we might all be damned."

"I'm just not sure I can kill," he said wretchedly.

"I'm confident you'll do the right thing when the time comes," she said, leaning closer.

She kissed his cheek with her soft lips.

"We need to practice a few of the other new powers we have so we can be fully prepared when Jacob gives his speech."

"That'll be fun. I feel like I'm Superwoman and you're Superman."

Robert seemed distracted, in another place as he glared out the window. "What do you think of The Cleansing?"

"It makes sense, except that all the males on this planet are not going to accept giving up their dominance to us poor helpless women," she cooed. "They've had too much control for way too long to want to lose that. If they are the first that need to be changed, then we have to fool them into reading *The Pallasian Covenant,* and once that's done, there'll be no turning back for any of them."

She laughed.

"If this is the new way, then women's liberation will leap forward light-years," he smiled, rolling his eyes back, egging her on.

She gave him a bashful look as her smile wrinkled her nose, a cute habit he loved. "How bad can that be?"

They spent the next few hours digesting every aspect of The Cleansing. All the failures that Rebecca's family had made over the years astounded them.

Robert saw a flaw in what The Family had done. They had misunderstood the needs of all humans, even though the clues were staring them right in the face. Using prayer to seek answers from a divine being had hindered man's growth instead of expanding it. But, man needed answers that he could see, not his prayers of faith, or the mantras he recited. Those words or rules he had been forced to abide by did not really provide man with the whole truth he sought. Devotion was not tangible; man needed something more solid. Loyalty had turned out to be the one thing that powerful men could use to control masses of people for their selfish purposes.

The hopeless scenario that Jacob had created allowed all the powerful religious leaders to gain more and more control. The common man was considered unworthy of making important decisions and deferred to those whom he acknowledged had the wisdom to lead him and mold his quest for the truth. As Robert kept reading, he could see why most men would not question their leaders and would do their bidding in the name of God. Those who questioned their leaders were ostracized or even put to death as sick and evil people.

As prejudice and hate spread, the first cleansing went dormant, and man continued to evolve into an aggressive and war-like species. The problem Robert and Katie had was that in such a short period of time they would have to break down the barriers that man had erected and activate The Cleansing. After Dável's recent message, the world would fear anything coming from Jacob or his messengers.

Robert's mind drifted, wondering if his new powers would allow him to seek out all who would never change, no matter what proof was before them. He imagined sending out a vapor that would only affect the men with the true damaged gene, killing them upon contact. The thought of that much power gave him the shivers.

"It's a nice thought," Katie said interrupting his trance. "It could be the only way to get a jump start on what Jacob and the Supreme Council want from us."

Robert didn't seem too happy with what she said and just shrugged his shoulders unable to reply.

Katie and Robert agreed on one thing: the hardest job would be changing how the religious leaders around the world viewed God and their religions. They understood that these men would not want to relinquish the power that they had accumulated.

"Do you think your meeting with Cardinal Richman will make a difference?" Katie asked.

"If anyone can make a difference, this man can."

"He's going to piss off a lot of powerful people and put his own life in danger. I hope we can keep him safe."

"That will be a good way for us to test our new powers," he answered, jokingly putting his fists on his hips like Superman.

"You've comprehended well all that's been thrown at you these last two days," Rebecca interrupted.

"You've been listening all this time?" he remarked, surprised he has not sensed her thoughts before.

"You were distracted with other brain impulses and didn't pay attention. It will get easier for you to focus on countless thoughts around you. This will have to happen or you might be caught unaware."

"Unaware of what?" he asked, unwilling to talk to her telepathically. "Talk to me! Stop with this telepathic shit; it's exhausting, and I'm still not fully energized from yesterday's grueling training."

"Dável and his family. They're active again and ready to cause disruption. Yesterday we captured his two sons and took care of that problem. But Dável and his daughter are still out there, and they're going to be unbalanced after what we've done."

"What can we do?" he said. "I don't feel ready to engage in conflict."

"Don't try too hard, and it will be there," Rebecca said soothingly. "This is our last chance to destroy Dável and his daughter. You have to succeed or all will be lost."

Rebecca vanished, and Robert, overwhelmed, wished he and Katie were on an island, far away from their troubles. He took

Katie's hand, brought it close to his lips, and in a nonchalant way asked her to run away with him.

She was shocked to see the deep blue ocean pounding against the white sand on the beach at Sunrise Island.

"What just happened?" she asked Robert.

"I'm not sure. I was thinking of being on a deserted island with you, and here we are. I think I've just tried out one of our new powers."

"This would not have been my choice," she told him mischievously.

Just then he was standing outside Katie's house in Wexlee, Ireland, watching her sway back and forth in a wicker rocker on her porch.

"That's amazing!" she giggled loudly.

"Care to show me around?" he asked as the bright sun disappeared behind the largest puffy white clouds he had ever seen. "I can see why you love it here so much."

He was impressed with the quaintness of her parents' cottage. The antique replicas of her childhood furniture gave him a sense of how it had once looked before the British burned it down.

The living room was small. A love seat, a Queen Anne chair, and two end tables surrounded the large river-rock fireplace that had not seen use in a long time. The dining room, she told him, had been rebuilt and furnished with an exact reproduction of the dining room table and hutch that her mother and father had owned. The look on Katie's face said how much she missed her parents.

"Let's go into town," she said, pulling his arm as they darted off to the shed. "There are two bikes in the shed. I want to show you how beautiful the countryside is this time of year. I'll finish your tour in my bedroom later."

The road to the village was a mixture of dirt and rocks. They traveled the entire ten kilometers very slowly, stopping for short breaks so Katie could share her wonderful childhood memories. They stopped many times, Robert completely taken in by the green flowing grass that blanketed the hills. He was hypnotized by the gentle sway of the tall grass on the hills as the winds changed directions.

"This place is so peaceful," he told her.

"I know. That's why I came back."

She looked beautiful. Her red hair sparkled as the sun filtered through its flowing strands, caught up in the wind. The cool air flushed her cheeks, adding to the glow she already had as fond memories came surging back. She began pointing to certain sites that had some special meaning to her, explaining the folklore that was part of Wexlee.

Robert pulled her closer and gave her a big kiss and then he put his arms around her shoulders and whispered in her ear.

"When this is all over," he whispered, "can we come back and live here forever? I know that France was once our home, but that was centuries ago, when we were different people. I want to mesh my soul with yours, and Wexlee seems the right place to start."

Her eyes became moist as she looked up into his eyes, not saying a word. Nevertheless, he knew what she was thinking. They kissed once again, but this kiss was different. He felt the love she had for him and for the second time felt a release of feelings. Tears cascaded down his cheeks, which Katie kissed, capturing his emotions inside of her.

Robert looked deep into her eyes, wanting to ask her something. He had been thinking of their past marriage and wondering if they were still technically married. He wanted to renew their vows and thought Cardinal Richman would be the right person to bring them back together.

"Katie, there's something I've been thinking about."

He felt her finger against his lips.

"I know," she said. "I've been thinking the same thing. When do you—"

She was interrupted by the explosion that vibrated around their feet, breaking their tranquil embrace. Then the sky lit up with an orange glow over the village.

"Shit, they're at it again!" she cried.

"Who's at it?"

"The IRA and the British!" she screamed. Her eyes welled up as she thought about her parents and what the war had done to her country. "It was over for a time, but the hate had never gone away."

"Take us there," he begged her, "and let's see what's going on."

They materialized in front of O'Hare's Tavern, which was

right in the middle of all the gunfire. Without thinking, she raised her arms, sweeping them in opposite circular motions. In an instant, the gunfire stopped. Blank stares were affixed on the soldiers' faces as they madly tried to continue firing.

Katie walked to the center of the street, turning slowly, scanning the buildings that had become riddled with bullets.

"It's over!" she shouted. "Put your guns down and come out of hiding now."

"What are you doing?" Robert asked.

"Practicing my newly acquired powers," she said angrily.

"Go girl, go! Let's see what you've got," Robert clapped.

Two British soldiers came rushing at her, knives drawn, ready to attack this unwanted visitor. Their savage screams at first alarmed Robert, but he just watched this young, beautiful lady take charge.

The first soldier was knocked to the ground hard, hit with an invisible punch that sent him tumbling backward in the middle of the cobble stone street. The second soldier stopped to help his comrade. Seeing he was just knocked out cold, he ran toward Katie, lunging with his knife. As if he had hit a cement wall, the impact held him upright for a second, then he slid down in slow motion to the pavement, his face a bloody mess, his eyes in a daze. Seeing their friends injured, five more Brits came to their rescue.

This time Katie didn't wait for them to get close. She looked at them and watched them levitate above the buildings, suspended in midair, thrashing wildly. All that could be heard were their screams of terror.

The other men who had been fighting, including the IRA soldiers, cautiously came forward, fear written on their faces. The two tanks at opposite ends of the street were immobilized. The young British soldiers reluctantly climbed out of their vehicles, apprehension on their faces, as they looked around for their captain.

The men moved toward Katie like zombies under the control of a powerful force. Her message was brief and to the point.

"I'm Katie O'Riley and this is Robert Phillips. We're messengers sent by The Family. This fighting will stop right now," she paused, as a tingling rushed through her body. She could feel that her powers were getting stronger. Her thoughts had

begun to slip inside the soldiers' heads. The men fell to their
knees, crying, hands locked in prayer.

"Witness *The Pallasian Covenant,*" she said.

In front of all the men copies of the new holy work
materialized. Katie wasn't sure how she did it. The book was
opened to the first page. Katie read the first chant. The prayer
swam inside their heads, flowing throughout their bodies. She saw
the change take place instantly.

The street echoed from the mutterings of the men as they
chanted. Instead of firing bullets, they released years of fear and
hatred that had controlled their actions. It was seen clearly on their
faces; the pain had been removed. When it subsided, they began to
embrace one another.

"How'd you do that?" Robert asked her.

"I'm not sure. It just happened," she remarked joyfully.

"I've got an idea. Watch."

Robert blew a cool mist from his mouth that drifted like a
fast-moving fog, blanketing the town.

By the feet of each soldier and IRA dissident and inside
every home in Wexlee, *The Pallasian Covenant* appeared.
Watching the reactions, amazed the two of them. Men wept as
they read.

Katie was the first to feel it. A magical calm had come
over her town.

"This must be what The Cleansing is supposed to do," she
said to Robert, showing her thanks for what he had just done.

"Let's go somewhere else and try this," he said.

In a flash they were standing on the battered streets of the
West Bank. Robert tried to do like Katie but could not muster the
power she had shown on the streets of Wexlee. He gave her a
hopeless look and shrugged his shoulders in disbelief that there
was something he couldn't do.

"Let me try," she said, pushing him aside.

The gunfire stopped, and the same thing that had happened
in her village happened on the West Bank. Israelis and
Palestinians chanted and embraced.

Robert was not as calm as Katie had been in Wexlee, but
since the results were just the same, he accepted that Katie had
stronger powers than he did.

"You go back to Manhattan and wait for me," he said. "I

have to tie up some loose ends in Springs River."

CHAPTER FIFTY-SEVEN

Robert stood in the middle of the Springs River police department lobby. Betty, the receptionist, was startled by his abrupt materialization.

"Hi, Betty. Did you miss me?" he said, a sheepish grin on his face.

"Chief," she stammered. "How'd you do that? And yes, we've all missed you. You're a big celebrity here in Springs River."

"Is Brad here?" he asked politely. "I need to speak to him."

He saw Betty give him the strangest look and then remembered she only knew him as an impolite drunk. She seemed uncomfortable seeing her boss act and look the way he did. She eyed his trim body and clear complexion through her thick glasses. She tried to clean her glasses to be sure what she was seeing was real.

"I'll buzz him," she said finally. "He'll be relieved you're back. His golf game has gone into the toilet with all his new responsibilities."

Robert smiled. "His golf game was already in the toilet before I left; he just wouldn't admit it."

Sitting behind the chief's desk was Brad Davis. He was now the acting chief of police, and his expression told Robert how much he hated his new job. Robert wondered how he would take the news that it was now going to be permanent.

"It looks good on you," he teased his friend.

Brad started to get up, gesturing for Robert to sit behind his old desk.

"Am I glad you're back!" he said. "This town's gone crazy with all of your shenanigans. We've become a tourist town. That Cardinal Richman has marked the area where the old shack was as a possible miracle spot, and the traffic and crowds are keeping us very busy. Are you back for good now?"

"We need to talk," he said. "Let's hit the links, and I'll bring you up-to-date."

As they walked out, the rest of the department just stared. Their police chief had changed. He looked fit: younger, and sober. Before he reached the front door, Robert turned and waved goodbye. Some ducked, afraid of what he could do. They must have seen his powers on TV. The others closed their eyes, expecting some divine power to bless them. Brad did not notice what Robert was doing, because he was out the door. Robert blew them a kiss and watched the gentle mist float from his lips and blanket their bodies. They opened their eyes to find on each of their desks a book, opened to the first page.

"Read the truth and be saved," he told them, his words filling their minds.

* * * * *

Brad was the first to hit. His tee shot went straight down the middle, skimming the surface of the fairway and coming to rest about a hundred and twenty yards from the first tee box.

"Shit," he shouted. "See what your absence has done to my game?"

"It doesn't look much different than what I remember," he laughed.

Robert had not been much of golfer, either, but he had always enjoyed his time with Brad out on the course. With a slow takeaway and a rhythmic follow through, Robert's tee shot seemed to hang in the air as its velocity kept climbing before it dropped almost three hundred yards straight down the middle.

"Whew. That felt good," he smiled.

"What have you been doing? You've never been able to hit a golf ball like that before."

"Guess being sober has helped my game."

Brad hit his second shot better than his first and was about ninety yards short of the green. Robert, only forty yards from the pin, hit his second shot and controlled the ball, allowing it to land a foot from the cup. Brad continued cursing as his approach shot dropped into the sand trap. It took him another three strokes to finish the hole. For the next three hours, Robert talked about what had happened to he and Katie and their new responsibility to the world.

"Why have they picked the two of you?"

"That's still a mystery to me. They say we're some pure form of human. They've given us special powers that I'm scared to use. With just my thoughts I can end a life, just like that."

"That's got to be difficult for you. You've always been such a peaceful man, even when you were drunk."

"What frightens me is that, as I'm getting stronger, my attitude toward criminals is hardening and my patience is becoming very short. I'm terrified what will happen to me when I exercise my new gift and take a human life. I'm now judge, jury, and executioner."

"The guy I know will not fall victim to those temptations. You've been living in a snake pit for too long to go back there and become as bad as this Dável character. I'm sure you'll make the right decisions. If you have to end a life, it will only be after you've tried every alternative." Brad put his arm around his friend. "Now let's see if you can end your round the way you started it."

When they finished, Brad had shot a ninety-six and Robert a fifty-four.

"That was the most amazing round of golf I've ever seen," Davis said.

"I cheated," said Robert, embarrassed. "I used my new powers to control the ball so you could see that what I've told you is true. I won't be coming back. You'll be a great chief of police, a lot better than I ever would have been."

"What's this?" Davis said, holding up *The Pallasian Covenant*.

"Read it. It will change your life. Just trust me. I've got to go. You've been a great friend. I'm leaving you with this gift."

Brad sat alone in the golf cart, staring at the book. He breathed in a sweet tasting mist that sent tingles throughout his body. As he read the first page, he felt The Cleansing. He looked for his friend, he was gone, and understood what was happening.

"Good luck, Robert. And thank you."

* * * * *

Dável sat on his red clay throne, his hands cradling his head. He was distraught. The obstacles Jacob had created were making him angrier and angrier. He looked different to Ruth. His actions seemed more bizarre, his thinking more preoccupied with delusions of grandeur.

Ruth was not sure how she should address her father. She felt sadness for him, because she knew his plan was failing.

"These two have some very special powers that could prove troublesome to us," she said to her father.

"Not if we destroy them before they get stronger," he answered curtly. His eyes were like molten lava as he watched his daughter slump her shoulders in fear.

"What about the weapon?" she asked.

"We've got time. Let's deal with Katie and Robert first. And this time stay calm so we can use them," he scolded her. His mood seemed to turn against his daughter.

"It's not going to be easy this time. They have powers they didn't have before."

Dável's face turned fiery red. The vapors from his nostrils looked like steam.

"Robert still has his doubts toward Jacob," he said, jumping up from his seat. "Maybe a little manipulation can provide a nice opening for us, and then it will be too late for Jacob and his messengers to react."

His piercing laughter bounced off the hard clay walls, hurting Ruth's ears.

CHAPTER FIFTY-EIGHT

Cardinal Richman tried to read his friend's face. Archbishop Stallsworth had not shown any reaction to what he had heard. He then looked at his other friend, Abdeljalil Tahmass, the Islamic cleric leader in the United States, whom he called Jalil because it was easier to remember.

Jalil seemed interested, but wanted to meet with Katie and Robert first. The cardinal wished he had a copy of *The Pallasian Covenant.*

Rabbi Feldman had sat quietly, squirming occasionally, adjusting his tie as he waited and listened pensively. He wasn't sure if he should tell them about the voice. Had it been his imagination?

Cardinal Richman looked over at Rabbi Feldman, hoping for some support.

"Help me here. You believe, don't you?"

Rabbi Feldman nodded. "I do think there's a possibility that what we've understood for so long to be God and religion might be wrong. I'm not saying that God is nonexistent; He's just not what we thought him to be." Feldman wanted to say more, but he held his tongue about the voice.

They paid their check and decided to continue their meeting at Saint John's Episcopal Cathedral by Morningside Park, where they could have more privacy.

They strolled leisurely through the Columbia University grounds, acknowledging the students who were rushing by to make their next class.

They were an interesting sight to see: the cardinal, in his red and black robe; the archbishop, with his reversed collar; Jalil,

in his flowing robe with a hood that covered the top of his head;
and the rabbi, dressed in black, his yarmulke fastened tightly to his
head. The students passing by did a double take, grinning at the
four of them decked out in their religious garb.

Lagging a hundred yards behind them were two of the
Guardians of the Cross that waited for the appropriate moment to
end Cardinal Richman's folly.

Behind all of them strode Kubota, his watchful eye alert, his
body ready to protect the man he loved.

Rabbi Feldman had always found Saint John's Cathedral a
masterpiece of God's work in progress. The large ornate metal
doors were embossed with religious friezes that should have been
preserved in a museum.

"You Christians have always known how to build a house
of God," he joked.

They walked toward the back of the cathedral, passing the
most beautiful sculptures, exhibits supporting poets, and
monuments that acknowledged other religions. The vaulted
ceilings went hand in hand with the openness that was practiced in
this house of God.

"If what you say is true," the archbishop began, "then we
have a major problem. The difficult task will be re-teaching the
truth of God and implementing it throughout the world. It won't be
easy to explain that we have misinterpreted all these centuries the
meaning of God. I for one will need more proof than what I've
heard today. I hope you have a plan."

"I agree," the cardinal said. "I've been having the same
confusing thoughts. And no, I don't have a plan. Maybe when we
meet with Robert and Katie it will become clearer."

Rabbi Feldman at first hesitated, then he interrupted the
two men. "I had a visitor last night."

The cardinal seemed amused at his comment. "A visitor,"
he grinned.

"It was a voice inside my head. It told me to trust you and
believe in a new message, some type of truth."

The archbishop gave his friend a contemptuous look.
"How much schnapps did you have last night, Abraham?"

"I've heard the voices, too," the cardinal jumped in. "This
family has powers that are far beyond our imagination. This just
may be the voice of God and his angels giving us one last chance.

Moses heard a voice. So did Mohammad."

The archbishop didn't know what to believe. But he trusted his friends. "I hope their messengers, Robert and Katie, will have those answers for us."

Jalil had been listening and finally put his opinion out in front of his friends. "If this is true, and believe me, I want it to be true, maybe my people can find some real peace in their lives. For Islam, it's easier than you think to inject a new theory. Most want to have peace and grow old in a calm and tranquil world. We do have some fanatics who have bastardized our religion, but once the masses fall in line, they too will have lost their desire to inflict terrorism on all non-Muslims."

"The meeting's tomorrow at the Plaza Hotel at twelve-thirty," the cardinal told them.

* * * * *

"Your Grace," the security officer following Cardinal Richman said to Cardinal Gironde, "Archbishop Stallsworth, Islamic cleric Abdeljalil Tahmass, and Rabbi Feldman appear to be in support of the cardinal's blasphemy. What would you like us to do?"

"You said they're meeting with the messengers tomorrow?"

"Yes, at twelve-thirty at their hotel."

"Silence Cardinal Richman tomorrow," Cardinal Gironde ordered. "Then it will be over."

"Yes, Your Excellency," the guard reluctantly said.

* * * * *

Esther had been monitoring the surveillance of the Guardians of the Cross. She walked into the next chamber and handed the printout to her husband as he reviewed it with his children.

"Should I stop them now, Father?" Rebecca asked.

"No, let's see how Robert reacts. He has to test his powers. Besides, our web is being nicely woven to catch Dável."

Rebecca was the first to feel it.

"Father," she said, "I'll remain close just in case."

She knew what was happening. The red diode on her wristband kept blinking. She was in a frenzied panic. She signaled her father and brothers to be silent.

She accelerated her metabolism to ten times normal,

reaching a higher frequency that she knew Dável could not scan. Her father and brothers followed her lead.

Flushed with rage, she looked at her father. "Father, we've been compromised. They've discovered our frequency."

"I know; I've sensed it also. He's testing his ability to find us, so when he has the weapon, he'll know where to look. It's only Ruth doing it. Dável must be watching Robert and Katie."

"I don't know how long I can stay at this rate without draining what little power I have left," Rebecca said. "I'm frightened Dável will win this time. We're all running out of time."

"Don't worry; he can't harm us yet. Robert will handle them. Don't agonize so much, everything will be all right."

* * * * *

Esther was alone at her communicator ready to give the Council her weekly update. She had to whisper in order to avoid being detected by her family. She was saddened by the deception she was forced to commit. But she had no choice.

CHAPTER FIFTY-EIGHT

CIA Director William Thomas watched patiently through the soundproof glass as three UWS scientists worked hurriedly to complete the Pulsar XR-36 and the RX-666. Rudy Glickman sat nervously, puffing on his cigarettes. He kept looking around to see if someone was in the booth with them.

"Get a grip, Glickman," Thomas said. "The boogeyman is not coming to get you..."

"Boo!"

Glickman jumped out of his chair and looked up, his eyes swollen. Thomas guffawed.

"I don't understand how you can remain so calm after what happened to you," Glickman said, snuffing out another half-finished cigarette.

Thomas remained composed as he thought of alternatives for his problem.

You're crazy, he told himself. *Dável is just a man. Soon I'll have the power, and then we'll see who'll be dishing out the fear tactics.*

He was startled by the cold hand on the back of his neck. *"Don't wish for something you won't be able to handle."*

He couldn't move as the cold air flowed over his body, paralyzing him.

"Show yourself, you bastard!" he shouted, trying to break free.

Rudy dove under a table when he saw Thomas being grabbed by his invisible friend.

"I like it that you're not scared of me," the voice said

menacingly. *"With my help, you can be a very powerful person after we destroy The Family. I've helped many men over the last five thousand years have the power they've always wanted. It could have worked well for Hitler, but he was too crazy and had a big ego. I like crazy, but don't ever think you can beat me. You can't. What I give I can easily take away."*

"I need to know who I'm dealing with," Thomas shouted again, refusing to speak to Dável telepathically. "If we're going to work together, I should be able to meet you face-to-face."

"In due time. I'm a lost patriot who has been fighting against The Family for too long to remember. They're attempting to control Earth and all its inhabitants. With the Pulsar XR-36 and RX-666, I can focus on their weaknesses, and we can defeat them. Then I can restore my people to the position we had a long time ago."

"How do I know you're not the bad guy and just want to control Earth like your enemy does?"

Dável became uneasy as he listened to Thomas' ridiculous questions. His mood changed, and a demonic laugh filled the observation room. Without warning, he clutched Thomas' throat, slowly compressing his larynx, enjoying the sensation that such a big man was being drained of life. He saw Glickman crawl out from under the table and cower in a corner by the door.

With what little voice he could muster, Thomas sent up a white flag. "All right, you're the man. I won't defy you anymore." Dável dropped him like a sack of potatoes to the cold hard cement floor.

Thomas slowly stood up, coughing uncontrollably, as he adjusted his shirt. A smile of respect came over his face for this powerful partner he believed was now his friend.

"I've moved up your schedule. I need the RX-666 done in two days. Forget about the XR-36 for right now."

"That's impossible," Thomas said. "We'll be lucky to make the original deadline."

"I've lost my two sons and won't tolerate any objections!" Dável screamed, out of control. Thomas put both his hands tightly on his head, acting like he had the worst headache. *"Just get it done, or you and your friend will suffer the worst possible death you can imagine."*

He was gone as quickly as he had arrived, and Thomas just

stood there laughing, an eerie, nervous laugh that was out of control.

"He's nuts," Thomas said out loud. *If he's going mad, then his powers must be getting weaker.*

Rudy wrapped his arms around his knees and rocked back and forth. "Don't get too overconfident. We have to do what he wants."

"You'll see that your big, bad friend is not so tough," Thomas bragged, puffing out his chest. "Now get up, you sniveling piece of shit. The weapon needs to be completed in two days, or we're both fucked. You remain here and make sure these guys work around the clock to get it done."

CHAPTER FIFTY-NINE

Jacob's sons David and Ian had returned. Their report was not good. The dismantling of weapons by most countries had come to a complete halt. It appeared that Dável's message had made an impact. Most countries had begun to appease him rather than The Family.

"Father, it seems that man has reverted back to his basic instincts of distrust and fear," David said. "We've got to set an example or Dável just might win."

If there was any good news for David to report, it was that smaller countries that had a stronger religious foundation sided with The Family. They had dismantled their weapons and siphoned money to the poor countries around them, happily assisting their neighbors to increase their standard of living.

David's list of troublemakers was long, but it appeared that Japan, China, Germany, Iran, and France had other plans.

"What shall we do, Father? You give me the word and I'll punish them."

"I'm surprised at their arrogance. However, what I don't understand is how they could believe Dável's message. I think you're right: we need to set an example. But Robert should be the one."

"Father!" he pleaded. "This is my job."

"It's time for this planet to stand on its own two feet. The Council's army will be here soon enough and will solve the problem if Robert and Katie haven't."

"I think we've put Earth in this position," Rebecca argued, "and should find a more logical solution than totally turning it over to Robert and Katie."

"We've been trying for way too long. This is our last effort, and if it fails, then we fail. We'll then go home as failures and face the consequences. I won't hear any more arguments from any of you. Do you hear me? We can't solve this problem for them. We've given the two of them enough of our powers. It's time for Earth to cure their planet."

"Calm down!" Esther said noticeably upset. "This time it will all work out; you'll see. Rebecca has done a remarkable job. Don't scold her. She still has a romantic vision. Her desires are not malicious, just quixotic."

Jacob didn't like being reprimanded by his wife, especially in front of his children. He gave all of them a scornful look and stormed off the bridge as fast as his feeble body could move.

Esther, as if nothing had happened, went back to looking at her monitor. Her children stood dumbfounded.

CHAPTER SIXTY

Katie and Robert reserved a small meeting room at the Plaza.
They laid out a full buffet of cold cuts, breads, salads, and pastries.

The four men were a contradiction. To their parishioners,
they were living saints. But to Robert and Katie, they were just
men who wanted to help save a troubled world, no matter how
their respective religions fared.

Robert almost didn't recognize Cardinal Richman. He was
dressed in khaki slacks, a light blue oxford shirt, a dark blue
blazer, and penny loafers, with pennies tightly affixed to the shoes.
If it weren't for the baseball cap with the crucifix above the brim,
he could have been anybody.

Rabbi Feldman had dressed a bit more conservatively. Dark
Blue tweed sport coat, with a blue and white tie with multiple Stars
of David imprinted on it. The archbishop wore light denim jeans, a
Loyola University sweatshirt, and running shoes sans socks.
Abdeljalil Tahmass looked like a hippy in his tie-dyed shoulder-to-
floor robe.

The four of them looked like a ragtag group of college
professors attending a teacher's conference, ready to cut loose
when the meeting was adjourned. Robert greeted his guests and
made sure everyone was introduced to Katie. After some
pleasantries, they all sat down at one large round table. It was
Katie's idea to keep everyone relaxed and comfortable.

Robert hoped that the meeting would go down in history: Newsflash-six ordinary people had come together from different walks of life and saved the world. He stared at them. Their eyes told the story. Robert knew they had come to help. For the first time in a long time, he had a broad smile on his face as he thought about his plan.

"I want to thank each of you for coming," he said. "I hope Cardinal Richman has filled you in on *The Pallasian Covenant.*" Robert was pleased that all three heads nodded in unison.

"What lies ahead of us is, well, more than reinterpreting God's word. The world as we now know it will be destroyed if we cannot get everyone to comply with The Family's demands."

Cardinal Richman lifted his baseball cap and scratched his head. "What do you mean by *destruction?* You didn't tell me our world might be destroyed. This throws a different light on things."

"I'm sorry," Robert said awkwardly. "I didn't think it would make much difference in how each of you could do your part. I didn't mean to deceive you."

Rabbi Feldman loosened his tie and wiped the sweat from his forehead, looking a little shaken at the finality of Robert's words.

"Who's going to destroy us? Can we negotiate? Our world does not have such a good track record when it comes to hate and prejudice. If we can't change that part of our human nature, war will continue to go on."

"Then we have a lot of work to do and not much time," Robert said apprehensively.

"How do you know we've agreed to help?" the archbishop interrupted in a calm, low voice. "I, for one, need more information and proof that we're not being lead down the wrong path. I'd like to see this *Pallasian Covenant.*"

"That's going to be part of what I'm going to tell you today. I only warn you that what I'll be telling you will sound like some science fiction novel. Trust me: it's not fiction. In fact, what've once believed was God with all the heaven and hell aspects was the true science fiction.

Both he and Katie spent the next two hours bringing the four men up-to-date, explaining why it was important that all the weapons of destruction on Earth be dismantled. They gave them examples of their new powers, and Robert laid out his plan to save the world.

"It seems that history recorded the events that guided our religions," Cardinal Richman said. "But they manipulated the true facts to gain power over a weak human race. How are we going to change the world's belief that God as we've known Him did not create the Heavens and Earth and that he's actually an alien from another planet?"

"Maybe we won't have to," Archbishop Stallsworth said calmly. "We've reinterpreted the Bible from time to time and introduced new ideas."

"That's true," Rabbi Feldman said, "but it was done through our religious leaders, at their discretion, and not through our congregations. We all know how competitive all the sects are and how egotistical their leaders can be. It will be impossible to get all of them to agree, let alone, change, on this new theory."

"The Vatican has suspected for some time that God is not the divine being we've idolized him to be," the cardinal said. "There are documents in the Vatican's archives that support other alternatives to God's existence. My fellow cardinals and the Pope have treated followers like children who need an easy, believable lie about God, His teachings, and the afterlife. If a new theory were to be proven correct, it would destroy the Catholic Church. They did not receive my words well on my last visit."

"I can't believe that the Church has kept these archives hidden," Katie said. "How arrogant."

"It was not arrogance," the cardinal explained, "but fear of putting the world in a panic. People need the hope, faint as it might be that a higher being is out there protecting them as long as they obey God's laws."

Katie didn't seem to be buying his answer, as she bit her lip. "Can we get those documents and verify the information?"

"The Guardians of the Cross, the Vatican's Secret Service, watch over the archives. They're protected better than Fort Knox."

"I guess the Ten Commandments are not their mission statement," Katie said sarcastically.

"Have you seen these documents?" Robert asked the cardinal.

"I worked on the project to interpret them."

"Do you remember what you saw?" Katie asked.

"I can do better than that," he said, handing a manila folder to Katie. "I've kept my notes and the copies I scanned just in case I needed them for a special day. I guess today is that day.

Cardinal Richman took in a deep breath, knowing perfectly well the can of worms he was opening up. "What we, the Vatican, have been able to discern is that Nostradamus was a space traveler who intentionally came to Earth to settle here. The pages from his logbook, which I was able to copy, were deciphered. But, we're still unclear about where he came from or what his purpose was here. The leaders of the Church intentionally misinterpreted Nostradamus' writings and made his predictions conform to biblical doctrine.

Katie intently read through the file, surprised that she could understand his language. Nostradamus had written in an ancient sacred language used by scholars on Pallas. It was a mixture of Arabic and Hebrew.

"Nostradamus was one of them," she told Robert telepathically. *"He mentions Jacob and the family. I think he was Rebecca's uncle and traveled here on his own to try to help his brother."*

"Why haven't they told us about him?"

"It appears that he died twenty years after arriving, when his brother was on one of their return trips back to their planet."

"What was he trying to do?"

Katie tried to hide what she was doing from the other, but the expressions of their faces told her they could tell she was keeping a secret. She continued anyway. *"He was trying to enlighten everyone about The Cleansing, but he failed because the religious leaders didn't take him seriously. They thought he was senile. I think he was forecasting the future as a way to show the world what to expect if Dável's poison was not removed from their souls.*

"Are you two all right?" Rabbi Feldman asked.

"We're fine," Robert said. "Just baffled by what's in this file."

"I believe you know what it all means, judging by the surprised look on your faces," the archbishop remarked.

"We do," Katie said, "and it throws a whole new light on what we already know. It seems that Earth has been visited by these space travelers for thousands of years and not just by The Family. Other than the ultimatum we've been given, there might be another reason why we're being asked to weaken our defenses. I'm just not sure what it might be."

"What do we do now?" Cardinal Richman asked.

Before Robert could answer, Jalil stood up. "You keep calling this group The Family. Don't they have names?"

Robert seemed surprised at his question, and he bristled at the thought of another possible deception by Jacob. His face contorted as he slammed the file down.

"I'm sorry if I upset you," Jalil said.

"I wasn't reacting to your question," Robert said. "It's just that I don't think we've been told everything about these travelers and their true purpose. I can give you their names. Jacob is the father, Esther is the mother, Rebecca is the eldest, and David and Ian are the two sons. You should know the names of Dável's children. Ruth is his eldest, and Ian and Cain are his sons. His sons have been recently captured by Jacob, and only Ruth and Dável are left on our planet."

"Rebecca, I feel you," Katie said loudly. "You've been listening, so tell us about your uncle."

Everyone in the room sat straight up.

"They need to be able to hear you? So, if you're willing to speak to them, please don't use your telepathic abilities."

"That's reasonable," Rebecca said aloud. "I want all of you to understand about my uncle. We've always known that other scientists from Pallas traveled to Earth, but for observation purposes only. Their orders were to never conduct experiments or interfere with my father's project.

"When we returned home during your sixteenth century, my uncle, who loved his brother more than life itself, vanished and was never seen again. Upon our return, we discovered that he had settled on Earth in 1536 somewhere in France. We found his logbook in the Vatican's archives and discovered he had tried to set in motion The Cleansing. He hoped when we returned in the next century the planet would be functioning as originally planned."

"It didn't happen, did it?" Robert asked sarcastically.

"Sadly enough, it backfired on him. After slowing down his metabolism and functioning as a normal human on Earth, he started to age at an accelerated rate. He expressed the words and messages from The Cleansing poorly due to the onset of schizophrenia. They were considered the ambiguous ramblings of a madman."

"It seems that no matter what your family does," the cardinal said, "The Cleansing does not work."

"It can work," Rebecca replied desperately. "It just has to be implemented by all of you so that your world will believe."

A copy of *The Pallasian Covenant* sat in front of each man, giving off a static charge that instantly traveled through each of their bodies.

"You now have the new word that needs to be spread to every male on this planet. Begin with your religious leaders and then move toward the political leaders. Inside each male is a chemical that has been blocked for centuries, and *The Pallasian Covenant* will ignite the fuse and trigger The Cleansing."

"What about all the females?" Rabbi Feldman asked.

"Katie can fill you in on that phenomenon. I've got to go now. I will keep in touch."

Then she was gone.

Katie stared with a devilish grin at the four men.

"All I can say is that men have had the luxury of screwing everything up until now," Katie winked at the four of them. "But that will change. I think I know a way to trigger The Cleansing and give us a head start on bringing some order to this planet and letting man's feminine side blossom."

Robert just sat there and listened. He felt proud to watch the woman he loved show her assertiveness. Her red hair seemed on fire as her face glowed with fervor.

"We must go and begin our work," Cardinal Richman said. "I'm off to get another audience with the Pope. This time he must listen."

The archbishop had already made appointments with the leaders of the Church of England before coming to the meeting. Rabbi Feldman told everyone he was going to meet with the members of his organization before leaving for Israel. Jalil was silent as he wondered how his religion would accept these new words, especially regarding the defect in men's hearts and the superiority of women. The new terrorist order of Islam enjoyed their power too much to let it be taken away without a fight.

They were out of the room, and with them went the hopeful energy that would save Earth.

CHAPTER SIXTY-ONE

"Bravo! Bravo!" Dável cheered, clapping loudly. *"Excellent performance."*

"*Dável,*" Robert answered with an air of confidence. "*I've been hoping you'd stop by for a visit.*"

"I've been meaning to have both of you over for coffee and cookies, but I've been a bit occupied trying to save my life," he mocked. *"I've come to offer you a deal that will save your planet."*

"*What could you possibly have to offer us that we don't already have?*" Robert responded.

"A way to defeat the Council's army. I know how they operate. And I know how to stop them from destroying Earth. They're not coming to evaluate your planet. They're coming to see if The Cleansing has taken effect so they can overtake your planet and build a new race of super-humans to help fight their enemies in their solar system."

"*I'm listening,*" Robert said. "*But understand, I know what you and your daughter tried to do to us once before at our chateau. You've lied before, and I suspect you'd lie again to save your family.*"

I'll never forgive you for killing my children, Katie interrupted. *So you better be truthful, or I'll kill you right here and now!*

    First, Katie disappeared to Robert's amazement. Then, he too vanished. They were both staring at Dável; his stunned look mesmerized them as he adjusted his robe. He did not look as old as Jacob; his short beard and long flowing red hair were not characteristics they had imagined. His height was commanding at six feet, four inches. His arms appeared old, but very muscular, like a construction worker's. His eyes were the eyes of a madman. His mannerisms were akin to those of the mentally disturbed that roamed the cold city streets.

    "Your powers are stronger than I had imagined," he said, his head twitching as he looked at them.

    "You haven't seen anything yet," Robert said impetuously.

    Dável could see they were looking at him with contempt.

    "Excuse my condition," he said. "This is what happens when people from our planet cannot regenerate. But, believe me when I say my mind is very lucid. Don't judge me by my appearance or you will underestimate my abilities. I've been like this for thousands of years."

    Dável appeared nervous. He had for century's evaded capture, and now these two humans were staring at him, something no one from Pallas had been able to accomplish since his escape from prison. Nevertheless, he attempted to tell them about Jacob and his family and what they had been doing since Mars had been destroyed. He explained that what they had been told by Jacob was a lie. That he was not the one who had poisoned the Earth. What had happened was the result of all the experiments that were conducted on the first inhabitants.

    "They've been trying to build a super race to use as their army."

    He continued to come across as very believable. He countered everything Rebecca and her father had told them, making a case like a good defense lawyer would do when arguing for his client. He told them that Jacob's plans rested on a belief in the ineluctable superiority of raw power.

    Dável, his eyes like empty pools of black oil said. "The mass murders you've witnessed these last few weeks are a good example of how Jacob intends to break down Earth's resolve and take control, using both of you as his surrogates."

    Robert seemed puzzled. "What about the murders you've done

to the young and innocent these last few weeks also? You do not have clean hands either."

Dável ignored his remarks. "Look at how Earth has progressed;" he told them, "Do you really believe that you have evolved from a poison I created? You flatter me."

Katie looked at Robert and knew he was drifting toward Dável point of view.

"Your story might be believable," Katie said, "except as I read your thoughts, I can tell you are lying to us."

Dável looked surprised. "You can't read my mind without my knowledge!"

"You don't have a clue what I can do—" Katie said her tone filled with contempt. She noticed the fear in Dável's eyes and tried to grab him.

Dável disappeared without any warning.

"Shit, we had him."

They were standing alone in an empty void. They returned to their hotel room, digesting their first confrontation with Dável.

"How did you do that?" he asked her.

"I'm not sure, but I'm glad I did. He was very believable."

"What about what he told us about the Council's army and how these new weapons could defeat them?"

"I'm not sure. Let's keep this to ourselves. I'm not sure Rebecca and her father would understand our talking to Dável and not capturing him."

CHAPTER SIXTY-TWO

Katie and Robert found Rebecca more easily than they had anticipated. She was startled, finding them inside the transporter.

Robert was not smiling as he faced her. His thoughts were not hidden or clouded. He wanted to confront Rebecca and her family. However, he ruled on the side of caution. He controlled his anger as he fought with himself to make the right decision.

"Rebecca, we met with Dável yesterday. He came to us, and we talked to him face-to-face."

She was shocked.

"In all the years we've chased after him, we've never seen him," she said. "Your powers are stronger than we thought. Don't misunderstand me—that's a good thing."

"He's very convincing," Robert said, watching her reaction. "We have some questions."

"Okay," she blushed. "Speak to me."

"Why would you choose Katie and me for this job, when there are more qualified people? Cardinal Richman and Rabbi Feldman, for example, would have been perfect choices."

"It's very complicated. Let's just leave it at that. You don't need any more surprises."

Katie rolled her eyes in disbelief. "After what you've had us do for you, I can't imagine anything that could shake me up anymore. Dável has said some very disturbing things about you and your family and what your true purpose is here on Earth."

"I agree with Katie," Robert said. "I want to know everything, and now!"

"Let's get back to your hotel. You'll thank me later for this suggestion."

Rebecca seemed nervous about talking on her ship. She kept her voice low as she tried to hush Robert.

Robert looked at her with contempt. "I'm not going anywhere until you answer this one question. Have we been bred to become slaves for your planet?"

Rebecca seemed genuinely surprised at his question. "That's ridiculous! My father has tried to make this planet a utopia, free from hate and prejudice. He has always hoped for one world with cooperation and freedom for everyone."

"How can I believe either one of you?" Robert scowled. "We could just be pawns in a political experiment that went awry. I'm still not convinced that your fear of our planet possibly threatening your world is the only reason you're here."

"The threat is real," she said, hurt. "Especially if Dável gains power. He knows far too much about our world, our weaknesses, and space travel. If he builds his army with the Pulsar XR-36 and RX-666, we could be at war with your planet within twenty years. I've told you that The Cleansing will defeat Dável and possibly save your planet."

She was on the verge of tears.

"What's this 'possibly save our planet?' All I know," he sighed, "is that we're not even close to space travel of the magnitude you're talking about. And without proof from you or Dável, it comes down to 'he said, she said.'"

"Why would we give you the powers you have, if we were not sincere about what we're doing here?"

"I'm not sure about that. Maybe it's only temporary until you achieve your goals."

"I can tell you that your powers cannot be taken away once your cells have changed," she said, aggravated by the two people she had thought she could trust. "You'll have to believe us or not believe us. It's your choice. Our only mistake has been our inability to maximize the potential of everyone's brain electrical impulses sooner. Dável, believe it or not, has been keeping your planet in its infant stage for thousands of years. That's the only way he can remain in control. Now my father's cleansing agent can reverse that and rid your world of your own poison. You've already seen how The Cleansing has worked. Why do you still doubt my father's sincerity?"

Katie smiled. She had been reading Rebecca's thoughts and knew she was telling the truth.

"Robert, leave her alone," she said. "I believe her more than I believe that bastard Dável."

He felt Katie had sideswiped him. He had hoped she would have doubts, lending him some support as he searched for the right answers. He had agreed to listen to Rebecca's explanation, under protest. He told them he was reserving judgment until he could sort out all the facts.

"Stop for just a minute and don't think like a detective," Katie scolded him. "You've been given an opportunity to do something of great magnitude. Your attitude that mistakes are a flaw, a deception of sorts that cannot be trusted, is bullshit. Rebecca is human like us; her father and mother feel pain like we do. Have some compassion. Open your heart and mind to the fact that they are the ones to be trusted, not that madman, Dável."

Robert blushed. He kept silent as he listened to Rebecca continue her explanation. It took her two hours to make clear what the Council expected of them. The job was a difficult one: to get the attention of the world in an unrealistic time frame.

It seemed impossible to Robert at first. He protested, not comfortable with what he had to do. Once Katie reasoned with him again, he finally realized that, for the good of the majority, it would have to be done, and done swiftly, without hesitation or remorse.

Rebecca seemed relieved that Robert was supporting her wishes. She could see that their powers had grown stronger, and she was hopeful that the new caretakers of Earth would succeed against a stubborn world and an unpredictable Dável. She knew that by all indications Dável was functioning like a wounded animal, ready to do anything to survive.

Rebecca was now more frightened than ever. She knew that Dável if he lost all hope to survive, like a suicide bomber, take his life in a way that would destroy Earth.

CHAPTER SIXTY-THREE

Cardinal Richman had sent Kubota ahead to bring his car around. His bodyguard protested, not feeling right about leaving him alone. He had parked the car a distance from the elevators on Level 2 of the hotel's garage.

Kubota initially wanted to use valet parking, but the Cardinal insisted that he did not want to spend the church's money frivolously. It was the same argument they had had many times before, but today his gut told him he should have been sterner, he was in fact in charge of protecting his friend. He instinctively knew something was wrong and became alert as he approached the Lincoln Mark VII. It felt like a trap had been set.

A second after he inserted the keys in the car door, a man came at him from his right. He then saw, out of the corner of his left eye, another attacker approach. His space to fight adequately had been limited to a two-foot area between two cars.

His body remained facing the Lincoln as he thrust his right leg out from his side, striking the first man's breastbone and cracking it with one powerful thrust. The first attacker fell like a rag doll. No screams, he was out cold.

The second attacker was too close for a second kick with his left leg. Kubota, with lightning speed and force, double-punched the second man—his two fists moving in lightning speed across his chest to its target. He felt his hands break rib bones. Then his fingers penetrated the skin under the rib cage, grabbing the wounded man's heart. With one hard squeeze, the man's life had stopped.

The cardinal! he thought. He stepped over the body that was to his right and began to run toward the elevators, fearing that his friend was in mortal danger.

He was just twenty-five yards from the elevator when he saw the cardinal walk toward the waiting area. He tried to call out, to tell him to get back into the elevator away from the impending danger. His words became muffled, hard to get out of his screaming mind. He felt a sting on the side of his neck, and pulled a dart out of his skin. He tried to force himself to remain strong, but whatever drug had been put on the dart had a very quick and powerful effect on his body. He was on the cold cement floor, fighting to get up, but could only watch in horror.

An officer from the Guardians of the Cross came out of the darkness toward Cardinal Richman. He had his orders and regretted having to carry them out on such a great man. He had the greatest respect for this man and the unselfish devotion he had given all of his life to the people of the world. But, he had a job to do, and did not want to upset Cardinal Gironde.

A white panel van cut off the cardinal before he reached the area where Kubota was to have brought his car. He saw his bodyguard lying face down on the cement driveway, not moving. He tried to go over to assist him when he felt someone behind him push him abruptly toward the panel door that had slid open. He stumbled and tried to reach for something to grab onto, when two more men grabbed him and pulled him into the vehicle. He banged his head hard on the bare metal floor of the van, passing out as they sped out of the garage and toward the private jet that waited to take them back to Vatican City.

After twenty minutes, the cardinal began to stir, propping himself up against side of the van and rubbing the blood off his forehead. He felt the warm blood from the wound on his head sting his eye. He forced tried to shake the fog from his head.

"I've been waiting for you," the cardinal said, seeing the astonished looks on the men's faces. "Did you harm my friend?"

"He'll have a bad headache when he wakes, but he will be okay, unlike two of my men."

"I'm sorry for that, but his job is to protect me and risk his life if necessary."

The guard gave the cardinal a look of contempt. "He didn't do that great a job, your Grace."

"I've been serving the Church for too long to not know that your orders existed and that my friend Cardinal Gironde feared what I was doing." His voice was calm, his mood very congenial.

"I'm sorry for what we're about to do to you," the young guard said, unable to look at him, "but we have our orders and must obey."

Cardinal Richman reached out and touched the guard's leg, patting it gently. "I'm happy I had time to receive *The Pallasian Covenant,* that the world must hear before I die," he replied without any expression.

He opened the book and began to read the first message.

First, a light mist was released, as the words traveled lightly on the air and was breathed in by the men. To the cardinal's amazement, the transformation had begun. The men fell on their knees, grabbing for his hand, begging for his forgiveness.

He closed the book in wonderment. The sparks that tingled through his body as he touched the book had given him the power to speak The Pallasian Covenant and ignite what he hoped had been The Cleansing.

"I can't wait to hear how it went for the others," he mumbled softly. "They are in for a wonderful surprise." He now prayed that it was going to go this easily when the court of Cardinals and Pope met with him.

CHAPTER SIXTY-FOUR

President Hopkins sat at his desk in the Oval Office, looking out past the lawn, his stare fixed on the Washington Monument.

"I'm making a big mistake."

"A mistake, sir? What kind of mistake are you talking about?" Thomas remarked apprehensively, wondering if Hopkins had found out about his current dealings with United Weapons Systems.

The president spun his chair around, his eyes riveted on his CIA Director. "I'm not comfortable disrupting the UN meeting and what The Family has to say. They've only showed aggression toward the true enemies of the free world. Maybe we can learn from them."

"I think you're failing to appreciate the severity of what's been going on," Thomas objected adamantly. "We're being held hostage by an unknown power that, if left unchecked, could imprison us."

"Sorry, I'm pulling the cameras and our agents. Do you have a problem with that?"

"I hear you, sir. And for the record, I object. But you're the boss."

Thomas excused himself and left. The color returned to his face; he was relieved that he had not been found out.

The president's secretary stuck her head inside his office. "FBI Director Smith on line one."

"Gail, what have you got for me?" President Hopkins asked.

"Thomas has been meeting with Rudy Glickman at United

Weapons Systems. They're up to something. Our surveillance can't penetrate their security!"

She was agitated. She tried to hide it, but was pissed that her lover had betrayed her and more than likely used her. She was now going to make him pay and keep her promise.

"Weren't we supposed to close them down and confiscate all their research data?" President Hopkins asked.

"That was stopped after Allan Vincent died. Glickman put his signature on the order to stop the takeover by the DOJ and my office."

"What's Glickman's involvement in all of this?"

"I'm not sure, but trust me, I'm going to find out!"

"Get in there and close them down today, and lock it down. No one goes in there without written authority from me. I don't want any research data leaving that facility."

"I'll be back to you this afternoon," she said before hanging up.

President Hopkins was beginning to wonder what was happening to his country. First his military tried a coup, and now it appeared his Director and Deputy Director at the CIA was involved in illegal arms sales.

I'm the goddamn leader of a Kleptocracy, he thought. *Thomas and Glickman must believe our government is so corrupt that it would not discover their antics. That's going to stop immediately.*

"*Very good, Mr. President,*" the voice said. "*Welcome to the real world. There are no real democracies anymore. Do you really believe that you are a president that helps his people? I don't think so. You are ruled by money and all the people and corporations that control it.*"

"Who are you?" he asked anxiously. "You're different than the other voice who communicated with me before."

"*Very intuitive,*" Dável said, his voice menacing. "*I'm your worst nightmare and you do not want to interfere with what I'm doing at United Weapons.*"

"What are you doing there, if I might ask?"

"*Saving what's left of my family.*"

"I can't let you do that."

"*How childish of you to think you can stop me,*" Dável's agitated voice reverberated inside the president's head.

Hopkins felt pressure restrict his airway, and then his body lifted off his chair. Kicking wildly, he struggled to get free, but it was impossible. His mouth had become dry; his tongue felt swollen as it dangled out of his mouth. Panic filled his body, and the blood vessels in his eyes were ready to burst.

The pressure eased as he fell to the carpet, gasping for air.

"Why are you trying to kill me?" he shouted. "It won't do your plan any good. If you kill me, I'll be replaced, and you'll have to kill all of us. And I don't think The Family will allow that."

"You don't know the first thing about my enemy," he raved. *"We've been battling for thousands of years, and I've survived so far. So don't be too over-confident about the cavalry you've been promised. I'll be watching you!"*

President Hopkins lay there, holding his throat, wondering what had just happened.

"Shit, we have God and the Devil battling on our planet."

He couldn't stop rambling as he reached for a glass of water to cool his burning throat.

He struggled to stand. His knees shook wildly. As he pulled himself up, he hyperventilated and fell back to the floor.

After a few minutes, his head cleared, and he was back at his desk. At first, he didn't notice the book that appeared on a stack of papers in front of him. His eyes caught the small static charges that jumped off its cover. Intrigued, he picked up the book and turned to the first page, not noticing the light mist that floated into his nostrils. As he read, a warm current began to flow through his arteries, warming his brain and igniting thoughts he had for so long left locked up inside.

"Find Phillips and O'Riley," he screamed to his secretary. "See if I can meet with them immediately."

CHAPTER SIXTY-FIVE

Yesterday, Robert and Katie had exercised their powers without mercy or regard for the outcome. They each had become prosecutor, judge, and jury as they attempted to stop the continued bloodshed incited by Dável.

Robert knew that before they could change the world they had to save the United States first. They had started in the East and moved west toward Los Angeles. Katie and Robert had begun to take on all individuals and groups that used guns for any purpose, including the NRA. The first of these groups to be addressed were the most powerful gangs that had terrorized cities in each and every state. Crimes of murder and intimidation had escalated to new heights. Greatly outnumbered and overpowered, the police were helpless. They were undermanned and limited in their firepower as a result of years of lawsuits stemming from police brutality claims. Now, the law enforcement community was happy to have help from Robert and Katie. They both knew that after the gangs were gone, so too would be the hate groups that had used a free society to promote their fanatical hatred, hiding behind the Constitution that protected them.

Robert, with the approval of all the governors, went on every local network and every loudspeaker that could be heard through the emergency broadcast system. He had one simple message that began at eight in the morning in every time zone:

"All persons bearing any type of weapon must lay them down. All weapons must be brought to your city hall within eight hours of this message. This includes every citizen and every criminal, young or old. Everyone who doesn't comply will die a most uncomfortable death. Exempt are law enforcement personnel and the military. HEED MY WORDS: BY FOUR THIS AFTERNOON, IF YOU STILL POSSESS A WEAPON OF ANY TYPE, YOU WILL DIE!"

Tomorrow, other cities around the world would hear the same demands. Robert hated what he was doing. He understood that if the world was going to be cleansed, the scum of the Earth had to either change or be destroyed.

In each of the time zones, they waited for the results at 4:00 p.m. The East Coast was the first test. Inside his head was a list of the men, women, and teenagers that did not take him seriously. That day turned out to be the worst day of Robert's life. The death toll reached 110,000 Americans, mostly criminals. But there were a few complaining NRA members who still clung to their constitutional rights that they thought would protect them. Instead, they died for their misunderstood principles.

As word spread, on every news channel, around the country of the quick and horrible deaths the defiant had received, more and more guns began to pile up on the steps of every city hall. Robert's ultimatum was working. His body was exhausted from the use of his powers.

* * * * *

Katie woke up first and showered, letting Robert sleep. She stared at herself in the mirror behind the bathroom door, using her towel to wipe away the steam.

She turned sideways, looking for a sign that she was carrying their child.

"Nothing yet, silly," she said. "It's only been a few days."

"It's a girl," the menacing voice said. *"They've planned this one very well."*

She covered her naked body with her robe.

"Who are you?" she called out, not recognizing him at first.

"I wanted to be your friend," he said, *"but your association with my enemy will not work."*

Dável, get out of here before I kill you.

"I had to rush out the other day and never finished my story," he said. *"Is this a good time?"*

"This is as good as any time," she replied out loud, hoping

Robert would hear her.

"You're being suckered into a false notion about me that will be your destruction. My people made the same mistake thousands of years ago, when they told us about their problems."

"Why are you telling us this?" she asked, attempting to get control of what was happening.

"Myself," he hesitated, *"and my daughter are the only remaining survivors of Mars. Once we're gone, Jacob's biggest mistake will be eradicated."*

Katie stopping talking telepathically so Robert could hear what was going on. "From what I understand about you and your daughter, that's not a bad thing to have happen," she said unsympathetically. "Your history on our planet leaves a lot to be desired. You're the Devil, Satan, and have caused too much pain and sorrow in my world."

"That's what they want you to believe. But that's a lie!"

"Right! I know you're lying out of desperation. I'm not feeling sorry for you."

"Mars was a planet like yours with oceans, mountains, forests, animals, and a special beauty before they came to harvest. After I settled there with my friends and family, we were a people that had desires and dreams for our future. We had families that we loved. Our race was a peaceful one, evolving slowly, safe from hate, prejudice, and greed."

"How do I know you're not lying?" she remarked, pondering his words that sounded believable. She tried this time to read his deep thoughts, but he must have learned from their first meeting to block her out.

"Your planet's history is filled with proof. You're just not willing to accept it. Throughout time, their scientists have been coming to this solar system, experimenting with the life forms they found here. In the Peruvian desert, there are rock engravings that show step-by-step heart transplant operations and a Caesarean section surgery. The Black Death that killed one third of the European population in medieval times was another experiment gone wrong."

"Why shouldn't I believe it was your people that did what you're telling me?"

"I can't prove it to you. You'll just have to seek out your own truths and decide. I can continue giving you more examples,

*but I sense you still won't believe me. Their propaganda is more
believable, since they've had the power all these years to make you
believe they were gods watching over you to protect you if you
followed their rules. Now they are at it again, threatening to
destroy all of you if you don't activate The Cleansing. I know you
can read my thoughts and separate the truth from a lie. Be open-
minded with what I've said, or you'll end up like Mars, a barren
desert planet."*

"That's just it; I can't read your mind like I did the other
day, where your lies were out in the open. You're blocking me out.
What are you hiding?"

The banging on the door startled Katie. Robert was
shouting at her to open it up.

"What's going on in there?" he screamed. "I sense trouble.
Are you all right?"

"I'm fine," she replied, backing away from the door as it
swung inward.

He was able to feel Dável's presence. He knew who he
was instantly. Robert grabbed something solid by the shower stall.
He felt him struggle, but held him tightly, ready to squeeze the life
out of him.

"Let him go, Robert. He can't harm us. He's very weak
now."

Once he loosened his grip, Dável was gone.

"What was he saying to you? I was blocked out and
couldn't read his thoughts."

"I'll tell you after I finish dressing," she replied.

* * * * *

"Father, he's got powers we didn't know existed," Ruth said. "This
is a problem. I think it's all over. We've lost."

"I think I was able to mask my lies. I saw Katie doubt her
new beliefs. If she hesitates next time we meet, we'll have her."

"I hope you're right. I'm too weak to continue much
longer."

"We'll not end this way. I have one last plan that will
insure our future and create a new race of stronger beings. Katie's
pregnant, and maybe, just maybe, that will be our last hope for
survival, a new Messiah for Earth's people to bow down to."

CHAPTER SIXTY-SIX

Robert was not sure what to make of what Katie had told him about her conversation with Dável. After what he had done yesterday, he tortured himself with the thought that Rebecca had lied to him. His newfound strength and power continued to shock him; the power of being a god had him trapped. His guilt consumed his body. He was unable to blank out a lifetime of faith in God, believing that if you were good your reward would be received in heaven alongside God. Now, everything was topsy-turvy. There was no reward for being good or no punishment for being bad.

Katie scowled as she told him about Dável's last-ditch effort to win them as allies. "He appeared to be desperate. I felt his many years of pain he had stored inside his mind. The strange thing is that there was only one voice, unlike what we hear when Rebecca speaks to us."

"What do you make of it?"

"I'm not sure. What he said was another side of the story that we haven't considered."

Katie could tell that Robert was once again thinking like a detective. He had that constipated look he's been getting digesting everything he's been told by Jacob and Rebecca.

"What if he's telling the truth..." he said solemnly... "that we're being setup to be defenseless? We might have a wonderful ten years after the cleansing. Then, Pallas' army arrives and we're caught with our pants down."

"I've something to tell you," she said, frowning.

"You seem worried. What's got you looking so sad?"

"My pregnancy. Dável knew it was a girl. If we're an experiment, could our daughter have been implanted? Is it going to be another mutation by a mad scientist?"

"Let's get tested and see if it's ours. That should relieve your mind," he assured her. "We do have powers now, and if Rebecca and her family were lying, why would they expose themselves like this?"

Katie held up her hand signaling Robert to stop talking. "Well, it's pretty clear to me," she said positively.

"We need to confront Rebecca again?" Robert asked puzzled.

"I don't believe so. I'm sure Dável is lying. I'll bet my life on it. You need to stop doubting and begin working on saving our planet. What you did the other day was not bad. The world has only lost its criminals."

Robert gave Katie a worried look. He was dismayed at their predicament. "We have six days before Jacob speaks. It might be too late to do anything."

Katie put his head in her cupped hands and held him tightly so he could see her eyes. "We have to side with what we believe is the good that is going on in our heads. I will risk my life and my baby's life to side with Rebecca and her family. Dável is evil and cannot be trusted. Shake those questions and doubts from your mind and trust my intuition."

Robert took a step back from her and smiled. "You're right. I can't keep torturing myself trying to be one hundred percent sure of anything. You seem to see deeper into people's hearts and minds to find the truth, something I can't do yet. I hope that someday I can see what you see and feel what you feel. You're a wonderful person."

CHAPTER SIXTY-SEVEN

Rabbi Feldman ran his hands through his thick curly black hair; the goose bumps chilled his entire body as astonishment exploded on his face. Today had become the happiest of his life as he watched his devoted followers become absorbed with a new spiritual change the *Pallasian Covenant* had inspired. He had handpicked forty of his most loyal and devout Jews. First, they had to believe in God and the waiting for the Messiah. Second, they had to be his most flexible and open-minded in his congregation. Otherwise, what he was going to tell them was not going to work.

Rudy Stein, his right arm of the movement, had been given advanced warning about The Cleansing and what The Family was all about. He had at first had some doubts; then, after touching and reading *The Pallasian Covenant,* he rejoiced that he could see in himself what God had originally intended.

"There will be no Messiah," Rudy shouted with delight. He never believed the Jews were really waiting for someone or thing to come and rescue them. Jews for sometime had been on their own surviving their cruel world.

Rudy Stein had always been more melodramatic than the other men; nevertheless, his enthusiasm spread to Rabbi Feldman's appointed leaders. Feldman's strategy had worked; the electricity in the room was contagious. Each of his appointed council had changed noticeably. They began acting as if they had been touched by a divine power.

After spending four hours telling each of them the story of The Family and their plan for the world, he left Rudy in charge to continue spreading the word to all Rabbis throughout the States. Now rabbi Feldman was off to Israel to begin what he knew would be the most difficult task to accomplish with the most stubborn Jews in the world.

* * * * *

Archbishop Stallsworth had similar success, but in a grander manner. He was an expert on what he called "mass marketing of religion."

The Archbishop was a great salesman. "God's message needs to be provided to the masses by whatever means his servants can find," he would preach to the media. "Since God directed us to create stadiums, the electronic highway, and satellite TV, it's my job to obey his wishes, even if God was not exactly what I imagined him to be."

His methods were controversial, but his true love of all mankind made him one of the most widely accepted religious leaders, second only to Cardinal Richman.

His followers in the Christian world were not Catholic; however, they devotedly embraced the message of Jesus Christ and the desire for harmony and peace for all mankind. Compared to the way the Pope directed the Catholic Church, the archbishop directed his church like a benevolent general, inspiring his troops to follow him to the ends of the Earth.

He knew that exposing God for what he really was had to be done very delicately. He had to walk on eggshells and hoped he was not going to crush the inner core that held his congregations together.

Stallsworth held his first of many planned religious concerts at Madison Square Garden, where it was to be televised on every religious channel across the United States and in most of Mexico, Central, and South America. If it worked, over a hundred million people would be exposed to *The Pallasian Covenant.*

It only took thirty minutes, and The Cleansing began to spread rapidly through the packed arena on that tiny cement and concrete island in the heart of New York City. Everyone attending or listening to the broadcast found on their laps a copy of *The Pallasian Covenant*, written in their native tongues. As if a fog had rolled into God's temporary house, the people inhaled the sweet aroma of the words that floated out of the archbishop's mouth.

At first, the change seemed, on the surface, nonexistent. However, a softness of sorts began to appear on every male face that stared at the archbishop.

With memories intact, the men seemed to enjoy the feelings of tranquility and friendship. African Americans, Hispanics, Whites, and Asian Americans hugged and talked. A new reunion of brotherhood had begun to emerge. The archbishop looked out at the thousands of staring eyes and knew he had done the right thing.

In his dressing room, he heard reports about the changes taking place around the United States, Mexico, Central America, and South America. Hate crimes were being replaced with neighborly compassion and acceptance. Where foreign governments had ruled with martial law and mass arrests, soldiers put down their guns and cried to God for forgiveness.

The archbishop and his leaders kept spreading the message. They traveled around the world to Europe, Africa, and Asia. The hardest job was sitting down with the Muslim leaders, but he felt his Muslim friend would be able to handle his task. He could not wait for the four of them to stand in front of the world with *The Pallasian Covenant:* united and transforming the world into one religious order.

He knew that if this really worked and there was no differences for people, then fear would be gone and with it hatred. What a great world there could be with everyone believing they were one loving family.

* * * * *

Rabbi Feldman, more of a realist than his friends, had serious concerns about what was happening. He was from the old school, remembering the concentration camps and the Nazis' promises that they would be safe if they came along peacefully. He rationalized that he was resistant to change, but he felt something was just not right.

He had seen the changes: the hate evaporated, and the fear that once cried out from the anti-Semites vanish from the faces of his enemies.

"If it will take The Cleansing to eliminate wars and hate around the world, then so be it," he persuaded himself.

He placed *The Pallasian Covenant* back in his briefcase as he heard his flight announced. He was on his way to the Middle East, along with fifteen of his faithful staff.

"If another Jew has to be nailed to the cross for these radical ideas, then this meeting will be the catalyst," he told his men. "We're heading into the lion's den, where for thousands of years an angry, unmerciful beast has ruled and controlled peace between the Jews and Arabs. I hope this works."

Overwhelmed with anxiety, he wondered whether meeting with hardcore radicals from both sides was the smart thing to do.

"I must be crazy to think this is a good idea," he said in Yiddish as he sat back and closed his eyes for his long journey.

* * * * *

Abdeljalil Tahmass arrived in Egypt the day after he met with Katie and Robert. The new premier was not open to his new ideas and objected to letting him talk to his people. Leaders from Saudi Arabia, Pakistan, Jordon, Yemen, Iraq, Afghanistan and Iran reacted the same way. Fanatical terrorist groups that survived Robert and Katie's justice wanted him dead.

Jalil was a silent man who, like a turtle, walked slowly, but always made it to the finish line first. He was friends with Ammar Abuzahra, the owner of the Arab version of CNN. Ammar's American nickname was Tom because he looked identical to TV star Tom Selleck. Jalil knew his friend very well because they had been college buddies at Princeton, where they became close friends. Their ideologies were the same, but they handled their jobs differently. Jalil was still upset with Thomas because he had only covered the propaganda of Bin Laden and would not let the United States tell the Arab world their side of the story. It had taken a while for Jalil to warm back up to his friend, but he now had to swallow his pride and ask for his help.

Jalil was in the Middle East for three days before a luncheon with Thomas could be arranged. If Thomas would not help, he had no other way to get his message across to a region where none of the leaders could even remember why they hated all non-Muslims. The Cleansing was the only alternative, and he knew he had to be very cautious with Thomas or risk losing him as an ally.

The restaurant Ammar had picked was very intimate so they could speak privately. The greeting was friendly: hugs, kisses on cheeks, and kind words of hello. Jalil knew these gestures meant nothing; all Arabs greeted friends in the same manner, even if they didn't trust them.

"Tom, it's been too long," he said, forcing a smile.

He saw his friend's eyes become little slits as his brow furrowed with caution. Telling the truth was always a safe bet; it allowed one's opponent to feel in control.

"I'll admit," he said, "I'm not fully over the anger I had for you ten years ago. Maybe I'm being childish, but I'm still uncomfortable."

Tom seemed to relax. A broad smile came over his face.

"Now that I can look back on it, I know what I did was wrong. You had every right to be angry with me. I hope we can still be friends."

He reached his hand out just as Jalil was doing the same. Both their eyes welled up, and the Muslim leader knew everything was going to be all right.

"My first reason to see you was to see if we could rekindle our friendship, which seems to be happening. The second reason was to ask for your help on something of worldwide importance—"

"If there is anything I can do to help you," Thomas interrupted, "my services are open to you."

"Thank you for saying that before you know my request. I hope after you hear me out, you'll still be willing to help."

Tom nodded his head, signaling him to continue.

"I'm sure you've heard about The Family and what they want all of us to do before their talk at the United Nations."

"I'm not sure I like where this is going," he said. "I have a tremendous distrust for whoever this family is and what they've been doing to our people."

Jalil searched for the right words.

"They have not been killing our people," he said gingerly. "They've been killing all Muslim fanatics, our known terrorist groups around the world. It has not been just Arabs. The Ku Klux Klan has almost been eliminated. The neo-Nazis around the world have been eradicated. The Arabs killed were not blessed by Islam and did not speak for our religion or the entire Arab world. The Family has come to the surface to bring peace to our world. Think of them as the God we've always searched for. They have a new message that needs to spread around the world. As we speak, Christian leaders and Jewish leaders are introducing *The Pallasian Covenant* to their people, and we need to do the same. You're the only person capable of doing this for the entire Arab world."

Jalil took a sip of water and watched his friend's expression. There was none at first, and then he said something that shocked him.

"Unless I can get a consensus from all the Arab nations, I won't help you. I owe them that much for all the financial support they continue to provide me."

Jalil, his face drained of color, felt like he had just failed his friends. He was lost for words because he knew that Thomas would get the same response he had gotten. Distraught and feeling ill, he asked to be excused. Then his friend began to speak again.

"I don't mean to hurt you or not act like your friend. But our clerics need to first review this new message and approve of it. It is our custom."

Jalil felt a new surge of energy. A perfect plan had surfaced.

"Do you have a copy of this book, so I can read it and form my own opinion?"

"Yes," he stammered, looking up, "I have one here with me. You can look it over during lunch."

He reached into his satchel and pulled out a book the size of the Koran. What followed next was amazing. He saw the look on Thomas' face change from seriousness to calmness.

"What are you feeling?" he asked his friend.

"It's hard to explain, but I feel like a weight has been lifted from my heart. A lifetime of doubt, hate, and prejudice seems to be gone. There will be no need to see the clerics first. I'm convinced this cleansing has to be given to all our people. But, first tell me how this is happening?"

"I do not understand it myself," he said. "It's like when we pray, we feel good at that moment. When we laugh, hate evaporates if only for a time. *The Pallasian Covenant* triggers some chemical hormone in our brain that removes our natural desire to hate and mistrust. How the books get to the people is another story I do not understand. I hope when the Family speaks, that too will become clearer."

"I can have a special newscast ready for you tomorrow. Be at the studio at eight in the morning so we can prep you on what to do."

Jalil stood up and gave his friend a big hug and wet, mushy kisses on his cheeks.

"You are a true friend," Jalil said. "Do me one last favor. Do not tell anyone about your special show until after my broadcast. Once I speak from The Pallasian Covenant to our people, all who listen will change like you have."

"That's a promise," Tom whispered in his ear.

* * * * *

Cardinal Richman arrived at the Vatican in the early evening, just as the sun was setting, shining its pink rays across the Vatican's dome. The young officer from the Guardians of the Cross grudgingly handed him over to the Vatican police, where the Church placed him into custody. Their rules were different and more severe. The Cardinal, with a smile of reassurance, had told the young man not to interfere, but to go back to his command post.

Handcuffs were placed tightly on the Cardinal's wrists, pinching his skin and drawing blood.

"Is this necessary?" he calmly said. "I'm not going to escape."

"If I had a wooden cross for you to carry, I'd strap it to your feeble body for what you've done to the Church," the tall guard said, sending a chill down the Cardinal's spine.

Cardinal Richman saw the fire in the guard's eyes and wondered where all his hate and anger came from.

His long walk down the cold marble corridor to the Pope and his cardinals was awkward. He knew his old friends waited to condemn him for turning on the only Church they believed the world should respect. He imagined how Christ had felt as he was asked to denounce that he was the Son of God. He thought if The Family was the God he had all his life believed in, then Jesus was this God's Son.

Cardinal Richman knew what they were going to ask of

him and what they were going to expect. He also knew what his answers were going to be.

A small trail of blood marked his path as he stumbled on. The unusually aggressive Vatican police officer kept pushing him forward to speed him up. On one of his falls, he dropped his copy of *The Pallasian Covenant* and watched as it slid across the floor. The officer picked it up, but did not hand it back to Richman immediately. The Cardinal hoped the book would affect this man, as it had the men who had brought him here. He was surprised that the guard had no reaction from touching the book. He turned toward the guard and caught him sneering at the book he had been holding.

Are some people immune to The Cleansing? Cardinal Richman wondered.

The guard looked at him, wanting to respond to his foolish thoughts, but held himself in check.

"This is evidence of your crimes and will be used to convict you," the policeman said mockingly. His strange, ominous look unnerved the Cardinal.

"That's not evidence of a crime, my son," the Cardinal said, out of breath. "It's *The Pallasian Covenant*. Once it's read, we'll all be cleansed of our sins."

The guard just laughed.

"There's only one word that matters to me," he snickered, "and that is from the Pope. You're an old fool who has outlived his usefulness."

Dável's irrational behavior had become excessive. He seemed to have lost his objectivity, as he continued harassing the Cardinal.

The Cardinal just smiled. He whispered a prayer for this misguided soul. The large, heavy doors swung open, and the officer gave him one last push, causing him again to fall and this time to hit his head hard against the cold marble floor. The fall reopened the wound he had received in the van. He struggled to rise, but couldn't. Two other guards rushed over and gently walked him over to his seat, where he would be tried and convicted of his crimes.

His head kept spinning as he held on to the carved wooden arms of his chair. He could see Pope John being handed what appeared to be his copy of *The Pallasian Covenant*, but he was unsure; his vision remained blurred from the impact his head had taken when he fell coming through the doors.

The Church's prosecutor, Cardinal Gironde, stood to the left of the Pope, dressed in his formal red and black robe. There was no one to defend Richman. The Vatican Court did not allow outsiders to be a part of their proceedings. If another cardinal wanted to defend Richman, he could do it, but no one stood to challenge Cardinal Gironde. The only person left to defend the cardinal against the Church and God was the accused. Cardinal Richman knew that the only way he could save his career was to disavow what he now believed to be the truth of his existence. He would have to recant, both verbally and then in writing, or he would be sentenced to a lifetime of seclusion, locked away deep in the Vatican dungeon. *That will not happen,* he assured himself.

The prosecutor spoke for just five minutes, presenting his case with innuendos and circumstantial evidence. There was no concrete evidence offered to the court, just rumor and supposition. The prosecutor ended his case and sat back down with the other cardinals. He was ready to cast his vote, not really interested in what Richman had to say.

The Pope was appalled. He was in disbelief over what he had just heard. He tried to speak, but his voice was weak. His head wobbled like a bobble-doll resting in the rear window of a car, while his hands trembled wildly on his lap. His multiple sclerosis had gotten worse since Richman's last visit.

"Cardinal Richman, are you ready to address this court and recant your crimes against the Church and God?"

The Cardinal could not stand. He continued to feel lightheaded and nauseated. The little he knew about medicine told him he had a concussion.

"Please excuse my rude behavior, but I'm unable to stand to defend myself. I didn't expect God's servants to be so abusive."

"You can sit," Cardinal Gironde called out smugly.

"I'm saddened that I've been tried and convicted before any of you have investigated what I have brought you."

He panned the chamber; no one moved or changed facial expressions. If he had not noticed their robes moving with each of their breaths, he would have believed he was talking to mannequins.

"I'd like to begin with a quote from a great Indian leader,

Cochise: 'You must speak truth so that your words may go as sunlight to our hearts.'"

He watched the confused looks, the disapproving gestures, and realized he was truly on his own.

"I've been given a new message by the God we believed to be an all-powerful being," he continued, "but not exactly in the image we'd imagined. We have from the beginning, since Christ was nailed to the cross, misinterpreted this God's original messages. Our world will be destroyed if we don't redeem ourselves and read his new Bible. We'll all be doomed to eternal hell. We've seen his power over the last few weeks and will hear his final message shortly. I hope he'll find each of you worthy of carrying on his New Message. The book I've brought, *The Pallasian Covenant,* will give you all the answers, the truth to our lives, and eternal peace for all of you and for all of mankind. All I ask is that you read it."

He watched the Pope touch the book with his fingers and pull his hand back as the electrical sensation startled him. The cardinal was disappointed. He had hoped the Pope would be unbiased but realized he was scared of change.

"Open your minds," he pleaded, "and see for yourselves. You have nothing to lose."

"Are you not going to recant you sacrilege against God and this Church?" the prosecutor shouted madly, his actions exaggerated for the benefit of the other cardinals.

Cardinal Richman's face glowed as if an energy force had consumed his body. "I've read *The Pallasian Covenant* and have recanted to my new God. I'm at peace now and will be forever, no matter what you do to me today. If you have prepared my crown of thorns, then I am ready to face your judgment."

The Pope picked up the book and placed it in a carved wooden box that would be stored in the Vatican archives, never to be looked at again. As he picked it up, he felt again the electrical charge flow through his fingertips. Then he dropped it into the box and closed its top, a frightened look on his face.

Cardinal Gironde stood. "Take him to his cell. Tomorrow he will be prepared to pay for his crimes."

You did well, Sir Pope, the voice playfully said. *My father will be very pleased with your actions. That book needs to be destroyed before it poisons the world and puts you into bondage.*

The Pope did not know what to make of the female voice. He looked around the room to see if anyone else had heard it, but by their expressions, he knew he was the only one. He had heard voices for some time, but not since his illness consumed him years ago had he heard a voice so clear and frightening.

* * * * *

Later that evening while sitting in his soft arm chair in his bedroom, Pope John tried to meditate. The box with the book in it had begun to emit a purple glow, disturbing his hour of relaxation. He lifted the box and opened its cover. The book appeared to be breathing.

Frightened, he closed the cover, tossing the box across the room.

"What's going on?" he asked himself out loud. "I can't change at this stage of my life. I'm too old and sick. God, please help me!"

When he opened his eyes, the box had returned to where he was sitting, the cover opened, the book revealed. He reached down and placed it on his lap. His hands felt the static rush enter his body.

* * * * *

Down in the musty damp holding cells, the rusty hinge of the cell door squealed, as it opened to where Cardinal Richman had been jailed. Standing over the guard who lay knocked out was the young officer from the Guardians of the Cross who had first captured the Cardinal. Cardinal Richman was surprised to see his rescuer holding a rifle.

"Why have you come here?" he asked, a disapproving look on his face.

"When I heard about your sentence, I couldn't let this happen," the young officer said. "I'm here to take you to safety."

"I'm not going anywhere. If I must be sacrificed to see that The Cleansing begins, then that is God's will."

"There's no God as we once believed," the young officer reminded him.

Cardinal Richman held the guard's hand, squeezing it tight. "God has always been inside all of us. Now, we have the answers to all our questions. We have to trust our own judgment and act upon those answers so we can discover the true meaning of why we are living here on Earth."

"I'm frightened for you," the guard cried.

"I'll be fine, my son. The Pope will find the right answers before it's too late. Now go and see that the guard you hurt gets medical attention."

CHAPTER SIXTY-EIGHT

Ammar had kept his promise and not told anyone, even his staff, what the special segment was going to be. But Dável had followed Jalil. He knew he had to stop him or the entire Muslim world would be free of his control and Jacob would win.

Dável waited until Jalil and the commentator were seated in the soft armchairs. He wanted to show the entire Islamic world his power.

It was nine o'clock, and the director behind the camera was holding up his hands and mouthing the countdown with his fingers: *five, four, three, two, one.* He pointed to Ammar, the signal that they were on the air.

"To all my brothers," he began, "Allah be praised."

"My good friend, Abdeljalil Tahmass, the cleric leader for our brothers in the United States, has a wonderful message for you that will change each of your lives and bring a new peace to your hearts and souls."

He looked at Jalil and saw beads of sweat forming on his forehead.   "I'm here today to bring a New Message about God and how we need to live in our troubled world," Jalil stuttered. He held up what looked like the Koran, but in Arabic it read: *The Pallasian Covenant.* "This will be the only book you'll ever need to read to find peace and tranquility."

He started to open the book to page one when he felt a vise-like grip around his neck. At first, he thought it was nerves, but as the invisible monster lifted him off his chair, he knew it was real. He tried to speak, but could only think.

"You're Dável, correct?" His mind was in a panic.

He could feel the grip get tighter and tighter, as his lungs were starving for the air they so desperately needed. He could hear his friend shouting at the invisible monster and see him swinging his hands wildly at the force that seemed to be killing his guest. At that moment, Ammar, too, felt a hand grip his neck, and now both men hung in the air suspended, thrashing wildly, as the life was being squeezed from their bodies. The room had begun to spin before their eyes and grow darker, a voice rang out in their ears.

"Dável, let them down, or you'll die right here and the world will witness how weak your powers are compared to mine," Robert materialized in front of the cameras.

Robert then disappeared and was standing next to Dável.

He reached out and put his hands around Dável's neck and began to squeeze as hard as he could. It looked as if Robert and Dável were in a Mexican standoff. Dável seemed surprised, mostly shocked that he was suspended, while at the same moment holding both Jalil and Ammar in each hand.

Dável gave him a horrified look, as if he had never before been touched by a powerful opponent. Robert tightened his grip, forcing Dável to let go of Jalil and Ammar. Once he saw that the two men were safe and okay, he told them using his telepathic powers to resume what they had been doing. He would now protect them.

Dável was more powerful than Robert had expected and he broke free from his grasp. Instantly, Robert swung his fist into Dável's midsection. The power from his blow lifted Dável up and threw him across the room, leaving an indentation in the studio wall. Robert could see that Dável was stunned for a moment, but he jumped up ready to fight. Just then, he heard a message Dável was getting from his daughter Ruth.

"Something you wanted me to watch is going wrong. You need to get back here immediately or all will be lost."

Before Robert could react and grab hold of his enemy, he was gone, leaving no trace.

"Damn, that slippery bastard is worse than a greased pig who doesn't want to go to slaughter." He knew at this time it really didn't matter. What mattered was that Jalil was able to get *The Pallasian Covenant* out to his people.

Ammar and Jalil kept rubbing their throats and drinking cold water to stop the fire that was in their throats. Ammar was the first to see the indented outline of a rather large man in the far wall, twenty feet away from where they were sitting.

"Who's this Dável?" he asked. "A friend of yours?"

Jalil gave him a harsh scowl. "Not my friend or anybody's friend. He's fighting against The Family, hoping to control our world and keep us in constant turmoil. Can we get started again with the show?"

Ammar nodded and signaled his terrified director to begin the show again. Ten seconds later, they were back on.

"I am very sorry for what you've just seen," Jalil said. "As you begin to understand *The Pallasian Covenant*, you'll understand the evil that has plagued our world for over six thousand years."

He opened the book and read the first message. He saw immediately the change come over everyone in the studio as copies of *The Pallasian Covenant* appeared at their feet, each opened to the first page.

Ammar was getting called off the stage by his director. "The phones are ringing off the hook. From what we've heard already, Muslims around the world that have heard *The Pallasian Covenant* are thanking you. It must be working. How, I don't understand, but it doesn't matter. I feel such a relief."

Ammar stood by the side of the camera and gave Jalil two thumbs up, letting him know it was working. The show continued for the next hour, and Jalil was exhausted when finally he got the signal that they were off the air.

"I thought we were goners," Jalil told his friend. "I can still feel his hand around my neck. I'm still seeing spots."

They hugged and agreed on an early breakfast before he

had to return to the United States.

CHAPTER SIXTY-NINE

Jacob and Esther needed more time in their regeneration chamber, which was not a good sign this close to the United Nations meeting. They had miscalculated their time on Earth and had grown weaker than expected. Rebecca looked at her parents; tears filled her eyes. She knew how vital it was to get them home immediately.

She remembered the weeks before her mother and father left Pallas in their final attempt to find a remedy for Earth. Her argument for them not to go, fell on deaf ears.

Her father had become too weak and was in his last years. If he lost too many of his brain impulses during this trip and couldn't get back to Pallas's atmosphere in time, his molecular sensor circuits would be lost forever.

Her mother was the stronger one in the family and always had shown compassion and empathy for what drove her husband in his work. How much patience did she have left? They had been married 10,000 years, Earth time.

The day before they were to leave for Earth, a cold winter snow had blanketed the four acres on their ranch. The birch trees that made a tall fence around their house had lost their leaves and were covered with a coat of snow.

Their horses romped through the freshly fallen snow, carving a serpentine trail through the once-green pasture that they grazed on in the warm spring months. The windowpane she had been looking through continued to fog from her heated breath, as she shouted her disapproval at her father.

"You're too weak to travel," she said. "Your last visit

should have been it, and this one should be turned over to my brothers and me. I've proven myself. This is pure folly on your part to think, in your condition, that you can finally after so many failures correct the problems on Earth."

"It's all right. My time with all of you has been precious, and I wouldn't have missed it for anything. Being able to work with all of you made my job more meaningful. I've lived a full and happy life."

"But you don't have to die like this so far away from home."

"It's my destiny. My failures can't be what I'm remembered for; I won't permit it. Earth's survival depends on what I'm bringing this time. I made man in my image and won't let Dável ruin my legacy. This is just how it has to be. Please don't argue. Respect my wishes. I, more than ever before, need your support and help this time for everything to work."

"You know I'll support you; I just can't feel happy about the consequences of your actions. I love you and will be there for you. Please understand, I'm going to try my best to see that you get home to enjoy your final years on the ranch."

She heard some stirring in her parents' master quarters and was brought back to the present. Her mother was the first to greet her.

"Your father's still resting," she said. "He's not very strong. I'm not sure how he's going to handle his speech in five days at the rate his sensor circuits are fading. Showing himself to the world could kill him before he's completed his message."

"Let me handle it," Rebecca asked. "They don't know who's expected to present the message, and I'm fully versed in what he wants to say."

"You know that he won't permit that to happen. He has something else on his mind that you and your brothers have not been briefed on."

"You've kept something from me?"

"You're still our child, and our decisions as your parents do not have to be part of a group vote."

"You have the power to stop him and end this so he can go home."

"Yes, I have the power to end everything, but don't wish to. I feel your father has a good solution to this problem, and if it means that he dies for his beliefs, then so be it."

"How can you say that about someone you love and have been with all these years?" Rebecca asked in disbelief.

"It's because I love him that I can support him and help him see a successful solution. You'll learn when you're older that unconditionally loving someone means accepting their internal needs that can heal their soul, even if the outcome hurts. A true loving relationship is when each partner can be selfish and know they can do whatever they want to do and not hurt the other person, no matter what the result." Esther had begun to show some emotion, but caught herself. "I cannot break that bond I've built with the love of my life. Your father and I have had a long and fruitful marriage, and I believe in him."

"I know you're in pain, and I'm not going to let this happen if I can help it."

She was gone before her mother could respond. She decided it was time to get Robert and Katie to help her.

* * * * *

Esther's briefing with the Council was brief, as Jacob slept in the other room.

"The Cleansing is moving along and should be fully completed sooner than the ten years we once thought we'd need. No one has suspected what I've been doing. Dável and his daughter will soon be captured, and we'll be free to complete our final harvesting."

She closed her communicator and turned, shocked to see Jacob standing by the archway to her work area.

"Esther, is the Council pleased with our progress?"

She wasn't sure what he had heard and acted like everything was normal. "They're very pleased. They can't wait to praise you for your wonderful accomplishment."

"Good," he said, returning to his quarters to get dressed. "Very good indeed."

A sigh of relief filled her body. She hated having to deceive her husband.

CHAPTER SEVENTY

Director Thomas sat inside the United Weapons System's laboratory booth watching the successful test of the RX-666. He smiled when he saw how destructive it was. Dável had deceived him about what he wanted built, maintaining that the Pulsar XR-36 was his weapon of choice. The RX-666 was no bigger than a business card and undetectable to any known monitoring devices. The remarkable power of this small device could be confined to a small room when sensor pads were placed inside. Unconfined, it had a range of one hundred square miles without the use of any receiving transmitters. The weapon was efficient, durable and the most powerful weapon ever created. It only destroyed life, leaving buildings intact, eliminating for the conquering country the cost involved to rebuild the infrastructure that was part of war.

He respected the beauty of its power and how its quick, vicious capabilities could rip apart the internal organs of its victims. As he called inside the laboratory to continue the testing, he had the scientists bring him the device so he could learn how to use it. With the sensors inside the lab, two large German shepherds were placed inside. One of the scientists handed him the device and showed him what combination of buttons to press. It was easy. After pressing the start button, he pressed a green button and watched the two dogs explode inside the confined room, leaving all the equipment and furniture intact.

"Holy shit...wow...mother-fucker!" he shouted loudly, lifting his hand in the air and looking for a high-five from the scientist.

All he got was a blank stare; the man didn't know what was expected of him.

His delusions of grandeur gave him a hard-on as he thought of how many countries he could topple without destroying one piece of property. War would be cheap because there would be no more cleanup and reconstruction.

"I could destroy every Arab and control the oil fields," he laughed.

"Very good my friend," Dável said. *"You've done wonderfully. Now I'll begin a new chapter in Earth's history and provide a more orderly existence for everyone."*

"With this weapon, the United States will dominate the world," CIA Director Thomas ranted, as though he hadn't heard a word Dável had said. "I've made a deterrent that will bring the world to its knees and earn us the respect we once had."

"That's not exactly what I had in mind for this weapon," Dável said harshly as he lifted up his large prey like a sack of feathers.

The glass observation window, which was constructed to withstand a sledgehammer, cracked as Thomas was hurtled against it. His feral grin pissed off Dável, igniting a rage that reverberated throughout the laboratory booth.

Director Thomas gasped for air as his windpipe began to be crushed. He tried to fight, but it was hopeless. It was over quickly. His face turned blue and his tongue hung out the side of his mouth. The blood vessels in his big round black eyes exploded. His eyes filled with pools of blood.

Rudy Glickman bit his lower lip, drawing blood, as Thomas lay dying at his feet. He watched the large giant of a man twitch uncontrollably, the violent spasms of death slowing down as the remaining life drained from him.

Rudy Glickman knew he was next; however, he was still alive, wondering if he had been saved. The three scientists who were cleaning up the splattered remains of the dogs tried to escape from the laboratory, but the doors were sealed. The only exit from their tomb locked as they heard a monster howl inside their heads.

Dável held the device as if it were a young, frail baby, caressing it like a magic lamp that would grant him any wish he desired. The four terrified men closed their eyes as the device floated like a paper airplane in the air-conditioned room outside their chamber. The men knew what was about to happen and in a frenzied panic tried to dismantle the transmitters, and Glickman tried in vain to run from the observation room, but his exits were locked also. He had not noticed the transmitter inside his room.

"Father, do it and let's get going," Ruth said. "We're running out of time."

The first toggle went up. The green light indicated the transmitter was on. With a smile, he pressed the button. He felt the vibration ripple through his body as he watched the only people who knew about the weapon explode and die a painful, horrible death.

"It's been a long time," he smiled, "but we've got our power back. Redemption will soon be ours once we get our new bodies and then we can go home again."

CHAPTER SEVENTY-ONE

Rebecca had been staring at Robert and Katie for forty-five minutes, reminiscing as they slept. The Manhattan morning noise clattered inside their room: traffic, horns blasting, and garbage trucks waging war with the metal receptacles that did not want to be disturbed. The symphony of earsplitting sounds would have woken a normal couple; however, this morning they both slept, exhausted from the aftereffects of their new powers. On this day, fatigue had won out, and they did not budge from the earthquake of sounds that rumbled their suite.

Rebecca's pent-up emotions had gotten the best of her, as she fantasized about a life she had never had, only imagined. Seeing how much Robert and Katie loved each other only made it hurt worse.

She had never stopped yearning for someone to love and share her life with. She had understood long ago that her commitment to her family and this project took precedence over her personal feelings and desires. Nevertheless, the pain of loneliness was beating up her feelings—crushing her dreams as she devoted herself to save a planet she did not call her home. Too many "what ifs" kept dancing inside her mind. Would she have been a great teacher, a caring mother? *Or, maybe just an average citizen on Pallas, enjoying a peaceful life free from tragedy and death.* A smile tried to crack through her sad face, but it couldn't because self-pity had gotten the best of her.

She did not have a selfish bone in her body and had allowed her life to take a backseat to the goals of her father and his

work. Her commitment and devotion had put her in line to
succeed her father, if the project could ever get back on track. It
was looking like that was not going to happen, especially with the
Council's army coming to destroy their life's work.

  She was having doubts. She wondered if the two lovers
who were fast asleep, wrapped tightly in each other's arms, were
strong enough to save Earth and their project? She had not told her
father that she had been giving Robert and Katie additional DNA
from her body, giving them more powers than her father, even the
council could imagine. Unfortunately, this sacrifice was making
her very weak giving her little choice, but to go back to Pallas to
live out her years.

  She knew her father and mother would have chastised her for
giving them her genes, but that did not matter. For her failure was
not an option. With each meeting with Robert and Katie, she
donated another part of her life, knowing she was creating two
powerful, unstoppable human beings. She knew this was her way
to leave a part of herself, to have a life she never would have on
her own.

  Her loud moan turned to a deep cry, as she fell to the floor
shaking. The pain was excruciating. Someone from her family
was being killed.

  Katie sat up against the headboard, startled. "Rebecca, is
that you? What's wrong?"

  "My brothers are dying! He's killing them! He's killing
them!"

  Robert sat up in bed, rubbing his eyes, trying to focus.
"Who's killing them?"

  "It's Dável," she sobbed. "I hear them crying. They need
me. I have to go now."

  "You don't sound too good," he said. "Are you all right?"

  "I'll be fine. I must go now before it's too late to capture
their brain impulses."

  Katie was out of bed getting dressed. "We're going with
you. We want to help and won't take 'no' for an answer. Where
are they?"

  "The Vatican!" she said helplessly.

  "Shit," Robert cursed. "Cardinal Richman's there too."

CHAPTER SEVENTY-TWO

Dável's rage burned. He was upset to see the Pope holding *The Pallasian Covenant.* He saw immediately the change in him. He then left Pope John's bedroom and found that the cardinals had just finished reading their books. Dável knew it was too late. None of these bodies would accomplish what he needed them to do. He screamed; his howl broke windows and cracked the walls inside the Vatican's courtroom.

The cardinals' eyes were wide with terror as they hid behind their chairs. Cardinal Gironde just stood there in an arrogant pose, holding his crucifix, his chest puffed out.

With the weapon in his hand, Dável knew the killing would be painful, something he enjoyed dishing out to the people who disappointed him. He dropped two sensor transmitters on the floor and stood outside the big wooden doors, Ruth was close by his side. He did not feel lenient or compassionate because the world was changing from The Cleansing and he was losing any hope of defeating The Family. If he couldn't have it his way, then no one would live, especially Jacob and his family.

He heard the screams, the torment of their bodies being ripped apart. He just grinned at his daughter.

"See, we now have the power. I'm going back to visit to the damn foolish Pope and make him pay for his stupidity."

He had so hoped that the Pope's body would be the perfect shell he needed to carry out his ultimate plan as he squeezed the life out of him. He imagined that the billions of followers of the Christian Church would listen to him once he occupied the Pope's body. Finally, he realized he was too old and frail and did not have the support, as Cardinal Richman had, from the world his predecessors before him had enjoyed.

"Everything happens for a reason," he grinned.

He was in a wild, untamed state, savage, fire exploding from his eyes, as he kicked the Pope's body across the bedroom floor. He watched the limp body lift up and glide helplessly, arms flapping, legs split apart, as the holy father smashed into his dresser, shattering the mirror he would never use again to check his appearance.

Dável knew he had drained some of his energy when he occupied the Vatican guard's body the other day. He knew he had to find a suitable body soon. He needed a lot of energy to complete a takeover or die on the planet that had been his hell for all these years. It had gone on much too long, his running, his hiding from the crimes he knew he was falsely accused of committing on Pallas.

Dável knew that, after so many years of hiding and avoiding capture, he and his daughter were the only remaining true survivors from that massive prison breakout orchestrated by his Ruth and his sons.

Ruth was standing near her father inside the Vatican Secret Courtroom where the cardinals lay dead, their bodies twisted in final repose.

"Father, what have you done?" she scolded him. "What are you going to do now?"

Cardinal Gironde's body lay bent and twisted from the internal explosions that had ripped him apart.

"There's a stronger one down in his cell. I'll have one last opportunity to leave that body shell before I take over the one I truly want. Cardinal Richman's shell will allow me to be accepted and followed without much complaint, until Robert can be fooled."

"I didn't mean that," she said, pointing over at the corner of the room.

Jacob's younger son, David, struggled helplessly for life. The damage the weapon had inflicted on his molecular structure was devastating. The friction from the rapid deceleration had heated his body so much that his skin had melted and was dripping off his bones. He looked like a mannequin in a wax museum that had just burned down. He did not die immediately but begged for mercy, his skinless hand reaching out for help. Without a word, Dável's foot slowly pressed his head. It exploded into a charred cloud of ash.

"An eye for an eye, my dear," he said, stamping his foot a few times to shake the filthy mess from his shoes. "Now they will know the pain I've had to suffer at their hands. We're all alone now, and after we complete our swap, the power will be ours again."

Ruth looked dismayed at her father's incensed state.

"When will I take over her body?" she asked. "I'm getting too weak and might not have the energy left to execute what needs to be done."

"We have to distract Robert. His energy is very strong. With him around, she's well protected. Go back to the compound and wait for me. I have an idea and if I'm right, will give you a new body and baby in a few days."

Dável seemed to have a renewed energy, believing for the first time in a long time he was truly going to win and save himself and Ruth.

CHAPTER SEVENTY-THREE

They were all there in a blink of an eye. Her younger brother's body burnt beyond recognition, except for his ring that Jacob had given him on his thirteenth birthday.

"He's got the weapon!" Rebecca cried. "How could Dável do this to him?"

She looked around for her other brother. He was nowhere to be seen, and she prayed he had escaped.

"He's just a kid," Robert said, looking at David's charred remains. "How could your parents allow a baby like this to be exposed to this type of life?"

"Don't criticize something you know nothing about," she scolded.

"I apologize," he said. "It's just so upsetting seeing someone so young die this way."

"We have to find my other brother. He's still alive. I can feel his brain waves, but we don't have much time."

Lying face down behind Cardinal Gironde's overturned chair, Ian clung to life. His body, like his brother's, was badly ripped and torn. His skin dangled on his broken skeleton, flapping loosely with every breath he struggled to take.

Without warning his head and torso levitated, with his legs

and feet pressed firm on the marble floor. Katie realized he was resting in Rebecca's arms, cradled by her chest and legs. It was over in minutes, and he again lay on the floor. This time the life force had left him forever.

"Did he tell you what happened?" Katie asked compassionately.

"Yes, it's my worst nightmare. My family has no defense against what Dável has in his possession."

"Were you able to harvest his brain impulses?" Robert asked.

"Yes, but it won't do me any good if I can't get him home."

"What are you talking about?" Katie questioned. "Why can't you go home?"

She raised her finger signally Katie to stop talking. "He's still here," she said frightened. "I need to go and think about all of this."

Before Katie could speak, Rebecca vanished. "Do you think he meant Dável is still here? I can't sense him at all."

Robert seemed baffled. "I'm getting no sense he's here either. Let's follow Rebecca. I want to find out what just happened."

CHAPTER SEVENTY-FOUR

Cardinal Richman heard the metal cell door open. The squeal of
the dry hinges made him jump. He felt the moist, moldy air get
cold. A chill blanketed his body. The cubical he had begun to call
home became inundated with a fine mist that, with every nervous
breath he took, filled his lungs with a sweet aroma. He stood up,
ready to be marched out and executed. There was only silence.
No orders, no demands. No one was out there. He noticed the
guard lying on the jail floor, dead. His tongue dangled out of the
corner of his mouth, and his throat looked like it had been crushed.
The indentation where his larynx used to be looked like a small
crater. He walked over toward the door and stood under the
archway, peering around to see who was out there. His breathing
got heavier, and with each rapid breath, he drew in more of the icy
cold mist. The sweet mist burned his lungs, making him cough.
He could taste the foul bile that coated his throat. He felt his
arteries constrict and his heart rate increase, as if his chest were
going to explode. He fell to his knees, then on his back, rolling
from side to side in the worst pain he had ever experienced. Wild
spasms were replaced by convulsions. He appeared to be having an
epileptic fit.

      Then it stopped, and for the first time in years he felt

stronger with more energy.

Something was forcing him to move.

"We're now one," a voice spoke, *"and your memories will be mine forever."*

The cardinal's mind went dark, as if he had been unplugged.

He no longer existed.

CHAPTER SEVENTY-FIVE

Rebecca's explanation did not go over well, especially with Robert. He was belligerent. He exercised a vocabulary that even shocked Katie. Rebecca's face drained of color as he kept shouting profanities, frustrated that he once again had been deceived.

Katie tried to calm him down as if she understood the reasons for all the deceptions. But, Robert was out of control. She had become very fond of Rebecca and realized if they were to complete their mission, they had to remain focused and think things out. Dável and his daughter were not going to give up that easily, and if his madness was getting worse, she knew his fury with this new weapon would be devastating.

Robert felt frustrated. Even though he knew who Dável was, he was upset at how foolish Jacob had been to think he could stop this madman the way he'd tried for centuries. Now, The Family's archenemy was more dangerous than ever before. Why hadn't Jacob instructed he and Katie to find the weapon first and destroy it totally? He repeated the question over and over in his head.

Rebecca tried to tell them the story of Dável's escape and what his crimes had been, but was interrupted. Robert's rage was uncontrollable.

"How many more surprises are we going to have thrown in our faces, as your problems get more and more out of control? If you would have trusted us from the beginning and told us everything, especially about this weapon, I could have stopped this from happening. But, no. Your father's stubbornness has set in motion something that Katie and I might not be able to stop, even with our powers."

Rebecca did not have an answer as her chin slumped to her chest. She seemed lost. Katie wanted to hold her and comfort her as she again tried to tell the painful story of Dável and his murderous rampage after escaping from Mars. She wished Robert would just let go of his anger and let her grieve for her dead brothers.

Rebecca wiped her eyes and tried to regain her composure.

"Katie, thanks for wanting to help, but he's right. We've completely bungled the hunt for Dável. Many times we had the opportunity to kill him, but my father could not be his executioner. Each time we thought we had him cornered and ready to harvest his brain waves, he got away. During the times we were back on our planet, he punished us, inflicting his poison upon Earth and forever changing the quality of life my father had dreamed of for your planet."

Robert took a deep breath, as he tried to control himself, the rage still boiling in his eyes. "All I know is that Dável has evolved in all of us, changing our genetic makeup. He appears to be our true father that you're asking us to destroy."

His comments might as well have been an elephant stepping on her chest. She folded her arms tightly across her body.

"That's partially true," she said. "But remember, you also have our genes. Not everyone has reacted to Dável's poison. Your planet's history up until now has been about fighting the good and evil that plagues man. There are more people like you and Katie in the world than there are like Dável. The noble ones have always been too weak to fight Dável's followers. You didn't have the power to eradicate the truly poisoned souls that ruled Earth until now. The righteous people remain hidden, afraid to speak or show their true feelings. It's the dark side, the snake pit of evil that has to be removed for all of you to survive. Dável's a cancer that cannot be put into remission this time. He has to be cut away and destroyed and forever removed from every corner of your planet."

Rebecca paused, taking a big breath, trying to allow Robert enough time to digest what she had just said. He started to nod. She prayed he was beginning to understand, but based on how his moods had been oscillating recently, she just wasn't sure.

"The fight with Dável and his daughter will come down to who is the smartest, not the strongest. Remember, he's delusional and can be led into a trap if we're smart. Since he has the weapon, I'm not going to be able to help you. He knows your powers and will feel he needs to beat you in order to feel superior. His twisted ego will be his undoing."

"If we've begun to activate The Cleansing," Katie asked, "what will happen to all of us if Dável wins?"

"With any luck, nothing to you. I've given you enough of our genes to counter anything he has. Losing is not an option. If you fail, he'll kill all the cleansed souls and build an army of slaves from the remaining humanoids that still have his mutated DNA. He's always wanted to go to battle with Pallas and eventually destroy a race he once called his own. He believes he can do it now with this weapon; I just hope his madness is his downfall."

"Then we should stop The Cleansing until we defeat him," Katie objected.

"No, on the contrary. It will make a big difference if everyone, or almost everyone, has been cleansed. He would not have enough slaves to form his army. Let's stay focused and try to destroy him and not get ahead of ourselves. I can't say it any clearer. Everything depends on the two of you. If you are to defeat Dável, you have to be stronger and smarter."

She continued telling them about her family and how they all were not going to make it back home. Once Katie heard about their sacrifice and how they had risked everything to save Earth, she was more committed to helping them and seeing that they got home safely.

"What we first have to do is understand this weapon. It begins at United Weapons," Robert said, finally calming down. "I'll go there to see what I can uncover."

Katie was eager to help also. "I'll check to see how Cardinal Richman did at the Vatican. Maybe he can bring us up-to-date on how the rabbi and archbishop are doing."

Robert looked pensive. "I'm not sure you should be alone after what happened at the Vatican. I want us to stay together. We are more powerful as a unit. Also, I know I have stronger powers that can control Dável."

"I've been taking care of myself long before you arrived on the scene and can handle any man, even if he is the so-called Devil," she replied bluntly. "We don't have a lot of time, and we need to find him and his daughter. They need to be stopped before they harm any more of Rebecca's family."

"You be careful, and don't take any unnecessary risks," he pleaded. "I'll be able to hear your thoughts. Just call me, and I'll be there in an instant."

He gave her a hug and then disappeared.

CHAPTER SEVENTY-SIX

When Robert arrived at United Weapons Systems, he was surprised to see that the FBI had it sealed off. Guards armed with assault rifles were posted at every entrance and exit. They were on high alert after someone had savagely murdered Thomas, Glickman, and three UWS scientists.

FBI Director Smith was on her cell phone to the president, her face ashen from what she had just seen.

"Now the group has shown us they can kill without mercy. Sir, it was horrible. I've never seen anything like it before. Their internal organs were heated with such intensity that there's nothing for the coroner to examine except a slimy glob of body parts."

Robert wasn't surprised at how these people had died; he had just seen the slaughter at the Vatican. And he wasn't shocked that William Thomas and Rudy Glickman were killed. He knew that Dável did not want any partners.

Robert was amazed how easily he could become invisible and then return to his normal state. His body did not seem to suffer the side effects that Rebecca had told him her family would experience if they rapidly slowed down. His mind raced. He knew now how to defeat Dável at his own game.

Robert knew he had to find the plans for the weapons that Dável now had. He had to destroy them.

Sitting at a computer in the laboratory, unseen by the guards, he scrolled the database, searching for anything that might refer to this new weapon. He scanned hundreds of files in seconds, each containing code signs that meant nothing to him. He checked the computer's trash bin, just in case the files he needed had been erased. He prayed that the madman had not dumped the trash bin.

"Eureka!" he shouted, spying the deleted file. He highlighted the file and double clicked the mouse to be sure the file was what he needed. Even these plans were beyond anything he had ever seen. He copied the files to a memory stick. There was more than one deleted file in the trash bin, so he copied all the files, just in case. The data was copied in less than thirty seconds, and he was back at his hotel room to tell Rebecca and Katie the good news. To his surprise, they were gone. *She can take care of herself,* he assured himself, not wanting to receive Katie's wrath again. He toyed with the idea of finding her first and then working on a solution for the counter-weapon.

He knew he couldn't waste any more time and decided to see an old friend in Los Angeles. Jasper Billings was an ex-CIA operative and a weapons expert. If anyone could figure out the weakness of this thing, he was the one.

He stood in front of his friend's desk, in the den of an early Californian cottage, unnoticed at first. He noticed how Jasper had aged since he had last seen him. His dark brown curly hair had turned albino white, and, with his light blue-gray eyes, he looked intriguing, but only from the eyes up. The extra weight around his mid-section and under his chins showed his age and how poorly he was taking care of himself. Robert looked around his office and laughed silently that Jasper had not changed. The room was piled high with files, loose papers, and compact disks with no labels. This was Jasper's organizational system. It worked for him. When he died, it would take years for someone to sort through what he had left behind.

After Robert lost his family, Jasper was the only friend who stuck by him when he sank into the dark pit of alcoholism that almost ruined his career. He had brought him back, sobered him up, and supported his transfer to Springs River. Now he needed his help more than ever and prayed his friend could help.

Robert kicked the desk hard, laughing as Jasper jerked straight up and toppled backwards onto his chair. His dangling feet were the only body parts Robert could see. However, he did hear the cacophony of profanities at the unwelcome surprise.

"I see your reaction skills are still as sharp as ever," Robert laughed.

"Where the hell did you come from?" he growled, turning his chair to its upright position and straightening his tie. "I didn't hear you come in. How long were you standing there?"

"Almost five minutes," he chuckled. "You look like shit."

"Well, it's nice to see you, too, you old fart. What brings you to Los Angeles from that easy-ass job you have in the desert? Looks like you've been working out, or maybe a little cosmetic surgery?"

"I see you still don't follow the news."

"Not lately. I've been very busy. Tell me how you've kept so fit?"

"That's another story."

"Then what are you doing here at this ungodly hour?"

"I need your help on something that's a matter of life and death. I pray you can help me."

He spent the next hour explaining about Dável and the weapons that were on the disk he handed him. He told Jasper what the weapon could do. And Jasper was impressed with the advanced technology. He had heard about it, but understood it to be mostly science fiction and something that was at least ten years away.

"It's been built and has already passed a devastating test run. Twenty-three people are already dead. And if I can't stop it, more will die, and the number could reach seven figures."

"I'm not sure I can figure this out that quickly."

"You're the best. You have to!" Robert pleaded. "This is some serious shit we have here. I need a counter-weapon, and I need it fast. Like yesterday."

"I've heard rumors about this Pulsar XR-36, he pointed to the file on his screen, but they didn't include what you're telling me about. There's another weapon?"

"I hope the disk has everything. There are a dozen files on it. See what you can come up with. All I know is its code name: RX-666"

"Very appropriate code name for this weapon. After what you've said this Dável is like, he's got the devil's weapon."

Robert looked puzzled.

"You know, the number of the beast: 666." Jasper tore off a corner from some papers he was working on and handed it to Robert with a pen. "Where can you be reached?"

"Just call my name and I'll pop right in again," Robert laughed.

"You're so full of shit. Either give me your cell or get out of here and let me work," he said.

When he looked up from his computer screen, Robert was gone.

"He was always a crazy mother-fucker," he muttered as he scanned all the files.

CHAPTER SEVENTY-SEVEN

Katie located Cardinal Richman; he had flown back from Rome and happily agreed to meet with her the next day at Saint John's Episcopal Church in Morningside Park. Her conversation was brief. He seemed encouraged that he had gotten the support from the Vatican, before the murders of the Pope and his Cardinals.

"I'm saddened by the tragedy that happened in Rome," the cardinal said, trying to sound believable. "It's horrible that Dável would do such a thing to so many great men. As the Vatican's newly elected leader, I feel we'll be able to continue The Cleansing without any resistance. If this was God's will, then so be it."

Katie sensed something was not quite right. When she asked him about the Pope and the Cardinals, he didn't seem too disturbed by their deaths, chalking them up to God's will.

If he was cleansed, why would he say that? she wondered, *and why did he specifically want to meet with me alone?*

There was a familiar ring to his words; she just couldn't put her finger on it. Katie decided she'd wait until they met. Maybe by then she could figure it out.

"I find his attitude strange also," Rebecca said. "Something just doesn't seem right."

"Have you been here all this time?" Katie said, surprised.

"Yes, I was hoping to get some private time with you. There's something I haven't told you that I think you need to know."

"Another deception?"

"No, just a more detailed description of the truth that only you should hear."

"Okay . . . "

"As you know, Dável and his daughter tried once to take over your bodies back at the chateau. Since he failed, we've never worried about him attempting it again, until now."

"Are you telling me, both of us are at risk?"

"Only you."

"What about Robert? Is Dável trying to take over his body?"

"No, that's impossible. I've made Robert too strong for him to even get close and harm him. Dável has probably already assumed a body. It's his daughter he's trying to help. I think with your powers and your pregnancy, we've given him a wild opportunity that he won't be able to resist. I didn't mean for it to happen this way, but you've turned into the bait in my family's cat-and-mouse game with Dável."

"What the hell am I going to do?" she screamed. She became repulsed that her body could be violated in such a way.

"Robert can't be away from your side until we find Dável and his daughter."

* * * * *

Dável held up *The Pallasian Covenant;* its power flowed through his hand. He did not like how it affected him while he was inside the cardinal's body. He threw it down immediately, as if he had touched the fires of hell. A frightened look came over him.

"How could it be?" he muttered. "I should be immune to all of this."

CHAPTER SEVENTY-EIGHT

It was 6:30 in the morning when the ranting voice rang out in their room.

"Who's is this?" Katie's voice was tired, but pleasant.

"Jasper Billings," he replied.

"Who?" She just looked at Robert confused. "Who's Jasper? And why isn't he using a phone?"

Robert raised his eyebrows innocently. "I told him to call me and he took it literally."

She rolled over, tuned out Jasper and buried her head under her pillow, her hands pulling the corners tight over her ears.

"Jasper, have you figured it out?"

"Are you going to tell how we are talking like this?" Jasper said his voice cracking.

"Later," Robert said. "Tell me what you discovered."

"It looks like United Weapons Systems has unleashed the worst weapon of mass destruction since the A-bomb. You owe me big-time, Robert. But, it wasn't the Pulsar XR-36 that killed those people. It was the RX-666, which has enough destructive power to wipe out an entire city with just the push of a button."

"Stop the jabbering, and tell me if you figured this thing out!" he shouted back into the phone.

"Are you aware of what this shit can do?" he shouted back at his friend.

"I've seen the results. I just don't understand how."

Katie propped herself up against the headboard. She looked bewildered, tugging at Robert' arm for his attention, wanting to know what was happening on the other end of the conversation. Then she remembered: she could eavesdrop.

"The Pulsar XR-36 is a great weapon, but the RX-666, that's one hell of a piece of destruction. Whoever controls it will be undefeatable. Used together, these weapons would make any army unbeatable. The RX-666 is small and carries a large wallop. The test results on animals are devastating. If what you witnessed was done by this device, we're all in big trouble."

"Stop being so melodramatic and tell me if we can stop it?" Robert shouted as if he were grabbing someone's neck during one of his interrogations.

"It appears that one of the scientists had the foresight to create a countermeasure just in case the weapon got into the wrong hands. It's not going to be easy to replicate. I'm just not sure I can get it made within your time frame."

"What will it take for you to be able to build it by yesterday?"

"I'll need access to United Weapons Systems laboratory. If I'm correct, your counter-weapon is there, inside their database."

"I'll meet with the president in one hour and get you the clearance you need," he said. "Stay by your phone."

"Right, you're meeting with the president in one hour," he laughed.

Silence.

"You're not joking, are you?"

"When this is all over, and if we're still alive, I'll tell you everything," said Robert.

CHAPTER SEVENTY-NINE

The president was sitting up in bed, just staring at the wall. He did not see them at first by the door, where they stood holding hands.

He looked over; they could tell he had been crying.

"I've been waiting for you. We're standing in a whole lot of shit, aren't we?"

"We could be, Mr. President," Robert said. "But we're here with a solution."

Once the president had heard their story, he was on the phone with FBI Director Gail Smith, ordering her to let Jasper Billings have full access to anything he needed at United Weapons. He also ordered that she see to it that he was flown there immediately.

Robert interrupted Hopkins. "I'll get Jasper there quicker than your planes. Just get him clearance. He'll be arriving shortly.

"Well, it's done," the president said. "My God, if we still have one, I hope he has mercy on our souls."

* * * * *

They were back at their hotel cleaning up when Katie burst in to the bathroom crying. She had just hung up the phone, shocked at the message she had received.

"What's wrong?" he asked, removing the shaving cream on his face with his towel.

"Rabbi Feldman and his wife were killed a few hours ago.

The police don't have a clue. Who would do this to him? He was such a good man."

"I've got to get to the crime scene and see if the MO is similar to what happened at the Vatican. It might be Dável and his daughter."

"I'm meeting later this afternoon with Cardinal Richman at Saint John's," she said. "I'll try to convince him to let us protect him."

"I don't want you going by yourself. I'll go so we both can twist his arm."

"I can handle him," she smiled. "You go find the archbishop first before Dável finds him. We'll meet up later."

Her kiss felt like it was going to be the last one he'd ever get. He had a flashback to the chateau and the morning he had left to work the farm. He had wanted to stay with her and make love, but she had said the same thing in French:

"We'll meet up later."

CHAPTER EIGHTY

The cathedral's lighting was poor because it counted on the sun's rays to shine through the beautiful stained-glass windows that illuminated its interior. Today, an unexpected storm had hit Manhattan, filling the skies with dark gray thunderclouds that hid the warm rays of the sun.

Katie was not sure where Cardinal Richman had said for them to meet. She was early and slowly roamed around the perimeter of the church. It was adorned with paintings and exhibits, reflecting a misguided history of religious events. How sad, she thought, that it would soon end and a new understanding would be taught in its place.

His cold hand startled her. She was surprised she did not feel his presence.

"Cardinal, I'm glad to see you're all right."

"What do you mean? I feel all right."

"I guess you haven't heard. Rabbi Feldman and his wife were killed earlier today."

"Oh my God. I met with them earlier today," he said, his inflection unnatural. "It must have happened right after I left. Who would do something like this? First the Pope and now my dearest friend."

Katie thought it strange that he would have the same reaction that he did to the Vatican murders. She sensed he was not terribly upset. His thoughts were unclear, hidden even, which made her uncomfortable. Something was blocking her out of his mind. She tried really hard, but she couldn't get an accurate read on him.

No more than twenty-five feet behind her, also hidden from her thoughts, was Dável's daughter Ruth, waiting for her father's signal to overtake Katie's body and become one with her molecular structure.

The Cardinal led Katie to an outer office away from the main part of the church. He had recently modified it to handle what he had in mind for Katie. He had lined the small room with a lead-based wallpaper coated with a red clay adhesive that would keep them cloaked from Robert's or The Family's scanning abilities—like the cave that had kept his family safe for centuries.

Although Katie entered reluctantly, she felt confident she had the power to protect herself against any danger. She heard the door slam shut and found herself for the first time since Sunrise Island once again alone in her thoughts. The silent void frightened her, as she realized she had lost contact with Robert. She panicked, wanting to escape, but some of her powers seemed to have vanished. She no longer had the ability to will herself to another location.

"What's going on here?" she shouted.

"There's been a little change in the plans you have for yourself and your baby," Cardinal Richman said, his tone menacing.

His face was bright red, his eyes glowed, and his nostrils steamed, as his warm breath filled the cold room.

"Let me go, Dável," she cried, realizing that Dável was now the Cardinal. "I know you've tried this once before. Your plan to have your daughter take over my body didn't work then and won't work now."

"How smart of you. But it's too late. Detective Robert Philips can't protect you here. You're on my turf now, with my rules. Don't resist. It will be over shortly, and you'll rule the world with me. We'll create a dynasty for our daughter that lives inside your womb. Then the world will truly know that the new Messiah has arrived."

"That will never happen. I'd rather die first than be part of your plan."

"Unlike the chateau incident, this time you'll not die. You're powerless here. So shut up, and let me get set up."

He nervously fumbled with the equipment he had laid out on a table. He was organized as if he were about to perform a major operation. He noticed that Katie was inching her way closer to him. She thought she still had her strength and jumped on

Dável's back, her right arm across his throat, her left grabbing tightly her other hand in a police choke hold Robert had taught her. She squeezed as hard as she could and felt Dável jump up, twirling madly, trying to rip her hands off his throat. Katie felt her strength, but it only lasted a minute before her prey broke free and kicked her in the head, tossing her across the small room. Her jaw felt broken. She tried to mend herself like she had practiced, but Dável was all over her and threatened to break her neck like a twig. She knew she was outmatched for the moment.

She sat down, trying to think how her powers could help save her. At the same time, she tried to call out to Rebecca, who she hoped had followed her today like she had yesterday.

* * * * *

Inspector Lefebvre had gone unnoticed by Katie. His first instinct was usually the one to trust, and what he had seen told him she was in some trouble. After listening for days to their conversations with the young girl named Rebecca, he speculated that this Dável had consumed the cardinal's body. He knew Cardinal Richman very well, and when the cardinal had brushed him off earlier in the church, he knew something was terribly wrong.

He followed them to the back of the cathedral to the room that Katie was pushed into. He tried to dial his cell phone to call Robert, but the thick concrete walls would not allow his phone to roam. He did not want to leave, knowing that Katie's life might rest on the precious seconds he might have to save her. He glanced at his watch. It was 3:30 in the afternoon.

"It's been a long time since I was a hero," he told himself, as he pulled his revolver out and checked to see if it was fully loaded.

Before he could use it, someone grabbed his gun and tossed it on the cold marble floor. He turned and was relieved to see the cardinal's bodyguard, Hirshumi Kubota, standing there, signaling him to wait.

CHAPTER EIGHTY-ONE

Robert found the archbishop. He was dead, killed in the same manner as Rabbi Feldman. Fear filled his mind; he sensed that Katie was in danger. He had to find Abdeljalil Tahmass before he turned up dead also. He started to scan for the cleric's brain waves and found him alive in England.

His nickname to his American Friends was Abe. No one really knew how to pronounce his first name properly.

"Abe, this is Robert. Rabbi Feldman and Archbishop Stallsworth are dead. You're not safe to return to the United States until we capture or kill Dável."

Abe was more than agreeable, which pleased Robert. He then reached deep inside his head to find Katie. It was like she was not on the planet. He had to find the Cardinal and Katie to warn them, but didn't know where to begin. He searched his mind, struggling to feel for Katie's presence, but it was as if she did not exist. Panic filled his head that she could be dead already. He was overtaken with emotions as tears filled his eyes. He prayed she was safe. He did not want to lose her now that his life was so happy and fulfilled. He had to make an immediate choice. Sadly, logic prevailed, and he just hoped the love of his life was safe.

He was back at the laboratory at UWS. He had to get what Jasper was building first. He couldn't leave without it. He had to be ready for Dável's arrival.

"Katie will be all right," he mumbled unconvincingly, as he paced fretfully around the laboratory, her last words echoing in his mind. "She can take care of herself…she can take care of herself."

"You're making me crazy," Jasper scolded. "I'll be done shortly."

Robert anxiously checked his watch. It was 3:30 in the afternoon in Manhattan. *Where the hell is she?* he tortured himself.

"Can you hurry up?" he said anxiously. "We're running out of time!"

"I'm moving as fast as I can. I'll need to test it before you go."

"I haven't the time. I'll have to test it on my own."

"Here!" he said, handing the small box to him. "I hope it does what you need it to do."

Robert smiled at his friend and gave him a hug. "You've never failed me before. I know you've found our solution."

He vanished, holding the small black box with the one switch on it and a short rubber antenna. He hoped the gadget would work.

Jasper rubbed his eyes in disbelief.

"I'm starting my twelve-step program tomorrow," he promised himself as he took a drink from his flask.

* * * * *

The day the world had been anxiously waiting for had finally come. This was the day Jacob would give his message to the world. The streets were lined with people, blocking all means of traffic around the United Nations.

News trucks had positioned themselves on the main courtyard, meshed in between the tents and sleeping bags of the people who had been camping out for over two weeks. A gigantic digital TV screen hung from the building, displaying interviews with religious leaders around the world, as everyone speculated about what The Family would reveal this day. The world seemed happy and ready for Jacob's words. The Cleansing had seemed to work on a majority of the world's population.

The speech, which most believed was God's final message to his children, would be broadcast live. Even though the world heard that Jacob was from another planet, they still believed he was God and had come back to Earth from Heaven. Their faith seemed to forget about Dável and his battle with The Family.

Little did anyone know what would happen if Dável was not stopped before The Pallasian Covenant was released.

Like innocent children playing silly games, the youth who had been waiting for weeks began to release their whirling-dervish energy, encouraging adults and the elderly to join in a celebration of redemption and salvation. Every major religion had predicted that one day God would return and save all of his believers and now everyone at the United Nations had a renewed hope for their lives.

* * * * *

Robert was at the UN, where he had hoped to see Katie waiting with Cardinal Richman.

"Where's Katie?" Rebecca asked, worried.

Robert kept pacing anxiously in circles.

I can't locate her or Cardinal Richman. I'm worried about her safety after finding the archbishop dead.

"It won't happen again," Rebecca said. "He won't get her."

"*I'm glad you can read my mind. I just couldn't bring myself to say those words. I'm not ready to lose her again!*"

"Neither am I," Rebecca said with confidence. "*I've got to go and help bring my father in. He'll be extremely weak from slowing down his metabolism for the speech. Keep searching for Katie inside your mind. She's out there.*"

Robert paced the lobby, hoping Katie would appear and everything would be all right. He could not concentrate. The other voices in his head interfered with his search.

"It's happening again," he whispered, frustrated he had no control and discouraged by another flashback.

* * * * *

Riding in on his horse, he had a feeling that Katherine and his children were in danger. In the distance, he could see their house and a strange glow that appeared to grip the wooden frame. As he rode faster and faster, the house was shaking violently, ready to explode. He was closer now and could hear his children crying and his wife screaming.

He ran toward the front door, grabbed a pitchfork, and with his foot kicked it open. Inside he saw Katherine flailing her arms, swinging helplessly at the empty air that filled the house.

Had she gone crazy? But then he immediately felt it himself. There was a hidden force trying to squeeze the life out of him. He struggled helplessly as the force was much too great for him to fight off. Before he collapsed, he saw Katherine being thrown in the air, gliding helplessly toward the pitchfork he was holding.

She came faster and faster. His weapon would not drop from his hands; a strong force held it upright. It continued to point at her as she floated toward him. Fear gripped him, as the sharp blades pierced her heart and lungs. Before he lost consciousness, his wife's eyes locked with his.

"I love you," she said, coughing her last breath. "We'll be together again someday."

His eyelids froze in a position of ascension as the room grew darker. He hurled his scorn at the ghosts who were killing his family, his eyes full of bloody intent, but he remained powerless as the life escaped from his body.

* * * * *

The picture was so real; he began to tremble in anticipation of what might be happening to Katie. Cardinal Richman entered briskly. Robert scanned the doorway, but did not see Katie. Pushing through the crowd of reporters, he was able to corner the Cardinal before the news media kidnapped him.

"Where's Katie?" he asked, pulling hard on the Cardinal's sleeve.

"I haven't seen her," he replied.

A look of disgust came over his face. He angrily removed Robert's hand from his robe. "She never kept her appointment with me. I couldn't wait any longer. I didn't want to miss the speech."

"Weren't you at Saint John's?"

"No," he replied, surprised. "We were supposed to meet at Saint Michael's."

"Shit, something's happened. I've got to find her. You'll have to protect The Family while I'm gone."

"Protect The Family? I can't raise my hand in anger. I'm a man of the cloth. I can't harm anyone, even if they're evil." He was pleased his lies were hidden from Robert' probing thoughts.

"All you have to do is press this button when Jacob begins his speech. You'll not be harming anyone; in fact, you'll be saving lives. Please don't argue. Just take this box. When the speech starts, press this button and don't move from your spot. Dável is out here somewhere, and he has a weapon that can kill everyone in the room, including Jacob. We can't let this happen."

Robert was gone before the Cardinal could say another word.

"I guess I'm living right," Dável smiled, tossing the box in the trash receptacle. *It will soon be over, and the hunted will finally find peace with his new family.*

* * * * *

Dável had always wished that things had turned out differently for him. His trial could have taken a different path, if only he had been allowed to defend himself. Unfortunately back then, the accused were assumed guilty until proven innocent. For him, there were no witnesses, and his fingerprints had been found on the gun that killed his partner at his laboratory. As far as the court was concerned, it was an open-and-shut case for the prosecution. Even then, he had lost his identity. His name, Eli, which his wife loved, was reduced to just a number throughout the trial proceedings. He tried to keep his name visible, but the court would not allow it. "Prisoner 666, please sit down, or we'll have to restrain you!" he remembered the judge shouting at him.

It had not mattered that he was Pallas's leading microbiologist, who had been working on new genetic combinations to cure all diseases.

Then one day he discovered that his partner tried to steal his ideas and make them his own. Eli had been working late at the lab as he often did when his partner attacked him. The attempt was ill prepared. Eli was faster and more agile than his partner was. He used his gun to stop what at first he imagined was an intruder who was there to steal their secrets. It was only after the shot was fired that he discovered it was his partner and long-time friend holding a long knife in his hand.

Even though he pleaded self-defense, he was sentenced to twenty-five years in prison on the barren desert of Pallas. A normal life span on Pallas was five hundred years, so he accepted his fate, knowing he would still be a young man when he got out.

His life took a drastic turn one day when his wife came on her weekly conjugal visit. His wife was taken to a small room equipped with a double bed and a small bathroom. One of the guards, the cousin of his partner, had given Eli problems since his arrival. That day he denied him his visit with his wife. He told him he had broken some fabricated rule during breakfast. There was no one to appeal to, so he was sent back to his cell.

Meanwhile, his wife was preparing herself for the visit and lay naked on the bed, awaiting his arrival. The lights had been dimmed, and when the door opened, the bright light from the hallway shined like a beacon through the doorway. Silhouetted was a man she thought was her husband.

"I've been waiting so long for you and need you now," she teased romantically.

"If it's a real man you've been waiting for," the guard replied, unzipping his pants, "then your wait is over."

She realized he wasn't Eli.

"Where's my husband?" she screamed, trying to pull the blanket over her exposed body. "Get out of here and leave me alone."

He was too fast and was on top of her, forcing himself inside her. With his strong hand, he covered her mouth to stop her screams, and with his heavy legs, he spread her apart. She fought him, scratching at his skin.

"You bitch," he shouted, cracking her cheekbone with his fist.

She was out cold when he had finished with her. He fastened his pants and left her there. He ordered the female guard to escort her out in fifteen minutes, patting her on the rear, as he swaggered down to his barracks to brag about what a great piece of ass Eli's wife had been.

Two weeks later, Eli received a note from his daughter that his wife Lea had killed herself in the woods behind their house. As he read on about what drove her to choose death over life, he felt an evil take over his mind. Unfortunately for Eli, the harvesting procedure on Pallas had not yet been perfected and her molecular cells were lost.

A month passed. He was ready to execute his plan. When the guard who had raped his wife came by his cell to harass him as he did every day about what a wonderful piece of ass his wife had been, he was finally ready for him. It was over so fast—but not so fast that he couldn't tell the guard why on this day he would die. Eli's strong hands and arms overwhelmed the guard. Every prisoner heard the snap. They banged on their bars in unison. The bastard who had tormented them was now finally dead.

Killing an officer of the court was a capital offense, and he could still hear the horrifying words from the Judge: "You've been sentenced to Pallas's worst punishment." A week later, he was scheduled for his planet's eternal death, which would effectively make him a deaf mute, paralyzed, unable to move. With just his thoughts crying out for help to a black void that would not respond. The torment each day would grow unbearable. Suicide was out of the question.

His five children could not understand why he was being punished after what the guard had done to their mother, and so they planned their father's escape. Eli was surprised when his children kidnapped him and set off for Mars. Eli made sure to take with him several of his fellow prisoners, whom he knew would stand by him until death.

The Council's Special Police Unit had looked everywhere for the escapee they now called Dável, the name given to someone who kills a protected individual. With his wife gone, Eli wanted to forget his given name, so he accepted his new title, as his medal of honor for avenging his wife's brutal rape.

* * * * *

He knew that after this day at the UN he still would not be able to reclaim his former identity, but he would finally be at peace, away from the hunters of Pallas.

The TV monitors were turned on. The cameras scanned the theater. Everyone knew they would be seeing a show unlike any other. Dável in his stolen body shell positioned himself under the TV monitor in the lobby and close to the chamber doors, the RX-666 in his hand. He had already placed the receptor cells around the assembly room, unnoticed and undetected by the FBI's scanners. He was safely outside ground zero, protected from the devastation he was about to inflict on everyone who was inside.

* * * * *

"You look the same as you did in 1746," Ruth said arrogantly to a frightened Katie. *"This time I'll win."*

"Not without a fight," Katie replied defiantly, not able to communicate telepathically.

"You have no powers in here, so don't be silly. If you just submit, it won't be painful."

"Give it your best shot," Katie said, gesturing for her to make her move. She crouched down like a soccer goalie ready to make a save.

She hoped that Dável's daughter would lose her temper, as she had done before and make a mistake in her weakened condition. With her remaining powers and strength, Katie felt that she could defeat Ruth.

Then it had happened. She could feel another entity inside her, traveling around her brain as if it were looking for a place to settle. The smell nauseated her. She could feel the entity inside her become powerful, draining her energy, as it latched on to every cell inside her body. She was at the door kicking and screaming for help. The blunt sounds her fist made told her that the door was very thick and that the room was soundproof. She didn't give up and continued throwing objects against the door and walls, banging her body against the door in futile attempts to break it down.

She started to feel weak—both in physical stamina and mental stability—as Ruth kept getting stronger. She was losing, feeling her body submitting to Ruth. Katie fell to the ground. There was no strength left in her. She understood it would soon be over. She cried out for Robert, but this time he was not around to protect her.

"I'm sorry, my love; I tried," she wept as her vision dimmed. "I'll always love you."

To Katie's surprise, the thousands of voices that had plagued her these last few weeks returned. She rolled over on the floor and saw that the door had been kicked opened. Standing over her was Inspector Lefebvre holding his gun, looking for someone to shoot.

"Are you all right?" he asked.

Kubota searched the room, sensing something was not right. He helped Katie up and pushed her behind him, acting as her shield.

"I will be now," she said, getting up and feeling her powers returning.

As if releasing a powerful cough, Katie shot Ruth's vapors from her mouth, slamming them against the far wall of the room. Katie immediately found Ruth's frequency and was standing over a young, frail girl. She was naked without her robe and terminally discolored. She looked the same age as Rebecca. Her emaciated face and arms inspired sympathy. Her hair was knotted, years of dirt imbedded in it. She tried to stand, holding on to a table to steady herself. Katie could see that Ruth knew it was over, but she still had contempt for her and what she had done to her children at the chateau.

"You didn't even have the respect to wash up before entering my body," Katie laughed at the young girl, who began to weep. "It's over. Now all we need is to stop your father, and the reign of terror you've inflicted on our world will soon be over."

Katie watched Ruth feebly try to come at her. She stumbled pathetically, exposing her twig-thin legs. The fury in her eyes mixed with her tears made Katie feel empathy for this monster. As she stumbled, an invisible force hit her. It was strange to see a human hand enter Katie's invisible world, and she watched with curiosity. As the large powerful hands grabbed tightly around their invisible enemy's mid-section, they were drawn inside the space that Katie had traveled to. Kubota had a strange expression on his face, as he wondered where he was.

"Thank you, my friend," Katie said as she grabbed Ruth harshly from Kubota's vise-like grip. "You saved my life. It's okay. I can handle her from here."

Kubota slowly relinquished his prize. Then he bowed to Katie, which she returned out of respect. Katie saw Kubota go back into his defensive stance, as another woman materialized right in front of his eyes. Katie turned and smiled.

"I'm glad I found you," Esther said.

"Esther, what are you doing here?" she asked.

"I'm here to help." She walked over to the dying girl, pushing Kubota away from her.

Kubota started to defend himself when Katie told him it was okay.

Katie and Kubota watched, as a computer screen floated toward Ruth, positioning near the back of her neck. It sounded like a vacuum searching for dirt to suck into its bag. The chill in the air gave Katie goose bumps. They watched the screen float away and disappear.

"It's over. She's gone forever. That was too close. Another sixty seconds and she would have won."

"How did you find me?"

"My sensors picked up your lingering brain waves inside the church—something you haven't been taught to do yet. I had a hunch you were still there. When the door to your room opened up, I was able to locate you."

"Wait a minute," Katie said. "I'll be right back."

She held Kubota's hand, and they both disappeared.

Inspector Lefebvre had been shocked when Katie disappeared. But when his new friend also disappeared, he found himself alone in an empty room. He almost fainted before Katie miraculously appeared holding Kubota's hand.

"I want to thank you for finding me," she said, giving each of them a big hug and a kiss on the cheek. "The two of you saved my life. Meet us at the hotel later, so we can thank you in a more respectful manner."

She was gone again in a blink of his eye.

They touched their cheeks. "You've thanked us more than enough."

"We have to find Robert," Katie said, returning to Esther. "Dável has taken over Cardinal Richman's body."

"He's already into his final phase. He must be thinking his daughter has consumed you. We need to hurry."

Katie heard Robert calling her. "Katie, where have you been?"

"I'm fine," she said. "Get back to the UN; Dável has taken over the Cardinal's body."

"Oh, shit. I just gave him our only defense to protect Jacob and Rebecca."

Katie and Esther both appeared in the front courtyard of the United Nations among the crowds of worshipers. Seeing them materialize silenced the onlookers. The surprise did not cause a panic. Instead, it brought them to their knees, their hands locked in prayer, chanting whatever came to their minds out of respect for the angels that had dropped from the heavens.

On the large TV screen positioned around the outside of the building, they could see that the speech was getting ready to begin.

"We don't have much time," Robert said. "Once we find Dável, we can't just grab him; it would start a panic. I don't want to lose any lives today, so let's try to be cautious."

He wanted to kiss Katie and hold her tightly in his arms, but he knew time was of the essence.

"I have an idea that might work," Katie told him as they disappeared inside the building.

CHAPTER EIGHTY-TWO

Rebecca walked slowly, steadying herself the whole way, as she approached the podium. Her eyes remained fixed on her feet, watching them intently, as they touched the firm ground that she had not felt in such a long time.

She was beautiful, tall and slender, with long blonde hair that tumbled down her back. Her olive skin, more Middle Eastern than Hispanic, accentuated her beautiful green eyes. She seemed to have had a make-over.

Robert read her thoughts. Fear was consuming her. It surprised him that someone so powerful was now so vulnerable, exposed to a danger she might not overcome. He knew that she could not come in and out of her increased metabolic state more than once without causing severe damage to her cells. He felt sad for her, he had begun to feel very close, and promised himself he would not let anything happen to her or her family. Robert tried to believe that Jacob and Rebecca had good hearts and cared very much about Earth. Further, he now believed Jacob could really be the Holy Father the world's major religions prayed to and that this God wanted a workable solution to save what he believed were his children.

Rebecca's voice cracked; a slight stuttering made her first words hard to understand. She bent closer to the microphone and repeated her greeting.

"My...my name is Rebecca. I am from a planet named Pallas. My father Jacob will be addressing all of you shortly."

She raised her head to look at her audience. She sensed everyone had noticed her nervousness, and she felt how flushed her complexion had become. The representatives from around the world buzzed with anticipation.

Katie felt her heart ache, as she watched her friend struggle to gather her strength. It was obvious that this metabolic state was harmful to her and would be harmful for her father also. Both of them were truly sacrificing themselves to save the world.

Her introduction to the group was brief. She told them what to expect and that they should remain in their seats. Any outbursts during her father's speech would be dealt with as an act of aggression. As she finished speaking, her father materialized. There was no smoke, drum roll, or bright lights. Jacob seemed serious and ready to get down to business.

He touched her arm, and looked straight into her eyes. He thanked her with his warm smile, which started her tears flowing. She kissed his cheek, as if it were a fine piece of china. Katie watched, her emotions welling up, remembering the day her parents were killed; she had not been fortunate enough to kiss them goodbye, as she ran to save her own life. She understood why Rebecca wanted to kiss her father, since this might be her last chance.

To the astonishment of everyone watching, Rebecca vanished. Jacob was now alone—ready to tell the world the truth about how Earth was created. Robert thought Jacob appeared much older than when they first met him on the transporter. He wondered if his appearance was just for show. Did he want to depict himself as the God everyone had imagined he would look like, or was he truly weakened?

The audience gasped. His white flowing robe and long white beard blended perfectly with his long silvery hair. His eyes were an icy-blue, cold and hard as he stared into the cameras. He hypnotized the assembly. The deep lines on his face told a sad story of pain and struggle. The world was not looking at a savior, or a God, but at just a man who had endured a long life of hardship and suffering.

As he spoke, the weather began to change outside. The black clouds that had been ominous all day turned to white puffy cotton balls. They floated apart, allowing the blue sky and the warm sun to shine through. The crowds outside shuddered, not from the warmth, but from the divine power they believed they were witnessing on the huge TV monitors.

Jacob's voice was deep and old-sounding. His words struggled out of his mouth, shaking wildly, as they floated, searching for attentive ears that begged for some meaning.

"For ten thousand years Earth time, my family has watched over your planet, trying to keep it safe and at the same time allowing you to evolve into a world that would be welcomed into our universe." He paused, frozen, as if he had forgotten what his next words were going to be. "I have led you to believe that I'm an all-powerful God that would provide internal sustenance in each of your lives. I am sad to say it, but that was a misleading lie, one that has brought your planet to a very unfortunate state. What was supposed to be various religious groups based on goodness and charity has not happened. Earth has evolved into a war-like state, using me as a motivator to kill or control for financial gain. I'm saddened for what I'm about to tell all of you; however, it must be said today. You will better understand the seriousness of my words by knowing that the prophesied Armageddon will soon be upon you, unless you heed my words. I will be gone from your lives shortly and will never return. As you will hear I will not leave you without a solution, as well as two messengers who can rehabilitate your planet."

The crowds outside, in the lobby, and in the corridor moaned with fear and despair. One woman slit her throat out on the sidewalk; others began to run irrationally about, not knowing where to hide.

"Don't panic!" he shouted out feebly. "The solution is within each of you. For centuries, I unfortunately believed that you needed a higher power to follow, when all the answers you needed were inside each of you.

"When you begin to believe that the truth to all your questions lies within your heart and mind, then and only then, you and your planet can be saved."

His hands shook as he steadied himself against the podium. He spent the next hour telling his audience the entire tale of Earth's creation and how the bibles they've read were works of fiction. He went on to explain how all religions were created and how they manipulated the truth, their leaders consumed by a DNA poison created by Dável.

The faces that he could see were emotionless. Their eyes struggled for comprehension, for something that could make sense of this stranger's message. The faith they had carried around all their lives was now shattering right before their eyes. Their most fundamental belief—that another world awaited them if they followed the rules God had given them—was now destroyed.

"All of you have the power to find peace and happiness without your old misguided values. Free your minds of the hate and prejudice that continue to plague your planet. All human beings were created the same. White, Black, or even Brown are just pigments, nothing more. Differences should not be feared, but held with respect and compassion. Rid yourself of the selfish greed that has motivated you to become a world of segregation ruled by wealth and power. There is no one race, religion or human better than anyone else. These differences were created so you could recognize where people came from. You need to learn to embrace and understand all walks of life. Every human being on Earth has something positive to offer your world and until you learn to accept that fact, wars, poverty, and prejudice will control you."

He went on to explain The Cleansing and the wonderful results it was having on people around the world. He told them it would require that a hundred percent of the humans on Earth be cleansed. This demand must be met.

He told them about *The Pallasian Covenant* and how it would replace the competing dogmas that had once controlled mankind. He told them about Dável and his poison and how the Devil's dark side was within each of them. He blamed his archenemy for all the horrible wars that had been waged for greed and power. He told them how their weapons of mass destruction threatened the universe and his planet, Pallas.

He explained the reasons for the recent killings and what needed to be accomplished before the Council's army arrived. He called their arrival a day of atonement, a day, which, if they were fully cleansed, would yield true paradise on Earth.

He noticed the room had begun to stir; the atmosphere inside grew tense.

"I sense most of you can't bear to let go of your fears and your dislikes and the dark side that has consumed you all your lives. But now, a cleansing will instantly take place, and you'll be free to love and feel safe on the planet you call your home.

"You will have to believe and trust what *The Pallasian Covenant* has to offer you. Practice, from this day forward, all its teachings; it will begin to reshape your mutated DNA and free you. I promise each of you that if you allow your minds to release the hate and prejudice that is inside you, you will finally have the answers to all your questions. Then, and only then, will you experience peace and tranquility for the rest of your lives."

He lifted the book with his two hands and held it high over his head.

"This will be your salvation!" he shouted. "The Cleansing has the power to remove any impurities inside your DNA. Once your bodies are pure again, then your planet will evolve to its full potential."

Jacob noticed a man whose anger and rage could be read clearly. He acknowledged the man with a wave of his hand and invited him to speak.

"I want to know why you've killed these last few weeks so many people!" the representative from France shouted. "Why should we follow a murderer and practice his teachings?"

"If those men had not been stopped, we would not be having this meeting today," he stuttered, nearly exhausted. "All those who have died were involved in a destructive scheme to start a world war that would have destroyed your free world and would have put them in power. I could not let that happen."

"We have laws we all live by. We can't condone or accept your unilateral justice," the French delegate said. "I will not endorse your blackmail of the world to accept your word as the gospel. Your Pallasian Covenant sounds more like Darwin's Pallasian Doctrine. We are not a people that will be domesticated. I won't allow my country to be controlled by you."

Jacob's icy stare stopped the man in his tracks. As if paralyzed, he stood frozen.

"If you don't agree to change, a harsh punishment will be brought upon you. Don't defy my demands; you've seen how powerful we are. We've given our powers to our messengers, Robert Philips and Katie O'Riley. They will police your world and make it ready for a positive evaluation from our Council's army."

"Sit down, and shut up," several people around the French delegate shouted at him.

The president of the assembly stood. "Please excuse his rude behavior. He can be damned if he likes, but you have our support. The French like to complain, but never have any positive solutions for our world. Please, continue."

    Rebecca's father, with much effort, opened *The Pallasian Covenant* to the first page. Ignoring the scorn that had been heaped upon him, he adjusted himself and held tightly to the edges of the podium so he would stop shaking. He looked up, his eyes warm with the love he was about to bestow on the world. His words began to flow out, floating toward all who would listen. The room grew quiet. All their attention focused on Jacob and the mist that gently blanketed the room, filling everyone's lungs with his power. He was remembering the time he spoke to Moses and regretting not speaking to all the Hebrews who had fled Egypt. It might have helped them cope better back then as they roamed the desert. *I always expected more out of these humans,* he told himself.

    This time he could see the tears of joy trickling down their cheeks. Hands were cupped in amazement, as the message, the change, The Cleansing, flowed through their minds and bodies. Resting on each representative's legs was a copy of *The Pallasian Covenant.*

    He looked at his children and exulted that they had returned and their minds and bodies this time were able to accept The Cleansing.

    "Esther, it worked!" he called to his wife. *"This time, Dável can't defeat us!"*

CHAPTER EIGHTY-THREE

Dável just stood there listening to first Rebecca and then Jacob, shocked how his brother had aged. His eyes full of bloody intent, his thumb on the button that would finally kill his most hated enemy. He knew that once The Cleansing Poem was heard by the world, it would be too late for him and his daughter to rule.

"You're all alone now," Robert said, his voice echoing inside Dável's head. *It's all over.*

He turned to see Katie standing next to Robert. Instantly Dável knew something was wrong.

Dável, his nostrils flared. He was noticeably alarmed. *"Where's my daughter?"* he screamed, his eyes glowing like an ocean of fire ready to consume everything in its path.

For the first time in his life, he felt isolated. The emptiness that burned inside him left only one choice. Without his daughter, life was finally not worth living. He wanted to make the world pay for his pain—make Jacob's family suffer like he had suffered, and finally kill the two new mutations that Jacob had created.

His eyes met Robert', and with a sadistic grin he put his thumb on the button.

"Jacob First," he shouted, "then the rest of you."

As he saw the horror on Katie's face, he winked at her and gestured with a bow of respect.

Suddenly, without warning, the doors to the General Assembly burst open. The people standing near the cardinal were startled when the heavy doors slammed against the concrete walls like cymbals smashing together to signal the finale of a great musical composition. Dável's murderous plan had taken an unexpected turn. Jacob and Rebecca were gone from the assembly room, and only Robert and Katie stood in his way. His finger stiffened on the button, and the weapon began to activate.

Dável felt his rage escalate when he realized the death toll would be huge if he pushed the button at that moment. Under different circumstances, he would not have concerned himself with that fact. But he knew he would die along with everyone else, and he was not ready to end his quest until he saw Jacob and his entire family dead at his feet. He had more fight left in him.

He knew his new nemesis, Robert Philips, was the cause. He had no choice, but to release his finger or die a savage death. Until his revenge was complete, he had to lure Robert and Katie away from the opened chamber doors. He frantically searched for a means of escape, as Robert inched closer, extending his arm to grab him.

Her voice shocked him, like someone had squeezed his heart in a vise. She had found him like she had found the others.

"I've captured your daughter," Esther said, emotionless. *"You've lost. Let's make it easy and spare yourself any unnecessary pain. I've searched for too long to let you escape this time. Your madness is finished here. Your punishment awaits you."*

Robert was surprised at how much Rebecca's mother sounded like a police officer apprehending a criminal.

Who are you, really? he asked, as she lifted her monitor, the capturing incubator that would store Dável's brain impulses for transporting back to Pallas.

"I'm exactly who you know me to be: Rebecca's mother. I just have a different job than my husband. I'm a captain in our criminal police unit. My assignment has been to search for and arrest Dável."

"I was right," Robert said, curtailing his anger for the moment. "Katie and I were bait all along."

"I didn't use you as bait or set any of this up. Rebecca's intentions, along with my husband's, have been exactly as they appeared to be. I just knew that if their plan worked, then Dável would surface and I'd have my prisoner, and we'd all win. I just used what my daughter and husband did to my advantage."

Dável was upset he had fallen for this deception. It was like his mind had exploded. Despair filled his body. He was now dangerously isolated, the hunted all alone to survive. He trembled at the thought that his family was finally gone. There was now no one. They had finally isolated him in a world that was empty of the people he loved and cared for. He had one last idea that might bring his children back to him, but he must act quickly and try to get take Esther's incubator. Killing Esther was not going to be easy, nor would gaining control of the device that stored his children's molecular brain waves. He could feel Robert's power trying to blanket him in a force-field swaddle. He knew that there was too many forces at work and he first had to try to escape.

The distraction of their conversation gave him the opportunity he needed. With the swift movements of a cat, the cardinal, Dável, fled down a stairwell. All that was left to see was his robe flaring as he headed down the steps to the building's garage. Handicapped by the body he occupied, he couldn't move fast enough. The garage was filled with vehicles, restricting his means of escape. He needed a plan and needed it quickly.

Robert and Katie, not having the same mobility restrictions, were standing ten feet away from him as he continued to search frantically for a suitable escape route.

"It's over, Dável," Katie said sadly.

Both of them sensed that Esther had followed them down.

"Should you be here?" Katie asked, worried that Esther should be with her husband and daughter to protect them.

"I'm a cop who has a job to complete," she replied. "Robert should understand that."

"She's a murderer who has killed off my children without mercy or regard for the truth!" Dável hurled contemptuously. *"The Pallasian Covenant..."* he said, his tone desperate, *"it's a plan to domesticate the entire human race. Why do you think they need to have everyone exposed to Jacob's vapors...do you really believe the Council's Army is coming to give you a passing grade? They are coming to see if their slaves can be controlled."*

He tried to tell his sad story of how he had become who he was, but sensed he was about to be captured before he could finish. He knew he had only one choice and that was to die and take the three of them with him. His thumb returned to its previous rigidity. Robert was the first to read his mind and panicked at the thought that they all would die.

* * * * *

Meanwhile, upstairs in the lobby, a small boy who was bored waiting for his mother, as she watched what she told him was an "important speech," had wandered off to explore his surroundings. He stood on his tiptoes, his chin resting on the edge of a dirty trash can. His eyes like radar scanned the array of used wrappers of discarded food, used soda cans, and newspapers. A blinking red light caught his attention. Tipping the can gently, he reached in and grabbed what he thought looked like a discarded toy, not knowing it was the counter weapon Dável had thrown away.

Holding the black box tightly in his hands, his palm sliding over the detonator button, his fascination and imagination lit up his face. He rushed over to his mother, yanking on her dress, demanding attention to his newfound discovery. She just patted him on the head and reminded him to be polite while Mommy was watching the TV screen.

He told his mother he was going to play with his new toy. She just replied, never taking her eyes off the TV monitor, "That's fine, Johnny," and continued listening to the speech.

The crowds of giants made no space for him to sit and play. He found a door that had a lighted sign in red letters, which he couldn't read. He struggled at first, pulling hard on the door handle. Then with his shoulder he pushed the heavy metal door open. The stairwell was empty— a perfect spot for him to be alone with his new toy.

Totally engrossed in what he was doing, he flipped the toggle switches up and down, pressing the detonator button. The pretty lights went out, and he worried he might have broken his new toy. He pushed the toggle switch back to the 'up' position. His smile returned as the blinking red light came back on. He put the box down and was ready to push the only button near the oscillating light, when a man in a red flowing robe rushed past him and down the stairs. The next thing he heard were shouts coming from down below.

He held the stairwell railing tightly with his left hand, and locked his new toy securely under his right arm. He meandered slowly down toward the noise that had piqued his interest. The door to the garage was too heavy for him to open. Since he did not want to put down the black box, he decided that this space was as good as any to begin his imaginary play.

* * * * *

Dável hesitated. He felt a twinge of guilt for what he was about to do. It was the cardinal struggling inside him, trying to reason with the troubled man. The cardinal's cleansing was conflicting with Dável's rage and hate. Trying to block out the hope Cardinal Richman was trying to instill in him, he fell to his knees, holding his head in anguish.

"Leave me alone, and let me die in peace," he cried. "I want to finally rest from this gruesome life I've led."

Robert and Katie stood there frozen, unsure of what to do next. Then the unthinkable happened. Dável stood, his faced contorted with the decision he had made. There was a certain finality in his expression. The cardinal's eyes were on fire, his face beet-red, as he pushed down on the green blinking light.

"If I can't live, none of you shall you live either!"

Before Robert could react, the button was pressed. He grabbed onto Katie and held her close.

"Maybe in another lifetime we could try this again," he whispered to her.

Nothing happened.

Dável pressed it again. Still nothing. He looked around nervously. He saw the young child standing by the exit. In the child's hand was the box Dável had discarded in the trash can, its green light blinking.

"Stupid! What a stupid mistake!"

Robert was the first to react, knowing what the boy was holding, and was by Dável's side, his powerful arms wrapped around his body before he could react and get over to the boy.

"Now it's finally over. Give up peacefully."

Dável had been distracted and was not aware of the monitor that was approaching him from behind. Katie knew what it meant and stood her ground, as she watched the device prepare to capture its prey.

Robert took his eyes off of his enemy for just a second and focused on the monitor that floated behind Dável's head. The cardinal's robe flared like a matador's cape. The box he had been holding dropped to the concrete floor, shattering and exposing the intricate circuit boards that were meant to kill them. The cardinal fell like a sack of potatoes to the floor, his head hit the ground hard, and the sound of cracking bones echoed off the cement walls.

Katie was the first to go to Cardinal Richman to see if he was alive. She caught herself from falling, as her foot slipped on the pool of blood spreading outward from his head. She kneeled down and felt for a pulse.

"He's alive! Call an ambulance."

"Not so fast," Robert said. "This might be Dável."

"It's not," Esther said, disgusted. "He escaped before I could capture him."

Robert walked over to the shocked little boy, still standing frozen in disbelief. The box easily slipped out of his hand, and Robert told him to go back upstairs and find his parents. The boy looked at Robert, then back over at the pool of blood that he imagined was spreading toward him. Without any further hesitation, he was running up the stairs, screaming for his mother.

"Let me look at him," Esther said.

Katie moved aside and watched as her hands gently touched the cardinal's chest. The frozen impressions from her fingers rolled over his entire body.

His body became stiff. He was lying on his back. His eyes opened. They seemed fixed on the exposed steam pipes fastened to the ceiling. His body started to lift, and a light mist of cold air surrounded him forming a cocoon. His arms and legs were swaddled against his body, as the cool vapor appeared to massage and treat his wounds. The pool of blood spun like a mini-twister, kicking up the dust and loose dirt that carpeted the floor where the cardinal had lain motionless.

The funnel of blood found the broken opening from where it had exited and, as if the crack in his skull were a vacuum, was sucked back into his body. The fracture closed up as the cardinal's body slowly came to rest once again on the garage floor.

His eyes began to focus, and Katie cradled him in her arms.

"Just relax. You've been through a lot just now."

"Where am I?"

"It's a long story, but I'm glad you're okay and back with us."

"I've had one hell of a dream," he remarked, crossing himself to ask for forgiveness for his disrespect.

"We'll tell you all about it later," Katie assured him. "Are you up to listening to the speech?"

"Just help me up and point me in the right direction."

Standing by the stairwell were Inspector Lefebvre and the cardinal's bodyguard and friend, Kubota. They were both smiling as they walked over.

Kubota looked at his friend with tears of joy. "Cardinal, you all right?"

"Yes. I just need to listen to the speech. Can the two of you help me?"

The inspector introduced himself and began telling the cardinal about Dável and what had happened.

"We have a bigger problem," Robert told Katie.

"I know, but I don't have a clue what to do."

"If his MO still fits his pattern after a major defeat," Esther said, *"he'll be hiding upstairs, looking for one last way to reap his revenge on all of us."*

"He's powerless," Robert said, "isn't he?"

"Dável's weak, but not harmless. If he's ready to die, then he's more dangerous to all of us. He can cause extreme harm with one last burst of energy."

Robert was frustrated. "How can we stop him this time?"

"I'm not sure, but it will be a final showdown one way or the other."

* * * * *

Dável was breathing heavily as he hid inside the assembly room, waiting for Jacob to reappear. Then he realized Esther would have warned Jacob to stay on his transporter. He searched his mind to find any recent energy signatures.

"So that's where they've been hiding."   He was weak and was taking a long time to try to transport himself to Jacob's location. "A few more minutes, and I'll be ready to move."

He knew if he could reach the transporter, there was a chance he could occupy Jacob's weak body and returned to Pallas undetected. He knew it was the only hope he had at the moment. If it didn't work, maybe he could kill his archenemy and brother so he could rest in peace.

CHAPTER EIGHTY-FOUR

During the brief episode outside the chamber doors, Jacob had followed Robert's orders and sought refuge on the transporter. The speech continued from the bridge of their ship. Jacob apologized for the abrupt departure he'd had to make, choosing not to explain to the world what had actually happened.

But, the calm that had started to blanket the room had now turned to agitation, both inside and out. People were buzzing about Darwin's Pallasian Doctrine and beginning to panic. The French delegation had begun to take control of the conversations, igniting the chamber into an uncontrolled shouting match. Arguments, as well as fist fights, erupted about what Jacob was going to do the Earth.

Jacob realized that he could not control the room from where he was and decided that for his plan to work he had to return, regardless of his safety, and finish the speech face-to-face, just like his son did before and was crucified.

The chaotic atmosphere in the room had spread to the streets. And as he appeared back on the podium, people began to hurl obscenities—as well as wadded-up balls of paper—at him.

Robert watched in shock, surprised at the mob mentality that had taken over the room.

"Shit, it's happening again," he whispered to Katie. "Are these leaders not being affected by The Cleansing?"

Without thinking, he approached the podium. Rebecca's father looked at him and nodded—relieved that he was being rescued. Like a traffic cop trying to stop oncoming traffic, Robert' shot his left hand straight out in front of him.

The General Assembly became silent, even though everyone's lips continued to move. The muted room was finally at peace. Then, calm began to fall over all the agitated bodies that had been jumping up and down. Like frightened animals that knew that a more powerful creature was about to consume them, they settled down to listen once again.

"All of you should be ashamed," Robert said scornfully. "Today you've learned the truth that should set you free, and you are rejecting it as if you have something better to cling to. Our world has been all screwed up with our old, misguided beliefs, and we need a better direction to follow. We can no longer be a divided planet, harboring our prejudices in the name of a God our religious leaders want us to believe in. We have to begin to look inside ourselves, to find the answers and truths that have been within us all this time. We will no longer submit to some imaginary divine being to control us."

He paused, taking the hand of Rebecca's father and raising it high above his head.

"This man has a message for all of us. I pray that you accept him and his words as the New Truth, The Pallasian Covenant, which will cleanse our world. We have for thousands of years thought the essence of life was given to us by God in all his beauty and wonderment. *We* are the gods that control our world and the time we have on it. If we truly want peace and happiness, The Cleansing must be accepted. Let your minds accept, let them expand. A new and better way awaits all of us."

As Rebecca's father resumed his speech, Robert felt a presence that made him shudder. *It's Dável,* he thought, panning the room to see if he had taken over another body.

He left the podium to find Katie—together he hoped they could end this.

They both felt Dável's thoughts. Robert knew that he was planning on going back to the transporter and taking over Jacob's body or killing him there and taking off with the transporter. Robert looked at Katie and understood she had read his thoughts, too. *We need to capture him now or on the transporter before Rebecca, Esther, and Jacob return.*

Dável homed in on their thoughts and knew his plan wasn't going to work unless he defeated them first. He decided to lure them away from the assembly room and outside into the open, where he would attempt to separate them and then destroy them one at a time.

* * * * *

Jacob reopened his book, preparing himself to read the next few pages.

"After today, the reading of *The Pallasian Covenant* will have to be done every day for it to continue to work and bring peace and harmony to your lives. Your poisoned genes will take at least a year or two to be fully restored. You've already seen how easily it will return if you don't follow my rules."

He looked down and began to read from the new scripture.

* * * * *

The cat-and-mouse game had begun. Dável had been weaving in and out of the crowds, randomly striking down innocent victims he felt were being cleansed. Katie stopped to heal the fallen people, which she found easy to do, while Robert raced after Dável, ready to apprehend his prey and end this fight.

Robert felt he had cornered Dável, but could not focus clearly on his thoughts. He turned around, seeing Katie in the distance, and then realized the cat had separated the mice. The game was not to chase him, but to separate the two of them.

A mist had formed behind Katie. Robert knew then what was happening.

"He's behind you!" he screamed.

She turned, facing the hovering fog that was trying to enter her body. *"Dável, I've been waiting."*

"It's time we became a team," he said, his voice more menacing than when they met earlier that morning.

"Not this time," Katie replied.

"You're foolishly naïve. You don't have the power to defeat me," he said. "The Family has failed, and so will you."

"But I do," Robert replied.

His breath shot a cold vapor of air that wrapped around a ghostlike figure, freezing it in a surprised pose. Like a child compressing fresh snow, Robert neatly formed a well-rounded snowball, holding in his hands the essence of Dável, trapped in a frozen hell.

A crowd had gathered around, keeping a safe distance as

these new gods fought their battle. Cheers resonated as the people danced with each other. These cleansed souls realized an evil had been removed from them and their world.

"I'll take it from here," Esther said as the monitor converted the icy vapors into a fine mist, swiftly sucking it into its confinement chamber.

"What will happen to him now that you've ended your pursuit?" Katie asked.

"He'll be taken back to be deprogrammed, then sent back into society in a few centuries."

Robert had a confused look. *"After all he has done, you can forgive him and give him a new life?"*

"We've known for a long time what made him and his family become the menacing killers that they were. And yes, we can forgive, since this started from our own mistakes. Once he's been rehabilitated, it would be as if he had never left Pallas."

"How can you be sure he can be deprogrammed and fit to live in your society once again?" asked Robert.

"While we can't bring back everything he lost, we can give him back his children, whom we've held in our confinement chamber," she replied calmly. *"My pursuit cost my family a lot of pain and hardship, especially losing three of my children. I had a job to do, and now that it's done, I'm going to try to get everyone home."*

"I feel we've been lied to again."

"I couldn't agree with you more," she said coldly. *"Nevertheless, your planet's survival is still in your hands. Ridding your planet of Dável's poison will still not be easy, especially before the Council's army gets here."*

Her tone had lost all compassion—something not unusual for a police officer. She had to, at all costs, avoid becoming personally involved with the victims of a case that had finally closed. He respected her detachment and fully understood it. He just did not like being left to clean up this cop's garbage. Robert realized the difficult nature of what he was being asked to accomplish. He was fearful that he and Katie with their daughter were now going to be the world's superhuman protectors, spiritual policemen, the caretakers left behind to prepare for a possible war with an unknown power that was speeding toward their planet. Suddenly, he realized he had no clue where to begin.

Robert let loose his frustrations. *"Go back to where you came from. We'll figure all of this out and defend ourselves without your help. Earth has survived thousands of years, even with all the misinformation you've thrown at us. We'll survive this time, too. And this time, we'll be in control of our destiny."*

Esther was gone. No goodbyes or a thank you. She apparently did not want to confront him, because she knew all too well that whatever the Earth had been able to accomplish before was due to their own intervention. Robert just stood there staring at Katie and, for the first time since they had been together, felt extremely alone.

Jacob had just concluded reading *The Pallasian Covenant*. The Cleansing had begun again. He knew only time would tell if Earth could be saved.

Katie looked at Robert, worried. "Are we prepared to do this?" Her eyes begged for some assurances.

"I'm not sure," he replied, exhausted throwing his arms in the air. "I just hope Cardinal Richman and Abdeljalil Tahmass will help get the remaining religious factions on board, and then we'll work with the political leaders. That's our first step. Then we'll build a defense system, just in case the Council's army has other plans for us."

"You sound so confident. Remember, humans have a short attention span. It isn't going to be easy once we're not front-page news."

"I'm not confident at all. I'm scared to death. I don't have the foggiest idea what to do as a superhero. We'll just have to learn as we go."

Katie reached for his hand and squeezed it tightly as they walked slowly back toward the UN.

"Let's find Rebecca and see how her father's doing," she said.

They both felt at peace for the first time in over a month. The crowds were back dancing on the sidewalks. Strangers were hugging strangers. The homeless were being brought in to the festivities. Katie and Robert thought that if this was how it worked at the beginning of The Cleansing, in six months the world could be ready for the Council's army. Robert smiled at Katie, hiding his doubts and fears for their future.

Inside the lobby and the General Assembly chamber, the

scene was the same. Delegations that had never spoken or touched before were hugging each other. They cried with joy from the release of hate and distrust they had kept locked up all their lives.

Rebecca and her father were nowhere to be found. Robert used his powers to try to reach them. He felt as if he were getting a disconnected number with no forwarding message. The distant voices were gone, as if they had never been there at all.

"Katie, can you still hear me?"

"Yes! I guess we still have our powers to help our world. I wish we could have said goodbye to Rebecca."

"Me, too."

CHAPTER EIGHTY-FIVE

Waiting for liftoff, Rebecca sat on the side of the cot where her exhausted father lay. Tears of joy rolled down her cheeks, and she was relieved that he had started The Cleansing and was going home.

"Father, I can't go home with you. They need me here to help them prepare the world and deal with the Council's army."

"You can't stay. You wouldn't survive for more than six months in your present condition. You're all I have left, and I don't want to lose you. I allowed your brother to stay and he was met with scorn and fear. Robert and Katie will have to figure things out now."

A disturbing sadness had come over her. She stared into her father's eyes. "My brother refused to use his powers to help the world, believing his words and actions would be enough to bring peace to a troubled world back then. I have a different alternative that might work," she said patting her father's hand.

Jacob was not happy, closing his eyes as Rebecca continued explaining her idea. "I've spent thousands of years sacrificing for you and mother, watching you experiment with so many life forms, and supporting mother in her obsessive hunt to find and capture Dável and his family. It cost us my three brothers and a life that I never had. I'm willing to sacrifice myself for six months if it would mean that I could experience some peace before I die."

Her mother stepped over, placing her hand on her daughter's shoulder. "I'm sorry for what we've put you through. Denying you the life of a woman for the sake of our self-righteous beliefs was not right. I don't want to lose you, but I do understand and will reluctantly support your desires."

"How can you say that?" her father cried feebly, too weak to move.

"Our time is almost up. We'll have only a few years left when we return, and if Rebecca returns with us, she will suffer that same fate. We've waited too long here, and our bodies have suffered irreversible damage. Let her have a life, even if it is for a short time."

Rebecca, her tears rolling down her cheek, was unfamiliar with her mother actually showing emotion and compassion for her. "What I was really thinking is that I could start a new life in a new body and be strong enough to help Katie and Robert."

Esther had a curious expression. "What have you in mind?" she asked.

"Let me occupy Katie's baby, just like we did with my twin brother. But, this time I will retain my powers, since the baby will have both Robert's and Katie's new DNA. By the eighth year, I'll have my memories and knowledge, which, combined with her baby's DNA, will help me live for seven hundred Earth years. That will allow me more than enough time for a new life. Maybe I can find a husband and have children when I'm older, multiplying a new breed of humans to help change Earth."

"It's possible, but it will take a few days to reconfigure the confinement chamber. You know it could be all over when the Council's army gets here."

"I know, but I really think I can help give Earth a fighting chance to truly survive this time."

Esther was already typing codes into her equipment and at the same time talking to Rebecca. "I'm going to reconfigure our procedures we have to re-occupy a body and let you become their new baby without affecting who this new life force is. As the baby grows, so will her abilities and powers she's gotten from her mother and father. Memories about you will begin to appear sporadically after the baby turns five instead of eight. You'll not have any memories of us or Pallas. I cannot allow you to have that much of an advantage over the Council's army. The baby will grow, learning quickly from the molecular cells you once had. From there, I can't predict what will happen. Who knows if you will ever remember Rebecca or your mother and father? This is the only way you'll have a chance to live on Earth and have a life."

"I'll take my chances, Mother. Maybe Katie will instruct her daughter about me and where I came from. At least I'd have those memories. Please begin immediately; I want you and father to get back to Pallas in time to be regenerated. Maybe you're wrong about your damaged cells; it's worth a try."

For the first time in a long time, she kissed her mother and gave her a hug. Esther brought her in closer and kissed the top of her head.

"I'm sorry I've been a poor mother to you all these years. And I'm sad that I had forgotten how wonderful you feel in my arms. I love you very much and will miss you tremendously."

CHAPTER EIGHTY-SIX

Two weeks had passed since The Cleansing had begun, and the world, as Katie had predicted, was slow in adapting to the change. The important thing was that the world for the first time was truly at peace.

Small radical factions in isolated sections around the world that wanted to maintain the status quo attempted violence, but were stopped before any deaths or destruction could happen. Robert was swift with his justice: either read *The Pallasian Covenant* or perish. Katie was happy that a violent alternative had not been chosen.

The United Nations elected a New World Council that included all the existing presidents, prime ministers, and dictators who had previously controlled their countries. Nationalism gave way to the global village. But, it was not happening as quickly as they would have liked. Katie adopted a new, progressive philosophy that emphasized small steps toward big goals. After all, they did have ten years, she would remind the man she loved so much.

Robert saw to it that United Weapons Systems was dissolved and that all the company's data banks were fully erased, leaving no trace of the RX-666 or the Pulsar XR-36. As a precaution, he kept the data for the Pulsar XR-36 and the RX-666 on compact disks—just in case he needed to hedge his bets when he came face-to-face in ten years with the approaching army of machines. While the world was beginning to trust and feel secure, he wasn't. He wanted a fail-safe scenario if the Council's army did not want to leave them in peace. He still had his doubts about the

Council and its desires for Earth. While the Pallasian Covenant was making the world a better place, it was Darwin's Pallasian Doctrine and what it stood for that had Robert on edge. Did Darwin come in contact with The Family or some other traveler from Pallas and was able to develop his theories on evolution? Did he also, have information about a domestication plan for earth? Robert thought.

These questions spun wildly inside Robert's mind, as he tried to set up a plan to bring lasting peace and harmony to the world, while at the same time prepared a defense system to protect Earth.

Two days after Jacob's speech, Katie felt something enter her body and affix itself inside her womb. For just a brief moment, she heard a familiar voice say thank you, and then it was gone. Her motherly intuition told her it was Rebecca and that she was going to be around to help them.

Cardinal Richman was elected as Earth's new Spiritual Leader, a new title created for the one religion being observed around the globe. Each day he read one prayer from *The Pallasian Covenant*, which was broadcast over a worldwide network of TV, radio, and Internet stations. Abdeljalil Tahmass was always by his side, repeating the message in all the Arab tongues. Richman's first official act was to unite Robert and Katie in holy matrimony. This was something he was honored to do, especially after he found out that they had been married to each other in another lifetime. He believed in new beginnings, and this union was the beginning of a wonderful future. He prayed their daughter would be the new Messiah, who would come to bring peace and hope.

Crime was reduced. It was not completely gone, though, and Robert and Katie dealt with the criminals. In most cases, it turned out that these unfortunate souls had not listened to or read *The Pallasian Covenant,* and once they were arrested and given the chance to read it or die, they happily agreed to be exposed to it. They had become fully rehabilitated.

* * * * *

Six months passed, and Robert had become dismayed at what he still felt was a major deception by Jacob. He kept pondering why, right from the beginning, that everything at United Weapons Systems was not destroyed. He knew they had the power to do it, but they didn't use it. It just seemed too opportune that Jacob had focused so much on The Cleansing. As powerful as Robert had become, his human frailties had not gone away. He knew his new powers required sharpness to safeguard the world he and Katie were entrusted to protect.

Katie had slowed down, taking care of herself as her pregnancy progressed. She tried to reason with her husband on many occasions that his paranoia had no foundation.

"Can't you appreciate what is happening around the world? There's no war or poverty. People are living in harmony for the first time ever. Economies are stronger than ever before, and people have enough of whatever they want."

He gave her a skeptical smile. "I found Dável's lair. He was a madman, but he also understood what was really happening to him. He kept a journal. It's dated back to when he was in prison on Pallas."

"You don't think he was telling us the truth, do you?"

It was obvious that Robert was being pulled back into a life of doubt and caution. "Some of what he recorded makes sense. Dável believed the experiments were conducted not only to eradicate what The Family thought was his poison but to build an army of supermen to harvest and take back to Pallas to be put into their military to fight their Million Year War. While he doesn't mention The Pallasian Doctrine, what he writes does seem that the human race was being domesticated for other purposes."

"You've seen how peaceful their planet is," Katie argued. "I can't believe what you're saying is true."

"All I know is what they told us. They showed us what they wanted us to see and believe."

"Why did they give us these powers, if they were not serious?"

"I'm not sure, but I believe Dável has those answers somewhere in his journals. I placed a small group of researchers in his cave to find some answers. Right now, I want to begin to prepare for the Council's army. I really don't believe they're coming to evaluate us. I'll bet you they're coming to capture the strong. Our history is filled with stories of alien abductions, and this might be the most horrendous one ever, if we're not prepared and ready. We've theorized for so long that aliens were one day coming to invade our planet. What if the plan was to create an army of superhuman people, controlled by The Pallasian Covenant and have them ready to die, like suicide bombers, for their ongoing war.?"

Katie looked frightened as she felt her baby kick. "I've something to tell you. I'm sorry I haven't said anything until now. But you're really frightening me. We're having a child and for just once can you show some positive encouragement for our world?"

Robert looked bewildered. "What's going on?" he asked.

"I'm not totally sure; it could just be my desire to have Rebecca near us again. But, two days after the speech, I thought I felt her enter my body and fix herself to our baby." She started to cry, overwhelmed by his doubts. "I can't believe that Jacob and Esther would have left their daughter here if she would have been in any danger."

He walked closer to her and gave her a hug.

"I know how much you miss her. I miss her, too. Dável, in his journal, wrote that Jacob and his children had been duped by the Council and Esther. I did find it very strange that Esther never participated in The Cleansing, always remaining distant."

Katie nodded. "She was a strange one. Different from the others. Robert, I trust your judgment. Do what you think will protect all of us. I'll help, once the baby's born."

He smiled. "I will. My first goal is to try to have Earth speak a universal language. I should help to break down some of the remaining differences and fears people still have. I just don't know if I have the power to do it."

Katie nodded, lost in thought as Robert kept speaking. "I'm sure you've already thought of this, but let's name our daughter Rebecca. Even if it was just your imagination that she entered you, our daughter will have her name as a reminder of a good friend."

CHAPTER EIGHTY-SEVEN

Somewhere, light-years away from Earth, the ship taking Jacob and Esther and the confinement chamber back to Pallas had become damaged by a meteor shower.

Jacob was weak and slowly dying and could not help Esther repair their ship. She was still strong, but had no knowledge of how to repair their transporter.

She had to advise the Council and prepare them for what to expect. Her transmitter still worked, but was low on energy, and she knew this would be her last chance to talk to them.

"The Cleansing has begun. They'll be ready for occupation when your ships arrive. There will be no weapons or army to fight you. The Cleansing will have rid their bodies of Dável's DNA, and they'll be ready for Phase 2. I'm sorry it has taken so long to complete my mission."

"You've done well, Esther," the digital voice told her. "As promised, your mother and father are still safe and anxious for your return. We've scanned your ship. Where are your children?"

She thought for a while, looking over at her dying husband. She knew that his frail body was not going to make it home.

"They were lost in our battle with Dável. It's just the two of us now, and I don't think we'll make it back alive. Our ship's been damaged by a meteor shower. We're adrift two hundred thousand light-years from you."

The president of the Council, without emotion or hesitation, gave her an order: "Place yourself in the incubator. Your sensor circuits should be intact until our ships arrive."

She did not respond immediately. She saw that Jacob had

been listening to her. His look of scorn hammered deep inside her heart. She was embarrassed that she had deceived him and her family about her true mission on all their trips. She continued with her communication.

"There's just one small problem that might affect your mission—"

The bridge became dark, and the power went dead before she could complete her message.

She was unable to repair the damaged transmitter. She accepted her fate, content that her mission had been a success. She took the cot next to her husband, placing his hand in hers, and closed her eyes.

She didn't expect her husband to have the strength to speak, as he turned his head, trying to hold it steady as it trembled from his weakened molecular cells.

"I knew what you were planning. I had intercepted one of your transmissions long ago. I just never understood why. Your plan won't work. I've left Rebecca with enough of my molecular sensor circuits to fight the Council's army. She has enough of my knowledge to create a counter-weapon to defend Earth."

Esther started to weep.

"I'm sorry, but I had no choice. My parents were being held captive by the Council and would have died if I hadn't followed their orders. I'm ashamed, but I didn't know what else to do."

"It's all right. This will be an important test for Earth. We've left them with the ability to defeat our army. I'm confident Robert and Katie with Rebecca's help will make Earth a powerful planet in a troubled universe."

He smiled at his wife and then closed his eyes; death had finally consumed him.

She knew she would remain adrift, alone in a dark, silent cave for the rest of her life—the punishment she deserved for deceiving her family. She placed the incubator across her chest, and then hesitated, not wanting to live with her guilt. As a tear rolled down her cheek, she gently placed the incubator on the table next to their cots and closed her eyes. She finally knew that Earth was about to open a new chapter in their history and for the first time wished for their success. She knew that it would be next to impossible for them to defeat Pallas' army.

www.ingramcontent.com/pod-product-compliance
Lightning Source LLC
Chambersburg PA
CBHW051545250626
47157CB00001B/197